D1325340

WITHDRAWN
FROM STOCK

Memoirs Are Made of This

Also by Swan Adamson

Confessions of a Pregnant Princess
My Three Husbands

Memoirs Are Made of This

Swan Adamson

First published in 2007
by LITTLE BLACK DRESS
An imprint of HEADLINE PUBLISHING GROUP

1

Cataloguing in Publication Data is available from the British Library

ISBN 978 0 7553 3365 3

Typeset in Transit511BT by Avon DataSet Ltd,
Bidford-on-Avon, Warwickshire

Printed and bound in Great Britain by
Clays Ltd, St Ives plc

Headline's policy is to use papers that are natural, renewable and recyclable
products and made from wood grown in sustainable forests. The logging and
manufacturing processes are expected to conform to the environmental
regulations of the country of origin.

HEADLINE PUBLISHING GROUP
A division of Hachette Livre UK Ltd.
338 Euston Road
London NW1 3BH

www.littleblackdressbooks.co.uk
www.headline.co.uk

To Steph, Caro and Cat

'You should write a memoir,' Whitman said.

He didn't look at me when he said it. My faux pa was carefully studying the menu at a new Italian restaurant where he and my birth sire, John Gilroy, were treating me to dinner.

I felt horrible, inside and out. This wasn't a celebration, it was a funeral. I'd just filed for an uncontested, no-fault divorce from Tremaynne, one month after our wedding.

'A memoir?' I let out a blurt of something that might have been laughter, but was probably closer to despair. 'Why?'

'To help you get over it,' he said.

'Over what?'

'Your life. All the mistakes you've made.' He looked up at me with his piercing blue eyes. 'Not many girls—'

'Women,' I corrected him.

'– your age have been through what you have.'

'They're lucky,' I muttered gloomily.

'Three husbands, two gay dads, a mother who believes UFOs are the cause of high gas prices . . .'

That got my dad's attention. He shot Whitman an incredulous look. 'Carolee believes that?'

'Mm.' Whitman held his menu up in front of Daddy and pointed to something on the menu. 'That's not how you spell "carciofi". I wonder if I should point it out to the owner.'

Daddy caught my eye and smiled.

'What do you think?' Whitman asked Daddy. 'Should I let

him know? It reduces credibility when you're trying to be upscale and misspell a word on your menu.'

I looked at my dads as they bent their heads together to discuss the matter. They were so tuned in to one another, so united as a unit, with over twenty years of shared experiences. They were so sophisticated, so knowledgeable, so successful, and so much in love, still. And here was I, their daughter, a disappointment on every front, a flighty flop who'd fucked up everything and was apparently doomed to a lifetime of . . .

I sniffed in a big gob of self-pity, raised the menu up in front of my eyes, and began to blubber.

'Oh, sweetheart,' Daddy said, reaching over and taking my hand.

'I know you don't want to hear this,' Whitman said, trying to sound sympathetic, 'but you're better off without him.'

'No – I'm – not,' I sobbed.

And yet I knew I was, and I knew Whitman was right. I just couldn't admit it to myself. Admitting it meant acknowledging that I'd made yet another bad choice, that my judgement was seriously flawed. And if my judgement was that out-of-whack, what did it portend for the future? My entire unlived life hovered there in front of me, a wasteland of loneliness.

'Drink some water,' Daddy said, handing me a glass of Pellegrino.

'I know you don't want to hear what I have to say,' Whitman said. 'I know that you think I'm judgemental and somewhat severe—'

'Whit,' Daddy said, 'maybe this isn't the time.'

'I'm sorry,' Whitman said, 'but it *is* the time. Venus can't go on the way she has been. Sort of drifting around like a jellyfish.'

I let out a horrified squawk, then a hiccough from the fizzy Pellegrino.

'It's when you're at your lowest ebb, pressed up against the wall,' Whitman said, 'that you show the world what you're really made of.'

What was I made of? I no longer knew. Losing Tremaynne,

my third and best-loved husband, to a radical environmental group had undermined the little self-confidence I had. My husband had chosen nature over nurture. *My* nurture, *my* arms, *my* body, *my* love. OK, it was noble and I could see that it was even necessary, the world needed eco-warriors like Tremaynne. But where did it leave me? Possibly pregnant, with no prospects in sight. And with hiccoughs.

Sitting there, lost in my misery, it seemed like the events in my life that I always thought would be major and lasting turned out to be temporary as hiccoughs. My first hiccough was Sean Kowalski, the guy I married at nineteen (what Whitman called my 'starter marriage'). OK, what do you know about love at nineteen? Nothing. You think riding around in a big souped-up car is romantic. I wanted to get out of my mom's house, fast, and Sean had the wheels to get me out of there. At first I thought it was cool that Sean was a convicted felon; later, when we were married, I realized he was permanently pissed-off and horribly homophobic, which didn't sit well with my dads, for obvious reasons.

After Sean was gone, I hiccoughed my way, or maybe ricochetted, into the arms of JD, the lead singer for a punk-rock band. It was my first lesbian love affair, and of course I wanted it to last for ever because JD was so totally awesome, with her band, her groupies, her big gleaming Harley, and attitude up the wazoo. It took me a while to figure out that cool, in her case, meant frigid. The worst sex of my life, and I always had to start it. Plus, JD was into drugs. I wanted a heroine, not heroin.

Peter Pringle, my next hiccough, disposed of dead pets for a living. Pete was permanently broke but he was boyishly cute and mine, all mine. I'd ride around and make out with him in his Pet Away van, soaking up his adoration and the smell of formaldehyde. I shouldn't have married Pete, but he was absolutely crazy about me – or maybe just plain crazy. Neither one of us had a clue about money (except how to spend it), and I danced topless and did lingerie modelling in secret to keep us afloat. But our marriage tanked anyway, weighed down with unpaybackable credit-card debt and my growing realisation that Pete was on the obsessive-compulsive side.

And then came . . . Tremaynne. He was *not* a hiccough, I was sure of it. From the moment I first laid eyes on him in bankruptcy court, Tremaynne was the love of my life. He was a man with *principles* (a new concept for me), someone who worked for a greater cause, on behalf of the *entire world*. He also happened to be the sexiest man I'd ever laid eyes on. We connected physically in a way that possibly ruined me for life, because no other man alive could possibly make love the way Tremaynne did. I talked him into marrying me and for our honeymoon the dads took us with them to a fabulous new wilderness resort. My pa John, the architect, had designed Pine Mountain Lodge and my faux pa Whitman, the travel writer, was writing about it. Pine Mountain Lodge was where Tremaynne and I last made love, without birth control . . . which meant that now, possibly . . .

'You're too smart, Venus, to go on this way,' Whitman said, snapping me out of my reverie.

We all froze when the waiter came over with glasses of wine for Daddy and Whitman. Oh, I wanted one too, a big glass of ruby-red Italian Chianti, preferably accompanied by a cigarette, but I'd refrained from ordering wine because I wasn't sure yet if I was carrying Tremaynne's baby or not.

'Sure you won't have a glass?' Daddy said. He and Whitman didn't have a clue about my possible pregnancy, and I wasn't about to tell them until I was certain. The whole thing filled me with a crazy kind of ambivalence because of course I wanted Tremaynne's baby, but a baby was the last thing I wanted.

They clicked their wine glasses to my glass of fizzy Pellegrino.

'Every ending is a new beginning,' Whitman said. 'A new opportunity.'

'To do what?' I asked. 'Hic.'

'Well, your father and I have been talking,' Whitman said. He pulled a clean, folded handkerchief from his pocket and handed it to me. 'Here, sweetheart. Dip it into the cold water and pat the area around your eyes or they'll get even puffier than they already are.'

I obeyed. It was easier to obey. I dabbed and hiccoughed.

'We've been talking,' Whitman went on, 'haven't we, John –'

'Mm-hm,' Daddy nodded, stroking my hand.

'And we feel somewhat responsible for what happened. Well, I feel somewhat responsible. Since it was my idea for you and Tremaynne to spend your honeymoon with us at Pine Mountain Lodge.'

And the whole story came pouring back into my head and my heart, like some rerun you've seen a thousand times before but can't stop watching. The trip to Pine Mountain Lodge, Tremaynne's disappearance, my terrifying wilderness trek to find him, the way we barely escaped death at the hands of those drunken rednecks, how we were saved by my dads, and then Tremaynne's announcement that he was staying, that our marriage was over, that he was going out into the wilderness to become an eco-warrior. Scenes flowed past quick as a dream.

'I don't blame you for what happened, Whitman,' I said. 'Hic. You and Daddy saved our lives.'

'Well,' Whitman said, 'that's what fathers are for. But at this point, Venus, we can't save you any more. Unless you want to be saved.'

I looked from Whitman to Daddy and back to Whitman. Something was up. I can always tell.

'Do you?' Whitman prodded.

I was cautious. 'What do you mean by "saved"? Hic.'

'I mean getting out of the endless rut your life always seems to be in. I mean going back to school. I mean having a career. Like the intelligent, responsible adult I know you really want to be.'

Ugh. Yes, he was right, much as I hated to admit it. But at that moment, dabbing my eyes with chilled Pellegrino and trying not to cry through my hiccoughs, I didn't want any responsibilities. I didn't want a career. I just wanted to crumble up and disappear into an emotional coma and not wake up until I felt better.

'It just so happens,' Whitman said, 'that I've been asked to write a monthly travel column for *Aura* magazine.'

'For *Aura*? Oh my God, Whitman, that's huge. Isn't it?' I knew virtually nothing about his world of freelance travel writing, except that it kept him constantly on the go.

'It's potentially huge,' he admitted. 'But it's an enormous amount of work.'

'It's a good thing you're – hic – a workaholic, then,' I said.

'I've never turned down a challenge,' he said. 'And this is a huge one. But I need some help.' He sat back as the waiter placed a mixed salad in front of him. 'Research help. I've got to come up with a year's worth of story ideas and present them to the editor-in-chief in New York next month.'

'Hic. So you're going to be travelling even more?' My caesar salad looked really good and I lifted a leaf to my mouth. Yummy, even in my misery, with just the right amount of garlic, olive oil and parmesan.

'Some of it I can recycle from other pieces I've done,' Whitman explained. 'I looked at my resumé the other day and it's a mile long. But I need someone to do some research for me.'

The romaine leaves were perfect and perfectly crisp. I bit into another one.

'You know how to operate a computer, don't you?' Whitman asked.

I looked up.

'Yes, honey,' Daddy said. 'Whitman wants *you* to be his assistant.'

'Temporary assistant,' Whitman clarified. 'Paid, of course. So you won't have to go back to working in that dirty-book store.'

I cleared my throat. It's awful trying to think practically when all you want to do is wallow in the mud of your misery. 'I don't know that much about computers,' I said. 'Hic.'

'Well, you know how to search the Web, don't you?'

'I don't have a computer.'

This admission seemed to astonish Whitman, who sat in front of his high-speed wireless flat-screen computer for hours at a time, day after day. When he wasn't at his desktop, he was on his laptop. 'You don't have a computer?'

'Hic. I don't need one,' I said.

'*Everyone* needs a computer,' Whitman said. 'How on earth do you—'

'We can get her a computer,' Daddy said. 'And send her to some computer classes.'

'She can have my old laptop,' Whitman said. 'I need to get a new one anyway.'

Some part of my brain was registering all this and trying to accept it. Another part was fighting the whole notion with a kind of a primitive anti-Father Knows Best reflex action. Granted, there were dreary realities to be faced. I knew I'd have to find a job, and I knew I didn't want to go back to Phantastic Phantasy, the porn store where I'd worked right up to the day I married Tremaynne.

Doing research work for Whitman didn't seem so awful. But he was such an exacting person, I was afraid I'd do something wrong.

'How does that sound?' Whitman asked. 'Twenty dollars an hour. And an all-expenses-paid trip to New York.'

'Hic. New York?' My heart, despite its pain, skipped a beat. 'When?'

'Next month. My subletter is leaving for China so we can all stay in the apartment again.'

'Just like old times,' Daddy said.

And just like that, my hiccoughs disappeared.

Old times. New York.

As I left the restaurant and set off across town, thinking about the Big A helped vanquish some of my divorce-related gloom. In three months I'd be legally single again. Mom had lent me the money and helped me with the on-line filing.

I hadn't been in New York for nearly ten years, but once

upon a time I flew out there on a quarterly basis to spend time with the dads – well, with John, my birth dad, because I basically hated Whitman back then. The dads had a small rent-stabilized apartment with a garden on the Upper West Side of Manhattan. Whitman had found this place before he met Daddy and he'd kept it even when he moved to Portland with Daddy.

Since Whitman came from one of the oldest families in Boston, and took things like table manners very seriously, it always seemed odd to me that he lived in a cramped, roach-infested apartment in a 'transitional' neighborhood. I always pictured him gliding around a penthouse on Park Avenue, telling the servants to polish the silver. Eventually I learned that his family had disinherited him because he was gay, and without old family money to prop him up, he had to make his own way in the world. So the apartment on West 102nd Street between Broadway and West End Avenue meant a lot to him because it was part of his life history. It was where he lived as a struggling writer, and where he and Daddy lived together for several years. It was a home that he'd created for himself, and they'd created together. Just as he and Daddy had created a new home for themselves up in the West Hills of Portland, with a fabulous view of downtown and Mount Hood.

I didn't have a home. Not really. I'd been expecting to make a home with Tremaynne, but now I saw what a pitiful fantasy that had been. Oh, I didn't want a big house. I would have been happy in a cute little Portland bungalow, like my mom's. Or even in a one-bedroom apartment. But that was my fantasy, not Tremaynne's. His idea of home was a tent in the forest or a platform high in an old-growth tree. He'd been happy to crash and make love in my tiny studio apartment in Portland, amidst the debris of my life, but he never aspired to the idea of moving up to more square footage with our name on a lease. I thought maybe he would, and burning all my bridges, as usual, I gave up the apartment when we got married.

So when I returned husbandless from what was supposed to have been my honeymoon at Pine Mountain Lodge, I didn't have any place to go or any money to rent an apartment. I stayed with the dads for a few days, then, when I couldn't stand their unwavering neatness any more, I moved over to my mom's. It was like being a kid again – you know, always looking for your little bit of private space away from *them*.

I still had my decrepit old Toyota and my ancient cellphone. Those two items were my lifelines, allowing me the illusion of independence. But even they required money.

Everything required money.

Life required money.

I had to start thinking about the future.

I was in no position to turn down Whitman's helpful offer of employment. Since my break-up with Tremaynne a month earlier, I'd been floating. That's fine if you're a balloon, but scary if you're not. And *really* scary if you're floating and possibly pregnant at the same time. I knew I had to do something, develop a plan of action, but emotionally I felt like I'd been hit by a stun gun.

As I sped across town to my mom's, I tried to get excited about the computer classes, tried to imagine myself with a 'career'. It was weird, like trying on a dress that doesn't fit and is not you at all. I vowed that no matter how successful I became, I would *never* look like one of those briefcase-toting women I first saw on the subways in New York, wearing carefully tailored suits and running shoes.

Mom insisted she wasn't waiting up for me, but of course she was. Since moving back in with her, I'd gotten a peek at her private life and the rituals that kept her afloat. She could barely keep her eyes open after ten o'clock.

She was stretched out in her favorite pink robe on the too-soft sofa that I slept on, watching an old Marilyn Monroe movie as a fan oscillated up and down her body. 'Hello, sweetheart. How was dinner?'

'Good.'

'What was the restaurant?'

'Mangia Mia.'

'Good?'

'Great caesar. Whitman said the pasta wasn't quite al dente enough, but I liked it.'

'Whitman is very sensitive about things like that,' Mom said. She pointed the remote control at the TV and froze Marilyn Monroe, who was wearing a low-cut gown, long gloves, and weighed down with jewels.

My mother, Carolee, had a great fondness for sexy female movie stars from earlier eras, especially if she knew that beneath all the glitter and the glamour they were abused and miserable. Mom dropped out to become a hippie back in the Sixties and never quite dropped back in again, except to marry Daddy. He was a hot-shot architect, and she was a hot-shit stunner. I'm the product of that culture clash.

When Daddy came out as a gay man and fell in love with Whitman Whittlesley III, Mom was devastated. But she was always civil to Whitman because she truly loved Daddy and wanted him to be happy. If not with her, as she'd hoped, then with Whitman. Jilted and generous, that's my mom. She's totally wonderful, in her own unique way, but she'll believe anything, no matter how weird or wacky, because 'there's always an alternative for what we call reality'.

'How's your father?' she asked me now, hoping I'd throw her a nice juicy titbit. She was always ravenous to know about Daddy and Whitman's glamorous life.

'OK.'

'How's Whitman?'

'OK.'

'How are you?'

'OK.' Over the past few days, and earlier that afternoon, we'd been crying together, Mom and me, and I could tell she was hungry for some more blubbering. She loved it when I cried in her arms and she could cry along with me, offering meaningless words of comfort as she held me close. But I was sick of crying. It didn't get you anywhere. It didn't lead to any insights, except that you were miserable.

'Have you been thinking about Tremaynne?' Mom

prodded, nudging my tear ducts. She tsked and sighed. 'Oh, sweetheart, I'm so sorry about what happened.'

I sucked in a ragged breath, determined not to go there, to her land of boo-hoo. 'Whitman's hiring me to do some work for him,' I said, kicking my shoes off and flopping down on her recliner.

'Whitman is? Oh, that's nice.'

'They're sending me to computer classes.'

'Computer classes?' Mom eyed Marilyn Monroe's image and fluffed up her own nest of red hair, squashed at the back from lying down. 'I didn't know you were interested in computers.'

'I'm not, but I'm going to do some web research, so—'

'Because my computer just sits there,' Mom said. 'You've never even turned it on. You've never used it, except today when I helped you to file for your divorce on-line.'

That word again! Divorce! It was like pressing a sore tooth. She just had to remind me, to see if it would turn on the eye taps. 'And we're going to New York next month,' I said.

She gasped like a game-show contestant. 'New York! Who is?'

'The dads and me.'

'For something special?'

'Whitman's subletter is leaving. So we're having an old times visit.'

'Lucky you!' Mom cried.

'He has to present some stories to the editor of *Aura* magazine. They want him to write a monthly travel column.'

'*Aura*! That's my favorite magazine!' Mom searched through the stacks of junk on her coffee table. 'It was here a minute ago,' she muttered.

'Never mind,' I said. 'I'm not as New Age as you are.'

'I was New Age way before I was Old Age,' Mom said, continuing her search, 'and *Aura*'s the only magazine that honors my belief in alternative realities.'

I rolled my eyes and sighed. Mom and her alternative realities. Sometimes I thought she'd be happier if she just looked life in the eye and gave real reality a chance. But reality, I had to admit, didn't offer much fun or comfort.

'Maybe I took it into the bathroom . . .' She hoisted herself up from the sofa and went to check. 'Aha!' A moment later she returned, waving the magazine with a triumphant flourish. 'It's not all totally New Age, you know. There's a column in here I just love.' She flipped through the pages. 'Here it is. "Nothing to Hyde" by Susanna Hyde.' She scanned something and let out a cackle. 'Listen to this. "Dear Susanna, I am a virgin and because of my deeply held religious convictions I intend to remain chaste until my wedding night. My boyfriend says I can perform fellatio on him and still remain a virgin. Is this true? Signed, Pure but Puzzled." '

'What does this Susanna What's-Her-Name say?'

'Hyde, Susanna Hyde. "Dear Pure but Puzzled," ' Mom read, ' "It's true that a blow job will not rupture your hymen, but neither will it give you much physical satisfaction. Apparently your religious leaders and your boyfriend didn't inform you that sexual relations are supposed to be mutual. The solution is some good, old-fashioned tongue for two: he eats you while you suck him." ' Mom nodded thoughtfully. 'That's good advice, don't you think?'

'I guess. It's hard to believe anyone could be that stupid, though.'

'You mean Pure but Puzzled? Oh, I disagree. I think women are still in the Dark Ages when it comes to sex.'

'I'm not.'

'Well, you've had a lot of practice, sweetheart. But when I was young, why, a blow job was something you got at the beauty parlor. I didn't have a clue what fellatio was until I married your father.'

'You gave Daddy—'

'That's why it's so good to have columns like this Susanna Hyde's,' Mom said, not answering my question. 'We all want to know these things but we're just too shy to ask.'

'Well, I'm never having sex again as long as I live,' I vowed.

'Don't say that, sweetheart. You're just feeling down on it

now because of Tremaynne. Because of what happened.'

Oh, the lovemaking. I ached for him. Tremaynne was the sorcerer of sex. He could make me feel sensations that required vocal accompaniment.

'You're still young and pretty,' Mom said. 'Another man will come along and sweep you off your feet.'

I shook my head. 'I'm going to concentrate on having a career.'

Mom stared at me, her mouth slightly open, as if I'd just morphed into a werewolf.

'I am. I really am. I'm sick of never having enough money and not doing anything with my life.'

'Is that what you think I've done?' Mom asked, her voice quavery.

I didn't want to answer that one. 'I'm tired of always being in an emotional quagmire, Mom.'

'Emotions are a primal legacy of womanhood,' Mom said defensively, 'and denying the goddess within just to fit into some man's version of the world is sick. Sick and anti-feminine.'

'They're just a big fat drain of energy, Mom.'

She sucked in a startled breath as if I'd just slapped her. 'Emotions remind us that we're feeling human beings, not heartless machines. Emotions remind us that we're connected.'

'To what? Our delusions? Our mistakes?'

'To our loved ones,' Mom said.

'No.' I shook off her suggestion that I should make myself comfy in the messy nest of my emotions. Mom fed on emotional chaos but I wanted something else, something clearer, something surer, something out in the larger world and not so eternally bound up with a guy. 'Whitman and Daddy are giving me a chance to do something with my life, and I'm going for it.'

'This sounds serious,' Mom said, getting more and more agitated, maybe because she knew it meant that I'd leave her. 'Why don't we go over to Saturna's for a tarot reading? She's got a two-for-one special this week.'

'I don't need a tarot reading, and even if I did, I don't have any money for one. That's the problem, Mom. I don't have any money, or any prospects, and I've just sort of frittered my life away, always thinking that having some guy was going to make it all better. And it never did. It was just wishful thinking.'

'So now you're going to start thinking about yourself,' Mom said.

'Yes. I'm going to start thinking about my future.'

Which made me think about the baby I was possibly carrying, Tremaynne's baby, and of course that made me cry, and then Mom, my crying-buddy, eagerly joined in, and soon we were sobbing and eating Oreos and watching Marilyn Monroe sing 'Diamonds are a Girl's Best Friend'.

The following Monday, determined to be prompt for once in my life, I walked into a windowless computer classroom at 8 a.m. sharp to begin my new life. Panic struck almost immediately. *School*. I stared at forty strange faces and forty strange faces stared back at me. At first I thought maybe it was because my halter top or red micro-mini was inappropriate. But then I realized it was because I was late. I'd misread the schedule and the class began at 7.45 a.m.

'Ah – Ms Gilroy.' I thought he'd be pissed, but the instructor seemed to brighten when he saw me. He nodded sympathetically when he heard my excuse. 'Just have a seat here, in the front row,' he said, indicating a computer right in front of him.

Maybe you weren't supposed to wear heels to school. Maybe that was why all eyes were upon me. A horrible dreamlike sensation of being shamed or exposed in public brought heat to my cheeks as I clicked over to my assigned chair. I straightened my back and tried to look rapturously interested as the instructor backtracked, just for me, and explained how to boot up a computer. He looked about Daddy's age but twice as old, his skin gray-green in the wash of overhead fluorescent light.

I assumed that this computer class would be filled with geeks, but that wasn't the case at all. Some of the students were older than any living creatures I'd ever encountered. One guy was ninety. There was a woman in her eighties who said she wanted to be able to send e-mails to her grandchildren. There were a few nervous housewives, and some guys whose enormous hands looked more cut out for heavy manual labor than tapping a computer keyboard (it turned out they were there for 'career retraining'). Almost everyone was older than me and every time I turned around a guy's staring eyes would quickly dart back to his computer screen.

It was fun and boring at the same time. I knew far more than most of the students, but what I knew was haphazard, stuff I'd picked up here and there. To me, computers run on magic.

After learning the basics of booting up, we dived straight into the World Wide Web. Of course I knew the Web was out there, but it had never really interested me. There was nothing in my life or about my life that made it imperative for me to sit down in front of a computer and navigate through cyberspace.

But now I was sort of intrigued. When the instructor told us to search for the website of something we wanted to know more about, I typed in 'Aura magazine' just for the hell of it. I got *Aura*'s website and typed in 'www.auramagazine.com'. And suddenly there it was, with some cool music in the background and shifting images on the screen. Magic.

Then the instructor told us to type in the name of someone we wanted to know more about. It didn't have to be a famous person, it could be anyone. So I typed in my dad's name, John Gilroy, architect.

I couldn't believe my eyes.

My dad existed in cyberspace. There were even photos of some of the buildings he'd designed. Including – oh my God – Pine Mountain Lodge, the luxury wilderness resort where I'd gone with Tremaynne for what I'd thought was our honeymoon.

Suddenly I realized the obsessive possibilities of the Web. With the right skills I'd be able to navigate and explore a whole new universe. Far from being a geeky pastime, it immediately threatened to become a way of life.

I Googled Pine Mountain Lodge and clicked on the link.

There it was, heartbreakingly beautiful, with a live Web cam tour of the grounds, the public rooms, the spa, and the guest suites.

Then I went one step further: I Googled Tremaynne. And – oh my God – there were dozens of articles, written at the time when he became an environmental celebrity by sitting in an old-growth redwood down in southern Oregon and refusing to leave because a timber company wanted to cut it down. I sniffled and clicked on one of the sites.

His photo appeared.

I couldn't help myself. I blurted out a sob.

'Is something the matter, Miss Gilroy?' the instructor asked.

'N-n-n-o. Just allergic to something.' I shook my head and quickly clicked the 'Back' icon to return to the Pine Mountain Lodge website. I didn't want the instructor to see Tremaynne's too-gorgeous image.

The instructor looked at my screen. 'Pine Mountain Lodge. It looks fantastic. Are you going there for a vacation?'

I shook my head. 'No. Just got b-b-b-back.'

'Perhaps you'd like to take a break for a minute. There's a water fountain right outside.'

Nothing like crying in front of your entire class. I burned with embarrassment . . . until I noticed all the guys were smiling at me in sympathy.

Because *Aura* had a New Agey edge to it, Whitman was going to call his monthly travel column 'One Thousand Places To Enjoy Before You're Reincarnated'. 'It's a brilliant idea,' he said, 'because I can spin off all the magazine stories into a travel book with the same title. And Stuckey Universal Media will probably publish it.'

'Stuckey Universal Media?'

'That's the media empire owned by Lord Farrell Stuckey. He owns *Aura* magazine. Along with half the other magazines and newspapers in the world, and some television and radio stations, and a publishing house or two.'

'Oh.'

We were sitting in Whitman's home office and he was telling me about my new job. He'd given me his 'old' laptop, which was a thin, sleek, beautiful machine with a pixel count in the billions and amazingly high color resolution. By now I'd finished my computer classes, so I knew about stuff like that. I was turning into a geekette who spoke Computer, throwing out words like gigabyte and modem. I was now enrolled in a quickie typing class because, as Whitman said, 'typing forms the basis of modern civilization.' He wanted me to be 'fluent on a keyboard'.

As Whitman explained what he wanted me to do, I got more and more nervous. Because none of it was black and white or cut and dried. In my last job, my duties were clearly defined: clean and arrange the DVD and video boxes for all the porn movies, make change so men could go back to the 'viewing booths', and operate the cash register. It didn't require skill so much as a certain amount of bravery, given what the customers were buying up front and doing in the back.

What Whitman wanted me to do, though, was collect information. And ferret out interesting titbits that he could use in his travel stories.

'Why don't you start with Angkor Wat,' he suggested, handing me a five-page list of possible destinations.

'Angkor what?'

'*Wat*. You know, the state temple in Cambodia.'

'Um – how do you spell that?'

I pecked out the letters as Whitman spelled Angkor Wat, then Googled. Hundreds of articles and websites appeared. 'Am I supposed to read *all* of this?'

Whitman folded his arms and worked at being patient. 'You'll have to learn how to be quick and selective,' he said. 'Scan and skim, or you'll be days on one destination.'

I flipped through that daunting list. 'How long should I spend on each place?'

'Half an hour, max. Find something that gives you a quick summary of what's there. Jot down a few key phrases. Like, "twelfth-century temple with quincunx of towers and highly decorated bas-reliefs. National symbol of Cambodia. Spiritual Mecca, first Hindu, then Buddhist." Stuff like that. And pull out any intriguing little bits and highlight them for me.'

I nodded, my head spinning. What was a quincunx? It sounded dirty. What were bas-reliefs? Something to do with sheep? How could I possibly ferret out anything especially intriguing when it was all so utterly foreign to me?

'Type up each one as a brief summary. Four or five sentences. And at the end, note the website address of national tourist offices or any public or private agency that looks useful.'

'And I've got half an hour to do all that for each one of these thousand places?'

'Fifteen minutes would be better.' He must have seen the look of panic on my face because he came over and put his hands on my shoulders. 'It probably seems impossible, but you'll get the hang of it. You're smarter than you think you are.'

'I hope so.'

'Look, darling, if you're ever going to make something of yourself, you have to learn to think on your own two feet. You have to accept challenges. The people who succeed the most aren't the ones who file widgets and count beans.' He planted a little self-conscious kiss on my cheek. 'And you couldn't ask for a better boss.'

I don't know how I did it, but I did it. By the time we were in Portland International Airport waiting for our flight to New York, I had summarized one thousand potential travel destinations.

I was surprised at how much I hadn't minded. Learning all those new skills had occupied my mind and kept me from obsessing 24/7 about Tremaynne. And it boosted my self-confidence. I now knew that I was capable of doing something completely unlike anything I'd ever done before.

And boy, did I ever learn a lot. Because of this work, the world was suddenly a much larger oyster, filled with exotic cities and strange customs and odd clothes and scary politics.

My newly acquired skills were becoming a part of my daily life. It gave me a weird geeky thrill to turn on my laptop every morning and hear its familiar clicks and whirrs and recognize its sequence of screens followed by the Microsoft finale. Sometimes, as my typing skills improved, I almost felt like a concert pianist. My fingers flew over the keyboard, fast and accurate.

Anyway, the impossible-to-please Whitman seemed genuinely pleased with my work. That was an enormous milestone.

'You see,' he said, 'I knew you were smart. I knew you could do this.'

'I wasn't so sure,' I said.

'You have a native intelligence,' Whitman said. 'Like your mother. It's just never been focused on anything creative or intellectual.'

'Maybe that's because I'm not a creative or intellectual person.'

'What are you suggesting,' Whitman said, 'that you're *ordinary*?'

'Is that so awful?'

'Look around you,' Daddy muttered.

I wondered what he meant. We were sitting in the new concourse waiting for our flight. I hadn't been in an airport for years. To me it was all tinged with the excitement of an impending journey.

'That's what I've always loved about New York,' Whitman said, 'and why I miss it so much.'

Daddy nodded. 'Nothing's ordinary in New York.'

'Well,' Whitman said, giving Daddy's neck the briefest and sweetest of strokes, 'you have to love a city where you fell in love.'

'Is that where you two fell in love?'

Daddy nodded. He and Whitman were looking at each other. 'Over twenty years ago now.'

'And we *still* can't get married,' Whitman said.

For although they *had* got married, in a quickie ceremony

along with three thousand other gay and lesbian couples, the state of Oregon had divorced them after voters demanded that marriage be defined as between a man and a woman. The official papers the dads had signed with such incredulous joy were now null and void and their registration fees had been returned with a curt official note that revoked the legality of their union. It was a real sore point with both of them, and ever since then, Whitman had been talking about moving back to New York.

And now it suddenly struck me – we were going back because the dads were thinking about doing just that. *Moving back to New York!* They hadn't said in so many words that this was their plan, but all the pieces fit together. Whitman's apartment was vacant. He was going to write a regular column for a magazine based in Manhattan. Daddy was taking two weeks off, which he never did, just to be in the old apartment and 'get in touch' with New York again.

I won't say I panicked, but the thought of losing them, of having them three thousand miles away, while I was stuck back in Portland with . . .

Before I could complete the scenario, my cellphone rang.

'Are you in the airport?' Mom asked.

'Yeah. Was there something you wanted?'

'Oh, no,' Mom said, her voice cracking. 'I was just thinking of how I used to bring you out there – to the airport – when you were a little girl, and you'd fly off all by yourself to New York to visit the dads.'

What was I supposed to say?

'I hope you have a wonderful time,' Mom said. 'I wish I was going with you.'

'Mom, you'd hate it there.'

'You mean the noise and the dirty air and the terrible weather?'

'For starters.'

'But there's just so much to *do*,' Mom said. 'I mean, from what you've told me. The museums and the theaters and the restaurants and the opera and the shopping—'

'Mom, you're afraid of flying, you're agoraphobic, and you can't stand it when the temperature goes above seventy-five.'

'Is it hotter than that in New York?' she asked.

'I just checked on the Web and it's ninety-eight degrees with eighty percent humidity.'

That silenced her for a moment. 'Well,' she finally said, 'maybe autumn would be a better time to visit. What's that song?' I didn't know, so she sang it for me. ' "Autumn in New York, why does it seem so inviting?" '

'Mom, they're calling our flight, I've got to go.'

' "Autumn in New York",' she warbled, ' "it spells the thrill of first nighting . . ." '

'Love you, Mom.'

But she wouldn't stop singing. ' "Glittering crowds and shimmering clouds in canyons of steel . . ." '

'Mom, I'll call you from New York.'

'*Bon voyage*, sweetheart! You're not a little girl any more.'

No, I was a big girl. A woman who menstruated. My period had come two weeks earlier.

I've always been a little irregular, and maybe the incredible physical stress of what Tremaynne and I went through at Pine Mountain Lodge had something to do with my missed period. But the moment I felt that familiar little ooze of moisture in my crotch my mind just went blank. It was such a huge deal that I couldn't deal with it. My first instinct was to cry, and my face was pulled in, tight as a mask, as I made my way to the ladies' room at Starbucks. Once inside, I could feel this swell of emotion starting to slosh around. Tears dripped from my eyes, which welled up as I fumbled with my change and inserted coins to buy a tampon. When I saw the blood in my panties I let out a big snot-filled gasp of sorrow and relief.

If the walls of that ladies' room in Starbucks could talk, they'd tell you all about the young woman – me – who sat on the toilet and sobbed her guts out. It was one of the most memorable cries of my life. I'd just bought a pregnancy test but I'd been afraid to use it. Now I had my answer.

I'd been freed from the burden of having a child by the man

I loved most and would have done almost anything to keep.

I wasn't ready for motherhood, I knew that in my soul. But in my fantasies, I sometimes gave birth to Tremaynne's baby and it magically reunited us.

With one internal flush, my life had changed. I was free of all biological ties with Tremaynne. Now if I could just dislodge him from my heart.

Whitman claimed the air was better in Business Class and he'd used over a hundred thousand of his frequent-flyer miles to get us up there. 'Otherwise it's like taking the bus,' he said, as the Business and First-Class passengers were ushered into the jetway ahead of everyone else. 'To think, we're not even fifty and we've already lived through the golden age of airline travel.'

It was kind of shocking. I hadn't flown for so many years that I didn't know how much the airlines had changed. People in Economy Class now had to *bring their own food*. 'And the smell of all that fat and grease just turns my stomach.' Whitman shuddered. From his carry-on he extracted three face masks, the kind you wear over your mouth and nose, and handed one to Daddy and one to me.

'Are you kidding?' I said.

'I am not kidding,' he said, slipping the elastic band over his head. 'I know it looks crazy and uncool, but even the air in Business Class is loaded with viruses.'

'I'm sorry, it's just too weird.'

'What's weird,' he said, 'is when you suddenly come down with an illness that nobody can diagnose and nobody knows where it came from and suddenly you're in a coma or dead.'

As if to prove his point, the man next to me let out an enormous sneeze and then started coughing without closing his mouth.

I put on the mask.

But took it off when the flight attendant asked if I'd like a pre-takeoff beverage.

'We'll all have some bottled water,' Whitman said through his mask.

'I'd like a margarita.'

'Alcohol is the *worst* thing to drink on a flight,' Whitman warned. 'It dehydrates you and makes you more susceptible to headaches and insomnia.'

'But it tastes good.'

The matter was settled when the flight attendant, a woman who looked old enough to be my grandma, said the airline didn't serve tequila except on flights to Mexico and South America. So I had water and dreamed of the red wine I'd order with dinner.

It would have been an on-time departure except that a safety check revealed that the landing mechanism needed a replacement part. That was reassuring news. The doors were locked and nobody was allowed off even though the mechanical problem took over an hour to fix.

Since we had to wait so long, the captain announced that we could continue to use our electronic equipment. Whitman and Daddy, sitting across the aisle from me, took out their laptops and cellphones and carried on as if they were at their offices. I hesitated but then did the same. I removed my laptop from its carrying case and set it on my tray table and opened it up. And at that moment I realized I was living in a new world. A new world for me, I should say. The 'new' Venus Gilroy, unpregnant, on her way to New York, was adept at making a slim, slender machine do her bidding. The 'old' Venus would never have had a laptop, or known how to use one. The old Venus would have whipped out the latest issue of *Vogue* or *Elle* for some serious browsing, eyed the potential love interest around her, nervously wolfed down an economy-size bag of super-salty potato chips, or slept off a hangover from too many margaritas the night before.

I'd crossed a personal and technological threshold. I felt *professional*, somehow. Important enough to sit in Business Class and use a laptop.

I looked at the executives around me, men and women, all

of them so busy, so intent on pushing their business forward and adding to the jackpot of their lives. I texted Whitman sitting across the aisle. 'Do you want me to reorganize the information for the thousand trips?' I heard the little dinging tone as my message entered his cellphone.

I watched as he read the message and texted his response. It was like a pingpong game. A moment later my phone dinged. 'No need to reorganize thousand trips,' his message read. 'Start writing your memoir instead.'

The heat slugged us the second we walked into the terminal at LaGuardia. Even with the air-conditioning it was hot. And muggy.

A deafening torrent of noise, the babble of people talking in a hundred different languages, roared in my ears.

Colors, shapes, clothes, *fashion*. We'd left the overweight whiteness of Portland behind.

A shiver, the kind a dog gets when it becomes excited, coursed through me. I was in New York again! I could feel the multicultural energy buzzing in the air.

Daddy stopped us in the middle of the concourse. 'How about a triple hug? To welcome ourselves back to the Big A.'

'I'll hug to that,' Whitman said.

'Me too.'

So we did a three-way hug. And, to my complete and utter shock and surprise, Whitman started crying. I'd never seen him cry before, except once – after he and Daddy had saved me in Idaho, on my honeymoon.

'I'm just so h-h-h-happy to be back,' Whitman sobbed. 'I feel like this is my spiritual home.'

Daddy patted his back. Me? I was too busy looking around. I wondered if New York was my spiritual home, too. Some of the men sure were cute.

The heat inside had been a mirage. The real heat hit us when we stepped outside the terminal to get a taxi.

We all stopped, slightly stunned by the impact. I said, 'Oh!' and Whitman whispered, 'Ay-yai-yai!' and Daddy murmured, 'Jesus Christ!'

I have to explain something here. When you live in Portland, Oregon, you live in a climate where the temperature usually seems to hover at about 50 degrees Fahrenheit. The air is sweet and rich because of all the rain and all the trees. For three months in the summer it gets clear and hot, but the heat is dry heat, blowing in from the deserts in the eastern half of the state. And no matter how hot it is during the day, at night the temperature drops twenty to thirty degrees and a breeze comes up, like built-in-air-conditioning. So really, it's never that uncomfortable out there.

But the weather in New York is dramatic, unpredictable and generally horrible. It all came back to me in a flash flood of memories. This humid heat was like something alive, a slippery, slithering, simmering force to be reckoned with. The sky was like a dirty gray sponge, sopping wet, waiting to be wrung out in one of those terrifying thunder storms I remembered from years ago.

'I hope you packed a winter parka,' Whitman said to me as we waited in line for a taxi.

'I can actually feel the dirt entering my pores,' Daddy said.

'Yes.' Whitman took a deep breath. 'And that weird metallic smell in the air. Isn't it wonderful?'

We were directed to a taxi and loaded our suitcases in the trunk. Whitman sat in front and gave the long-faced, dour-looking driver our old address. He said, as he'd always said to taxi drivers, 'One oh two between Broadway and West End.'

With a neck-snapping lurch we were off.

'This is the way we always used to come in,' I said as we sped along the Van Wyck Parkway.

Daddy smiled and took my hand. 'Excited to be back?'

I nodded. 'It brings back memories I didn't know I had.'

'I remember how frightened you were the first time I came out to pick you up.'

'I was eight years old and I'd just flown across the entire

country by myself. I was terrified that you wouldn't be there at the other end.'

Daddy pressed my hand.

Up front, Whitman was engaged in an animated discussion with the Russian driver. 'Where did they find the body?' he asked.

'In apartment,' the driver told him.

'And he'd been dead how long?'

'Two veeks. It vas the smell. Dot's ven dey got suspicious.'

'Nothing like that's ever happened in our building,' Whitman said.

The drive in from LaGuardia along the Van Wyck Parkway is not what you'd call pretty. It wasn't until we got near the Triboro bridge and saw the Manhattan skyline rising up through a steamy gray haze in the distance that my heart began to boom-box.

'Listen!' Whitman said suddenly, turning around with a goofy look on his face. 'Hear that?'

'What?' Daddy and I looked at each other.

'Frank Sinatra,' Whitman said. 'Singing "New York, New York". You don't hear it?'

The funny thing was, I did.

'Central Park,' Whitman announced as we crossed Fifth Avenue at 96th Street and sped into the park.

'Raccoons now,' the cab driver informed us.

'Raccoons in Central Park?' Whitman laughed. 'Deer can't be far behind.'

'Yes, deer,' the cabbie said. 'They're moving in from the suburbs.'

'Can't say I blame them,' Whitman said.

And then – there it was – we pulled up in front of the old five-storey apartment building in the middle of 102nd Street between Broadway and West End Avenue.

'We're home,' Daddy said as we got out and stood staring at the building. 'We're all back home again.'

'What's the name next to the buzzer for IB?' Whitman asked.

I squinted and tried to decipher the handwritten tag. 'Wang? I think.'

'Dingding Wang,' Whitman nodded. 'My subletter. He's gone now, so you can slip that little piece of paper out with your long fingernails and turn it over.'

I did as requested. 'Whittlesley-Gilroy' was neatly printed on the other side. I slipped the tag back in the slot next to the buzzer.

'Officially at home,' Whitman said, putting his key in the first of the two heavy doors that opened with difficulty and slammed ferociously if you let go of them for one second.

We all sniffed as we entered the hallway. It wasn't unpleasant, it was–

'Fried chicken?' Daddy guessed.

'Chicken something,' Whitman said. He put a hand up to shield his eyes. 'God, that new fluorescent light makes the hallway look like an operating room.'

'When did they install that?' Daddy asked.

'Dingding said they did it around Christmas time. And painted the hallways.'

We all stopped to examine the shiny walls gleaming under the fluorescent lights. Not white, exactly, but a kind of gluey gray with a dark brown trim along the moldings.

'Ghastly,' Whitman said. 'That's the one thing I hate about New York – you can't control the awful taste of your landlord.'

The building was five storeys tall, like all the buildings around it, and had two apartments on each floor, one at the front and one at the back, ten in all. There was no elevator, so the top apartments were called 'walk-ups'. Our apartment, 1B, was at the back of the ground floor and opened on to our own private garden. Whitman was just putting the key in the lock when something slammed against the inside of the door to 1A and a male voice cried, 'Oh God! Give it to me!'

As we stood there, the door to 1A began banging against its hinges and, just behind it, the hoarse male voice kept up its moaning encouragement. 'Ram it in! Farther! Farther! Ahh!'

It was like being back on the night shift at Phantastic Phantasy, the porn store with the viewing booths at the back.

We all looked at each other and tried not to laugh. 'Andy and Candy,' Whitman whispered.

'They're still here?'

'Apparently.'

A door opened in the hallway above. There was a loud scraping clatter and we all looked up in astonishment as a nun wearing an old-fashioned habit and inline skates made her way down the stairs, walking sideways and holding on to the banister so the skates wouldn't shoot out in front of her. Her face was turned away from us but when she reached the bottom she turned and saw us.

Or, rather, he turned and saw us.

'Hello,' Whitman said. 'Do you live up in 2B?'

'Just visiting.' And with that, the nun picked up the front of his habit and glided gracefully to the front doors and out to the street.

The moment the front doors slammed, the lock on another door, on a higher floor, clicked, the door was pulled open, and someone came out to the landing to peer down and say in a loud, piercing voice, 'Dingding, is that you?'

'No, darling,' Whitman called up the stairs, 'it's Whitman and John and Venus.'

The gasp was acoustically enhanced by the stairwell. 'Whitman! And John! And Venus? You're back? Oh. My. Gawd. Hang on a sec! I'll be right down!'

'Do you remember her?' Whitman whispered as we waited for 3A to come down.

'Just the voice.'

'Sheba Fleischbaum,' Daddy whispered. 'She's been in the building longer than anyone else.'

'She's rent-controlled,' Whitman whispered. 'Pays four hundred dollars a month.'

'Whitman! And John! And Venus! Oh my Gawd!' Sheba's sandals ticked as she made her way down the stairs. 'I have to walk slow or I'll pass out from the heat!'

'It's hot,' Whitman affirmed.

'Hot? Oh my Gawd! I'm schvitzing all over the place. They should mop up after me. Maybe the floors would be cleanuh.'

'How are you, Sheba?' Daddy asked politely.

Now we had a glimpse of her, stuffed into a one-piece swimsuit with a kind of thin, loose kimono wafting out behind her. 'How am I? Hot! I finally broke down and bought a new air-conditionuh, right? On sale down the street at the appliance store. They'd been sold out for weeks. So finally I get one and they deliver it and I have to pay extra to have this big cute Hispanic guy fit it in my front window, right? Venus! How are you, darling? Oh, I can't believe you're here, it's been at least a century. Look at you! So I'm in my bathing suit, right? Because it's so fucking hot, pardon my French. I'm way past the muu-muu stage, and my body's still pretty good for a sixty-year-old, don't you think? So this big cute Hispanic guy comes in to install my new a-c, right? He comes in, and I'm sitting there on the sofa in my bathing suit. He says, "Where you want it, lady?" And I say, "In the front window", and he says, "Someone might steal it." '

'And someone stole it,' Whitman guessed.

By this time she had reached us, but was continuing her apparently unending story. 'So I go out for dinner with some friends. Cute little new place up on 105th Street. Order the veal tenderloin if you go. So I'm gone for two hours, max, and I come home and I enter my apartment and it's so hot. I'm thinking, "Didn't I leave the air on?" '

'Did they take anything else?' Whitman asked.

'An air-conditionuh isn't enough? Do you know how heavy that thing was? I swear to Gawd, it had to weigh at least half a ton. Venus! Do you remember me, darling? I think you were about fifteen when I saw you last. You'd just had your hair permed and your dads had bought you some new clothes over at Bergdorf's and it was snowing and you were all on your way out to a Broadway show. *Cats*. I saw you here in the hallway.'

'You have a pretty amazing memory,' I said.

'Well?' She opened her arms, revealing the ample, pear-shaped body beneath the kimono. 'Give me a hug!'

I hugged her. Then it was Daddy's turn.

'So what's with living out in Portland, Oregon? Nobody ages out there? Look at the skin! On all of you! John, sweetheart, don't you have any unmarried bruthas? As good-looking as you? So how's business out there in Portland, Oregon? You building buildings?'

'Look in the new issue of *Aura*,' Whitman said. 'There's a feature on Pine Mountain Lodge, which he designed.'

'Pine Mountain Lodge. Oh my Gawd, doesn't that sound romantic? It's in *Aura*, huh? Too bad I hate that magazine.'

Whitman stiffened. 'Hate it?'

'Whitman's going to write for it,' I said.

Sheba Fleischbaum didn't miss a beat. 'Like I said, I *love* that magazine. I just can't understand why it's published.'

'I won't hold it against you,' Whitman said, giving her an air kiss. 'So this robbery—'

'Yeah. First one in ages,' Sheba said. 'They must have come across the roof and down the fire escape but how they got out again, carrying a half-ton air-conditionuh . . . The police think it might be one of the boys who clean the hallways. If you call this cleaning. So I don't know. All I know is that I'm hot, there's no beach, there's no place to take a dip, and the appliance store's sold out of air-conditionuhs again.'

'Who's the nun in 2B?' Whitman asked.

'Oh. Kenny?' She laughed. 'He's an illegal sublet. Like Dingding. Who went back to China, I hear. And you remember Norm up in 5A? Well, his arthritis got so bad he had to move.'

'Norm was also rent-controlled,' Whitman informed me.

'Norm and me and you,' Sheba said. 'We're the only ones left.'

'No, I'm not controlled,' Whitman said, 'I'm stabilized.'

'Well, you should of seen poor Norm. I swear to Gawd, my heart bled every time I heard him on the staircase. It took him an ow-wa to get down, and two ow-was to get back up, that's how slow he had to move because of the arthritis. Plus he was going blind, you know.'

It took us almost another ow-wa before Sheba stopped talking and we were able to get into our apartment.

The apartment was dark, the air was stifling, and the overwhelming smell was . . .

'Cabbage?' Daddy guessed.

'Feeuw.' As he groped his way into the darkened apartment, Whitman stepped on something which let out a scream and flew into the bedroom. 'Jesus! What was that?'

'I think it was a cat,' Daddy said.

'A cat? How did a cat get in here?'

'Maybe Dingding had a pet,' I suggested.

'And just left it behind? Great!'

'The window's open,' Daddy said. 'Maybe it got in that way.'

'Fleas and all,' Whitman said. 'Well, we'd better find the damn thing. I just hope it's not feral.'

While Daddy turned on lights, or tried to – half of them didn't work – Whitman ventured into the narrow bedroom. 'All right, where are you?' he demanded. 'Come out, we're not going to hurt you.'

We heard a yowl and saw a thin black shape dart out of the bedroom and into the kitchen.

'This is ridiculous,' Whitman said. 'This is New York – *wild animals don't come in through windows*. Look at my Louis Quatorze sofa – it's been clawed to shreds!' He pointed in horror. 'Cat poop! On my Persian rug!'

'I need to find some lightbulbs,' Daddy said. 'I don't remember it being this dark in here.'

'It wasn't.' Whitman peered out the barred windows in the living room. 'Oh my God! They've built an outdoor balcony right above our windows!'

Daddy and I went over to look. It was true. A balcony now protruded into the space right above the windows, cutting off the light that used to slant in.

Whitman was furious. He stormed back into the bedroom, unlocked and pulled open the old glass-paned door, unlatched the screen door, pulled back the bar on the heavy metal security door and pushed that open, then stepped out into his beloved garden. The moment all the doors were open, the cat raced through the apartment and outside where it tried in vain to leap up to the top of the wall that surrounded the garden on all sides.

'It's gone insane!' Whitman cried. 'John, do something! It's going to damage the Polygonatums and maidenhair ferns!'

Daddy and I ran out to the garden and watched as the huge, skinny cat ran back and forth, from one side of the garden to the other, hurling itself at the plaster walls. When Daddy cautiously approached it, the cat bared its fangs and hissed.

'Don't let it bite you!' Whitman herded us back inside. 'Let's just wait until it calms down, and then we can figure out what to do.'

'What's wrong with this air-conditioner?' Whitman tried all the knobs but nothing happened. He followed the cord from the air-conditioner down to an outlet hidden somewhere behind and under his desk. 'The cord's been chewed off!'

'By the cat?' I said.

'Or mice. Dingding probably never let the exterminator in.'

'It was an old air-conditioner,' Daddy said.

'Old,' Whitman said, 'but working perfectly when Dingding moved in two summers ago.'

'What happened to that fan we used to have?' Daddy asked.

As they rummaged around, Whitman exclaiming how filthy everything was, how they'd have to clean every square inch of the apartment and reupholster all the furniture, I sat on the shredded sofa that had once served as my bed and tried not to think of Tremaynne.

Something about coming back to New York, returning to the apartment, a place both strange and familiar, had squeezed out some fantasies that I shouldn't have indulged but did. Like, what if Tremaynne was here with me and we were moving into 1B ourselves, to start a new life together. How would I fix the place up for us?

But the fantasy fizzled and I couldn't go anywhere with it because I knew that Tremaynne would hate New York. He would hate everything about it. He wanted to live in the wilderness, a place without people. I wanted just the opposite.

That's why I loved New York. I loved the sense of being right in the thick of it. The wonder of this apartment, old and decrepit as it was, was that it was as quiet as the country and had a garden, but the minute you walked out the front door, you were half a block from Broadway.

Then I thought: what would it be like to live in New York on my own?

Start over. From scratch. Create a new document on my computer hard-drive and write out a new life for myself.

Something stirred in me, the excitement of possibility.

Why not? I could find a job. I had computer skills. I could type.

It would make even more sense if the dads were, in fact, thinking of moving back themselves. I wouldn't be all alone. They could help me search for an apartment.

'Heat got you down?' Daddy came over and perched for a moment beside me.

I shook my head.

He brushed my cheek with his fingers. 'Feeling a little sad?'

'I'm tired of feeling sad. I think I need some big new major change in my life.'

'I can understand that.'

'Daddy, are you and Whitman thinking of moving back here?'

He sat back, sighed, and rubbed his chin. 'We've talked about it.'

'Talked about what?' Whitman said from the kitchen alcove.

'About moving back to New York,' Daddy said.

'Yes, we've talked about it,' Whitman said. 'Why?'

I shrugged. 'I was just thinking – maybe – I don't know – maybe I could move here too.'

'To New York?' Whitman said incredulously.

'I could get a job.'

Both dads were silent. They looked at one another. Whitman ran a hand through his newly cut hair. 'Let's talk about it when the apartment's clean,' he said. 'That dang Dingding wasn't what I'd call a meticulous housekeeper.'

Whitman was serious when he said every square inch of the apartment had to be cleaned. 'Cleaning's my version of an exorcism,' he said, stripping down to shorts and tennis shoes, a bandana around his head to sop up the sweat.

It wasn't what I thought my all-expenses-paid holiday was going to be, but I got into it. We all did. We were a team. Daddy repaired, rebuilt, replaced and refinished. It wasn't that things had been damaged so much as that he had such exacting standards. He was an architect, so the fact that there wasn't a single straight line in the entire apartment drove him slightly crazy. Years earlier, he confided to me, when he'd first moved in with Whitman, he'd rebuilt the entire apartment as a 'love gift'.

So he'd done all this work, building cabinets and installing a new kitchen and bathroom. But over the years, his once-pristine work had suffered various indignities. A flood from the floor above had warped cabinet doors, ruined perfectly painted walls, and stained meticulously finished floors. And a succession of subletters – all of them illegal because in New York you are allowed only one two-year legal sublet for the duration of your tenancy – had proven to be what Whitman called 'irritating mistakes'. One, a drag queen, painted the entire apartment bubble-gum pink.

And so they fussed and repainted and made it livable again, according to their standards, because Whitman refused to give it up and went to absurd lengths to keep it. The idea of giving up his New York abode and becoming a permanent resident of Oregon frightened him. 'Do we really want to live in a place that revoked our marriage license?' he said.

I helped vacuum and ran a wet, soapy rag along various

surfaces that had turned black and sticky with grime. 'Rub, sweetheart,' Whitman said. '*Rub*. Think of it as aerobic exercise with a purpose.'

Whitman sang opera arias as he scrubbed, waxed and buffed the floors. Years earlier, before he met Daddy, he'd studied to be an opera singer, and he did have a pretty amazing tenor voice.

The heat continued unabated and there wasn't a single air-conditioner to be found anywhere in the city. 'It's awful,' Whitman admitted, 'but try to think of it as an extra-long hot-yoga class.'

Between sweaty bouts in the apartment, we stepped out into the garden for a breath of air. It was broiling out there, too, but the bittersweet vine Whitman and Daddy had planted on their first anniversary had crept across the telephone and cable line and up the back fire escape, creating a shady arbor below. This vine, in fact, looked as if it might pull down the entire building. Seeking light, it had climbed steadily upwards, following the slats and poles of the fire escape up all five storeys of the buildings.

But what to do with the cat?

It was the dirtiest, ugliest, scrawniest and scariest-looking cat I'd ever seen, but sort of weirdly loveable because of that. A hungry street cat, we decided, that had somehow managed to get into the garden, maybe to hunt birds, and from there had snuck through the bars of the window Dingding left open when he vacated the premises. The cat had obviously cased the joint, seen that it was empty, and was living like a squatter in 1B. But now it wouldn't come near us and couldn't get up the garden walls and back out to the street. It sat in high alert in a far corner of the garden with one paw partly raised. 'It's either an affectation or it's hurt,' Whitman said.

I'd grown up with cats. With Carolee I'd lived through fleas and parasites and enough kitty litter to fill Grand Canyon. 'Couldn't we adopt it?' I said.

'Are you out of your mind?' Whitman looked at me as if I were crazy. 'It's absolutely filthy. There's something *oozing* from its left eye. One of its ears is torn and one of its front fangs is broken – it would cost a fortune to have a crown put on. No, we can't adopt a cat and that's that.'

'OK.'

So the snaggle-toothed cat sat there in the corner of the garden, eyes oozing, covered with sores, its one paw held up as if it were holding a tea cup, staring balefully at us, the usurpers of his comfy domain. Periodically it would make a mad, futile dash to get out. But the stuccoed garden walls, which Daddy had built years ago, were about seven feet high and covered with ivy and Virginia creeper which the cat tried to latch on to and only succeeded in tearing down.

'How are we going to get it out?' Daddy asked. 'It can't climb because its front paw is hurt.'

'I think that's from when I stepped on it,' Whitman admitted.

We didn't know what to do, so we didn't do anything. That first night, the cat stayed out in the garden. I could hear it making weird sounds, maybe because of its sore foot, or maybe because of life's general miseries.

I woke up way too early the next morning and looked out to see Whitman crouched in the garden and murmuring something. 'Come here, you stupid old thing,' I heard him say. 'I'm not going to hurt you.'

The cat stared at him from its corner, as suspicious of this friendly overture as I was.

'Look, I brought you some milk. It's only one percent but that's all I have.'

The cat leaned forward, considering.

'I can't adopt you,' Whitman said, 'but I promise I'll take you to a vet and get you cleaned up and then bring you to a nice animal shelter over on the East Side.'

The cat rubbed its oozing eye and licked its good paw.

Whitman left the milk, came in, and went back to bed, but I continued to watch the cat. The moment it was alone, it hobbled over to survey the dogwood tree by the back wall. Then, without using its hurt paw, it slowly began to climb, the thin trunk of the dogwood swaying back and forth and threatening to snap under its weight.

Somehow the cat made it up to the top of the wall, but when it gingerly stepped off the tree onto the curved wall it couldn't keep its balance and with a yowl of indignation went crashing down into the shrubbery on the other side.

'Well,' Whitman said later that morning, 'it obviously knew the meaning of "animal shelter".'

On the day he was to go pitch his column ideas to the editor-in-chief of *Aura*, Whitman dressed in a linen suit with a shirt and tie even though it was almost a hundred degrees outside.

'You forgot to shave,' I said when he came out of the bathroom to model for us.

'No, sweetheart, carefully trimmed stubble is the recommended look nowadays.'

'Well,' Daddy said, 'you look hot.'

'I *am* hot,' Whitman said, pulling at his collar. 'The trick will be to remain unwrinkled until I get to midtown.'

'I meant *hot*,' Daddy said.

'Oh.' Whitman gave him a self-conscious kiss – he was always self-conscious about showing physical affection towards Daddy when I was around – and did the same with me. Then he picked up his smart new briefcase and left.

By that time – four days into our trip – the apartment was looking much better and Daddy and I decided to take the rest of the day off. 'Let's walk across Central Park and maybe stop in at the Metropolitan Museum,' I suggested. This is what we'd always done in years past, on my quarterly visits.

We dressed as coolly as we could and still look decent. I put on a pair of shorts, a banana-yellow halter top, a wide-brimmed straw hat, and slipped into a pair of sandals. Daddy wore what he called Bermuda shorts, a T-shirt and a Yankees cap. Even stripped down to the bare essentials, we started to sweat the minute we stepped outside. But everyone else was sweating, too, and no one cared what they looked like, so you just got into the shared heat groove and slowed way down.

We headed south on Broadway. It was like wading through molasses. The frantic pace of New York had slowed to a crawl. The only one who looked halfway cool was the middle-aged lady wearing the bikini and little gold sandals.

'Can you imagine being that unself-conscious?' Daddy said.

'Not with a body like that,' I said. Averting my eyes from the woman's lumpy overflow, I caught sight of a pair of dark male eyes staring at me in passing. I looked away, and right into the eyes of another man who gave me an up-and-down eyeball massage.

'It's like walking down Broadway naked.' Daddy sighed. 'Well, New York does drive people crazy. I've always thought that.'

'Mm-hm,' I said, trying not to smile at a really cute guy who lifted his eyes my way, then pursed his lips and blew me a kiss.

This was maybe the stretch of New York that I knew better than any other, Broadway between 96th and 103rd Street. It wasn't glamorous, but there was so much to look at. I marvelled to see so many changes in ten years. Everywhere you looked there was a new building or new construction. Daddy was in architect heaven. 'Look at that!' he said, pointing to a construction site. 'That used to be the Red Apple supermarket, remember? The one where the cashiers never looked you in the eye and just kept talking to one another.'

That depressing store with its stale smells and terrible produce and rude cashiers was gone. We stared up at the steel bones of what would be a new forty-storey luxury apartment building.

It was hard to believe, but in the ten years of my absence, Broadway above 96th Street had become gentrified. The whole city had. On the Upper West Side, one- and two-storey buildings had been knocked down and replaced by huge towers. Intriguing little neighborhood boutiques and bodegas had disappeared and were being replaced by larger brand-name stores. Hole-in-the-wall restaurants that served Cuban, Chinese and other inexpensive ethnic foods had vanished and were being replaced by fancy places where a hamburger cost twenty dollars.

But one thing had definitely not changed: the bold stares of the men. Daddy was oblivious to the appreciative comments and lewd propositions pitched so low that only I could hear them. I'd forgotten about the sexual bandwidths that flowed down New York streets carrying instant messages from eye to eye. It was so brazen compared to Portland, stuck in the gridlock of political correctness. Here the guys openly ogled and flirted outrageously to get your attention.

'Oof,' Daddy said as we crept along the steaming streets, 'it's like a jungle.'

It sure was, but probably not the kind he had in mind. A sloe-eyed guy passing by looked me up and down and said, 'Woof.'

We were in the European Paintings galleries, staring at a naked reclining woman painted by Renoir, when Daddy's phone rang. I could tell from the annoyed stares that it was not cool to receive phone calls in the Metropolitan Museum of Art.

Daddy turned away and lowered his voice. I heard him say, 'fantastic' and 'terrific' and repeat an address.

'That was Whitman,' he said when he'd switched off. 'He wants us to meet him down in Chelsea at six o'clock.'

'Did he get the job?'

Daddy grinned. 'They loved his ideas and they're giving him his own travel column.'

'Are we going out to celebrate?'

'We're going out for dinner, but Whitman wants us to come to a cocktail party with some *Aura* people first.'

I was instantly apprehensive. It's not that I don't like parties. The dads used to drag me around to parties when I was a kid, and all their childless New York friends would fawn over me until they got bored with my shyness. So I learned not to be shy, because really, they were all pretty nice people and did interesting things. But I wasn't a kid any more. I was in my late twenties, with nothing to show for my life. I'd been married three times and I'd nearly been killed on my honeymoon in Idaho. In New York, where having a career defines your life, I was a big fat zero.

Plus I didn't have anything to wear. I mean I did, but none of it was suitable for a chic New York cocktail party. When I voiced my fears, Daddy sweetly suggested we hop in a cab and head down to Bergdorf's.

'Do I look OK?'

'Sweetheart, you look wonderful. Really. Believe me.'

It was my first black cocktail dress, a form-fitting sheath with tiny straps. It moved like a dream and made me feel sexy and self-conscious and grown-up. I couldn't slouch wearing such a dress. I had to walk like I had a book balanced on my head. It made me realize just how much I'd let myself go since the split with Tremaynne. I was what Mom liked to call 'voluptuous', but I felt more like the 'before' picture in a weight loss ad. I'd never be skinny, never *wanted* to be skinny, but a little more definition would do wonders.

'I'll pay you back,' I said, slipping into the sumptuous black heels that went with the dress.

'Just enjoy it, sweetheart.' Daddy said. 'Enjoy being a beautiful woman in a beautiful dress in New York City.'

I hope I'm that sweet to my kids, if I ever have any.

The party was in a big loft-like space that was jammed and noisy and cold as a walk-in freezer. My sweat instantly turned to goosepimples.

'Do you see Whitman anywhere?' Daddy asked as we waded into the crowd.

'No.' Just a sea of impossibly beautiful people who knew they were impossibly beautiful.

'Wait right here,' Daddy said, 'I have to find a toilet.'

The minute he was gone, a very cute dark-haired guy not much older than me appeared at my side. 'Are you with the *Aura* crowd?' he asked.

'Sort of. Not really.'

'That's what I call an elusive answer,' he said. 'Wouldn't you like to be holding a drink in your hand?'

I smiled but kept my mouth closed because I'm self-conscious about my teeth. Carolee didn't believe in orthodontia and the dads' friends used to say those little gaps between my teeth were 'charming', but in the world of blindingly white perfect choppers, I knew I was dentally challenged. 'Everyone seems to be drinking wine or water,' I said.

'Biblical, isn't it?' He touched my elbow and motioned for me to follow him to the bar, where he ordered two glasses of Cabernet Sauvignon. He looked a little surprised when the bartender told him it would be twenty dollars, and fumbled in his wallet for the money. 'Ten bucks for a glass of wine,' he winced, handing me my glass. 'This must be New York.'

I nodded. 'Everything's so expensive here.'

He eyed the heart tattooed on my left breast and clicked my glass. 'Cheers to expensive New York.'

'Cheers,' I said, trying to rein in all sorts of wild impulsive urges. Oh God, this guy was beyond cute. He was drop-dead gorgeous. His face was sculpted so that all the parts fit together perfectly and added up to hot, hunky perfection.

'Writer?' he asked.

I shook my head, amazed that anyone would ever think such a thing.

'Model?'

'Not thin enough.'

'Financial analyst?'

I laughed – shrieked, maybe – then quickly clamped my mouth shut. 'I'm terrible with money.'

'Me too,' he said.

I smiled dumbly, tongue-tied in his presence. I felt his instant snap of attraction, but instead of honing in on me, his beautiful green eyes began darting around like fish in an aquarium. I assumed he was keeping an eye out for someone else. Someone else had first dibs on that strong square chin with the slight cleft in it that made my knees wobbly.

But then he turned back to me and asked if I was there by myself.

'I came with my dad.'

'Your—Oh.'

Right, I thought, let's get everything off to a good bad start by announcing that my dad is my date. What would this guy think? 'He's in this month's issue of *Aura* magazine,' I said dumbly. 'My dad.'

His eyes widened in appreciation or perhaps surprise. 'Is he a writer?'

'No, architect. My other dad's a writer.'

'How many fathers do you have?'

'Just two. And a mother, of course. It's a long story.'

'Yes,' he said, moving an inch closer, 'and I'll bet it's fascinating.'

'Fascinating?' I let out another weird-sounding too-loud laugh.

'Well, most ordinary mortals have only one father.'

'I guess I'm lucky.'

'I *like* lucky people.' His eyes moved across my cleavage and along my shoulders and up my neck. A shiver snaked down my spine. 'You know,' he said, 'people generally rub things for good luck.'

'Do they?' I was just about to turn and lavish all my lucky charms on him when I saw Whitman appear at the bar with a slender forty-fivish blonde wearing pale pink lipstick and – my heart sank – the same dress I had on. Whitman turned around, surveying the crowd, and saw me.

'Venus! Hey!' His face was cranked up in party mode, with flashing white teeth and a kind of loud, assertive hardiness that I feared and admired. He hugged me and then presented me to his cohort. 'This is Susanna Hyde. Susanna, this is my daughter Venus.'

He wasn't aware – men never are – of the acute and contradictory emotions that arise when two women realize they are both wearing the same dress.

'Your *daughter*?' She had a husky voice and an English accent slightly slurred from drink.

'John's daughter,' Whitman clarified. 'I'm her faux pa.'

Susanna Hyde laughed as she eyeballed me head to toe. 'Well, darling,' she said, 'your faux fille obviously has excellent taste in clothes.' Her eyes slid from me over to the cute guy, standing slightly behind me. 'What's your boyfriend's name?' she asked me. There was no time to tell her I didn't know because she suddenly left Whitman's side and took a slightly lurching step straight for him. 'Susanna,' she said, putting out her hand and wedging herself between us. When he extended his, Susanna clasped it and drew him closer, away from me.

'Josh,' he said.

'I'll bet you're here looking for a good fuck,' Susanna said.

He laughed, a little uncomfortably, I thought, maybe put off by her aggressiveness, and stepped back closer to me. 'And maybe some work,' he said. 'I'm a writer.'

'Oh,' Susanna said, glancing up at Whitman, 'so are we.'

'Yes, I know.' Josh shook Whitman's hand and turned back to Susanna. 'I've heard of you.'

Susanna let out a bored but pleased laugh. 'My reputation precedes me, Whitman. As usual.'

I'd heard of her, too, but couldn't remember where.

'I just had a story published in *Belles Lettres*,' Josh said.

'Ooh,' Susanna said with mock admiration. 'Well, I just had my *third book* published and I'm almost finished with my *fourth*.' She looked at him with a droll little smile, daring him to top her.

'Fiction?' Josh asked.

Susanna laughed. 'Sort of.'

'A memoir,' Josh guessed.

'Not quite,' Susanna said playfully, running her manicured hand down his arm.

I suddenly remembered where I'd heard of her. ' "Nothing to Hyde!" ' I blurted out. 'You write that sex column.'

'Darling,' Susanna said, 'to paraphrase Flaubert, I *am* that sex column.'

Whitman flattered her by saying, 'You're the best-known sex-advice columnist in the world, aren't you? After Dr Ruth?'

'Dr Ruth!' Susanna practically spat. 'Who would want to have sex after reading Dr bloody Ruth? It would be like masturbating in front of your grandmother.'

We all laughed. Josh moved a step away from me and a step closer to Susanna.

'Susanna's just been named editor of *Aura*,' Whitman informed us. 'She's going to bring it up to a whole new level, aren't you, darling? Make it the New Age *Vogue*.'

'That's my mandate from Lord Stuckey,' Susanna said. She kept her frosty blue eyes on Whitman, ignoring us. 'That's why I wanted you, darling. It's time you had a monthly column of your own. To express all those deep deep insights you have about travel and culture.'

I couldn't tell if they were flirting or not. Didn't Susanna Hyde know that Whitman was gay? Or maybe they were just old friends. Or maybe in New York everyone was a congenital flirter. I watched as Susanna, while she was talking to Whitman, angled herself closer and closer to Josh until she was practically rubbing against him.

'Now that you're editor,' Whitman said to her, 'are you going to keep writing your column?'

'My column's the most popular feature *in Aura*,' she informed him. 'People buy the magazine because of *me*. Just as they buy my books because the name Susanna Hyde is on the cover. I'm a *brand*, darling.'

'Who's your publisher?' Josh asked.

Susanna, practically in his arms, turned her head and looked up at him. 'I just left my old publisher because they never did enough to promote me. From now on I'll be publishing with Stuckey Universal Media.'

'Instead of a sex column,' Josh said, 'have you ever thought about writing a sex *novel*?'

Susanna drew back, narrowed her eyes, and studied him. 'Why? Do you have some dirty ideas up your sleeve or behind your zipper?'

The transition was complete. Josh left my orbit and entered Susanna Hyde's. I can't say that I blamed him. There was something mesmerizing about her, a magnetic quality that drew you towards her even as it pushed you away.

By this time Daddy had found us and Whitman introduced him to Susanna. And Susanna, in turn, introduced Josh. She did this by turning to him and saying, 'What did you say your name was?'

'Josh O'Connell.' He extended his hand to Daddy. 'I'm a writer.'

'Architect,' Daddy said.

Whitman kissed Susanna, 'I'm afraid we have to go.'

She was theatrically crestfallen and to convey her disappointment, she snuggled back into Josh's body. 'Must you?'

'Yes. So congratulations, new *Aura* editor.' Whitman kissed her on the lips.

'Thank you, darling.' Susanna smiled and brushed a strand of streaked blonde hair from her eyes. 'And believe me, I'm simply thrilled that you're going to replace that wanker Jerry. I did everything I possibly could to influence Larry's decision today. You know that, don't you?'

'Yes,' Whitman said, 'thank you.'

And thank you, Josh O'Connell, I said to myself, for being the first gorgeous New York man to almost ask me out on a date. If I'd had the flagrant nerve or magnetic fame of Susanna Hyde, we might be leaving together just about now.

'And you will keep an eye open, won't you?' Susanna said to Whitman. 'You'll toss anyone who looks even *remotely* promising my way?'

'Susanna's looking for a personal assistant,' Whitman informed us.

It was like standing on the edge of a diving board, blindfolded, and not knowing whether there was any water in the pool. I took a chance and jumped.

'Could I apply?' I asked.

They all thought I was kidding. But I wasn't.

Something had nudged me, some hidden streak of boldness or dare-taking. Standing there in that cold, crowded room filled with smart people who were or wanted to be somebody, I wanted to be somebody, too. I wasn't thinking about being famous or anything like that, but just becoming somebody other than the Venus Gilroy I had been. A new Venus in a new place with a real job that demanded something of me.

I didn't want to conquer the world. I just wanted to conquer myself. Do something interesting with my life besides getting married to the wrong guy. And New York, not Portland, was the place to do it.

'If you're serious,' Susanna said, 'give me a call and we'll talk.'

'I'm serious.'

'Then we'll talk. Whitman has my private number.' She smiled, ever so briefly, and turned her attentions to Josh O'Connell.

'You're not serious,' Whitman said as we left the party and made our way down West 18th Street.

'I *am* serious.' I shivered as my refrigerated body tried to readjust to the stifling heat.

'I didn't know you were serious about moving to New York,' Daddy said.

'Why shouldn't I? You guys are.'

'We're only *thinking* of it,' Whitman said. 'The great thing about this new column is that I don't have to go to an office. I can work from home.'

'Home here?' I asked. 'Or home in Portland?'

Whitman and Daddy exchanged glances. 'Well,' Whitman said, 'I *love* our little apartment here and I'll *never* give it up, but I just don't know if I want to *live* there any more.'

'It's pretty small,' Daddy agreed. 'And if we got anything bigger, the rent would be at least four grand a month. We couldn't buy anything here unless we sold the house in Portland.'

'You designed that house,' Whitman said. 'For us. I am not selling the Portland house.'

'Good,' Daddy said, 'because if we did, what we got for it wouldn't even buy a one-bedroom here. And I'm not willing to spend over a million dollars for a one-bedroom apartment.'

'I'm not either,' Whitman said. 'It would make more sense to stay in the apartment we have because it's so cheap. Come back as needed.'

The problem, as they explained over dinner, was that they'd become what Whitman called 'victims of lifestyle', accustomed to a much higher standard of living in Portland than they could ever have in New York.

'One can live a *reasonably* upper-middle-class life in Portland,' Whitman said. 'It's a bit dull, and something of a cultural wasteland, but it has its advantages in terms of quality of life.'

'Most of my clients are on the West Coast now,' Daddy pointed out.

'And I do love the house,' Whitman said.

Of course he did. Who wouldn't? It was all wood, stone and glass and hung out over a canyon above the city.

'So I guess what we're saying,' Daddy said, 'is that we're probably not going to move back to Manhattan.'

'The problem is, I need to keep the apartment as a pied-à-terre,' Whitman said. 'But I can't ask a subletter to just let me stay there when I need it.'

'Why couldn't I sublet it?'

They looked at me in astonishment and then at one another.

'You mean *live* here?' Daddy said. 'Without us?'

'*Alone*?' Whitman, like Daddy, couldn't quite grasp the idea.

'Why not?'

'Why not?' Whitman sat forward to make his point. 'Sweetheart, this is New York, OK? Not dear dull little Portland. You've never been here by yourself.'

'Well, I think it's time that I was. That I try. That I find a job and try to make something out of my life.'

That shut them up. For a moment.

'I applaud your newfound ambition,' Whitman said. 'Really *applaud* it.' He mimed clapping. 'But—'

There followed a long list of reasons why I shouldn't consider moving to New York. And, of course, the biggest reason was that they wouldn't be here to watch over my every move, to ride with me on the subway, to pay for my meals and everything else.

'It's time I learned how to do all that,' I said. And then, when I couldn't think of anything else to say, I said, 'And if I'm here, you can come back any time you want.'

They were silent. Then Whitman said, 'I'll consider it. If your father and mother will.'

Two days later I took my first subway ride without the dads. Does this sound ridiculous? Probably. But I'd never had a life of my own in New York, so I'd never gone anywhere without them.

You'd have thought I was heading into the uncharted wilderness, the way they carried on.

'Now remember not to accidentally *bump* or *touch* anyone in the subway,' Whitman said, 'and don't *stare*. Touching and staring can make mad people mad. Especially when it's hot and everyone's irritable.'

'Carry your purse like this,' Daddy said, demonstrating how I should keep my purse clenched to my side. 'Never open it while you're in the train or on the platform.'

'Are you sure you don't want to take a cab?' Whitman said. 'We'll pay for it.'

'No. I want to take the subway.'

'Do you want us to walk to the station?' Daddy asked.

'I think I'm capable of doing that. It's only a block away.'

'OK,' Whitman said, 'but you know that the subway doesn't use tokens any more.'

'Maybe we should go with her,' Daddy said, 'and show her how to buy a Metrocard.'

'I. Can. Do. It.' They were making me so nervous I wanted to scream.

'Now when you meet Susanna,' Whitman advised, 'just remember that she's into being important. Do you want to do a quick role-play situation where I'm Susanna and you're you?'

'No, I think I'll be fine.'

'She can be very bitchy,' Whitman said, turning me around so he could examine my interview outfit, 'but she adores me because I helped her out of a jam once, so she'll be predisposed to like you. Don't be afraid of her, OK?'

'OK.'

'You've got your new cellphone in case anything happens?' Daddy asked.

I flashed the new phone they'd purchased for me and let them see me putting it into my purse.

'And your apartment key.' Whitman handed it to me. 'We'll be here, but you should have a key just in case.'

I looked down at that key. I made a wish. Then I gave them both a quick kiss and headed out for my job interview with Susanna Hyde.

The feeling struck me before I reached the 103rd Street subway station. Well, it was three feelings, really, all appearing simultaneously.

The first was a kind of exhilarating thrill. Maybe it's what baby birds feel when they step out of the nest for the first time and start hurtling towards the earth. Some instinct they didn't know they had kicks in and they start flapping their wings. It's either fly or die.

The second was maybe less a feeling and more an awareness. I suddenly had the sense that everyone in New York was playing a role of their own creation. It was a place where people invented themselves. A place where the possibilities existed to let you invent or reinvent yourself. In New York, you weren't expected to think small.

The third was maybe best of all. It was a sense that I belonged here.

Aura magazine was owned by Stuckey Media Enterprises which was owned by Stuckey Universal Media which was owned by Lord Farrell Stuckey. They didn't have their own office, as I'd thought. *Aura* shared the twentieth floor of a newish fifty-storey building in Midtown with a bunch of other magazines. There was one reception area for all of them.

Before I reached the reception area on the twentieth floor, though, I had to sign in and wait while the security guard in the lobby called upstairs to verify that I was expected. Then I was issued an adhesive-backed tag that said VISITOR.

I shared the elevator with two girls carrying paper bags and Starbucks' coffee cups and swapping complaints about someone named 'she'.

'She's like, do this, and I'm like, do it yourself, bitch, and she goes, now, and I go, no way, so she's like, well? And I'm like, no.'

The complainers got off on the same floor I did and punched in a security code that let them in an unmarked door. I headed for the double-glass doors on the other end of the corridor. They were locked. By the time I figured out that I was supposed to ring a small bell, the doors had clicked open for me.

Inside, in what was basically a windowless cubicle, a beautiful black woman, maybe about thirty years old, sat behind a polished marble counter answering the phone and directing traffic and packages in and out of the office. Behind her gleamed the silver logo of Stuckey Universal Media, a Superman-looking S sitting in a U with 'Media' written out beside them.

'Are you Venus Gilroy?' she asked.

'Yes. I'm here to see Susanna Hyde.'

The receptionist reacted with a display of facial expressions I couldn't decipher. Surprise? Horror? Pity? She glanced up at me as if about to say something, but then decided to remain strictly professional. 'I'll tell her you're here. Have a seat. It might take awhile.'

There was an alcove with a piece of art, a grey leather banquette and a table with magazines neatly spread out on it. I saw the latest issue of *Aura*, the one with Whitman's story on Pine Mountain Lodge. Next to it was a magazine called

Lifestyle Home. Next to that was *Personal Health*. Then came *Fitness Today* and *Cat & Kitty*. And at the end, *Peeper*, with a winking, big-breasted blonde in an army uniform on the cover, and *Personal Fetish*, with a special feature on bondage for beginners.

I was confused. Were those two sex magazines sitting out on the table, like *People* magazine in a doctor's office, to help waiting clients pass the time? What a weird choice. I'd seen *Peeper* and *Personal Fetish* while working at Phantastic Phantasy, but I'd never read them because they came in cellophane wrappers.

I sat and waited. And waited. The receptionist kept glancing at me and then glancing away when our eyes met. At one point, the door to the inner office burst open and a young woman ran out sobbing. The receptionist watched as the crying woman rushed out to the elevators, then shifted her eyes over to me.

'What was that all about?' I asked.

'This was her last day,' the receptionist said.

'She must have liked it here.'

The receptionist shrugged. 'It was her first day, too.'

After I'd been waiting about twenty minutes, a young woman named Dorcas came out to fetch and shepherd me through a maze of cubicles to Susanna Hyde's office.

'I'm the administrative assistant,' she said, 'so I get all the shit jobs.'

'I'm sorry,' I said half jokingly.

She shrugged. 'I'm really a writer, but in publishing you've got to start at the bottom and work your way up. Unless you're a man, of course.'

'Of course.' We threaded our way down corridors and around corners and past dozens of modular cubicles where everyone seemed to be on the phone or staring at a computer.

'Doesn't anyone have an office?' I asked.

'Larry, the editor-in-chief, he has an office. And the art directors, they have individual offices. The editors, they get a closet without a window. Everyone else is in the mod squad.

Except Susanna, of course. She has a corner office with *two* windows.'

'Do you like her?' I asked, knowing I shouldn't.

Dorcas didn't answer, probably because we were standing right outside Susanna's open door. Inside, from behind her desk, Susanna was looking at Dorcas with a vaguely disdainful expression. She didn't say thank you, she simply shifted her attention to me and said, 'Come in. Close the door.'

Susanna's office wasn't very large, but it had two windows that looked south and east into a dense forest of skyscrapers and all the way down to the Empire State Building on 34th Street. The room felt colder than the rest of the floor; so cold, in fact, that I shivered.

Susanna leaned back in her ergonomic chair and said, 'I just spoke to your faux pa. He told me that you don't really have a professional CV.'

I stared at her. I didn't know what a CV was.

'A resumé,' Susanna said.

'Oh. Yes. That's true, I don't.'

She motioned for me to sit. 'But you do have some work experience?'

I nodded. 'My last job was at Phantastic Phantasy.'

'What's that?'

'It's a porn store. A chain.'

Her eyebrows went up. 'Oh really? What did you do?'

So I told her.

'I take it, then, that you aren't prudish or censorious about sex and sexual matters?'

'No.'

'Because so many girls are.'

'Men are just as prudish as women,' I said. 'Maybe more so.'

She pursed her lips, nodded, and scribbled something on a pad. 'I'm not asking for a curriculum vitae in sex,' she said, 'but how experienced are you? With men, I mean.'

'Don't women count?'

'Lesbian?'

'I fall in love with the person.'

'Bisexual then.'

'I don't like labels.'

'Except on dresses,' she said.

We laughed. I wondered if she was still smarting because we'd worn the samc dress to that party.

'I'm going to be frank with you, Venus, because I don't have time to be subtle. I'm in the business of sex. This is not a job for some blushing virgin who gets tongue-tied saying fellatio.'

'I understand.'

'I've got a schedule from hell and I need someone brilliant to help me out. Lord Stuckey's just made me editor of *Aura*, but I'm still in charge of the fitness and beauty departments, too, and I'm not giving up my sex column and I intend to continue writing books. I'm working on a new one right now.'

'You *need* an assistant,' I said sympathetically.

'I do indeed. But I was frankly hoping for someone with some experience in publishing. You have none. Where did you go to college? Smith? Vassar?'

'I went to a junior college.'

'I see. But you seem bright. Whitman told me you were very bright.'

'He did?' That surprised me. Not that he'd said I was bright – that was the sort of thing parents were supposed to say, no matter how dimwitted their kids were – but that he'd said it to Susanna. Because that meant he was giving me a boost for the job, and if he was giving me a boost for the job, he was obviously going to let me sublet the New York apartment.

'He told me quite a lot about you, actually,' Susanna said. 'He said you'd worked as his research assistant.'

I nodded.

'He's hoping that you're serious about having a career.'

'I am.'

The phone rang and she had a brief discussion with someone about a layout. Her manner to me had been friendly enough, but on the phone she turned steely and boss-like, demanding that some photos be reshot. Then, just as she was hanging up, there was a knock on the door and Dorcas came in carrying a pile of papers for her to sign.

'Just leave them there.' Susanna pointed to a corner of her desk.

'Larry said to have them ready by the three o'clock meeting.'

'Excuse me?'

When Dorcas started to repeat what she'd just said, Susanna interrupted her with: 'Perhaps you mean that Mr Weiner *asked* if I could *please* have them ready by the three o'clock meeting?'

'He didn't ask and he didn't say please. He just said to have them ready.'

If looks could kill, Dorcas Phinney would have died on the spot. She got out of Susanna's office as quickly as she could.

'That girl,' Susanna muttered. 'If there's one thing I hate, it's rudeness to a superior.' She glanced at her watch, then pulled out her BlackBerry and looked something up. 'Oh God, I'm late.' She made a quick phone call, this time her voice light and charming. 'Darling, I'm terribly sorry. I'll be there anon, as soon as I'm finished with this boring meeting. I'll be there by the time they bring my Martini, extra dry, with a twist. Yes, me too. Bye-bye.'

She continued the interview and got ready for her date at the same time, pulling out a cosmetics bag and a mirror and applying eyeliner, mascara, lipstick and blush.

'I can't remember what we were talking about,' she said.

'Careers.'

'Oh, right. Well, it won't be easy, this job. I mean, it's almost below entry-level and the pay's terrible, but if you're good . . .'

'I'll be good. At the job, I mean.'

'Right. And listen, this job is a personal perk for me. From Lord Stuckey. I said I wouldn't accept the editorship without a factotum. So you'd be a one-of-a-kind around here, and you'd have to deal with jealousy from all the other little people.'

'What does that mean?'

'It means none of the other executive editors has a PA. They all share Dorcas. Larry Weiner's the only one with his own PA.'

'Who's Larry Weiner?'

'He's editor-in-chief of all the magazines published here at Stuckey Media. The big weenie, as it were – although I've heard otherwise. Anyway, he's the only one with his own PA, so my PA will have to deal with some of the hostility that I'm already dealing with as new editor of *Aura*. Could you handle that?'

'Why is everyone so hostile?' I asked.

Susanna laughed. 'Because Lord Stuckey gave me a PA and not them.' She gave her silky blonde hair a quick brush and then fluffed it loose. 'There are a lot of changes going on around here. Big changes. And I need someone I can trust and someone who can do things without being told a million times. Someone who's sort of independent. And someone who can travel. Someone who's not tied down with a boyfriend or a husband and doesn't have kids.' She gave herself a final appraisal in the mirror and then turned to me. 'What do you think?'

'I'd like the job.'

'I meant me. How do I look?'

'Oh. Great.'

'You're hired.'

The dads were flabbergasted but my mom was stunned. 'You mean you're not coming home?' she cried. 'You're staying in New York?'

So I explained as best I could how I wanted to move on with my life, and how this opportunity had presented itself, and how crazy I'd be if I didn't take it. 'It's working for Susanna Hyde, Mom. I thought you loved her column so much.'

'I do,' she admitted, 'but that doesn't mean I want you to stay in New York and work for her.'

'Mom, some girls would kill for a job like this. Girls with college educations.'

'If you want a college education,' she argued, 'you can live at home with me while you go to school. For free, honey. I wouldn't charge you a dime. I'll do all the cooking, too. You'd be free to study twenty-four hours a day.'

'Mom, it's time for me to do something with my life.'

'Why can't you do something with your life here, in Portland?'

'Because there are too many memories there.'

'You can't run away from memories,' she said. 'Just because you have three ex-husbands here doesn't mean you should avoid Portland.'

There was just one ex-husband whose memory meant anything to me, but I didn't tell her that. 'Mom, you don't have to worry about me. I'll be fine. I'm going to stay in the apartment here.'

'But you don't have any friends there.'

'I'll make friends.'

'Let me talk to your father, please.'

So I put Daddy on the line and went out into the garden, where Whitman was having a conversation with Carmine Capistrano, the old Italian guy who was the building's 'super' even though he lived in Brooklyn.

'Carmine,' Whitman said when I appeared, 'you remember our daughter, Venus.'

Carmine looked at me with his squinty brown eyes and said in a gravelly voice, '*Mama mia*.'

I shook his leathery hand. 'Hello, Mr Capistrano.'

'*Quanti anni* – how old is she now?' Carmine asked Whitman.

'*Venticinque*. Can you believe it?'

'Twenty-five! Same age as my granddaughter. Mary-Joseph!' he called.

A short, lean, dark-eyed woman wearing jeans and a man's workshirt, her hair stuffed into a baseball cap, appeared from around the corner. 'Yeah?' Her eyes met mine and lingered for just a second before continuing on to her grandfather's.

Carmine nodded in my direction. 'Someone I want you to meet.'

'How yuh doin'?' Mary-Joseph, working a mouthful of gum, looked back at me with her big dark eyes. She wiped her hand on her dirty jeans before shaking mine. 'Excuse the dirt, we been down in the boiluh room.' She smiled and stepped to one side of her grandfather, keeping her eyes on me as she snapped her gum.

Something about her, the tiny tough-cookie directness that couldn't quite hide a shy vulnerability in her eyes, tapped faintly at my heart.

'Carmine,' Whitman said, 'Venus is going to be staying in the apartment for awhile. So if anything goes wrong, she can call you, right?'

Carmine made a funny noise in his throat. 'She canna call-a Mary-Joseph. She's gonna be the new super.'

Whitman and I looked at Mary-Joseph, who nodded and yanked the visor of her cap further down on her head. 'Same numbuh,' she said.

'Don'ta worry,' Carmine reassured us, 'she'll do a gooda job. She got all her licenses.'

'What about you, Carmine?' Whitman asked.

'I'ma retiring. I had enough broken terlets and clogged drains. So from now on, you call-a Mary-Joseph.'

'Same numbuh,' the new super reminded me as they left, flashing me a shy and unexpectedly charming smile.

In the days that followed, the dads gave me a crash course in New York life and life in the apartment on 102nd Street. It wasn't until the morning they were leaving that the immensity of what I was doing really dawned on me. I was both scared and excited, eager for them to go, but apprehensive about being alone. Mom wasn't happy with my decision, but there was nothing she could do about it. I told her she could come out and visit any time she wanted – which wasn't likely, given her fear of flying.

Whitman had a list about a mile long of things he thought I needed to know. 'OK,' he said, 'remember never to leave the apartment without locking the security door to the garden.'

'OK.'

'And you know how the toilet flushes – just a light press on the handle, once. Don't hold it down.'

'Yes, Whitman.'

'And the lock on the front door, you remember how it works: open the lock, open the door, close the lock and open it again with the key, then pull the door closed and turn the key to lock the door.'

'I'll remember.'

'You've got Sheba's number upstairs – don't be afraid to call her if you need to know something about the building.'

'I won't.'

'And you've got the new super's number.'

'Mary-Joseph Capistrano. Yes, you've got it written down.'

'Make sure you keep an eye on that drain in the garden. It gets clogged and then when it rains it doesn't drain properly.'

'I'll keep an eye on it.'

'And you know how to go down into the basement to turn on the water for the hose.'

'And I'll water the garden if it doesn't rain for a long time.'

'I've put a thousand dollars in your new bank account,' Daddy said. 'You remember how to operate the ATM? Dip your card and punch in your PIN.'

'Yes, Daddy. Thank you for the money.'

'And I'll waive your first month's rent,' Whitman said.

They were both being so generous, and I had nothing to offer in return, except to do well in my new life. I vowed there and then that I would never ask them for money again.

'If you have any questions about *Aura*,' Whitman said, 'e-mail me. You're entering a snake pit there but try to stay calm.'

'I will.'

Whitman hugged me. 'It's so weird – now we're the ones going back to Portland instead of you.'

Then it was Daddy's turn. 'Well, sweetheart,' he said quietly, 'we'd better be off.'

'OK.' Suddenly I was fighting back tears.

'You're starting a new life now,' Daddy said.

I sniffed and nodded.

'I want you to enjoy it.'

'We both do,' Whitman said.

I stepped into Daddy's arms and laid my cheek against his warm chest. 'I love you, Daddy. And you, Whitman.'

Whitman wiped his eyes. 'Would you open the door for us, sweetheart? Just so I can see that you know how to operate the lock?'

I did.

They rolled their matching yellow Tuomi bags out into the hallway.

'Now lock the door behind us,' Whitman said. 'So I know you know how to do it.'

I stepped back inside and flipped the lock.

I heard the wheels of their luggage, then the front door opening and banging shut behind them.

I was on my own in New York City.

I was supposed to begin my new job just after Labor Day, which meant I had a holiday weekend to get through with no backup from family or friends. But I had lots of work to keep me busy. Susanna had loaded me down with old and new issues of *Aura*. I was supposed to read them all to get a feel for what the magazine had been and what it was in the process of becoming under Susanna's editorship.

The weather continued hot and the stores were still sold out of air-conditioners, so I got a coffee frappuccino from Starbucks and hauled my stack of *Auras* outside to the shady spot under the giant bittersweet vine. Daddy and Whitman had set up a sturdy metal table there with four sturdy metal chairs; it was where we ate meals and hung out.

Whitman and Daddy's garden was a pretty amazing place. It was lush, overgrown, mysterious, like an enchanted garden in a fairy tale, only right in the middle of Manhattan. Whitman claimed there were over a hundred species of plants and that the garden created its own microclimate. The stucco walls were painted the color of Italian terracotta to offset the green of the vines and the profusion of plants, trees, and shrubs. Whitman called it a 'woodland shade garden' because two enormous ailanthus trees in neighboring gardens rose up in a canopy overhead.

I knew zilch about the plants, but this garden had lots of memories for me. I'd first seen it when I was eight years old. I'd been terrified and fascinated by the metal security door that led out to it, and bewildered by the way the garden was planted: so unlike a grassy yard in Portland. There were buildings all around, with back windows facing the garden, and it took me a long time to get over the scary sense that I was being watched by some maniac who'd sneak through the barred windows and into the apartment at night. On the cracked concrete around the planting area I'd demonstrated my tap dancing skills for the dads when I was ten. In the winter, when it snowed, we made snowmen and tossed snowballs and dared one another to run outside barefoot. Sometimes, on summer nights, the dads would light the garden with candles and throw parties so I could meet their friends. Those magical nights seemed to epitomize the romantic life the dads led in New York when I wasn't there. Fireflies blinked green and floated slowly among the plants, candles flickered, people talked and laughed and drank wine.

On the same chair where I sat now, I'd sat as a scared girl, a troubled adolescent, an angry teen. I'd made wishes out here that never came true, and dreamed up impossible futures, none of which involved living in New York City.

And now here I was, alone, on my own, trying as usual not to think about Tremaynne and my lost marriage. Where was he now, that eco-warrior who made love like no one else on earth? While I was sitting here, in this civilized little garden, was my ex-love hiding out in that vast wilderness where I'd last seen him?

Did he ever think of me?

Every time I felt myself drifting into a daydream, I pulled myself up short and redirected my attention to back issues of *Aura*.

Because what was past was past. Events would never happen again the way they had. It seemed like I'd had only a moment to grasp and enjoy those moments with Tremaynne before I'd been forced to let him go.

My heart was so bruised. The pain of it was something I could never tell the dads. Mom sort of understood, but even she didn't know how deep the hurt went. The Three Wise

Elders probably thought it was just their flaky daughter being flaky again, misjudging her marriage material and getting out of another relationship she shouldn't have gotten herself into. That was my history. What they'd never know was that Tremaynne had really been the one person I wanted and had been looking for my whole life. You know it when that happens. Something chimes in your heart and nods in your soul.

What I'd gone through with Tremaynne out there in Idaho, at Pine Mountain Lodge, had changed me for ever. Tremaynne and I had escaped death, together, and when you escape death with someone you love, you're bonded in some profound new way. For life.

But I had to let go of the past and look forward. I had to create new days for myself, new routines, new wardrobes, a new home. All my household junk – like the broken futon (one of the legs cracked during too-strenuous lovemaking with Tremaynne) – stayed in Portland, stored at my dads'. I didn't need to furnish the apartment in New York because it already had everything I needed. Clothes were the biggest issue. In Portland, working at Phantastic Phantasy, I could wear anything. But in New York, where I'd be travelling to a fancy office in Midtown every day, I had to look halfway decent.

Mom had shipped out a couple of boxes of clothes that I guess I once thought looked hot or fun. But what might have looked sexy in Portland looked a little ratty and soiled when I pulled it out in New York. The ketchup stains and unravelling seams and smoke-saturated fabrics seemed like gruesome reminders of a failed life. I'd cleaned and repaired what I could and figured out various combinations that might still work, but really I just wanted to throw out the whole lot and start over. I couldn't afford to, though. I *had* to be practical. That thousand dollars in my new checking account had to last until my first pay cheque. I couldn't charge anything because I'd lost all my credit cards when I declared bankruptcy. And even though I tried to be frugal, withdrawing only twenty bucks at a go, the money seemed to disappear the moment I pulled it from the cash slot.

Now it was the last weekend in August and the city was quiet as a morgue. Everyone who could afford to had left for their final summer fling. The only sound was the low humming drone of air-conditioners. I picked up another old issue of *Aura* and started flipping through the pages.

The magazine had changed drastically over the years. When it first appeared in the late 1970s, *Aura* was a cheap, sloppy-looking magazine devoted to new New Age ideas. Flipping through the old copies was like flipping through the weird-smelling 'Hippie' racks at a vintage clothing store, or watching reruns of sitcoms made before I was born.

But somehow, despite its amateur look and bad writing, the magazine stayed afloat – maybe because the people who bought it didn't care how it looked. They were more interested in the alternative ideas it contained. My mom, a former hippie who'd once lived in a commune, had been an *Aura* subscriber for years. I'd always ignored it because it didn't have any fashion or make-up ads and I wasn't interested in calling upon my inner goddess or planning a fertility rite.

Over the years, as New Age became more and more mainstream, *Aura* was sold to different publishers and went through a couple of half-hearted redesigns. Finally, Lord Farrell Stuckey, the British media magnate, moved in and bought the company that published *Aura* and a whole string of other magazines, including *Peeper* and *Personal Fetish*. Lord Stuckey then hired Susanna to completely rethink *Aura*. Whitman had told me that Lord Stuckey loved Susanna's syndicated sex-advice column, which had been running in *Aura* for a couple of years by then.

'She was just a freelancer, like me,' Whitman had told me, 'only she had the security of a syndicated column. And then suddenly she was an editor, and making God only knows how much.'

So now, under Susanna's editorship, *Aura* was starting to look like something suitable for a news-stand: glossy, well designed, almost glamorous. Susanna was beefing up the celebrity content and the advertising.

I knew nothing about magazine production, so before he and Daddy went back to Portland, Whitman had given me a crash course.

A magazine – usually called 'the book' – is divided into three sections: front of book, the well, and back of book.

The front of book is the most important part of the magazine and the most widely read. It's where the single-page monthly columns run and where single- and double-page ads cost the most because they have the highest visibility.

The well is the story section of the magazine, where articles are not broken up by any advertising.

The 'back of book' collects overrun from the well ('continued on page 142') and runs less glossy ads, which are smaller, cheaper, and not necessarily in color.

All the times I'd scanned through *Cosmo* or *Elle* or *Vogue* or *Vanity Fair* I hadn't given a thought to any of this. But now it was kind of fascinating to see how carefully all the pieces were fit together to make the final product.

I was on my tenth issue of *Aura*, reading about a glamorous star's past-life regression, when I heard the glass door on the balcony behind and above me slide open and a voice say, 'Feel the sun, Esmeralda? Doesn't that feel good?'

To look or not to look, that was the question. The balcony was maybe eight feet above the garden and recessed back by the fire escape, so it was impossible to ignore whoever was up there.

Finally I turned around and saw Kenny, the illegal sublet. Only now he wasn't dressed in a nun's habit but a pair of skimpy shorts, his white hairless torso exposed. He was bending over something on the floor of the balcony. I couldn't see what it was.

'Doesn't that feel good?' he said, apparently stroking something. I thought maybe it was a cat or a little dog, lying on its back in the sun as he brushed it.

'Hi,' I said.

He stood and looked down, scratching his scrawny white chest. 'Hello.'

'We met in the hallway a couple of weeks ago. I'm Venus Gilroy.'

He nodded but didn't introduce himself. 'I'm giving Esmeralda a sun bath,' he said. His voice had a soft Southern accent.

'Oh.'

'She likes to rub against the tiles and climb up the bars. It's sort of like a jungle gym out here.'

I thought maybe I'd misheard him. What kind of a pet could climb up bars? I prayed it wasn't a monkey. A friend in Portland had a monkey and it looked cute but it was the most horrible, scary pet, leaping all over, pooping everywhere, biting your finger. 'What is Esmeralda?' I asked.

And tried to keep a smile on my face as Kenny bent down and lifted up a long, heavy, muscular snake.

I hate snakes even more than I hate spiders. My heart began to race. I was twisted around in my chair and glued in place with sheer terror. I couldn't utter a sound but I was aware that my smile had turned into something that preceded a scream.

'Ain't she a beaut?' Kenny said, draping the snake around his neck. 'She's a red-tailed boa.' He raised his arm and Esmeralda slithered across it as if it were a pale white branch in a jungle.

I closed my eyes. Tried to swallow. I was certain that if I moved even an inch Esmeralda would lunge off the balcony, mouth wide, fangs dripping, and attach herself to my neck. I had a vision of myself being swallowed, slowly, inch by inch, as Kenny looked down from his balcony.

'You OK?' Kenny asked.

I tried to shake my head but it must have looked more like a nervous tic.

'She's completely harmless,' he said. 'She *loves* people.'

'I'm sure she does,' I managed to squeak. With a mighty effort I twisted back around, pried myself up from my chair, and made my way on wobbly legs back to the apartment.

*

That night was my first night alone in the apartment. My first night alone in New York. The first night of my new alone life.

If I was in Portland, there would have been lots of people I could call. Here, in the middle of one of the most densely populated cities in the world, there was no one – except people back in Portland. And frankly, I didn't want to talk to any of them. I didn't want to explain what had happened with Tremaynne, why I was single again, what I was going to do with my life now. I preferred to be lonely.

The heat had built up during the day and the apartment was like an oven. I'd ventured out to get a slice of takeaway pizza at Sal's, around the corner, but couldn't bring myself to go out into the garden to eat it. What if Esmeralda smelled the tomato and cheese sauce and came slithering out to find it?

When I was showering before bed, trying to cool down and wash off some of the sticky grit of the city, I looked up and saw an air vent I'd never seen before. Did it connect to Kenny's apartment, directly above me? Couldn't Esmeralda slide right down from his apartment into mine? I closed the bathroom door when I left, just in case.

It was my first night sleeping in the bedroom, on the dads' Murphy bed. This bed had always epitomized New York to me, and as I pulled it down from the wall to the floor I had a sense of being just another New Yorker living in a cramped apartment without space even for a full-time bed. I crawled under one sheet and stared up at the ceiling. The problem wasn't the bed, it was the fear I had of sleeping in the bedroom, as the dads did, with the security door out to the garden open and just a screen door between me and all of night-time New York.

I couldn't do it. Someone might sneak down the fire escape and jump into the garden, or scale the garden wall. I'd hear a rustle and wake up and look over to see a figure just outside raising a knife or a hammer . . .

I pulled the heavy security door closed and locked it. But then it got so hot I could hardly breathe. I set up the fan so it was trained right on me, but all it did was push the thick stale air back and forth.

Finally I decided I'd go sleep where I'd always slept, on the couch. That way I could get some air from the two windows beneath Kenny's balcony. These windows were double-barred and now had those little sliding screens in them, so Esmeralda wouldn't be able to slide in to say hello and swallow me whole.

It was almost too hot to sleep. I dozed. Then woke with a start, my heart racing. The sound was low but distinct and it came from directly outside the window. Not from the garden. *From the window ledge*.

It was a horrible sound, inhuman, a kind of sustained bone-chilling tone that went up and down as if it were gloating and threatening at the same time.

I turned my head just far enough to see a large black shape pressed against the screen.

Snakes didn't make noises like that, did they?

A cat? It had to be.

What cat?

The cat trapped in the apartment when we first came? The scrawny, scraggly tom that had run out into the garden and finally managed to climb the dogwood tree and disappear over the wall? Had he come back to demand his squatter's rights to the apartment? Part of me was tempted to let him in, take him under my wing, make him my first new friend.

But that sound – wasn't that the creepy sound of a cat in heat? Or maybe just a hot cat.

'Go away,' I whispered to whatever was out there.

Of course it didn't listen. I'm the one who had to listen, all through the night.

On the morning of my first day at my new job, I woke up in a panic, thinking I was late. It turned out that I'd awakened *before* the alarm went off, a totally new experience for me.

There was a Starbucks right across the street, and I was tempted to go over there in my robe to get a huge cup of wake-up-and-get-ready coffee, but of course that was out of the question. So without the aid of coffee, and with only a glazed doughnut to start me on my way, I carefully put on my first-day clothes. The weather remained murderously hot, sending my blow-dried hair into a frizz. Pantyhose – ugh – so scratchy on my freshly shaved legs. The skirt was cotton, mid-thigh-length, with big, zippered pockets that I thought might come in handy for pens and things. A tangerine-colored blouse with a modified Peter Pan collar completed my ensemble. And my purse, of course, filled with all the new paraphernalia I'd need as a New Yorker: apartment keys, Metrocard, employee identity card for Stuckey Universal Media.

I thought I had plenty of time, but when I looked at the clock again I had only half an hour to get to Midtown. I crammed the rest of the doughnut in my mouth, took a gulp of orange juice from the carton, jammed on my black heels, and dashed out into the steaming morning air.

I'll be just like everyone else, I thought, and get a Starbucks coffee to drink on the subway. That gave me my first thrill. I felt ridiculously sophisticated, sipping my coffee as I got into the air-conditioned subway car. But at 72nd Street the No. 2 train gave a sudden lurch just as I had tilted the cup back for another sip and coffee splashed out of that little hole it never splashes out of. Right on my skirt – which was black, luckily, so it didn't look too much like I'd wet my pants.

The first thing I learned on my new job was that Susanna wanted me to be at the office by 8 a.m. with a coffee yogurt that she would eat when she arrived at nine. It had to be a certain brand of yogurt, and the container had to be placed on a white china plate with a small silver spoon and a folded napkin beside it.

OK. I could handle that.

'Do you know how to make proper tea?' she asked.

I didn't, being an American coffee drinker, so she instructed me. She had a 'lucky teapot', an antique that had belonged to her grandmother. It had to be warmed with hot water before a tea ball filled with loose Earl Grey tea leaves was placed inside and boiling Evian water poured over it. The tea steeped for three and a half minutes exactly before the tea ball was removed. Susanna's first cup of tea was poured into a china teacup over half an inch of milk and two packets of sugar-free Splenda. The remainder of the pot she poured herself.

That was at nine. At eleven she had another pot of tea. Her lunches usually ran from one o'clock to three. At four she had more tea. She generally left the office at seven, usually for a dinner date or some social event, but often came back afterwards to work until ten or eleven.

She expected me to be there at least until seven, later if we were facing a deadline.

My first few days at *Aura* passed in an exhausting blur as I struggled to learn names and remember details and figure out new pieces of office information and technology.

'You'll be in charge of my shedjewel,' Susanna said, sipping her tea.

'Your – what?'

She flicked her eyes up at me, annoyed by the interruption.

'My shedjewel.' She saw I didn't understand and let out an aggrieved sigh. '*Sked*jewel, as you Americans say.'

'Oh, OK. Schedule. Sorry.'

'You'll be in charge of my shedjewel, so you'll have to coordinate my BlackBerry with yours.'

'I don't have a BlackBerry.'

Again the exasperated look. 'Well, you'll just have to get one, won't you?' She handed me hers. 'Tell me what my appointments are today.'

'I can't. I don't know how to work one of these things.'

'A *child* could operate a BlackBerry,' she scoffed, then heaved another one of her signature sighs. 'OK. Go down to Marty in IT and tell him you want a BlackBerry and that he's to show you how to use it. Go. Chop chop.'

My days were filled with events like this. First, I had to figure out what IT meant and where it was. Then I had to track down Marty and make my request: 'I'm here to get a BlackBerry.'

'What account?'

'Um – *Aura*, I guess.'

'You guess?'

'Well, Miss Hyde didn't tell me what account. She just said to get a BlackBerry and ask you to show me how to use it.'

'You don't know how to use a BlackBerry?'

I shook my head. 'I'm sure it's easy, I've just never—'

'Fill this out. And this one, too.'

'What is it?'

'A release form so you can't sue us if you get BlackBerry finger.'

'What's that?'

'You'll know when you get it.'

So many forms. Account numbers. Everything had to be tracked and eventually got back to Moira Paisley, *Aura*'s managing editor, who was always asking me to step into her small, windowless office. 'Venus, what is this charge for a BlackBerry?'

'Susanna told me to get one from Marty in IT.'

Hectic red dots appeared on Moira's pale, wide cheeks. 'Susanna told you to get a BlackBerry?'

'I'm in charge of her schedule. I have to coordinate her BlackBerry with mine.'

'I've never heard of – OK, I'll talk to her about it. Just remember, that BlackBerry is for work-related calls only.'

There was a tense vibe between Susanna and everyone who worked for her, but I tried to remain uninvolved. I had new computer programs to learn. A new phone system to master. New techno-tones to identify. Each beep, click, whir and buzz telling me to do something I hadn't done before.

I had to deal with the *Aura* staff, too . . . all of whom seemed to be cross-jobbing at other Stuckey Universal Media magazines. Nobody except Moira had just one job. And nobody ever seemed to have enough time to do whatever they were supposed to do. Chronic multi-tasking was the order of the day. If you wanted to keep your job, you had to do two, maybe three. Or four, like Susanna, who was Queen of the Multi-taskers.

Susanna was one busy lady. Not only was she editor, she also managed the Fitness and Health sections of *Aura*. And not only that, she continued to write her syndicated sex-advice column for Stuckey Universal Media, which meant it was published in magazines in both America and the UK. And not only that, she wrote books, mostly based on her sex-advice columns. Her new book, not yet completed and not due out until the following April, was already generating some buzz. I heard that it was going to go way beyond any sex-advice book ever written.

It's weird, when you're a nobody, to see how power works, and where it comes from, and what it does to people. And how hard it is to maintain.

Susanna was new at her job, like me, only hers wasn't a job, it was a high-paying career. I'd say she was pulling in close to two hundred grand a year.

I have to admit it was fascinating for me to watch the way her life unfolded. I had a front-row seat and got to see it all.

*

I was the odd-woman out at *Aura*, and Susanna had warned me that some people would hate me, not for anything I did, but simply because I was Susanna's PA. She sometimes referred to me as her 'perk'.

'Oh, that's Venus,' I heard her say on the phone when I'd transferred a call in to her. 'My new perk.'

I wrote that down immediately. I didn't want to forget it, or how it made me feel. Coming from ultra-nice and politically correct Portland, I was shocked. It was like hearing her say, 'She's my new slave.'

Which was basically what I was. But 'personal assistant' sounds nicer.

'Oh no, darling,' I heard her say to someone else on the phone, 'I've got a PA now. *She* can do that.'

Or how about this: 'I'll have *my girl* get in touch with your girl.'

When I heard these comments I smarted with resentment, but I was smart enough to know that resentment would get me nowhere. In general, I'm not a resentful person. So I tried not to take Susanna's denigrating comments personally. I was always reminding myself that I'd given myself a challenge, and I had to accept it.

Besides which, maybe I could actually learn something from Susanna Hyde. Growing up, I'd had no strong, successful female mentors. The dads were career nuts, but my mom was not. In a way, my mom's life was about avoiding responsibility. But accepting responsibility, I quickly learned, was what you had to do if you wanted a career. You had to perform, even if you didn't want to. Slackers did not have careers.

And then there was the fascination thing. Susanna fascinated me. She was one of those go-getter women who'd gotten everything. Who had everything. Who *demanded*. I'd never learned how to demand. My mom had never taught me because she didn't know how herself. Despite all her self-empowerment manuals and alternative therapies, Mom was totally passive and afraid of life. Life had let her down, she accepted defeat, and she felt she couldn't do anything to change it. Susanna, on the other hand, refused to accept anything less than exactly what she wanted. That was a breathtaking realization for me, and to see it in action was awesome. It induced both fear and respect in me, something I'd never felt for my mom. Could I ever be that demanding, I wondered? Would I want to be? Would it make me less desirable as a woman? Or – maybe – more?

Mom was completely selfless and Susanna was totally selfish. They were polar opposites. And there was I, stuck right in the middle, tugged in both directions.

My office wasn't a full module, it was half a module, a modulette, right outside Susanna's door. She got Wu Wee, a feng shui expert who was trying to wheedle a story assignment from her, to 'design' the placement of my modulette. The energy, said Wu Wee, should flow through Susanna's south-facing window, into her office, out her door, and not hit any obstacles as it poured forth into her domain, that section of the twentieth floor where *Aura* had its cubbyholes. So my half-module's partition wall went up to one side of Susanna's door, and my desk was placed at right angles to it. I guess Susanna's energy flowed underneath me, or over me, or maybe right through me on its way out her door.

Then a color therapist, Doris Chilling, was asked to help with a suitable color scheme for Susanna's office. Doris, like Wu Wee, was trying to interest Susanna in a self-promotional story about her amazing spiritual talents and was hauled in to provide a free consultation.

Susanna was very clever about getting people to work for nothing. She invited them to her office, ostensibly to discuss their story idea, and had me bring in tea, on a tray, with china cups and the lucky teapot and all that. It made the person feel special. Then casually, in the course of a chat, Susanna would say something like: 'I *am* curious about this color therapy of yours, Doris, but I need something more tangible to make me understand how it works in the real world. So, for instance, if you were doing a color therapy scheme for this office, what colors would you recommend?'

Because truth to tell, Susanna knew nothing about color. It was like she was afraid of it. She wore black, every day, and the only colorful touches in her office were her lucky tea pot and Royal Doulton teacups.

'Yellow's a *very* successful color,' Doris told her. 'By incorporating yellow into your daily life, you'll feel quite energized and be promoting success on a material and a spiritual level.'

'Mm. Fascinating. And what about my girl's area, out in front?'

Doris came out to survey my modulette. She was a thin, older woman with dyed black hair and an eye-catching magenta scarf around her shoulders. 'Pink or orange,' she pronounced. 'Pink if you want to bathe in affection, love, or enjoyment. Orange if you want to make a statement about confidence, ambition, or pride.'

Susanna got her yellow. Guess what color her girl got.

As September moved towards October, I came to understand why that song 'Autumn in New York' was written. It's because there *is* something truly magical in the air at that time of year, a mood that hovers between sweet and sad.

The light is different, the air is crisper, and the sky softer and more purely blue.

There's a definite change of season, and it tugs at your emotions. In the parks, leaves turn red and yellow and russet and drift to the ground or get blown off during sudden gusty rainstorms. There's a chill at night. Pumpkins and ornamental gourds appear in the greengrocers and supermarkets. Street vendors sell roasted chestnuts. Everyone is back from their vacations, back from the Hamptons, back from Fire Island, back from Maine, and Vermont, and the Jersey Shore and Europe. Manhattan bulges with all the extra bodies. The subways are crammed, everywhere the queues are longer, but everyone seems to enjoy autumn in New York.

Even Susanna, though fall for her was mostly a chance to show off her cold-weather wardrobe. I'm sure she enjoyed the glow of autumn between all her endless appointments.

Because a woman, after all, is only as successful as her schedule. Or maybe as crazy as her schedule.

With Susanna, scheduling was everything. It was hard for me, with my old West Coast slacker mentality, to understand how anyone could pack so much into a single day. When she wasn't scheduling meetings she was 'booking' things:

restaurants, theatre seats, massages, hair cuts, pedicures, manicures, dress fittings, veterinary appointments for her cat, workmen to fix or change things in her 'flat', personal trainers, facials, car services, horoscope readings, flights to London, train tickets to Washington, D.C. . . . The list was endless.

More than once she phoned me from her apartment and had me 'ring' for take-out food to be delivered to her.

Power lies in the details, I guess. I know for sure that power lies in the perks. Of which I was one, as were the two windows in her corner office. I couldn't believe how much envy and resentment I and those two windows generated.

Aura staff meetings were daily and dreaded occurrences. Dreaded because Susanna liked to change her mind. And nothing pleased her. And, she let it be known, everyone around her was incompetent, a drain on her vision for *Aura*. And if you were incompetent, Susanna wasn't above a little raiding party to another Stuckey Universal Media magazine where your counterpart was ever so much more talented.

Her senior editors, Eldora Button (in charge of the monthly 'Food and Feasts' column) and Petra Darkke (in charge of the monthly 'Celestial Navigator' and 'Your Lucky Numbers' columns), had probably been nice, ordinary women at one time. Maybe even happy. But working for Susanna turned them into suspicious, resentful harpies. They hated her, and they hated me for no other reason than that I worked for her. When Eldora or Petra passed my desk and looked at me, I knew they were just dying to fling an order my way. But couldn't, because as Susanna's PA I was protected by an invisible shield that only Susanna could penetrate.

I didn't mind that. I had enough multi-tasking of my own to do without taking on any of theirs. Their biggest grumble was that they had too much to do. 'For Christ's sake!' Eldora screamed in one staff meeting. 'Stick a broom up my ass, Susanna, and I'll sweep the floor while I'm doing everything else.'

'You might want to pitch that idea to *Personal Fetish*,' was Susanna's dry reply.

Her art director, Evan Bevins, entered every meeting like a

man on his way to the guillotine. His layouts were inevitably dismissed as 'boring', 'dull', and 'uninspired'. Poor Evan. I felt sorry for him. He was an older guy, in his sixties, and here he was taking orders from a woman twenty years younger. There was nothing flashy or fashionable about Evan. He was just one of those guys who'd spent his entire life working – not very hard – in New York publishing, starting long before anyone had ever heard of computer layouts, corporate takeovers, or media makeovers. Once he got the drift that she disliked him, Evan approached Susanna with the nervous trepidation of an old dog afraid he was going to lose his place by the fire.

Susanna was always horribly blunt. 'This is absolute shit, Evan. Boring, uninspired . . . Venus! Run down and ask Giles Travaille if he can give me five minutes.'

Giles Travaille, art director of *Peeper*, was 'brilliant', Susanna told Evan. 'He's got fresh ideas. He's into concept. Giles knows how to create a *look*.'

'Is it more glitz you want?' Evan asked.

'It's not what *I* want, Evan, it's what the *public* wants.'

'We've always gone for a kind of – um – *metaphysical* look with this column,' Evan pointed out.

Susanna blew up. I hurried off to fetch Giles Travaille.

Peeper and *Personal Fetish* had their own floor, up on twenty-one. They were accorded special status, I later found out, because they sold more copies than all the other magazines in the Stuckey Universal Media group combined. I'd heard rumors that their success was due in large part to Giles Travaille, the hot-shot art director who had a sixth-sense about selling sex. He'd 'discovered' several models whose unclothed bodies made *Peeper* fly off the stands.

The 'stands' I'm referring to were not just in adult bookstores like Phantastic Phantasy. *Peeper* had broken the crossover barrier and was now sold in grocery stores and news-stands. No wonder everyone loved Giles Travaille so much. *He'd increased volume*.

All the women on our floor went dewy- and doey-eyed whenever Giles's name was mentioned. 'Oh, that English accent,' they'd sigh. 'Oh, those tailored suits.' 'Oh, did you see how he had his hair combed today?'

To which I always wanted to say, 'You never met my husband Tremaynne.' Because in my mind, of course, when it came to handsome hunky men, no one could even approach my third ex-spouse.

But oh, oh, oh, Giles Travaille, Giles Travaille – the women watched and whispered and dreamed about him. If he glanced their way, they felt like they'd been singled out for some special blessing.

I'd never met him, nor had I ever been up on the twenty-first floor.

And was shocked at how different it looked.

So open. Hardly any modular units. Shiny marble floors instead of utilitarian carpet. Lots of low, sleek furniture. About one-third of the floor was a photography studio.

I asked a bosomy receptionist with dyed blonde hair and puffy pink lips where Giles Travaille's office was.

'What agency you from?' she asked.

'I'm not.'

'You here for a shoot?'

'No, Miss Hyde wants to see him.'

'Miss Who?'

'Susanna Hyde. From *Aura*. Downstairs.'

'Oh, her. The English lady.' By lifting the end of her finger, she was able to press the phone buttons without endangering her five-inch pink nails. 'He ain't in his office,' she said. 'Try the light box.'

'What's that?'

'The *light box*. Just left of PF's editorial.'

I walked in like I knew where I was going but quickly got lost because I didn't know what I was looking for. The light box was supposedly to the left of PF, whatever that was. I walked up to the desk of a pleasant-looking man with pierced eyebrows and chains that ran from his nose to his earlobes and asked, 'Excuse me, where's PF editorial?'

'You're in it, ma'am,' he said.

'I'm looking for the light box.'

He gave me some long, hopelessly complicated directions and must have seen my look of confusion because he said, 'I'd take you there myself, ma'am, but I'm chained to my desk.'

I thought he was speaking metaphorically. But he wasn't. This guy's ankles were clamped to his desk chair. That's when I finally realized what PF stood for. Personal Fetish.

'My boss is *very* strict with me,' he said. 'I'm not allowed to leave unless she gives me permission.'

A stern-looking woman wearing a long skirt and a high-necked blouse, with her hair done up in a tight bun, appeared in the doorway of the office behind him and stared at me.

I flashed a dumb smile and got out of there.

Finally I found it. The 'light box' was a separate room next to the photography studio. It had white, translucent countertops where you could view slides and transparencies, and grey wall boards where photographs could be pinned. The door was open and I could see through the glass walls that two men were inside, looking at what appeared to be dozens of Polaroids. One man was pointing and talking. He was tall, fair, and – from his right-angle profile – handsome. The other man was one of the ugliest people I've ever seen in my life. I don't mean he was unpleasant looking, or homely, this dude was *ugly*. He had a short, squat body with a fat ass and a barrel chest, a shaved head, thick, coarse features that all seemed squished together, a bad complexion, and an overbite. For some reason he reminded me of Bruce, the owner of Phantastic Phantasy, where I'd worked in Portland.

As I moved closer, I could hear them talking.

'The set-up's OK,' the ugly man said, 'but we gotta see more of his tongue.'

'Right,' said Giles Travaille. 'That means leaning her back a bit more and repositioning the left leg.' He had a deep, drawling, I'm-never-in-a-hurry voice. He was English, like Susanna.

'You lift the leg, you confront waffle,' the ugly man said. 'No waffle in *Peeper*.'

'The thighs are too large anyway. I'll reshoot with another model.'

'Get Cupcake Cassidy, I liked her.'

'Cupcake? I'll see if she's available.'

'Keep the guy, his tongue's photogenic.'

'Color's good, don't you think? All the blue from the pool?'

'Yeah. Let's call it "Laps". I'll get one of the interns to write up a teaser.'

Giles Travaille must have sensed my presence because he suddenly looked over his shoulder and saw me standing nervously in the doorway.

I cleared my throat. 'Mr Travaille?'

'Who wants him?' he said, his voice deep and teasing.

'Miss Hyde. At *Aura*. She was wondering if you could give her five minutes.'

'Miss Hyde wants a quickie,' the ugly man quipped with a barking laugh.

Giles Travaille never took his eyes off me. Not for one second. His eyes, dark as a camera lens, moved up and down and left and right, as if he were mentally positioning me for a photograph. I felt like I was standing there in front of him naked. 'Right,' he said. 'Take me to your leader.'

'What's your name, sweetheart?' the ugly man said as he was leaving. He was wearing way too much cologne.

'Venus Gilroy.'

He flicked his eyes over me, like I was produce in a supermarket. 'Want a job?'

'I've already got one,' I said.

'You ever need a job, Venus, you come up and see me.'

'Thank you,' I said.

'Don't *ever* go to see that whoremonger if you need a job,' Giles Travaille said quietly as we headed for the elevator.

'Who is he?' I asked.

'Fred Bjoner. Executive editor of *Peeper* and *Personal Fetish*.'

I didn't know what to say, so I didn't say anything.

'So you're Venus Gilroy,' Giles said as we waited for the elevator. 'Not quite what I expected.'

'What *did* you expect?' I asked, wondering if he'd really heard of me or was just making small talk.

'Susanna said you were marvellous.'

'She did?'

'She said you were a very good girl and did everything you were told.'

I couldn't tell from the tone of his voice whether he was putting me on or not. 'You could say that about a dog, too.'

Giles laughed – not a loud laugh, nothing about him was loud, but a kind of appreciative chuckle. 'I expected – I don't know quite what I expected. A mousy little sycophant, I suppose.'

The elevator arrived and we stepped in. I didn't say anything. I was racking my brains trying to think of what a sycophant was.

I looked at him out of a corner of my eye. He was about four inches taller than me, with thick, sandy-colored hair and long pale eyelashes. Mid-forties maybe, with lines starting to crease the sides of his eyes. He looked slightly sad, or maybe a little debauched. Worldly, anyway. There was a funny kind of languor about him, but also a sharp, sexual, self-confident tang. He was a very cool dresser.

'Giles! Thank God!' Susanna ushered him into her office, where glum Evan Bevins sat with his rejected layout. 'I need an artful eye here.' She closed the door, severing my brief connection with Giles Travaille.

When you're really busy with a job, it's easy to forget that you have a life.

That was how I wanted it. For now. And that's why I didn't complain too much about all the nutty, annoying things that Susanna made me do.

To tell the truth, I enjoyed working until seven o'clock because I was learning so much about New York in a back-door kind of way. Like where rich people got their dry cleaning done, and what salons they frequented, and their favorite restaurants, and where they had their housekeepers shop for cat food. I learned the price of everything I couldn't afford myself.

By the time I got on the subway to go home at night, I was completely exhausted, but in a good sort of way. All I wanted was to kick off my shoes and relax. Watch some TV. Listen to some music. Think about Tremaynne. Or, rather, try *not* to think about Tremaynne.

The city itself was a perpetual fascination, but most of its allures were way beyond my financial means. The change in prices between reasonable Portland and astronomical New York was surreal. What people paid for things in New York simply boggled my mind.

It made me realize just how lucky I was to be living in the dads' apartment. Dorcas Phinney, the administrative assistant at Stuckey Universal Media, paid over half her salary every month to rent *one room* in a three-bedroom apartment.

Food? Oh my God. No wonder so many New Yorkers are so thin. They can't afford to eat.

'Say yes to every party,' Dorcas advised me, 'every launch, every function, no matter how boring it sounds, and always help yourself to as much food as you can. That's my modus operandi for saving on grocery bills.' Dorcas always called me when she spotted something edible in the office, like a plate of stale doughnuts left over from a meeting. And she taught me how to troll for edibles myself. 'Try to walk by the test kitchen at about eleven every morning,' she said. 'That's when the stuff they've made is usually coming out of the oven and they want tasters.'

Dorcas wasn't a friend, exactly, but our paths were always crossing because we were the most junior people on the floor, the get up and go-fers who had absolutely no power of our own. She was a large, semi-geeky person, a little older than me, with small, rectangular glasses, greasy hair pulled back in a ponytail, and absolutely no eye for fashion. She was super smart but usually came across as rushed and resentful because she hated her job and thought it was beneath her.

Dorcas had been at Stuckey Universal Media for nearly a

year and was far more tuned in than I was to the gossip that flew around the modules on the twentieth floor.

'It'll all be useful when I write my memoir,' she said one day when we were waiting at the copy machine.

'You're writing a memoir?'

'That's what's hot right now.'

'What's yours about?' I asked.

'My life, of course.'

'Oh. Sure. But I mean, what about your life?'

Dorcas flipped back her ponytail in what looked like a defensive gesture. 'What about it?'

'Well, I mean, I don't know, but don't you have to have something special to write a memoir about?'

Her answer was a sarcastic laugh. 'And you think I don't?'

'I don't know,' I said clumsily, 'maybe you do have something special to write about.'

'If I don't,' she said, 'I will by the time I leave here.'

Dorcas was tight with Sharanda Williams, the beautiful black receptionist, and sometimes the three of us would go to a nearby Starbucks together – there was a barrista there that Dorcas thought was cute – or out for a sandwich or hot dog at lunch.

The rule in New York is that you never are what you do for a living. You're always something far grander. What you do is your 'day job', a boring interruption from your true calling. In Dorcas's case, that was being a writer. Sharanda, on the other hand, was a struggling actress – or *actor*, as she tersely informed me when I made the mistake of saying actress.

'You don't say sculptress any more,' she said as we waited in line for our plain drip coffees, the cheapest thing Starbucks offered. 'You say sculptor. Right?'

'Yeah,' Dorcas agreed. 'You don't say authoress, or poetess, you say author or poet.'

'You don't say bitch*ess* when you're talking about Susanna Hyde,' Sharanda said with a sly smile, 'you say *bitch*.'

'She's not a *countess*,' Dorcas countered, 'she's a *cunt*ess.'

I knew what they were doing: trying to draw me into their

clique by offering me an opportunity to carp about my boss. And there was a lot I could have carped about. But I just didn't want to. Susanna was difficult, but she wasn't impossible. And she'd given me a job. She'd even told Giles Travaille that I was marvellous.

'She must be hell to work for,' Sharanda prompted.

'It just goes to show you,' Dorcas muttered, but then stopped because she'd caught sight of the cute barrista and her face turned all bright and she quickly changed her order to a more complicated drink.

'Show you what?' Sharanda asked.

'How you can sleep your way to the top.'

'Susanna?' Sharanda let out a hooting laugh. 'She just writes about sex, she doesn't have any.'

'Don't be naïve,' Dorcas said, flashing a smile at the barrista. 'How do you think she got to be editor?'

'Hard work and talent?' I said.

They looked at me as if they couldn't believe their ears, and then decided I was being snide, which put me on their side.

'Writing about sex?' Dorcas said. 'That takes talent?'

'Anyone could do that,' Sharanda said dismissively.

'Anyway, that's not how she got to be editor,' Dorcas insisted. 'She had absolutely no experience. As an editor, I mean.'

'So who did she sleep with?' Sharanda asked.

'Who do you think, Sharanda?'

'Giles Travaille?'

'No.'

'Larry Wiener?'

'No.'

'Well, who then?' Sharanda wanted to know.

Dorcas looked right and left and lowered her voice. 'Lord Farrell Stuckey.'

'Girl,' Sharanda said after a moment's pause, 'you are talkin' biiiig scandal here. How do you know this?'

'Thanks!' Dorcas beamed at the barrista as he placed her drink on the counter. He nodded curtly. When I stepped up to get mine, he grinned and said, 'Sorry you had to wait so long. Here's a coupon for a free coffee next time.'

'Thanks.'

'I'll steam up a really good latte for you.'

'I'm sure you will,' I said, turning away with a smile. Which dissolved when I met Dorcas's suspicious eyes.

The line had been so long at Starbucks that our coffee break was over and we had to hurry back to the office.

'OK,' Dorcas said when we were on the street, 'I heard this from a couple of senior editors. Sheryl at *Cat & Kitty* and Corinna at *Lifestyle Home*. They were *shocked* when Stuckey made Susanna editor at *Aura*. There were tons of people who were *really* qualified. Eldora Button, for one. She's been at *Aura* for, like, fifteen years. All Susanna had done was her stupid column. She was a freelancer, for God's sake. But Sheryl told Corinna that she saw Susanna getting into Stuckey's limo one day, just before Stuckey made the announcement that she was the next editor.'

'That doesn't mean that they're having an affair,' Sharanda pointed out as we flashed our identity cards and headed for the elevators. 'Lord Stuckey's married. He's been married for about fifty years. To the same lady.'

'So don't believe me,' Dorcas said peevishly as we reached the twentieth floor and headed for our respective modules. 'But I'll bet you a double tall latte that Susanna Hyde's got her talons into Lord Stuckey's ass and she's not letting go.'

All fashion emanates from New York, but you'd never have known it looking at my paltry wardrobe. Sharanda had introduced me to a couple of secret, cut-rate, off-the-rack stores where you could find designer goodies for a fraction of their original price. But with what I was making, even a 75 per cent markdown often wasn't enough.

Five working days per week = five different combinations. Five different ensembles in a world where the women who saw you every day would know in two weeks flat every item you had in your wardrobe.

The thousand dollars the dads had put in a savings account for me shrank to five hundred despite my best efforts. Because things fall apart, get stained, rip. Zippers malfunction, buttons disappear, heels collapse, tights run. It's endless, and endlessly expensive to keep everything looking up to Inspection standards. How do you stay ahead of the nightmarish nothing-to-wear scenario when an essential garment you counted on suddenly requires repair or drycleaning, thus short-circuiting your obsessive mix-and-match schemes. You can't just go out and buy that cute (marked-down) skirt and blouse because you're not getting your measly pay cheque with all those infuriating deductions until the following week. You have to be creative and make do with what you have and endure the snickerings, piteous glances, and rolled eyes that you imagine are following you everywhere you go.

Not to mention make-up.

At some point, I was forced to pull out more of my Portland duds. I figured since almost everyone hated me because I worked for Susanna, it didn't really matter that much if I looked a bit . . . out of the ordinary.

Sure enough, it was my Portland clothes that got the most stares. From the women they were often Oh-my-God-look-what-she's-got-on-today stares, but from the men the stares were more like Whoa-baby-give-me-more. Susanna didn't act like a school principal defending a dress code or anything, but she could sometimes be rather caustic. 'Taking a lap dancing class?' she asked once. And once she said, 'All that color hurts my eyes.'

Well, it was all part of getting into the swing of New York. Finding out what worked and what didn't. Keeping body and soul together on a shoestring.

One night I was in the apartment frantically trying to iron a potential outfit for the next day when my new cellphone rang. I looked at the caller ID. Carolee.

'Are you out someplace fabulous?' Mom asked when I picked up.

'I'm trying to iron.'

'Iron?' I heard what sounded like the tinkle of ice in a glass. 'Since when do you know how to iron?'

'I didn't say I knew how, I said I was trying.' I waited to hear the ostensible reason for her call. She always had to have a reason.

'Well, sweetheart, I quit my ecstatic dancing class today,' Mom said. 'Do you think I should have stuck with it awhile longer?'

'I don't know, Mom. I don't even know what ecstatic dancing is.'

'Oh, it's a form of spiritual expression I practise. You go to this big room and you can wear whatever you want. I usually wear a leotard with veils. Then the music starts and you just twirl. You know, like those whirling dervishes, only not so fast. You twirl until it turns into ecstasy.'

I tried to suppress a vision of my mother wearing veils and

twirling in a room full of middle-aged, overweight Portland women. 'Sounds like good exercise.'

'Well, that's what I thought, until this woman in the class had a stroke. She was twirling really fast and then she just keeled over. So I'm thinking maybe I should just stick to my women's drumming group.'

'Mom,' I said, 'why don't you try something co-ed for a change. Maybe you'll meet a guy.'

She let out a squawking laugh. The ice tinkled in her glass. 'Me? Men don't want me. My breasts are too large.'

'Hello. Wake up. Men love big breasts.'

'Big *young* breasts, maybe, not big mature breasts.'

'I don't see why not.'

'Do you think I'm too old for breast reduction?'

'Mom, what the hell's wrong? You've never bought into cosmetic surgery.'

'Well,' she whimpered, on the verge of alcohol-induced tears, 'if my tits weren't so big, maybe I wouldn't get so many backaches and my balance would be better.'

'Oh, so now your breasts are making you unbalanced?' I couldn't believe what I was hearing.

'Sweetheart,' Mom said, changing the subject but not really, 'aren't you horribly lonely out there?'

'Sometimes.' But, more importantly, sometimes not. Even when I was by myself, which was most of the time. I was a party girl without a party, but I didn't mind, and it bewildered me sometimes that I didn't mind. Back in Portland I'd always hated to be alone. In New York, surrounded by seven million people, I kind of liked it. 'But I'm usually pretty busy, Mom.'

'Oh, busy.' The ice tinkled. 'What does staying busy have to do with not being lonely?'

'A lot, actually. I'm trying to build a career, and that takes up time and energy.'

'Don't you miss your car?' Mom asked.

The answer was no. Even though I was a West Coast girl who'd grown up in cars, and regarded a car as essential as a telephone, I didn't miss my junky old Toyota for one second. I loved taking the subway and the bus. I loved being jammed in amongst other New Yorkers, eavesdropping on their conversations, noting how they looked, sounded and behaved. It was so impossibly different from the car culture of Portland, where everyone's isolated in their own separate vehicle. In New York, I shared the sidewalks with millions of active, *walking* people. The streets were jammed. For a people watcher like me, it was like living in a carnival.

'Well, I don't believe that you're not lonely,' Mom said. 'Not for a moment. Unless you're seeing someone . . .'

'I'm not. I'm not ready.'

'You're not over Tremaynne, that's why. Oh, sweetheart, I'm so sorry about how things worked out –'

This was my cue to burst into tears. But, miraculously, I didn't. Until Mom told me that she'd just received my divorce papers in the mail that day. 'Do you want me to forward them to New York?' she asked.

So now it was final. Now it was officially over. I looked around the apartment. Looked at my blouse on the ironing board. Looked at my laptop, on the glass-topped coffee table. Sniffed.

'Oh, sweetheart,' she said, her voice miserable on my behalf, 'I know how it must make you feel.'

How could she, when I didn't know myself? 'Mom, I've gotta go now.'

'Oh sweetheart.' She sucked in a ragged, pre-sob breath. 'I wish I could be there for you right now.'

'Love you,' I said. 'Bye.' I switched her off before she could say more. Then I just stood there in a kind of daze, looking around the apartment and thinking, this is your new life. This is what you've got to work with. This is all you have, so you'd better make the most of it.

I went back to the ironing board. The familiar Tremaynne-pain throbbed in my chest, wanting the expression of tears, of sobs, of wails of grief.

I resisted it. I slipped on a sweater and went out to sit in the dark, quiet garden, looking up at the lighted windows in the apartments all around me. So many people. People everywhere. Ordinary folk living out their lives in small rooms and offices and modules. Getting up in the morning and going to work and coming home at night. Sometimes it seemed like that's all life was.

But no. It was more than that. The trick was not to shrivel up, or put electric fencing around your heart. The trick was to move forward, into new territory. I'd lost something I regarded as precious, but no amount of crying would bring Tremaynne back.

And really, I thought, as a fresh, chilly breeze blew off the Hudson River and over the tops of the buildings and down into the garden and across my face, what better place to start again than New York? I didn't want to run home. I wanted New York to be my home. I wanted to elbow my way into a future here. I wanted to have the grit and stamina it takes to be a New Yorker.

'New York always lets you know if you belong or not,' Whitman once told me. 'If you don't belong, it'll spit you out within six months.'

I still had about three months to go.

As the New York social scene ramped up, Susanna's name began to appear in gossip columns. This wasn't by accident. She wrote out little notes and announcements that I hand-delivered to various columnists.

'Slip this *under* her door,' she instructed in one case. 'Give the doorman ten dollars and he'll take you up to her floor.'

Did she mean bribe the doorman? Was that ethical? Of course at that time I didn't know what messages I was carrying. I only knew they were going to famous gossip columnists. But even so . . .

'Hurry. Chop chop. What are you waiting for?'

'The ten bucks.'

She frowned and sighed. 'I'm short of cash. No time to go to the ATM. Just pay him and I'll reimburse you later.'

Right. She was making two hundred grand and I was barely

able to afford coffee, but I was supposed to bribe a doorman for her. If I'm ever rich, I swear I'll never forget what it's like to be poor.

Sometimes I'd have to deliver her notes to a newspaper office. Or to a public relations firm. 'Make sure that *Micki* gets this,' Susanna would say. 'Micki Landis. I want you to personally put it into Micki's hand. Don't leave it with her receptionist. Don't lay it on her desk. *Put it into her hand.*'

So I did. I got into places and met people ordinary mortals never lay eyes on. And all because I worked for Susanna Hyde. Once when I was supposed to place an *extremely* important message in the hands of Aloya Pearlstein, who wrote the 'All Around Town' column, I couldn't get past a security guard in her building. I called Susanna and asked her what I should do.

'Shake your tits and give him a cute smile,' she said impatiently. 'It's imperative that Aloya Pearlstein receive that note immediately. They go to press in an hour. Just figure something out.'

So . . . I did. And it worked every time. You know why? Because men on the lowest rungs of the New York social scale – like doormen and security guards – are so accustomed to frowning, huffy, dismissive women. They love it when you smile and look pretty and ask nicely and don't hide your chest.

So all that fall I hauled ass around town, delivering Susanna's 'notes' without knowing what I was carrying. And then, sometimes, an 'item' would appear in one of the gossip columns and the twentieth floor would be abuzz and Susanna would walk in looking like the cat that ate the canary. Or act surprised, as if it were completely unexpected.

'Susanna Hyde, new editor of *Aura*, attended the lavish black-tie event honoring . . .'

'On hand was the multi-talented Susanna Hyde, London-born author of those blush-blush sex books and new editor of *Aura* magazine . . .'

'Lending sparkle to the festivities was that dynamic dynamo Susanna Hyde, whom Lord Farrell Stuckey recently named editor of *Aura* magazine . . .'

One of my jobs was to go through all the daily papers and cut out just the gossip columns. When I brought in her first pot of tea, Susanna would be poring over these columns so intently that she'd barely glance up to make certain there was precisely a half-inch of milk in her teacup.

When people called to mention that they'd seen her name, she'd give a little titter, as if she'd just been goosed by Brad Pitt, and then twist around to slam her door shut with her foot, so I wouldn't be privy to the conversation.

Oh yeah, I was beginning to see how the fame game worked.

And how my love life didn't. Was I getting rusty? Did I look like used goods? A designer knock-off instead of the Real McCoy? In a city filled with smart, beautiful women, maybe I came across as a dog. I got plenty of leers, occasionally from cute guys worth smiling back at. But every time I smiled I was stricken with this awful sense that I didn't mean it. It was an old habit that I hadn't broken. The only *really* cute guy I'd met and talked to since arriving in New York was that writer Josh, whose last name I didn't know (or I would have tried looking him up in the phone book). And he'd been snapped up by Susanna. I was beginning to see that available wantable men in New York were at a premium. The competition was really tough. And people didn't share. At least Susanna didn't. She never mentioned Josh, so sometimes I wondered if maybe he was free again, and out looking for someone just like me.

One morning in November, Susanna had an appointment with Gilda Cosmopolis, an 'aesthetic revitilizer' who did 'body readings' and advised women on the various kinds of cosmetic surgery best suited to their 'emotional auras'. Gilda, who looked like a slightly dazed contestant in a beauty pageant, was trying to pitch a story idea on spiritual makeovers.

As I brought in the ritual tea, I heard Gilda going on about 'the unfulfilled spirit that resides in a less-than-perfect body'.

What crap, I thought.

'It does make sense, of course,' Susanna said. 'We know when something could be better, don't we?'

'Our inner aesthetic knows,' Gilda confirmed. 'And when the physical change is made, we are profoundly revitalized within.'

I took my time pouring their tea.

'Well, before I can consider this as a story,' Susanna said, 'it would be useful if you gave me one of your body readings.'

'I'd be delighted,' Gilda said, holding up her slender, beringed hand when I offered milk. She did take four packets of Splenda, though.

A few days later, Susanna decided that she needed a more glamorous image to accompany the bits of print that were now sprinkling her name through the tabloids.

I didn't peg her as the makeover type because I thought she was a beautiful woman already, or distinctive-looking anyway: slender, sharp-featured, with cornflower-blue eyes, a smooth, lovely complexion, and an uncomplicated blonde hairdo. She came across as smart and sophisticated, not as someone who was insecure about the way she looked.

OK, maybe she *was* starting to show some wear and tear around the edges, but she was still beautiful.

So I was as surprised as everyone else when Susanna's transformation began.

And it began with: 'Venus, call Giles Travaille and see if he's got a few minutes for me this afternoon.'

They were always hanging out together, but I couldn't tell what, exactly, was going on between them. Dorcas was certain they were sleeping together; I wasn't so sure. It seemed more likely that Giles was sleeping with everybody *but* Susanna. Like all those super-endowed models he was always 'discovering' and photographing for *Peeper*. Maybe that increased his sex appeal in Susanna's eyes. And one thing you could say about Giles was that he was sexy. It was an inescapable fact.

He was sexy without swagger, sexy in the way that guys who know what they're doing are sexy. Tremaynne was like that. Guys like Tremaynne and Giles don't need to work at getting a woman's attention – the women just come to them. I guess you could call it sexual charisma. And funnily enough, that was exactly what Susanna didn't have, even though she'd made her name writing frankly about s-e-x.

Giles was a chronic flirt, I knew that much, and even though I saw it for what it was (or thought I did), his flirtatiousness kind of amused and turned me on at the same time. I liked the mixture of dashing style and laconic delivery. And when he flirted with me, which he did every time I saw him, it was almost like he knew that I knew it was all a game, to be enjoyed but not to be taken seriously. We connected on the flirtation wavelength, or so I liked to believe, almost as equals. And when my thoughts turned into late-night fantasies, with Giles as star, I just tried to laugh off the ridiculousness of them. Because he was so cool, and I was not.

'You've got something,' he said to me one afternoon when I was delivering something to him from Susanna. Before I could say anything, he snatched up a big camera and snapped a photo. 'I have a feeling you'd be great on film.'

I looked over and saw the layout he was working on. It was called June Bride. The model had on a long white veil and white high heels and nothing else. 'Don't make me laugh, OK?'

He snapped another photo. 'Ever done any modelling?'

'I went to modelling school for a while. For a month. Back in Portland. A few years ago.' I tried to dodge him as he swung around and snapped me from another angle.

'Brilliant! I knew it.'

'Stop it. Knew what?'

'For better or worse, Venus, I've got a sixth sense about these things. Flip your hair back, darling, and give me a smile.' He clicked again. 'Come on, open up those luscious lips. Let me see the pearly whites.'

I shook my head, frozen with embarrassment.

'Why not?'

'I don't want to.' That was why I left modelling school, after all. They told me if I didn't have my teeth fixed – which would have cost about $10,000 back then – I could never be a model.

Giles lowered his camera and studied me. 'You're really fresh,' he said. 'Innocent, but in a knowing kind of way.' He smiled in a knowing kind of way himself. 'You're real, that's what it is.' He lifted the camera and took another snap.

'OK, fine, but you're making me feel unreal.'

He just kept shooting. 'No cosmetic enhancements. A little out-of-kilter. All natural.'

'But not,' I said, getting out of his office, '*au naturel*.' Which got an appreciative laugh.

Later, when he came down for a meeting with Susanna, Giles smiled at me in that same knowing way he had in his office and leaned over to whisper in my ear: 'My camera's in love with you.' He tossed an envelope on my desk as he walked into Susanna's office.

'Giles,' I heard her say, very matter-of-factly, 'I need a new image.'

'Of what?' he asked.

'Of *me*.'

She needed several images, actually. She needed one for the front of *Aura*, to accompany 'From the Editor's Desk', her chatty overview of the current issue. She needed one for the jacket of her new, as-yet-unreleased book. And she needed one to send out for publicity purposes. 'But our photographers down here on twenty are so awful,' Susanna complained to Giles. 'They'll make me look like some sort of demonic New Age priestess. And for the book – well, that's about sex so of course they'll try to make me look cheerfully wholesome.'

'How do you want to look?' Giles asked.

'Sexy!' she exclaimed. 'Like I've got a man in my bed every night of the week and two on Sunday.'

'Well, you're hardly *Peeper* material. Too classy.'

'Not enough tit, you mean.'

'Your breasts aren't your biggest asset, darling.'

'Giles,' Susanna said, her voice turning softly seductive, 'you could make me look sexy, couldn't you?'

'Sex*ier*,' he said. 'Maybe.' Giles was the only man who dared to be completely honest with Susanna. I suddenly wondered if that's why she liked him so much. And if she didn't think she was sexy, didn't that mean that he wasn't sleeping with her?

'I don't want to look like one of your slutty tarts,' she said, 'but I do think it's important to freshen up my – you know – sex appeal. Don't you?'

'No, I don't.'

'You don't? Because you don't find me sexy at all?' She sounded hurt.

Their voices, low and intimate, carried right out to my ears. But then Susanna must have realized that I could hear every word because she twisted around and closed the door with her high-heeled hoof.

As if I would have listened in or anything.

I opened the envelope Giles had tossed on my desk. Inside I found . . . *me*. The photos he'd taken in his office that day. Oh my God, was *that* how I really looked? I stuck the envelope in my purse, afraid to cross-examine the images that confronted me.

A few days later I had to bring something I'd typed into Susanna's office and pick up the afternoon tea things. Susanna had been called into a meeting with Larry Wiener, the editor-in-chief of Stuckey Global Media.

Laid out across her desk were several head shots, some in color, most in black and white.

It was the strangest thing.

She looked *terrible*. Stiff. Unnatural. A smile that was so patently false that it looked pasted on. The English beauty I saw in real life was simply not there. If this was her attempt to look sexy, it hadn't worked.

'Horrible, aren't they?'

I gasped and looked up to see Susanna standing in her office door.

'Don't lie,' she said, coming in and looking at the photos herself. 'The photos don't.'

'I like this one,' I said, trying to be generous.

Susanna stared at it with distaste. Then she took a red marker and made a big X across the photo. 'That's what I think of it.' She X'd all the photos and then tore them in two and handed the pieces to me. 'Put them in the shredder.' As I was leaving her office, she said, 'Who tints your eyebrows?'

'They're natural.'

'Where did you have your breast enhancements done?'

'I don't have any enhancements.'

'Mm, you and Elizabeth Hurley.'

'The only thing I've had done are my tattoos.'

'That's too bad,' she said. 'Because you know they *never* come off, and as you grow older and your skin sags, they get all blurry and—' She stopped mid-sentence and asked me how old she looked. 'Don't lie. Tell me the truth.'

'I don't know.'

'Don't be such a bloody bore! I'm asking for an honest opinion.'

'All right. Forty.'

'Forty?' she said hopefully.

'Three.'

'Forty-three!' My answer seemed to take her aback. And her next question took me aback. 'Do I look like I have only one ovary?'

'I don't know how a woman with only one ovary would look,' I said.

'It's one of those hidden things, you know? One of those missing parts that screw up your chemistry. It's like having only one testicle.'

'I don't think anyone could tell that you have only one ovary just by looking at you.'

'Gilda Cosmopolis knew,' she said. 'She said it affected my inner aura.'

'Well, most of us aren't psychic,' I said, 'so we wouldn't know.'

'But *I* know. And I also know that having just one ovary affects one's hormones. And hormones affect one's skin. One's all-too-human flesh.' She patted her cheek, then prodded it. 'It's sagging. It's pouching. It's puffing. It's crinkling. It's wrinkling. And that's what you see on those bloody photos.'

I hovered in the doorway, holding the tea tray, not knowing if she wanted me to go or stay. The photographs had obviously agitated her, but something else was going on, too.

'We've got to reach out to a younger demographic,' she said, as if I were one of her editorial staffers. 'This is what I just said to Larry Weiner. Not just *Aura* – all the Stuckey Universal Media magazines. Younger, younger, younger. And sexier, sexier, sexier. We can't be afraid of it. We have to embrace it. If we don't, we're dead. The future lies in youth and sex and the Internet.'

'Sounds pretty grim,' I said.

'Well – Larry called us in because we just got our quarterlies. Subscriptions are holding steady but news-stand sales are down. And the demographic stats for *Aura*? What do you think they are?'

I shrugged.

'Average reader between thirty-five and fifty. We may as well change our name to *Lifestyle Death*.'

My arms were getting tired holding the tea tray. 'Do you need me for anything else?'

'Yes, call my wine store – number's in my BlackBerry – and have them deliver two cases of that French white from St.-Emilion and two cases of the Lascalles Bordeaux. Oh, and a case of Perrier.'

'Deliver to your apartment – I mean your flat?'

'Right. Then call Jacqueline' – she pronounced it jack-*leen* – 'at that catering firm –'

'Which?'

'The one I always use. Trois Framboises. It's on the BlackBerry. Ask Jacqueline if she can do hors d'oeuvres for twenty off the books. Those little cheese puff thingies and some timbales and that teeny chocolate tartlet with cayenne. Make certain you speak *only* to Jacqueline. And make certain you say "off the books".'

'What does that mean?'

'It means she charges me forty dollars a head instead of fifty. Ask her if she can deliver them by seven o'clock on Friday and provide two servers. Tell her they have to look and act like professionals.'

I raced back to my desk and scribbled furiously, trying to remember phonetically what she'd said. I didn't know French, so it was all guesswork.

Everything seemed to be going fine until I told Jacqueline that Susanna wanted two people to serve. This provoked a surprised gasp. 'Tell her this is not posseeble,' she whispered in a thick French accent. 'The cheese puffs, *oui*, the timbales, *oui*, the *tarte aux chocolat et cayenne*, *oui*. But the servers, no. She will have to find someone else.'

Which is how I ended up serving canapés at Susanna's party. It was a desperation tactic. I was paired with another last-minute employee.

The minute I saw him my heart gave a little flip. It was

Josh, the guy I'd met at the *Aura* party. The one Susanna had shoplifted from my side.

'You look familiar,' he said, squinting at me as we stood in the kitchen trying to figure out our respective duties.

'That's because we've met before,' I said.

He nodded. 'I never forget a face,' he said, eyeing my heart tattoo.

'We weren't together very long,' I said, feeling weirdly shy. He was even cuter than I remembered. 'I mean, we weren't *together* together, we just met and talked for a while.'

'And I didn't ask for your phone number?'

I shook my head, wondering if he'd ask for it now. But he didn't. 'I don't usually do this sort of thing,' I said nervously, tying on the starched white apron Susanna had insisted I wear.

'I don't either,' he said. 'I'm a writer.'

I nodded. 'I know.'

'Is it that obvious?'

'No. I just remember you saying that. Before. I mean the last time I met you. I mean the one time.'

'You're an actress, right?'

I shook my head. 'I'm Susanna's PA.'

'Oh. Oh, right.' He smiled and folded his arms and leaned back against the sink. 'That party.'

'Mm.'

'I had too much to drink that night. Someone else must have been paying.'

'It wasn't me,' I laughed nervously.

'But it was you,' he said. 'At that party. We were talking and – what happened?'

'You met Susanna,' I said.

'Ohhh.' He nodded meaningfully. 'Oh, right.'

It was time to get going with the party prep. I'd had some practice at my dads' parties and knew the basic outlines of Cocktail Party 101, so I sort of knew what to do and how to do it. But did he? 'So you're going to be pouring the wine?' I asked.

'I don't know,' he shrugged. 'I'm just doing this as a favor.'

'To who – whom?'

'Susanna. She called in a panic and asked if I'd please help her out. She said Lord Stuckey'd come to town unexpectedly and she had to arrange a party.'

'*I* arranged the party,' I said, lining up trays of Jacqueline's unbelievably minuscule hors d'oeuvres. I'd never seen edibles that small in my life, except maybe as free samples in supermarkets.

'Anyway,' he said, 'it's not every day you get an opportunity to meet a British publishing magnate.'

'What do you write, when you're not being a waiter?' I asked, eyeing the eats. If I ate just *one* of those tiny canapés it would mess up the strict symmetry of Jacqueline's trays. But if I ate an *entire row*, no one would know.

Josh reached over, nabbed a timbale, and popped it into his mouth. 'Well, I just had a story published in *Belles Lettres*. And I've been invited to Meat Loaf.'

'What's that?'

'A famous writer's workshop.' He snagged another canapé, as nonchalant as if he were a guest.

I tried to rearrange the tray. 'You mean you have to be famous to go there, or the workshop is famous?'

'Both. Sort of.' He regarded me with those beautiful green eyes as he chewed on a tartlet.

'Are you teaching there or what?' I asked.

'No, but I was accepted into Leon Dagger's creative fiction seminar. He only takes five students. And if he's behind you—'

We heard the sound of scurrying feet, the clack of high heels on wooden floors, then Susanna burst breathlessly into the kitchen. She was wearing a strapless aquamarine-blue silk dress that looked a bit pinched around her bosom. 'Right. People will be coming any minute now. Josh, you'll be an angel and take care of the bar. Offer wine first – it's French and there's a white and a Bordeaux. If anyone insists on a drink drink, we're set up for G and Ts and Scotch and sherry, right over here. But don't offer them a drink drink first, just wine, or you'll be constantly darting back and forth. Don't pour red into a glass that's had white, and don't pour white into a glass that's had red. If they're changing wines, offer them a fresh glass. I'll take care of Lord Stuckey. He'll be completely my responsibility. Venus, I want you to answer the door and to start passing hors d'oeuvres when about four or five people have arrived.' She stopped and studied Josh. 'Is that the best jacket you have?'

He was clearly embarrassed. 'Well – yeah – I mean I was in a hurry. You said it was an emergency.'

'Do you have a tie?'

The way she acted with him, bossy and intimate at the same time, indicated that something had developed between them. But Josh was at least fifteen years younger than Susanna. I watched the two of them with renewed interest.

'You didn't say to wear a tie,' Josh said.

'Because I thought it was *understood*,' Susanna said, sounding like a disapproving mother or exasperated girlfriend. She scurried away and returned with a black patterned tie. 'Here, put this on.' The doorbell rang and Susanna looked at her watch. 'Fuck. All right. That's Lord Stuckey. Venus, you answer the door and ask him to come in. I'll meet him in the sitting room.'

'The sitting room?' I said. 'Where's that?'

'The sitting room. The – the-what-do-you-call-it-here – the—'

'Living room?' Josh offered.

'Yes,' Susanna said. 'The living room. That's where you'll direct the guests, but most of them are Brits, so say "sitting room". Now answer the door. Chop chop. And say "good evening" when you open the door, not "hi" or "how ya doin' ".' She disappeared to take up her spot and await the appearance of Lord Farrell Stuckey, who maybe was and maybe wasn't her lover. I looked back at Josh as I was leaving the kitchen.

'I guess we've got our orders,' Josh said, an amused glint in his eye.

I nodded. He was Susanna's lover, too. How many did she have? It seemed kind of unfair.

*

A noxious cloud of smoke greeted me as I opened the door, and Lord Stuckey looked at me from behind an enormous cigar. 'This is Miss Hyde's flat,' he said, stating, not asking.

'Yeah – yes. Good evening. Miss Hyde is in the sitting room.'

'Miss Hyde is hiding in the sitting room, is she?' He barrelled past, streaming smoke like an old locomotive.

He seemed awfully rude and smelly for a British publishing magnate. And old. He must have been around eighty, with an upswept nest of stiff white hair guarding a bald patch in the center. He was a big man, tall and corpulent, a commanding figure with an outsize bluster and an ego that never went hungry.

'Farrell, darling,' I heard Susanna say, and the rustle of her dress as she walked across her sitting room to greet him. 'What a surprise to hear you were in town.' A moment of silence, maybe as he kissed her. 'Let me get you a drink.'

'Scotch,' he brayed.

'Of course. I've got your favorite. Sit here in my favorite chair,' she coaxed, 'and I'll be right back with your drink.'

I was hovering in a kind of no-man's-land in the hallway between the kitchen and the sitting room. Susanna shot me a glance as she passed by. 'I'll get his drink,' she whispered, 'but you bring out some canapés. Leave a tray on the table beside him.'

Lord Stuckey had the gravelly voice of a firmly committed smoker. 'You're a pretty gell,' he said when I came out and offered him the tray of cheese puffs.

'Thank you.'

'You a *Peeper* gell?'

'No, I work for Miss Hyde.'

He looked scornfully at the tray of hors d'oeuvres I was offering. 'What the hell are these?'

'Cheese puffs.'

He waved the tray away and returned to the pleasures of his cigar, tapping ashes on to Susanna's antique Persian carpet.

Susanna saw him do this as she entered with his drink. It was the briefest of eye movements, but I could tell that she did *not* want ashes on the carpet. 'Venus,' she said, 'would you bring Lord Stuckey an ash tray, please. A *large* one. Kitchen cupboard. Left side. Third shelf up. Waterford.'

When I returned with the ashtray and put it down beside Lord Stuckey's elbow, he said to Susanna, 'Didn't know you had a maid.'

So – I was her perk, her girl, and now her maid.

Susanna looked at me, imploring me with her eyes – to do what? Play along? 'Oh, she just comes in now and then,' she said, smiling at Lord Stuckey. 'I couldn't afford anyone full time. Not on that tiny salary you give me.'

'Ha ha!' His laughter turned to a cough, the cough to a loud hawking. For a moment I thought he was going to spit out a big brown gob of phlegm on Susanna's Persian carpet, but instead he fished out a stained handkerchief and spat in that.

'I'm going to take you to my Chinese herbalist about that cough,' Susanna said.

Lord Stuckey apparently thought this was a joke, for he spat out a couple of loud haw haws.

Half an hour later, I was so overwhelmed by my duties that I didn't know if I was coming or going. I raced from door to kitchen, greeting and directing and offering Jacqueline's delicious canapés and taking coats and showing people where the bathroom was and picking up empty plates . . . while Josh ambled about as if he were Susanna's co-host instead of a lackey serving wine. I caught glimpses of him talking, smiling, laughing with the guests. He was the kind of smart, relaxed guy who could assimilate in a high-powered crowd. Someone the dads would definitely approve of. Not like the guys I'd married, including Tremaynne, who had no social skills of any kind. Seeing Josh in this milieu made him even more attractive.

Parties have a life and energy of their own, and when twenty people drain four cases of wine in under an hour, you know some serious drinking is afoot. Most of the guests were rich Brits who either knew Lord Stuckey or wanted to. Some were apparently Lord Stuckey's friends, people Susanna didn't seem to know well or maybe not at all. It struck me that no one else from Stuckey Global Media was there, no other editors, not even Larry Weiner, the editor-in-chief. Susanna seemed to have a special, private hold on Lord Stuckey.

But that changed, and the party dynamics changed, when Giles arrived.

I opened the door and saw him standing in the hallway with an impossibly proportioned woman who looked like she'd gone to Doll School. 'Wellll,' Giles drawled, looking me slowly up and down, 'you can even make a bloody apron look sexy.' He'd been drinking, I could tell, and was in an upbeat, playful mood.

'Good evening, Mr Travaille,' I said, curtseying, trying not to laugh.

'Good evening. This is Ms Cassidy.'

'Call me Cupcake,' the woman said, extracting a mirror from her purse and examining herself from many different angles. 'Hey Giles, who is it lives here again?'

'Susanna Hyde.'

'The one who writes that sex column, right?'

'Yes, but now she runs *Aura* magazine as well.'

'And this Lord Stuckup, he's like a jillionaire publisher, right?'

'Right,' Giles said. 'Only his name is Stuckey.'

'You think he'd be interested in publishing my memoir?' Cupcake had Giles hold the mirror while she applied some fresh lipstick.

'I didn't know you were a writer, Cupcake.'

'I ain't. This is a memoir. You know, true. About my experiences as an adult superstar. I'm calling it *The Naked Truth*.' She turned to me. 'Good title, don't you think?'

'I'm sure Lord Stuckey will be all ears,' Giles said, following Cupcake into Susanna's flat. 'Is the old goat here yet?' he asked me in a passing whisper.

'Yeah, he's here.'

Susanna's sitting room went completely silent as Cupcake walked in behind her giant uplifted breasts. I have never seen a dress like the one she was wearing. How it was constructed was a complete mystery. It hung on her like a cobweb, yet managed to shore up the weight of her half-exposed mammaries, offering them up like shimmering desserts on a platter.

I slipped into the kitchen. Giles and Cupcake were standing right by the kitchen door, so I could see and hear everything that happened.

Susanna came over to greet the new arrivals. 'Giles, you made it.' She turned to Cupcake, or rather, Cupcake's breasts. 'Hello.'

'Susanna, this is Cupcake Cassidy.'

'Somehow I guessed that,' Susanna said. 'How do you do?'

'You write that sex column, right?' Cupcake said.

'Yes,' Susanna said. 'I'm internationally syndicated.'

'Me too,' Cupcake said. 'I was Miss Peeper of the year last year. How many copies did you sell that month, Giles? Worldwide.'

'Oh, about two million,' Giles said, lifting a cheese puff from the tray as I passed by.

'And my flicks,' Cupcake said to Susanna, 'hey, they break records every time one opens.'

'I didn't know you were a film star, too,' Susanna said drily.

'You didn't see *Da Vinci's Big Secret*?'

'No. Unfortunately.'

'*Kama Sutra Girls*?'

Susanna shook her head.

'*Zombie Doll*? That was my breakthrough role,' Cupcake said.

'I saw *Kama Sutra Gells*.' It was Lord Stuckey, drawn over by the flashing beacons of Cupcake's breasts.

An introduction was inevitable, but Susanna obviously didn't want to provide it, so Giles did. When she heard Lord Stuckey's name, Cupcake's entire demeanor changed. 'You're the one I wanna talk to,' she said, taking his arm and leading him away. 'Listen, I'm writing this memoir . . .'

Susanna nervously watched their departure, then glanced at Giles with what looked like annoyance. 'What a talented girl,' she said. 'But that dress is a bit frumpy, wouldn't you say?'

Giles laughed and turned away from her, meeting and greeting and shaking hands and kissing the ladies as he waded into the crowd. It was the first time I'd seen him out of an office setting. Handsome, somewhat sly. I watched him lean forward and tell a story in a low voice. Everyone around him leaned in, too, listening intently, until suddenly they burst apart again in a fit of laughter. A consummate party animal. And an unending flirt, which the ladies all seemed to love.

Every once in awhile, as I darted around offering canapés and opening the door, I'd glance over and see Giles looking at me. I'd be lying if I said I didn't like it. But it also made me feel a little weird, since I was so obviously the 'help' and not an invited guest. But when Giles looked at me, when he smiled, for just a second or two it was like we were in our own world, separate from everyone else, as if we shared a special secret.

The only one Giles didn't take to was Josh. He told Josh what he wanted to drink, and when Josh returned and tried to make some conversation, Giles nodded curtly and then pointedly turned around to talk to someone else.

Susanna, meanwhile, was anxiously fluttering around Lord Stuckey and Cupcake as the two of them wandered from spot to spot, deep in conversation. Well, maybe it wasn't conversation. Cupcake seemed to be doing all the talking while Lord Stuckey stared at her breasts.

But, as with any party, people moved around constantly and the social configurations were changing all the time. Intent on my duties, darting in and out of the kitchen, I lost track of Josh, Giles and Susanna. But then, at some point, as I was sort of hiding in the kitchen trying to wolf down a few hors d'oeuvres before they all disappeared, I heard two distinctive voices. Giles and Susanna were apparently standing close together just outside the kitchen door, on the other side of the wall.

'Did you speak to him?' Giles asked in a low voice.

'Not yet.' Susanna sounded annoyed. 'I will.'

'Nick Burden said he could get a hundred grand.'

'It has to be done carefully,' Susanna said.

They suddenly stopped talking and Josh came striding into the kitchen. He saw me eating some of the hors d'oeuvres I was supposed to be serving and came over to snarf down a few himself.

'There are some really important people out there,' he said excitedly. 'I made some really good contacts.'

'Try one of these,' I said, popping a chocolate and cayenne tartlet into his mouth.

'Mm. I've got to get this one lady's e-mail address before she goes,' Josh said, chewing the tartlet. 'She's starting up a new arts journal and looking for some hot new fiction writers.'

'That would be you, right?'

'She was really impressed when I told her about being invited to Meat Loaf. And my story in *Belles Lettres*.'

A deep, husky voice just behind us said, 'Oh, there you are.' It was the lady looking for hot new writers. She was pretty old, but impeccably groomed. She eyed me for the briefest of seconds before zeroing in on Josh. 'Have your agent call me,' she said, handing him a card.

Josh looked at the card, then smiled at her. Oh, that smile. It could open bank vaults. 'Hey, this is great, Mirella, but I don't have an agent. I'm working on that right now.'

She narrowed her hooded eyes. She had one of those hairdos that cover up excess wrinkles – you know, bangs down the eyebrows and sides that hang straight, right next to the corners of the eyes. 'Then I guess you'll have to call me yourself,' she said.

'OK. Sure. I'll do that.' Josh graciously squired her out of the kitchen. I heard a deep, husky laugh by the front door.

By eight-thirty, the only guests left were Susanna, Lord Stuckey, Giles and Cupcake. Susanna informed me that the four of them were going out for dinner. 'Oh, you can come too, Josh,' she added, as if it were an afterthought. 'Venus can clean everything up.'

I was accustomed to her dismissive tone and hardly thought

anything of it. But Josh stood in the hallway, his eyebrows raised in surprise, as if he'd never witnessed such rude behavior. 'Uh – no, that's OK. I'll stay here and help Venus.'

'Just stack everything in the kitchen,' Susanna said to the two of us on her way out. 'My cleaning lady will take care of it tomorrow.'

I started to pick up glasses and plates, watching Josh out of the corner of my eye as he came into the sitting room. I couldn't believe how nice he'd been, offering to stay behind to help me pick up party debris. But instead of helping, he poured himself a glass of wine, sat down on Susanna's frilly, chintz-covered sofa, and put his feet up on her coffee table. 'Great party,' he said. 'That's why I love New York.'

'The parties?'

'Yeah. All the different people you meet.'

And lose.

'I love talking to people,' Josh said. 'Even snobs and fools. You can learn something from all of them.'

'Like what?' I went around picking up empty glasses, discarded napkins, large, obvious crumbs, but I left the big crystal ashtray with Lord Stuckey's stinky cigar ash.

'Like – how they talk. If you're a writer, you have to know how people talk. How they act. What they do. Even if you don't always like it.' He watched me tidying up. 'For Christ's sake, leave that.'

I looked at him.

'You've done enough tonight.' He put out his hand, beckoning me to the sofa. 'Come sit down. Have a drink.'

'I wasn't asked here as a guest,' I pointed out.

'Well,' Josh said, '*I'm* asking you.'

I let out a laugh. 'It's not your apartment either.'

'I hang out here enough,' he said. 'If I want to invite you to sit down and have a drink, I will.'

'Just one, then,' I said. 'That red wine looked really good.'

'I stashed some.' Josh leaned around the side of the sofa, fished up a bottle, and poured me a great big glassful.

'To New York,' he said, holding up his glass.

'To New York.' I clinked my glass against his.

That was the night I finally got to talk to Josh O'Connell. In Susanna's apartment, of all places. And when I say we talked, I mean we *talked*. And when Josh talked – oh, he was just so much fun, and so interesting, full of sharp, unexpected observations and pitch-perfect impersonations that made me laugh. Josh was in hotblooded pursuit of fame as a writer, he was quite clear about that, and that was why he'd come to New York.

'How about you?' he asked. 'Why'd you come to New York?'

'It's a long story,' I said.

'I love long stories. Sagas, even.'

'Some other time.'

'OK.' Josh smiled. Oh, he could have bottled that smile. 'We'll meet and exchange narratives.'

'It's a date.' I leaned over and kissed him on the cheek. I wanted to do a whole lot more but refrained out of courtesy to Susanna. He was still hers, after all. Wasn't he?

I spent a lot more time in Susanna's flat, as it turned out. Whenever she went off on a trip, I had to go over to keep her cat company.

'I've seen simply too many neurotic pets in New York,' Susanna said. 'They get that way because their owners don't spend enough time with them. And then they turn mean and nasty.'

'The owners or the pets?'

'The pets. So you won't mind going over for a couple of hours a day, will you? To give Regina' – rhymes with vagina – 'some quality time?'

'I guess not.' It was weird, and added a couple more hours to my work day, but I thought it might be fun.

'She's quite finicky about her food,' Susanna said. 'It has to be served on one particular plate by a human who stands beside her, or she won't eat.'

'OK.'

'And her litter box . . .' That had to be cleaned daily, or Regina wouldn't do her business. She was so meticulous, according to Susanna, that she wouldn't even scratch kitty litter over her droppings.

Well, I like cats. Crookedy, the cat I'd loved most, was a Portland tom, in and out all day long, and not a fussy eater. I'd never encountered a cat like Regina.

To begin with, she was a long-hair as opposed to short. White, of course. She had a sour-looking squashed-up face, a long feathery tail, and the funniest little voice, a tiny squeak that was completely at odds with her true nature.

On my first visit, it took me two hours to find her. I wandered through Susanna's very large flat calling, 'Regina, Regina,' and making appropriate come-hither sounds with my tongue.

No Regina.

I couldn't feed her until she was present in the kitchen. 'She'll let you know when she wants to be fed,' Susanna had told me. So I began a deeper exploration of apartment 14C, peering under furniture and behind doors.

No Regina.

While I was looking for Regina, I was also looking more carefully at Susanna's flat. It was in a huge brick-faced building on Riverside Drive and 81st Street, and the windows were high enough above the trees so that I could see the Hudson River and across to New Jersey. The place was enormous compared to the dads' apartment where I was living. It had an entrance hall, a good-sized kitchen with a 'maid's room' off it, a sitting room, a dining room, and two bedrooms with an old-fashioned bathroom between them. More importantly, it had a 'good' address.

Whitman had told me how Susanna had gotten this apartment. When she first came to New York, sometime in the 1990s, she'd rented one of the bedrooms from a gay guy who'd been living there for ages. When the building went co-op, the guy was offered an incredibly low 'insider's' price. He didn't have enough money to buy. Susanna did, but her name wasn't on the lease. So she suggested to her landlord that they get married – strictly a financial arrangement, done so that they could get an expensive New York apartment at a rock-bottom price. They married, but what happened after that, Whitman didn't know, except that Susanna was suddenly a US citizen and the owner of a piece of Manhattan real estate that was now worth at least three million dollars.

All this flitted through my mind as I looked for Regina. 'Here, Regina. Here, kitty kitty.' I pulled a half-opened closet door and peered inside.

Clothes.

Oh, so many clothes. Beautiful clothes. Beautifully tailored. Luscious fabrics. But so much black. And shoes. A faint smell of leather hovered beneath the scent of Susanna's perfume. I was about to close the door on that enchanted realm when I heard a faint squeak from the back of the closet.

'Regina? Are you in there?'

She was, but she wasn't coming out. Nor could I figure out where, exactly, she was hiding. I got down on my hands and knees to look but I couldn't see her.

'Regina,' I said, using my best kitty-coaxing voice, 'I'm going to go in the kitchen and get your dinner ready.'

Then I went and waited in the kitchen, but she didn't show.

Back to the closet, more coaxing, a disdainful squeak from Regina – or was she in distress? I got down on my hands and knees again and crawled into the closet, over Susanna's shoes and beneath her clothes. 'Regina? Come on, sweetheart. Come out of there.'

She said something like 'Aow' before suddenly leaping out from a hidden shelf and raking my arm with her nails as she fled the scene.

It was almost midnight before she allowed me to feed her, and then she wouldn't eat, so I tried mashing the food up. Regina looked at me as if to say, 'What the bloody hell are you doing? I don't eat mashed food.'

'Goodnight, Regina,' I said, sometime around one in the morning. She sat in the hallway watching as I collected my things. 'Don't choke on your food or anything.'

Susanna called the next morning at 8 a.m. sharp to ask how her 'little precious' was.

'*She*'s fine,' I said, stifling a yawn and examining the long, thin scratch marks on my arm.

'Play some games with her tonight, would you? She's extraordinarily bright, and she needs stimulation. There's a box of toys in the sitting room.'

So I did. It took an hour to find her, and an hour to feed her, and then I pulled out her box of toys and tried to figure out what to do with them.

There was a feather on a long string attached to a pole, a small plastic ball which flashed colors and had a tinkly bell inside, and a fat cloth mouse filled with catnip. I dangled, rolled, and threw.

Regina didn't even bother to look at me.

Susanna was gone for a week that time. And in her absence I felt like I could relax a little, move at a more normal human pace, and not be so wound up and worried all the time about what I was or was not doing. It was like being on vacation. I found myself yawning a lot, daydreaming about taking naps.

One afternoon, delivering some stuff to Giles, I couldn't help myself and started to yawn.

Giles looked up from his light board. 'Am I that boring?'

I shrugged. 'Oh. No. Sorry. I'm just kind of tired.'

'Venus, we're all tired. Fatigue is the hallmark of the twenty-first century. Tired and wired.' He closed the door and motioned me over to his desk. 'Come do a line with me,' he said, digging a small packet of powder from the back of a desk drawer.

'No thanks.'

'It's pure. It's a great snort. Takes the yawns away.'

I smiled and shook my head.

'Don't worry,' he said. 'I won't do anything to you.'

'I didn't think you would,' I said.

'You didn't?' He sounded surprised.

'No. You're not that kind of guy.'

'I'm not?'

'You don't have to force yourself on women. Women come to you.'

He nodded, a bit morosely. 'Yes, that's true. But not always the women I want.' He put the cocaine in his shirt pocket and looked at his watch. 'Hey, let's close up shop and go out for a drink.' He sounded like a naughty little boy.

And just then I happened to feel like a naughty little girl. My fatigue vanished. I was rarin' to go. 'OK.'

I met him in front of the building and we started walking over towards Third Avenue, where Giles said there was a great new bar. I was freezing because the temperature had dropped twenty degrees since lunchtime. I'd worn a short skirt and heels that day and a piercingly cold wind now whistled up my legs. I shivered in my unlined denim jacket and hugged my arms tight.

'You look like you're bloody freezing,' Giles said. He put a sheltering arm around me and we walked on. But I couldn't stop shaking. 'Here.' Giles took off his long cashmere coat and wrapped it around me. It was soft and still warm from his body.

I tried so hard not to read anything into these gallant gestures. They softened Giles in my eyes, gave him a gentler human dimension, made him less intimidating. But I knew what was on his mind because it was sort of on my mind, too.

The bar was sleekly gorgeous, all chrome and wood and dark blue strip lighting along the walls. It was jammed with office escapees taking advantage of Happy Hour. Giles led me to a table and ordered our drinks and some tapas. I pretended like this was all par-for-the-course for me, but of course my brain was ticking like a taxi meter, totting up the cost of everything I couldn't afford.

'Well,' he said, 'how are things with our demanding Susanna?'

'Demanding.'

'She's always been that way,' Giles said.

'Have you known her for a long time?'

'We met at university.' He smiled at some private amusement, then laughed. 'We used to tromp around London together. God! We were so bloody poor back then. *Hated* it. Always looking for work, always being turned down.' He blew out his lips as if the memory still chilled him. 'Well, that's how we both got into sex, really. Susanna started writing a sex column for one of those neighborhood weeklies. It was sort of a lark and a way to make some much-needed cash until one of her books sold. But it just sort of took off and took over.'

'What about you?'

He ran a hand through his hair and let out a sound that was half-sigh, half-moan. I suddenly saw how wired he was, how hard it was for him to relax. 'Me? I switched to an art school so I could study photography. I was gruesomely artistic in those days. Loved scenes of urban squalor. The ugliness and injustice of life. But I couldn't find a gallery to show my work. I was desperate, so I took a job photographing weddings.'

'June weddings,' I said, remembering that photo spread of the naked brides with their long gauzy veils.

Giles laughed and clinked my wine glass with his double Scotch. 'But then I met this bloke who made a living by photographing nudes. That was his specialty. There's a huge market for photographs of nude women, in case you didn't know.'

'I know.' And I knew this because I used to work at a porn store, Phantastic Phantasy. 'Nude everything.'

'David Lyle, that was the bloke's name. He was so busy with his nudes that he needed someone to help him.'

'And the rest is history.'

'The rest is money,' Giles said. 'Power and money. Finding it, keeping it, increasing it.'

Power and money. To me they were just concepts. My problem was that I didn't have any special gift or talents to spur me forward or lubricate my financial dreams. All I'd ever wanted was to be happy with someone who loved me and whom I could love in return. It seemed like kind of a paltry ambition in the steaming career-cauldron of New York.

After downing his Scotch, Giles went to the men's room, and when he came back his energy had ramped up to party mode. I suspected it was the cocaine. 'Let's go somewhere else,' he said. 'I just feel like blowing off some steam.'

'OK.' I followed him out, nice and cuddly-warm now in his cashmere coat, buzzing pleasantly from the wine, and watched with admiration as he hailed a cab with one short, sharp whistle.

Party Girl finally got a chance to party. With someone who looked like a pro. Giles unleashed a kind of wild, manic energy that caught me in its updraft and sent me soaring. It's one thing to party, it's another thing to party in New York when someone else is paying. Oh my God. My mental taxi meter could hardly keep up. Cabs, drinks, cigarettes, tips – I stopped counting after he'd spent about two hundred dollars. *Just for fun*.

'I've never seen you like this,' I said as we danced our asses off in a huge hot club downtown. By then it was about midnight and we'd been going for six hours straight.

'Side effect of office life,' Giles shouted over the din, grabbing me by the waist and twirling me around. He was great on the dance floor. Every woman in the place was staring at him.

Around one o'clock I crashed and said I had to go home.

'I'll take you,' Giles said. We left the club and he hailed another cab.

I told the driver the address and added, just as Whitman always added, 'That's between Broadway and West End.'

When Giles pressed close to me in the cab and started nuzzling my neck, I was hesitant. He smiled and gave me a gentle kiss on the lips. Then we started making out like two teenagers.

I'd never kissed anyone in a speeding taxi before. I felt kind of glamorous and sophisticated.

No no no, I said to myself as he slid his hand into his cashmere coat and started caressing me. No no no, he's generous and handsome but you must not go to bed with him. No no no. It might be fun, but it would be a one-night stand because Giles sleeps with every woman who steps in his path. You'd be nothing special to him, but he'd never know how special he was to you.

Still, I couldn't deny that something was surging between us.

He's too old, I thought, running my hands through his hair, trying not to moan as he stroked my neck. He's almost got bags under his eyes. He snorts coke and he's probably an alcoholic. He's friends or lovers with Susanna.

But my God could the man ever kiss.

We were pretty hot and messed up by the time the cab pulled up in front of my building. I had to decide – should I ask him in? I was leaning towards yes. But as Giles reached for his wallet to pay the driver, meaning it was understood from his end that he'd come in, Tremaynne's image suddenly rose up like a genie and pulled the plug on my passion. Poof. Just like that.

'Giles,' I said, 'I'm not going to sleep with you.'

He pulled back and looked at me, more shocked than accusing. 'Well, I've never forced myself on a woman who didn't want me.'

'That's because every woman does want you.'

'Except one.'

I sighed. 'Giles, it's not you at all. It's something else.'

'Don't tell me. You're in love with some other bugger.'

'I'm trying not to be,' I said.

'Darling girl,' he said, reaching over to open the door for me. 'Don't waste too much time on him. Others are waiting.'

The next morning, I was standing in line at Starbucks with Sharanda and Dorcas, trying to sound half interested in their endless stream of office gossip as I nursed a major hangover. All I wanted was the biggest cup of coffee on earth.

'Now she's after Larry Weiner's job,' Dorcas said as she peered around looking for her favorite barrista. 'She wants to be the new Weenie.'

'Is Larry Weiner being fired?' The plots and counterplots at Stuckey Global Media flew so fast and quick I could barely keep up. The various magazines had a kind of feuding rivalry with each other, like countries fighting over dwindling resources, and all the editors spent as much of their time as possible trying to curry favor with Larry Weiner, the editor-in-chief.

'I heard that Larry Weiner was offered a job over at *Condé Nast*,' Sharanda reported.

'That's just what he wants people to *believe*,' Dorcas said, talking to us but smiling and trying to get the attention of her favorite barrista. 'Petra Darkke told me that she thinks Lord Stuckey wants to can old Weenie and put in a new editor-in-chief. Petra thinks Susanna's after the job.'

'That bitch doesn't have any experience being an editor-in-chief,' Sharanda said indignantly.

'No, but she's sleeping with Stuckey,' Dorcas said.

'How do you *know* that?' I asked. Because even I didn't know that for sure, and I was Susanna's PA.

'*Everyone* knows that,' Dorcas claimed.

Sharanda shivered. 'I wouldn't sleep with no old man, no matter what he gave me.'

My BlackBerry – Susanna's BlackBerry – played its techno-tune. I assumed it was Susanna, calling from London to load me down with some more tasks. But it wasn't.

'Hey. How are you?'

The voice sounded so familiar. I looked at the caller ID. 'Hey, Josh. Susanna's out of town.'

'I know. That's why I'm calling you. I didn't have your home number.'

He was calling to invite me to a Writers' Jam that evening. It was like a Poetry Slam, he explained, only for non-fiction. My head was throbbing and I couldn't hear with all the hub-bub in Starbucks, but I said sure, I'd go. Josh said to meet him downtown at a club in the East Village around nine. I couldn't tell if he meant for this to be a date or if it was a performance thing of some kind and he was inviting everyone he knew.

Back to basics. Meaning: back to being poor and watchful of every dollar. I prayed that Josh would pay for my admission, if there was one.

I practically ran home after work and immediately started to ransack my meager wardrobe. What did you wear to a Writers' Jam? Was it a dressy kind of thing or would everyone be all severe in black? Nothing! I pulled out everything, even the Portland rejects. Finally I decided on a long, tight tube skirt in black and a frilly fuchsia-pink blouse that Mom bought me for Christmas one year and I'd never worn.

The club, called Wordmeister, was up on the second floor of an old building in Alphabet City, with crooked stairs that looked like they'd been climbed for a hundred years. Little overhead lightbulbs. The a dark, crowded, smoky room with wooden tables and chairs and a tiny stage and a microphone at one end. It was a 'private club' so people brought their own booze or could buy bottled beer from a big cooler on an honor system.

I got the gist of it at once: everyone was broke or living on a shoestring.

'Venus! Hey, over here!' Josh waved me over to a table filled with a bunch of his friends. They were all writers, most of them in their mid-twenties, many of them graduates of Columbia. My discomfort had nothing to do with *them*, it all had to do with my own lack of educational pedigree. Two years at Portland Community College sounded laughable in this crowd. A lot of them were going on for advanced degrees.

I sat, the shy new girl at the party, taking in the sights and sounds and overall Wordmeister scene. I kept thinking Josh would direct all his attention on me, but he didn't. He was all lit up and all over the place, talking, laughing, telling stories. There was another girl at the table who was maybe in love with him. She followed him around with her eyes, just as I was doing, and bloomed into a hopeful smile every time he looked in her direction.

'Hey, want a beer?' Josh asked me after about half an hour. 'I've got enough for about one more.'

'I'll split it with you.' I followed him over to the beer cooler.

'Having fun?' he asked, beaming me that big, confident smile. He looked relaxed and sexy in his old blue jeans, the kind that fit like a glove, and a blue fleece.

'I didn't know there were places like this in New York.'

'Oh yeah. It's part of a huge alternative universe for people with gargantuan student loans and no money to pay them back.'

'Do you come here a lot?'

'Yeah. Sometimes agents are here.' His eyes darted around the room. 'Scouting new talent.'

'Is that hard, finding an agent?'

'Oh yeah. Brutal. But without one, you'll never get anywhere.'

As we chatted, I could feel the eyes of that other woman on me. Josh was open and friendly – *friendly* – and I finally relaxed and just let it all be what it was, which was a bunch of smart people who loved words getting together to have fun. Everyone at the mike had three minutes to read something they'd written on the evening's theme of 'embarrassment'.

They were all good, but Josh was best. Of course I was biased. He just had this charisma, like he wasn't afraid of anything or anyone. The very *idea* of standing up in front of roomful of people and speaking made me lightheaded. And he was funny. 'It's open mike for you,' he said, gazing around the room to get everyone's attention, 'but it's open Mick for me. Because I'm Irish.' And he launched into a three-minute story that was hilarious and hair-raising, about being so poor as a kid that he got caught trying to steal his mother's Christmas present, which was a statue of the Virgin Mary.

Pretty soon it was almost midnight and I had to go because I didn't like taking the subway alone late at night. I hoped Josh might offer to accompany me, but he didn't. It was like saying goodbye to a friend. And that wasn't so bad, except that the friend was so damned adorable.

Needless to say, I didn't mention going out with either Giles or Josh to Susanna and I assumed neither of them said anything to her. She'd only been back a week or so when she called me into her office and said, 'Look, I have to go back to London on business – it's absolutely essential, and unfortunately I'm behind on my column. So would you be an angel and write up some questions for me?'

'I'm not sure I know what you mean.'

'You know, questions. About sex.'

'Don't readers write in and ask those questions?'

'Oh God, no.' She made a face as if the very idea horrified her. 'I make them all up. Just like we make up all the letters to the editor.'

I stared, trying to comprehend this new information. 'You mean – all the letters are fake?'

'No magazine answers real letters,' she said. 'It's potentially litigious. Someone could say you gave them the wrong advice and ruined their life and sue you for millions.'

'So you want me to write down some questions . . .'

'I'd do it myself but I'm simply stretched to the limit. And it would be fun for you, wouldn't it?'

'I guess so.' I was afraid she'd fire me if I said no.

'I mean, you've obviously had *loads* of sexual experiences,' Susanna said. 'This is hardly virgin territory for you.'

'No, but I've never written anything before.'

'They're just questions, for God's sake.'

'All right,' I said hesitantly. 'I guess I can try.'

'And sketch out the answers, too, while you're at it.'

'You mean, ask the questions and then answer them myself?'

She nodded. 'Right. Ask for some advice and then give it to yourself. Is that so very difficult?'

'But wouldn't I be asking the question because I *didn't* know the answer?'

A Susanna sigh. 'Aren't you interested in pursuing a writing career? Like your faux pa?'

I'd never thought of myself as a writer. Ever. Whitman was the writer in our family. When he prodded me to write my memoirs, I always assumed he was teasing. But suddenly I thought: why not give it a try? How difficult could it be to write out some questions about sex and answer them? I had a sudden vision of myself as *fitting in* with all those writers down at Wordmeister.

'I'll try,' I said.

She rewarded me with a smile. 'The column's one thousand words, usually with three questions. E-mail me next week in London to show me what you've come up with.'

I started to leave her office, then thought of something and turned back around. 'Do I get some extra money for doing this?'

Susanna didn't mince words. 'No,' she said.

I never used to understand what the dads meant when they said that in New York your apartment becomes your castle. The apartments I had, back in Portland, were always like prisons, cramped and dreary, places to escape from, where being alone was no fun. But now, living in New York, I loved my cozy little apartment and actually looked forward to spending time there. It really was like my castle, a special place where I could tune out the endless rock and roil of New York. I didn't feel trapped and lonely there, by myself, the way I always did in Portland.

I was pacing around the apartment one November

Saturday morning, wearing a robe and slippers, trying to think up three questions about sex, when the doorbell rang. I pressed the intercom button and a voice said, 'Soupah.'

'Oh, right.' I'd called Mary-Joseph Capistrano, the new super, because the water wasn't draining properly from the kitchen sink. I buzzed her in.

She was tinier than I remembered, maybe five feet, but was bundled up in a thick flannel jacket with a baseball cap on her head, leather gloves, and carrying what looked like a really heavy tool case. She looked up at me, her cheeks flushed from the cold, but didn't smile. She was chewing a wad of gum, working it hard and fast in her mouth, snapping and popping it. 'Hiya. Which sink?'

I showed her and demonstrated how slow the water was to drain out.

'Yuh wash yuh hair in there?' she asked.

'No. In the bathroom.'

' 'Cause I can't tell yuh how many times it's hair. Washin' the hair without a trap, so it goes down and clogs.'

'It can't be my hair,' I said.

She looked at my hair, as if judging for herself, then shrugged off her gloves and jacket, which I politely took and hung on the back of a chair. The jacket was warm from her body heat. She moved into the kitchen area with her toolbox. 'I'll tryen unblock it for yuh,' she said, moving the gum to one side of her mouth and chewing on it with staccato bursts.

'OK. Whatever.'

Size-wise, she reminded me of JD, my one-time girlfriend. But, unlike JD, Mary-Joseph Capistrano had an air of dark, intense physicality. She was small and strong, like a sparrow on steroids. There wasn't an ounce of excess fat on her, and no sign of feminine curves or softness showed through her thick flannel shirt and heavy-duty work jeans.

And yet, when I looked, she had the smallest, most beautifully shaped hands. And such gorgeous big dark Italian eyes. She was very cute in an unaware sort of way. An Italian sparkplug with one of those thick New York accents I could never decipher: Bronx, maybe, or deep working-class Brooklyn.

'Any troubles with yuh terlet?' she asked, pulling a box from her tool kit.

'My – terlet?'

'Yeah.'

'Um – I'm sorry – I don't know what a terlet is.'

She gave me a funny look. 'Yuh don't know what a terlet is?' She clomped over to the bathroom in her dainty leather workboots and pointed at the toilet.

'Oh! I'm sorry, I didn't – no, the terlet's fine.'

'Flushin' good?' Mary-Joseph asked.

I nodded.

'You should have a new terlet. That's one of the old models. The new ones use less watuh.' She went back to the kitchen sink and started to feed a long flexible hose down the drain.

OK, I'm completely unhandy. I know what a hammer is, and a saw, and a screwdriver, but I've never *used* a tool in my life. I always admired the way Daddy could do that kind of home-handyman stuff. He can actually build and fix things. And it fascinated me to think that Mary-Joseph Capistrano could also fix things, that when something broke she had the know-how to get it working again. Fixing what was broken was her life's work.

'It's kind of unusual,' I said, 'to have a woman as a super.'

She didn't say anything and kept feeding the line down the drain. I wondered if I'd offended her.

'I admire people who can do things like that,' I said. 'Practical things.' She gave her head a flick to indicate that she was listening. 'Do you enjoy your work?' I asked.

'Yeah. Do you?'

'Yeah. I mostly do.'

'Whuddaya do?'

I laughed. 'If I told you what I was doing, right now, you'd think I was crazy.'

'I don't think yuh crazy,' she said, jamming the line down the drain.

'OK. I've got to think up three questions about sex, and then answer them.'

Mary-Joseph stopped and gave me an incredulous look. For a moment she even stopped chewing her gum. 'Get outta here. That's yuh job?'

'I have to do it for my boss. She writes a sex-advice column, only right now she's too busy. So I'm supposed to write the questions and the answers.'

Mary-Joseph shook her head and began chewing again. 'Now I've hearda everything.' She bent her head deeper into the sink and began a forceful circular motion with the hose. 'So whudjuh come up with?'

'Well, I figured they should sort of be general interest questions. Like, when your boyfriend asks how many guys you've slept with, what should you say?'

'Yuh should say, "None of yuh goddamn business, fuckhead" is what yuh should say.'

I liked her directness. New Yorkers will always tell you what they think. 'More than three, and they think you're a slut,' I told her. 'Less than three, and they think there's something's wrong with you.'

'Who gives a shit what a guy thinks of yuh anyway?' Mary-Joseph asked. 'It's what yuh think of yuhself that mattuhs.'

I was struck by the simple truth of her observation.

She cocked her head to one side and looked at me with those big dark eyes, a little smile on her lips. 'Right?'

'Right.'

'What other questions?' she wanted to know.

'Well, I thought maybe one of them should be about lesbians.'

The smile disappeared and Mary-Joseph quickly turned her attention back to the reamer. 'What about 'em?'

'I haven't decided yet.'

'Whudda *you* know about lesbians?' she asked.

'I know a few things.'

Mary-Joseph nodded into the sink. 'Seen that new show on cable?'

I knew she meant *The L Word*. 'I love that show.'

'Me too. But I never seen no dykes looked like *those* women,' Mary-Joseph said, shaking her head. 'They all look so gorgeous. Like you.'

I smiled, then laughed, then realized that I was showing my teeth and closed my mouth, but blushed and turned away to tighten the belt on my robe. 'Are you allowed to drink coffee on the job?' I asked.

'Depends on whose makin' it,' she shot back, chewing her gum real fast.

'I am.'

'White,' she said. 'Two sugahs.'

Whitman came to New York for some kind of big editorial meeting at *Aura*. Daddy was in California and couldn't come. He was working on a new resort he was designing in the Sierra Nevada, something like Pine Mountain Lodge only at a higher elevation.

'You won't mind camping out on the sofa for a couple of nights, will you?' Whitman said as he did an inspection tour of the apartment.

'No, I don't mind.' The sofa was where I'd always slept when I came out to visit as a girl.

'You know, sweetheart,' Whitman said, peering around the kitchen, 'there's an attachment on the vacuum cleaner that lets you suck up crumbs in all these really-not-so-hard-to-reach places. You're just inviting roaches.'

'I haven't seen a single roach.'

'That's because you don't sleep with your eyes open.' He was all business, never far from his laptop and cellphone, working on the little table where we ate. In the morning we took the subway together to the offices of Stuckey Universal Media. He went his way, I went mine. After work, he took me out to dinner at a neighborhood Szechuan place where we'd always gone when I came out to visit as a girl. They had a sizzling platter of shrimp, beef and pork with a spicy oyster sauce that we both loved.

'So, sweetheart, how are you making out in the Big A?'

'Fine.'

'And life with the Big S?'

'Fine.'

'She had mild praise for you when I saw her today. But coming from Susanna, that means you must be doing a fabulous job.' He smiled and patted my hand. 'Your father wanted to come with me, but this new resort is taking up all his time.'

Without Daddy, we were both kind of shy around one another. 'Have you seen Carolee?' I asked.

'Talked to her before I left. She said to tell you not to worry.'

'About what?'

'Her, I suppose.' We both turned our attention to the tableside preparation of the Sizzling Three Treasures. Our waiter dropped the shrimps and meat on to a hot platter, poured oyster sauce over the top, and mixed it all together. 'Are you meeting people, sweetheart?'

I nodded, ladling Sizzling Three Treasures over a pile of rice.

Whitman looked at me as he poured tea into my cup. 'Anyone we need to be worried about?'

'I wish you wouldn't worry about me so much, Whitman.'

'Well,' he said, 'just because I'm a surrogate parent doesn't mean I shouldn't worry. You don't know what it's like to be the surrogate father of an It girl.'

'Daddy doesn't worry as much as you do.'

'Well, your daddy does, he just doesn't say so. And I've been charged with bringing back a full report on your welfare. To both of your biological parents. So let's start with all the boyfriends.'

'No boyfriends. Just friends.'

'Names and occupations?' Whitman pulled out a pen and a small notepad. 'And also, are they leaseholders?'

He was kidding, but not. So over dinner I told him about my life in New York up till then. I mentioned Sharanda and Dorcas, Giles Travaille (suspicious look from Whitman), Josh

O'Connell (approving interest but qualified approval when he heard Josh was a writer) and Mary-Joseph Capistrano.

'I take it she *is* a lesbian?' Whitman said, picking up a shrimp with his chopsticks.

'Does it matter?'

'No, of course not. Your father and I always hoped you'd be gay.'

'I fall in love with the person, Whitman.'

'Yes,' he said, 'usually the wrong one. So are you *dating* Mary-Joseph? Or just letting her unplug the terlet?'

'We're friends, OK? Not even friends. She's just come over to fix a few things.'

'It's important to have working-class friends,' Whitman said. 'But what about this Giles person. I think I've met him. I thought he was a closeted homosexual.'

'No way,' I laughed, remembering my make-out session with Giles.

'And a writer.' Whitman shook his head and sighed. 'Now there's someone you need to keep an eye on.'

'Yeah, I'd like to. But I think he's Susanna's boyfriend.'

'Really?' Whitman looked at his notebook. 'Josh O'Connell. I'll see what I can find out.'

The next evening, as he was getting ready to fly back to Portland, he said, 'This Josh O'Connell? It's not serious.'

'What do you mean?'

'Well they *are* sleeping together,' Whitman said, 'but they're both writers, so I wouldn't count on it lasting very long.' He kissed me on the cheek, snapped up the handle on his yellow Tuomi suitcase, and headed for the door.

'Whitman?'

He turned.

I was longing to blurt out the news that I had written one of Susanna's columns. It was such a big deal for me, such a huge departure. I wanted my faux pa to be proud of me. But Susanna had sworn me to silence. Not even Whitman was to know that there was now another writer in our family.

'Do you need some money?' Whitman asked.

'No.' Yes, but no. I rushed over and gave him an impulsive hug. 'Thank you for giving me this chance, Whitman.'

He let go of his suitcase handle and took me in his arms. 'You'd never know from the way I behave, would you, how proud I am of you.'

New York goes crazy around holidays, mostly because everyone's trying to figure out a way to get out of town or invited somewhere. Being alone on a major holiday in New York is about the worst fate most people can imagine.

But I was looking forward to spending my first Thanksgiving in New York entirely by my lonesome.

A whole day off, to do whatever I pleased. Sleep late. Watch TV in the morning. Go for a walk. Or, conversely, get up early and go to see the Macy's Thanksgiving Day parade in person. I'd watched this parade on television every year since I was a kid, and now I was living in the city where it was held.

That's why I loved New York.

Daddy and Whitman offered to fly me back to Portland. But I said no.

Mom valiantly offered to fly out to New York. But I said no.

Sheba Fleischbaum in apartment 3A invited me up for her annual 'Thanksgiving Nosh'. I said yes. It was perfect: I could eat and wouldn't have to stay more than an hour.

As the big holiday weekend approached, the offices at Stuckey Universal Media went into frenzied overdrive. The day before Thanksgiving happened to be the deadline for the March issues of all Stuckey Universal Media magazines. And that was doubly important for *Aura* because the March issue would be Susanna's first with the new format she'd devised, utilising the colors of the chakra. These seven colors (red, orange, yellow, green, blue, indigo, violet), in the most luscious shades, would run across the top of the page for each department.

All this new color and format really made *Aura* sing in a way it hadn't done before. But getting there was a nightmare that left everyone even more pissed off than usual at Susanna.

Susanna seemed to thrive on fights, but even she lost her cool a couple of times. Doors slammed, angry voices were heard, sometimes crying. It was like living in a soap opera where the plot twists and turns in a new direction every day. I don't think Susanna knew how much pressure there would be when she became editor.

'This magazine was a joke when I took it over,' she said one morning as I was pouring her tea. She'd been in a foul mood since her breakfast meeting with Larry Wiener. 'A bloody *joke*. And when I told them what I thought it *could* be, they all agreed. They gave me a mandate to change it. But when I rolled up my sleeves and stepped up to the plate, what did I find?' She looked up at me, her face in a pinched frown, as if I knew. 'I found an organization entrenched in the past. Afraid to look ahead. And lazy. Bloody fucking lazy. And that shit Weiner has fought me every bloody fucking step of the way.'

'Because you're a woman,' I said.

Susanna flared her nostrils as she looked at me. 'That's what it always bloody comes down to, isn't it? Every time a woman tries to rise above her class or her station.'

She was really bristling.

'They'll always favor a mediocre man over an extraordinary woman,' she grumbled, sipping her tea. 'Unless she has big tits, of course.'

'Speaking of big tits . . .' I pointed to the photograph in the newspaper gossip column that was sitting on Susanna's desk. It was Cupcake Cassidy, shot from the breasts up and smiling magnificently.

Susanna unconsciously cupped her own breasts as she stared at Cupcake's. 'Giles took that photo. He told me she had her tits propped up on special boards and separately lit.'

'The article said—'

'It's not an article,' Susanna snapped, 'it's an item.'

'The item said that Stuckey Universal Media is publishing her memoir.'

'*The Naked Truth*. I'm sure it will sell millions. Especially with Giles's photos sprinkled through it.' Susanna didn't sound too thrilled. 'She *insists* they're her own. But I happen to know otherwise, and I may just have to let the air out of those giant balloons.'

'Your photo looks nice,' I said, trying to change the subject.

'Rubbish.' She glared at her own image, taken at the same party where Cupcake's publicist had announced her new book deal. Unfortunately, Susanna and Cupcake appeared together in the photograph. 'You can barely see me behind those dirigibles of hers.'

'Can she even write?'

'It's not her *literary* style people will be interested in,' Susanna griped. 'It's the photographs. Giles's photographs. Stills from her porn films.'

'Nobody buys a memoir just for the photographs.'

'Are you kidding?' Susanna sipped her tea and pulled out her mirror, primping for her next meeting. 'Venus, it's all about image now. The word is on its last legs. Literature is dead. Soon it will be nothing but pictures because people won't even be able to read.'

'Don't say that. It gives me the creeps.'

She continued with her new make-up regime as she spoke. 'We used to live in a word-saturated society, but now we live in one that's saturated with images. We're perennial voyeurs. Even our thoughts are advertisements.'

'Mine aren't.'

'Mine are,' she said, running an elegantly manicured fingernail along her redrawn and freshly tinted eyebrows. 'That's why I'm meeting with Charles Fabian of Fabu. I'm going to convince him to advertise big-time in *Aura*. The perfume, the whole cosmetics line.' Finished with her face, she kicked off her low heels and slipped into higher ones. 'If I can get the advertising revenue up, you'll be joining me in the editor-in-chief's office.'

So she *was* after Larry Weiner's job. It was kind of thrilling to be in on the secret.

'What's down for this evening?' she asked. 'Didn't I have some boring dinner date or something?'

I checked my BlackBerry. 'Josh O'Connell. Dinner at L'Albatross.'

'Oh God,' she moaned. 'Why is that boy so infatuated with me?'

I kept my mouth shut.

'I mean, the sex – yes – fantastic. He's totally and utterly divine in bed, now that I've trained him to do exactly what I like. But out of it . . .' She shook her head. 'The poor thing's got absolutely no talent. And no money. So boring.' She shook her head again, but this time it was to give her hair a fluff. 'He's a nothing, he'll never make a name for himself.'

If he's such a loser, I thought, why are you sleeping with him? Susanna's dismissal of Josh irked me. From the little bit I'd heard that night at Wordmeister, Josh was a really good writer.

But I said nothing and waited for her orders. No doubt she'd have me call Josh and cancel the date. But instead, she asked me what I was doing that evening.

'Nothing.'

'Tell you what. Go down to L'Albatross and have dinner with Josh.'

'What?'

'He may be boring but he's cute and he's single. And you're alone – poor thing – on the eve of a major American holiday.'

'Susanna, I can't afford dinner at L'Albatross.' I'd looked online before I made her reservation. Just a salad there cost twenty-five dollars.

I thought she might offer to pay for my dinner, and then I could demur until I accepted. Because L'Albatross was, after all, the hottest new restaurant in Manhattan. It was a miracle that I'd gotten Susanna a reservation because the waiting list was two months long.

But Susanna didn't offer to pay. 'All right,' she said, 'just go down there and meet him and have a drink and talk to him until I show up. This meeting with Fabu is really important and I may be a little late.'

I'd be in the first issue of the new *Aura*, too, only no one would know it. Susanna had taken the three questions and the answers that I'd written for her and was going to publish them in her March 'Nothing to Hyde' column under her own name.

On the subway ride downtown I read and reread the page proof that I'd printed out. It was strange and kind of wonderful to see my work in print, even if everyone would think it was Susanna's.

Susanna had polished up my clumsy efforts, editing and rewriting the work I'd so nervously presented to her. But she hadn't changed everything. Here and there I could still pick out sentences that were mine alone, that I remembered writing, and the thrill I'd felt when I came up with the right words.

But something occurred to me while I was obsessively reading the printout. This piece wouldn't just be in *Aura*. Susanna's 'Nothing to Hyde' column was internationally syndicated by Stuckey Universal Media. It appeared in SUM magazines all over the US and the UK and throughout the world.

I'd be international.

How about that.

Only nobody would know it was me.

I'd be in the same magazine as Whitman!

L'Albatross was downtown, in the meat-packing district. Which meant that the streets were filled with the Bridge and Tunnel crowd – 'the Yahoos,' as Whitman always called them. The city was in a revved-up mood because it was the night before a long holiday weekend.

I was bundled up in my long black winter coat, a garment that would have been completely unnecessary in Portland. But

New York was *cold*. I'd forgotten, in my years away from it, just how cold it could be.

I figured I could have one drink, maybe a glass of wine, and get away without paying more than twenty bucks. For that twenty-dollar glass of wine I intended to enjoy myself, and take in the scene at one of the city's hotspots with a cute, smart guy at my side.

'Reservation for Susanna Hyde,' I said to the maitre d'.

He glanced at his book. 'Of course. May I take your coat?'

'I'm freezing,' I whispered. 'Is it OK if I keep it on for awhile?' This was my ploy to save a five-dollar tip.

'Of course. Please follow me, Miss Hyde.'

'Oh, I'm not—' But he was already threading his way into the restaurant, so I followed.

It had that buzz – you know, the buzz of places that know they have a buzz? And the buzz was all about the people eating there. The see-and-be-seen scene. Very hot and very haute.

I was definitely out of my element and felt my spirits and confidence start to sag. But then I thought: hey, you're going to be a published writer, even if nobody knows it's you, so even if you do blow the twenty bucks you were planning to use for the *entire weekend*, at least have a good time.

Josh was already seated. He gave me a puzzled look as I slid in beside him on the red leather banquette.

'Susanna's going to be late,' I explained. 'I'm supposed to keep you company until she gets here.'

'Oh. Cool. How are you?'

I smiled and nodded, pleased to be in his company again. But Josh seemed preoccupied. Maybe he was disappointed it was me and not Susanna. 'Have you ordered a drink?' I asked.

'Uh, no. I was going to wait for Susanna.'

When I saw the drinks and wine list, I knew why he was holding back. The prices were twice what I'd expected. I frantically scanned the list until I found a glass of house wine for under twenty dollars. I ordered that, and Josh asked, to the waiter's disdain, if he could have a glass of tap water. 'I'll order wine with dinner,' he said.

He was so cute, with those wonderful jade-green eyes, but he looked crimped and nervous – maybe overawed like I was by the prices and the exclusivity of the place. You were supposed to be famous, after all, or at least *somebody*, if you dined at L'Albatross. Josh's wool jacket looked a bit wrinkled and threadbare among the five-thousand-dollar Armani suits.

'What's that?' I asked, pointing to a cardboard box on the seat beside him. He kept touching it, as if he were protecting something extremely valuable.

'My novel,' he said.

'Really?'

'I just finished it.' He couldn't suppress a proud grin. 'My first one.'

'Oh God. Josh. A novel! That must feel—'

'Fucking fantastic,' he admitted.

'Congratulations.' I lifted my glass of house wine and clinked his water glass. We're *both* writers, I thought; that should give us something to talk about.

'I'm going to give it to Susanna,' he said. 'She's going to help me get it published.'

'Really?' I took a sip of my wine. It wasn't very good wine, but I was determined to enjoy it.

'Well, I mean, she's right there at Stuckey Universal Media. An editor. She knows everyone. Stuckey Universal's going to publish her next book.'

'I just heard they're publishing Cupcake Cassidy's new memoir, too.'

'Who's that, a Western writer?'

'No, the woman at Susanna's party. The one with the huge –' I cupped the air about a foot in front of me.

'Oh, her. She wrote a memoir?'

'About her life as a porn star.'

'Memoirs sell,' Josh said. He looked down at his cardboard box. 'This is *kind* of a memoir.'

'I thought you said it was a novel.'

'It is.'

'Then it's fiction, isn't it?'

'Well, it could be either. It just depends on how they want to market it.'

'Either it is or it isn't,' I said. 'It's either fiction or it's non-fiction.'

'It's non-fiction thinly disguised as fiction,' Josh said. 'Anyway, all those old distinctions between fiction and non-fiction don't mean anything any more.'

'But when I read a novel, it's fiction,' I argued. 'When I read a memoir, it's supposed to be non-fiction.'

'Everything's made up,' Josh said. 'There's truth in falsehood and falsehood in truth. That's what Ivan Dagger says.'

'Oh yeah, Ivan Dagger. How was that seminar at Meat Loaf?'

'I didn't go,' Josh said after a long pause.

'Why not? I thought you were one of the five students he accepted.'

'I was,' Josh said, his green eyes flitting about the room, avoiding mine.

'So why didn't you go?'

'I couldn't afford it,' he said with a short staccato laugh. 'How's that for truth?'

I touched his arm in sympathy.

'Five thousand to get in, then another five if you want to be in his special group. The ones he helps get published.' He refused to look at me, maybe because he was embarrassed.

'Josh, I'm sorry. That really sucks big-time.'

'If I had the money,' he said angrily, 'I would have paid, all right? But my school loans – Jesus – and just trying to keep up in this city . . .'

'I know.' My BlackBerry buzzed. I pulled it out and looked at the caller ID. Susanna. 'Excuse me one second, Josh.'

I turned away and as I listened to her rapid, don't-interrupt-me voice, I felt my heart sink. I could hear a buzz of background noise and guessed she was at a restaurant not too different from the one where Josh and I sat. She'd been drinking – I could always tell because her voice was slightly slurred and louder than usual. She gave me my instructions and said she had to run. I put the phone back in my purse and took a sip of my wine.

'That was Susanna,' I said.

He put his hand on the box beside him. 'Is she on her way?'

I took another sip and looked out into the dining room, full of rich, successful and seemingly happy patrons. Well, they had every reason to be happy. Luck was on their side. Their number had been called. They had money and standing. Power and position. They didn't think about the price of a glass of wine. They ordered exactly what they wanted.

'Susanna's not coming,' I told Josh.

He didn't say anything. But now he looked at me, his face expectant and unprepared for the news I was about to give him.

'She said – I'm supposed to tell you – she doesn't want to see you any more.'

Josh sat back and cleared his throat. 'She told you to tell me that?'

I nodded. 'I'm sorry. It seems kind of mean.'

He picked up the cardboard box with his manuscript in it and carefully laid it on the table in front of him. Stared at it, self-engrossed and mournful, as if he'd just seen his hopes disappear in a puff of smoke.

'Should we go?' I quietly asked him.

He didn't speak.

'Josh?'

'Aren't you having dinner?' he said, his voice flat.

'No. I can't afford it.'

'I can't either,' he said, still staring at his box of manuscript. 'I was going to put it on a new credit card. Dinner. I figured it would be worth it if she—'

'I've got some frozen pizza at home. I could heat it up.'

'Some other time,' Josh said morosely. 'Now, how the hell do we get out of here without ordering dinner?'

'I'll take care of that.'

And I did. Because working for Susanna I'd learned how to

finesse every situation. Or, rather, I'd learned not to be afraid to try anything. I put twenty dollars down for my wine, got up from the table, and walked to the front of the restaurant to have a little chat with the maitre d'. Then I went back and motioned for Josh, who bolted up and followed me. He didn't have an overcoat, so we quickly made our way out to the street.

It had turned colder and windier. Josh, shivering, hands in pockets, the manuscript tucked under his arm, walked beside me as I headed towards the subway. I stole a glance at him. The poor guy looked so miserable, like his entire world had just collapsed. Maybe it had.

'What did you say to the maitre d'?' he asked.

'I told him the truth.'

'The truth?'

'You know, the truth? Non-fiction. I said she wasn't coming and we couldn't afford to eat there.'

'You said that? That we couldn't afford it?' Josh looked mortified.

'Look at it this way,' I said, 'you're the only person in New York who's ever got a table and a free glass of water at L'Albatross.'

'Water.' He shook his head in disbelief. 'I'm so fuckin' poor I go to L'Albatross and order water! That is fuckin' pathetic, isn't it?'

'No.' I put a hand on his arm and stopped him. 'Josh, no, it's not.'

His eyes were all fired up, burning green amethysts. 'Do you know what it's like to be *held back* because you don't have enough money?'

'Yes, I do.'

I couldn't tell if he'd heard me or not. Josh seemed to be on the brink of totally losing his cool, relaxed veneer. 'That's how my parents have lived their entire lives,' he said. 'And I swear to God I am not going to live that way myself.'

The hot flames of his ambition warmed and excited me. He had a *passion*. Just like Tremaynne. This whole episode had touched off something inside Josh that was really important. And I wanted to stay with him, even if it was just as a friend, nothing more, to help him celebrate completing his novel. 'Where are you going now?' I asked.

He shrugged and shivered. 'I don't even have a fucking apartment of my own. I've been crashing with this girl I know, over in Hell's Kitchen.'

I thought, *he could crash at my place*, but I quickly reined myself in before I could make the offer. That was exactly what had happened with Tremaynne. 'Well look,' I said, 'I could go to that ATM over there and get some money – enough for a couple of beers – and maybe we could go someplace . . .'

His face softened, turned kind of tender. 'You'd do that?'

'Josh, you just finished a novel, for God's sake. I know that must be a really big deal for you. So I think we should celebrate even if it's not champagne and dinner at L'Albatross.'

'I'll take you to L'Albatross one day,' he vowed. 'Just wait.'

'OK. I will.'

'Like Irish music? There's this Irish pub not too far from here. It's pretty cheap and there's no cover for the music.'

'Sounds great.'

'We'd have to walk, though, because there's no subway around there.'

'Let's go.' I put my arm in his and we went.

That was the night Josh really let me see who he was and where he'd come from and what he'd been up against. The pub was a fun, noisy place with musicians who played toe-tapping fiddle music and mournful songs with Irish harp.

Josh's Irishness fascinated me. I was part Irish on my dad's side but Josh was 'pure' Irish on both sides. His parents had left Ireland in 1970 and made their way to the US, where they lived as illegal immigrants. Josh, born in the US and therefore a US citizen, had grown up in hair-raising poverty. But he was smart and determined and wasn't afraid of a challenge. He had pulled himself up by winning awards and scholarships.

There seemed to be a perennial *striving* in his character, and the striving came from growing up so poor, almost like a fugitive, always on the move, always afraid his parents would be caught and put in jail or deported.

For sheer drama, his upbringing even surpassed my own. And if any of it was actually in that novel that he kept at his side all evening, I had no doubt that it would be a bestseller.

The next morning I was awakened by a phone call from Sheba Fleischbaum in apartment 3A reminding me to come up later that afternoon for her annual Thanksgiving Nosh. 'It's a little tradition I have,' Sheba said. 'Kind of a Thanksgiving potluck kind of thing.'

Which meant I was supposed to bring something. And I'd spent the twenty bucks that was supposed to last me all weekend on that glass of wine at L'Albatross. At first I was going to lie and tell her I had other plans, but then the thought of turkey and mashed potatoes and gravy kicked in and I agreed to stop by.

It was a clear, crisp day and I had this urge to go for a walk, maybe over to Riverside Drive and then down to the Hudson, past the marina and over to 72nd Street. But first the dads called. That was half an hour each. Then mom called. That was another hour.

The Parents were so *relieved* that I had 'someplace to go' on Thanksgiving. I didn't try to explain that I would have been fine being by myself.

It was noon by the time I got outside. And the streets were almost totally deserted. I felt like I had the whole city to myself.

As I walked, with dry leaves skittering along the sidewalk and swirling around my feet, I thought about Tremaynne. If we'd stayed together, we'd be together today. Where? In Portland? Or out in Idaho somewhere? At Pine Mountain Lodge, when he gave me the horrible news that he was going to leave me and go out into the wilderness to become an eco-warrior, I'd begged him to take me along. I told him I'd live outdoors, sleep on the ground, sit in trees, do anything he asked. That's how much I loved him. At the time I'm sure I meant it. I'm sure I would even have done it, and adapted. If our love was strong enough.

Mine was. His wasn't.

I knew that now. So why couldn't I peel him off my heart, like a dry scab? I looked at the linden and sycamore trees along Riverside Drive and thought of his fierce commitment to save the forests, his acceptance of personal discomfort, his valiant belief that he could help save the world from ecological disaster. I pictured him out in the woods, shivering, wet, hungry, hiding, hunted by federal agents working on the side of huge corporations. While here I was, living in New York City, loving New York City, symbol of everything he despised.

I wish you well, my eco-darling, I said to him in my thoughts.

And then I idly, and without guilt, wondered who would take his place in my heart.

Someone, eventually.

But I was in no hurry – for a change. And that surprised me and made me feel incredibly grown-up. I was no longer famished for love and hallucinating happiness with anyone who looked twice at me. Moving to New York and changing my life had given me some much-needed distance. I was a better observer of others and of myself.

On the way home from my walk, I stopped and bought five beautiful apples to bring as my contribution to Sheba's potluck.

'Oh, honey, they're *gor*-jus!' Sheba enthused. 'They'll look *perfect* in my centuhpiece.'

I'd never been in Sheba's apartment before. So when she opened the door and invited me in, I wasn't prepared.

She'd lived in the same one room for over forty years. And packed it, I mean *packed* it, with so much stuff that it was almost impossible to move. It was like having the contents of an entire house crammed into two hundred square feet. There was a giant sofa, two upholstered chairs, a coffee table, a china hutch, a dining table with six chairs, even a piano . . . so much furniture, all wedged together, that you had to squeeze along tiny pathways between the pieces. Where on earth did she sleep?

On top of which, she was one of those people, like my mom, who loved to theme decorate for every season. So amidst, atop, and beside all the furniture, there were autumn/harvest/ Thanksgiving 'displays' – ornamental gourds, fake branches with red maple leaves, wicker baskets spilling out a cornucopia of Indian corn and pumpkins.

'I love my tchotkes, but the dusting takes *ow-was*,' Sheba said as we navigated towards the dining table, where a giant cardboard turkey with an orange crêpe-paper tail presided over more seasonal produce and tableaux of pilgrims and Indians made of painted china. There were trays of turkey and some other meat and bowls of olives and pickles and coleslaw, everything tightly wrapped in cling film. 'We'll just stick these gor-jus apples in with the gourds and hope that nobody figures out they're real.'

'I brought them for people to eat.'

She shook her head. 'Too messy. I don't want any wet apple cores sittin' on my furniture or squashed on the floor. Attracts vermin.' She hid the apples among her plastic produce and then turned to me with a big warm smile, plucking affectionately at my feathery fake boa. 'Venus, you look absolutely gor-jus. How's life treatin' you, sweetheart?'

'Fine.'

'Those darling dads of yours are calling me all the time.'

'They are?'

' "Check on Venus. Check on Venus." Cute, but annoying. I said, "Look, Venus doesn't *wanna* be checked on. Venus wants to live her own life. Just like I did at that age" – how old are ya, honey?'

'Twenty five.'

'Barely menstruating. Anyway, parents don't get it, right? Mine didn't, yours don't. They just don't get that you *wanna* be away from them. On your own. Am I right?'

I nodded.

'Of course. A gor-jus young woman. Just starting out. Away

from home. She doesn't want someone older and wiser poking into her business. At twenty-five you don't want to be wise, right? You wanna be a little crazy. *Verkokte*, right? I know I did.'

She'd dressed for the occasion in a bright, slightly-too-tight ensemble of orange and brown wool offset by a little ornamental apron decorated with pumpkins and bundled sheaves of hay. A cornucopia, a harvest of costume jewels, spilled out across her bosom, but those were real diamonds, and pretty big ones at that, sparkling in her ears.

'So how many boyfriends?' Sheba asked as we threaded our way back to the tiny alcove that served as her kitchen.

'None.'

She turned to look at me. 'What? I figured you'd be beating them off.'

'No. I've been sort of getting over someone.'

'Ah.' She led me over to where she'd set out the wine. 'That nice Chinese lady in the liquor store recommended this one. It's white and she said it would go with turkey *and* corned beef. Mm? Sound good?' She poured and handed me the wine in a heavy, ornate glass. 'Be careful of the goblet, sweetheart. It's very old crystal. I'm terrified to take them out every year, but if you gottem, you gotta use 'em, right? You gotta take that risk. Sometimes things break. But you gotta risk it. Am I right?'

'It's a pretty glass,' I said, holding on tight.

'It's Bohemian crystal. *Very* rare. I'd offer you something to eat, but I don't wanna take off the plastic until a few more guests arrive.' We inched our way back to her sofa and sat down. 'So you're nursing a broken heart? Some guy out there in Portland?'

I nodded. 'We were married. Actually.'

'Married? Are you just separated, or divorced?'

'Divorced.'

'How long were you married?'

'About three days. Actually.'

'Three days?' She plucked at her sweater as if it were scratching her.

'He left me on our honeymoon.'

'Oh my Gawd.' She reached over and brushed the side of my face. 'You poor thing. Well, a first marriage is sort of like a trial subscription to a magazine, you know what I mean?'

I didn't feel like telling her that it wasn't my first marriage, it was my third. I didn't want to go into my past history and have to relive all my mistakes. 'Have you ever been married?' I asked.

'Me?' She let out a low chuckle. 'No. Had a couple of close calls, though. Big names in the Poconos. Back when I was a showgirl. You'll have to read my memoir to find out who.'

'Are you really writing your memoirs?'

'Yeah. I'm calling it *A Coffin With One-and-a-Half Rooms*.'

'That's an unusual title.'

'Cute though, huh? It's because I've lived my entiuh adult life in this studio apahtment. So when I croak, I wanna nice roomy coffin – one anna half rooms.' She lifted a finger as if something important had just occurred to her. 'Say. My friend Ellen's son Mark. Twenty-eight. Studying to be a dentist. *Loves* kids . . .'

'No, that's OK.'

'Gor-jus eyes. You could paint pickchuhs with his eyelashes, that's how long they are.'

'I'm not interested in meeting anyone new right now,' I said.

'You must have loved him a *lot*.'

I nodded. 'I did.'

'Well, whenever you're ready. Not that I'm a matchmaker or anything. I don't charge a fee, but you have to invite me to the wedding.'

Someone knocked and Sheba got up to answer the door. 'Andy and Candy. Come in, come in. Happy Thanksgiving, despite our present administration. You know Venus, your neighbor in 1B, right?'

I turned around and said hi to the couple from 1A. I'd hardly ever seen them, but I heard them a lot. From the sounds that periodically burst through their door, it was impossible to tell what, exactly, they were doing – it sounded like violent sex, but it could have been violent cooking because sometimes I heard what sounded like pots and pans banging.

Andy was a short, skinny, middle-aged guy with a bald head, goggly eyes, a thin rim of beard and a pencil-thin moustache. Candy, on the other hand, was a woman of morbidly obese proportions with small, scouring eyes and a weird, nervous, high-pitched laugh. It was impossible to imagine the two of them doing what it sounded like they were doing in the privacy of their apartment.

They'd brought a big homemade pie. But how Candy was ever going to actually enter the apartment and manoeuvre herself along its tiny pathways was a matter of speculation.

'Candy'd be more comfortable on a chair out here by the kitchen,' Andy said. But Sheba stopped him before he could extricate one of the tightly wedged dining-room chairs. 'Leave those,' she said sharply. 'I want the symmetry. I'll get another chair for Candy. Or how about this stool? It's nice and sturdy.'

Candy eyed me. 'You have mice?' she asked. 'We have mice.' She turned to Sheba. 'You have mice, Sheba?'

'I had a mouse in 1974,' Sheba said. 'I'm surprised I'm able to mention it without fainting.'

While Candy was getting settled and Andy was unwrapping their pie, more guests arrived, most of them people I'd never seen before. Some of them knew Daddy and Whitman and some of them were relative newcomers to the building.

The cling film came off the dishes. People oohed and aahed over the gor-jus table. Sheba commandeered every new dish that arrived, positioning it according to some exacting design plan in her head. I don't know how they did it, but people got into the apartment and found places to sit and started yakking.

I smiled and chatted and kept a firm grasp on my antique crystal wineglass as I inched my way to the dining table. It all looked so good. I couldn't remember the last time I'd had or even seen this much food. Economic necessity had turned me into a soup and salad girl with occasional splurges on hot dogs and pizza. Starch and cholesterol filled in the gaps. Food had become sort of like Tremaynne: always there in the back of my mind but an inaccessible fantasy. The good part was that I'd lost ten pounds.

I stared at the neatly sliced turkey like a kid dazzled by a display in a candy store, almost afraid to touch it.

Someone standing next to me said, maybe to me, 'It would be terrible if that turkey's tail caught on fire.'

It was Kenny, the illegal sublet who lived right above me in 2B. The guy with the snake. He was dressed in a tight synthetic shirt with a plunging neckline that showed off a pale, hairless chest that reminded me of a plucked chicken. A big round pendant on a thick gold chain dangled from his neck. His tight low-risers – no longer fashionable in New York – revealed thin legs and a flat little butt. Red jewels winked from the eye sockets of his skull earrings.

'Maybe we should just move that orange candle there further away from the turkey's tail,' Kenny said.

'I think that's a good idea,' I said, 'but I'd run it by Sheba first. She likes to position things in a certain way.'

'Tragedy can strike at the most inopportune moments,' Kenny said in his unhurried Southern drawl. He picked up a plate and speared a piece of turkey.

OK, I'll admit it: my horror of snakes (and spiders and mice) is such that even talking about them makes me uneasy. But I wanted to be neighborly, so I made myself ask Kenny, 'How's your – how's Esmeralda?'

'Oh, she's fine,' Kenny said. 'She just ate, so she's resting.'

I shuddered and gathered my boa closer around me. I didn't dare ask what Esmeralda had had for her Thanksgiving dinner. 'Do you – um – keep it – *her* – in a cage or something?'

Kenny was navigating the table, spearing or scooping up everything in sight. 'Nah. I just letter go where she wants to go and do what she wants to do. Sometimes she even likes to sleep with me.'

The image made me lightheaded. I took a deep breath and held on tight to my crystal wineglass with one hand and my boa with the other. 'You're joking, right?'

He stuck out his lower lip and shook his head. 'I'm terrible at telling jokes.'

'Listen,' I said, laughing nervously, 'I'm just terrified of snakes.'

'A lot of people are,' Kenny said, his mouth full. 'But you know what? Snakes are wonderful, despite what the Bible says. They're sleek and smart and beautiful and they can become attached to you –'

Eeek!

'– just like a dog or a cat.'

I looked down at my plate of food and tried to defuse the horror I felt.

'You all should come visit,' Kenny said. 'Es loves people. I mean, we're all like warm trees to her.'

'I couldn't,' I whispered, 'I just couldn't.'

'Well, I once thought I could never move to New York. But I did. And then I thought, you can't dress up like a nun and go rollerskating in Central Park. But I did. The truth is, nobody here gives a shit what you do. The restrictions are all in your head.'

'I still don't think I could ever – *touch a snake*.'

Kenny shrugged. 'Let me know when you do.'

If it weren't for that damned Esmeralda, I could have been friends with Kenny. And it would have been nice to have someone in the building I could hang out with now and then. But I knew I'd never knock on the door of 2B so long as there was a six-foot boa constrictor on the other side.

The big news in the building was that 5A had recently been burgled. Sheba was certain it was the same person who'd broken into her place last summer and stolen her air-conditionuh.

'An inside job, I'm telling you. Those kids they hire to mop the floors – if you can call it mopping – and put out the gahbage.'

'Those guys are too sweet,' someone else said. 'They're from Peru.'

'Who then, the new supah?'

'No,' I said, 'I've met her. She's really nice.'

'Nice schmice,' Sheba opined. 'She's got keys to all our apahtments, right?'

'It's not her,' I insisted.

'Well,' Sheba said, 'I think we should ask for more security. I for one do not feel safe walkin' around in my negligée. And I got my earrings to think of.'

And mice. Oh. My. God. As I was scanning the table, planning my next foray, I caught sight of two little black eyes peering out from Sheba's cornucopia. I watched, speechless, as a gray mouse climbed up on a fake squash, right next to my dangling scarf, and . . .

Everyone turned to look as I screamed and frantically shook my boa. 'A mouse!' I cried. 'It jumped on my scarf!'

But then it hopped off me and into an almost-empty bowl of coleslaw. Gasps, cries, pandemonium. The table got jostled as everyone around it rushed away. A candle fell over. Poof! The turkey's crêpe-paper tail was suddenly ablaze. Sheba let out a piercing shriek that brought me back to my senses. I flung my wine on the flames and then someone else shot seltzer water out from a bottle.

'My gor-jus table!' Sheba moaned, staring at the soaked, smoking mess. She looked up in sudden alarm. 'Where's the friggin' mouse?'

'I've got it.' Kenny raised his hand, a paper napkin balled in his fist.

'Get it outta here before I plotz!' Sheba wailed. She began shooshing everyone towards the door. 'OK, OK, party's ovuh for this year. I gotta lie down – maybe for the rest of my life.' She clutched my hand before I left. 'Thanks, honey, for puttin' out the fi-uh. I'm glad it wasn't you went up in flames.'

'Me too.'

She patted my cheek. 'You're a gorgeous girl, Venus. I hope you marry someone rich and nevuh have to live in a walk-up with mice.'

Then snow came, and bitter winds, and icy sidewalks.

I loved it.

What was wrong with me?

Each new season was a revelation, a new adventure in adaptation, helping to turn me into a real New Yorker. I'd grown up with moderate temperatures, in a place that stayed green year-round. Now I was battling my way to the subway through blizzards that dumped foot after foot of snow and sent razor-sharp Arctic winds slicing through my clothes.

Another major adjustment to the wardrobe was required. Hats or hoods were essential, no matter how ridiculous they looked, and of course New York had the aplomb to turn even hats and hoods into major fashion statements. Everyone seemed to be wearing those knitted Laplander-looking hats with long earflaps that you could tie under your chin (but didn't), and peaked tops that ended in a kind of thin, braided tail. I found a weirdly cool Chinese aviator's hat, nylon outside, fake fur inside, that fit like a helmet and had long earflaps that could be snapped under the chin (and were) or pulled up and snapped on top.

The dads sent a quilted down coat (overnight Federal Express) that made me look like the offspring of the Michelin tyre man and the White Queen in that old *Alice in Wonderland* movie from the 1930s. But I didn't care, warmth was all that mattered. Like the insulated mittens I wore – sorry, but thin leather gloves do *not* keep out the cold. Luckily I'd had the foresight to bring my fur-lined rhinestone-studded cowgirl boots from Portland. They were a reminder of my old wild ridiculous pre-bankruptcy days when I danced topless, earned thousands in tips, and bought anything my heart desired. How long ago was that? Several lifetimes. My cowgirl boots were pre-Tremaynne. In fact, it came over me in a rush as I hauled them out and pulled them on, I'd met Pete Pringle, my second husband, in that topless bar, dancing in these very boots.

So much history in a pair of boots that I now used as winter gear.

Huge storms blew in and tranquilized the city, turning it into something quiet and white and gor-jus. The garden shimmered like a frosted wedding cake. When the sun came out, this strange pure-white world burned with an ear-searing radiance, forcing me to put on my fake Gucci sunglasses ($20 from a furtive sidewalk vendor), or risk having my retinas seared.

You get the picture: I was quite a picture. Totally unrecognizable beneath my layers of extreme-weather gear, encased in garments that entirely hid body shape.

One day it would be freezing, with shrieking winds rattling the old sash windows in the apartment and sheets of snow blowing down, and then the next day it would be so warm that all the snow would turn to dirty gray slush and even a sweater made you too hot.

Was it global warming?

A city of extremes, New York. Weatherwise and peoplewise, it was totally unpredictable. But living in New York gave every New Yorker a common bond, and that's what I loved about it. Everyone in New York had something in common: New York.

Right after Thanksgiving, Susanna seemed to go into a state of permanent overdrive. I raced around town doing her bidding, delivering 'notes' to gossip columnists, picking up packages, returning unwanted items for store credit. I liked getting out of the office, even on the coldest days, so I didn't chafe at being her personal messenger. The stores were festive and full and for the first time as an adult, without my two fathers grasping my hands, I walked *by myself* over to Rockefeller Center to gape in awe at the giant tree.

It was a huge spruce from Oregon!

An honest-to-God *thrill* ran right through me.

I wanted to share it, so I quickly e-mailed Whitman and Daddy, sending a photo of the tree along with the e-mail. Whitman immediately e-mailed back: 'I think that I shall never see an e as lovely as your tree.' Daddy's came a minute later: 'Remember when we all went skating at Rockefeller Center?'

I looked down into the ice rink and saw myself, a thrilled and terrified nine-year-old, trying to keep my balance between the dads as we made a slow circuit around the famous icy oval.

When I got back to the office, Susanna called me in.

Queen of the multitaskers, she was always doing something else while she talked to me (or at me, I should say). I sometimes felt like a checkout clerk must feel when a customer stays on a cellphone during the entire transaction.

'I'm going to be honest with you,' she said. 'I am absolutely stretched to the limit. I've got the entire magazine to oversee, plus my column to write and my new book to finish.' She was flipping back and forth through layout pages on her computer as she spoke, making notes and answering e-mails. 'Can I trust you to do a couple things for me?'

'Sure.'

'You've really been keeping up,' she said.

My first flattery from an important executive! My heart swelled. I almost heard music.

'I feel I can trust you.' She turned from her computer screen and looked up at me for one brief second. '*Can* I trust you?'

'Of course you can.'

'Trust is about keeping one's own counsel. Not gossiping with your friends.'

'I know that.'

'I like you, Venus, because you're smart. And you're not a griper.'

'Griping doesn't get you anywhere,' I said.

'Right,' Susanna agreed. 'It's pointless, like asking for another person's opinion. Opinions mean nothing. To get something done, one needs to take action.'

'Right.'

'So first off – would you like to keep going with the "Nothing to Hyde" column?'

'You mean—'

'I mean, do exactly as you did before. Come up with three questions and answers every month, one thousand words total. I can't pay you or give you any credit because my contract with Stuckey forbids it. But you did such a fantastic job last time that I thought you might like to keep at it. It's a good way to polish your writing skills.'

My writing skills? Was Susanna Hyde actually telling me that I could *write*? I mean, write like a *professional writer*? I was speechless.

'But!' She raised a manicured finger. 'No. One. Must. Know. Not even your faux pa. If you want to do this, it's strictly undercover.'

'I understand.'

She told me I'd have to give her 'copy' by a certain date every month. 'And don't be afraid to delve into the darker side of sex,' she urged. 'People love that. The wilder, the better.'

'OK.'

'It's important that you don't miss any deadlines.'

'I won't.'

'It's good discipline. And if you're a writer, that's a good thing to have.'

She made it sound like she was giving me a gift. Like I should be grateful that she was allowing me to write her columns for free. And you know what? I was. I actually thanked her.

'And there's one other thing,' Susanna said before I left her office. 'I want you to call Nick Burden in London . . .'

*

It had to do with the lavish holiday party that Stuckey Universal Media was throwing for all Stuckey employees. Susanna wanted Nick Burden to photograph her entering the party with Lord Farrell Stuckey. And then photograph the two of them together throughout the evening.

But not just at the holiday party. Susanna wanted Nick Burden to photograph her and Lord Stuckey at other parties, too.

But I didn't know this. I just gave Nick Burden – or his assistant, I should say, since I never spoke to Nick Burden himself – a list of dates, times, and New York addresses.

Out of curiosity, I Googled Nick Burden.

He was a famous paparazzi-pack photographer. Even if you've never heard of him, you've probably seen his photographs. He's been sued on at least three different occasions, once by the royal family and twice by celebrities who said he violently intruded upon their privacy.

What did it all mean? Because of my new pact of secrecy with Susanna, I didn't mention it to Dorcas or Sharanda or to Whitman, the one person who might have shed some light on whatever unseen intrigue was in the works.

But all three of them mentioned the party because all three of them had received invitations.

'Apparently, it's going to be quite a *lavish* affair,' Whitman said. 'My sources tell me that Lord Stuckey wants to make a good show of it because it's his first year as the owner of all those magazines.'

'Why don't you and Daddy fly out for the party?' I said. 'Come for Christmas. Remember how much fun we used to have?'

'You only came out for *one* Christmas,' Whitman reminded me, 'and you spent most of the time crying for your mother. You always wanted to spend Christmas with Carolee instead of us.'

That was true, and it reminded me that I had to make a decision about Christmas very soon.

'You never wanted to spend Christmas with us in New York,' Whitman went on. 'You wanted the comfort of Portland. So I respected that. It broke my heart, but I respected it.'

'It broke your heart?'

'Of course it did. I wanted you to have some glamour and excitement in your life. I wanted to give you some . . . *alternative* to that downwardly mobile world you lived in with Carolee.'

'Well, now it's my turn to invite you and Daddy. Come out here for Christmas this year.'

There was a pause on the other end of the line. 'Well – sweetheart – that would be *lovely*, but this year it's impossible.'

Whitman and Daddy were flying to some sacred spot that just happened to be on a beautiful tropical island somewhere in the South Pacific, with white sand beaches and warm ocean breezes. 'It's *work*, of course,' Whitman assured me. 'I'm doing a story on it for the magazine. A resort there is flying us over first-class and putting us up in a beachside suite – otherwise, of *course*, we'd be spending Christmas with you in New York.'

OK, so they weren't going to be in the Christmas picture. That left my mom. But I didn't have the money to fly out to Portland and Mom, because of her deep-seated fear of flying, would never get on a plane.

'That's why I haven't invited you out for Christmas,' I explained to her late one night on the phone.

'Because you thought I'd say no?'

'Well, you *would* say no, wouldn't you?'

'I've always wanted to see New York,' she equivocated.

'But you'd never get on a plane to come out here, right?'

'I've *always* wanted to experience an exciting city,' Carolee insisted. 'But I just never had the opportunity.'

'OK, so what I'm hearing is that if I *did* invite you to come out for Christmas, you wouldn't say no.'

'I was watching *Breakfast at Tiffany's* just the other night. Audrey Hepburn is just so friggin' gorgeous. I thought of you there in New York and wished I could come out and see you.'

'Because there are new anti-anxiety drugs you can take,' I said. 'We just ran a story about it on the health page.'

'But I assumed you were so busy all the time that I'd just be in the way.'

'OK, Mom, listen. If you are telling me that you *would* actually get on a plane and fly across the country to spend Christmas with me, I'm going to invite you—'

'I understand that it's probably *healthy* that we're separated,' Mom rattled on, lost in her own self-absorption. 'I *need* to adjust to the fact that I'll be living alone for the rest of my life. But it's just a little more difficult around Christmas, that's all I'm saying, because Christmas was always *our* holiday. Your fathers had you on the Fourth of July and Labor Day weekend and sometimes for Thanksgiving, but Christmas was our special time, yours and mine.'

'Mom, why don't you come out here for Christmas?'

Silence.

'I only have a couple of days off, and it's the most expensive time of the year to fly, and the most crowded, but I'd come out to the airport to meet you so you wouldn't have to feel scared once you're here. And you could stay here in the apartment—'

'After all these years,' Carolee said, 'I'd finally see that apartment where you used to have so much fun with your fathers.'

'And here's the best – you could come with me to the big office Christmas party.'

'Oh, you'll have a date, I'm sure.'

'You'll be my date. We're all allowed to bring someone. It's a big fancy party in a famous hotel, and there's a sit-down dinner, and it would be so much fun if you could come out and—'

'It looks like they've still got one seat available on that direct flight on Delta,' Mom said.

'How do you know that?' I asked.

'Oh – I've just been checking out the website while we're

talking. If I click on this one button, I can buy it right now. Let's see –' In a low, breathless monotone she read off all the conditions and restrictions: the ticket was non-refundable and non-exchangeable.

'Maybe you should think about it for a day,' I suggested.

'Then I might not get this flight,' Mom said. 'Or *any* flight. Apparently this is going to be the busiest airline season in history, with every flight booked solid.'

'If you book it, you can't back out,' I warned. It was something of a miracle that she was even this close, but I'd seen her wobble in her resolve before. 'You can't get sick or make up some lame excuse –'

'Well, I *can*,' Mom said, 'but if I do, I lose a lot of money. That's sort of a good thing, in a way don't you think? Forces me to . . .'

'It's up to you.'

'OK.' I heard deep, jagged breathing on the other end, as if she were already trying to ward off a panic attack. 'I just bought it.'

For several days in early December Susanna didn't come into the office at all. She was working from home, for 'personal reasons', she said, without telling me or anyone else what those were.

I was at my desk every morning at 8 a.m., as usual, eating the coffee yogurt I usually brought for Susanna and picking up the first calls and e-mails. I was Susanna's office proxy, relaying her orders and running around to all the little cubicles and windowless cubbyholes where her staff worked. Eldora Button and Petra Darkke, those seasoned, resentful senior editors, still had it in for me, but I tried to deflect their caustic remarks with a bright smile and cheerful manner.

'Who the hell does she think she is?' Eldora blew up one morning when I relayed a message from Susanna that an article on ancient grains needed to be rewritten. 'Anna fucking Wintour?' She glared at me.

Petra and Eldora also tried to get me to do work for them.

Without Susanna there, it was difficult for me to say no. But I did say no. It was like a newly acquired skill. I marvelled at myself.

Hadn't that always been my fatal flaw? I couldn't say no. Everything was yes with me. It was a bad habit I'd picked up from my mom.

One day when I brought something in to Evan Bevins, the beleaguered art director, he looked at me with those sad, hangdog eyes and said, 'What's a pretty girl like you doing in a hellhole like this?'

'I kind of like it,' I said. 'I didn't know it was a hellhole.'

'Oh, yes.' Evan laced his fingers across his protruding belly and nodded solemnly. 'If you knew what publishing used to be, you'd know you were in hell now.'

Well, I didn't know how publishing used to be. I only knew how it was now. So I couldn't feel sad for the good old days.

I left before Evan could start crying on my shoulder. I knew from a couple of memorandums I'd typed up for Susanna that Evan's days were numbered. She wanted him out. 'He's one of those tired old farts who thinks he deserves some kind of special treatment just because he's got a dick hanging between his legs,' she complained to me one day. 'The man has absolutely no sense of what's going on around him, no sense of changing styles, no vision for the future, and no talent.'

'Just like our president,' I observed. Which got a rare hoot of laughter out of Susanna.

On the second day that Susanna was gone, I received an e-mail from Giles Travaille asking me if I wanted to have lunch.

I stared at the message, acutely aware that my heart was pounding. I hit 'Reply'. Paused to consider. I wondered if there was some connection between Susanna's absence and Giles's invitation. I remembered how he kissed. I pictured myself walking into a restaurant with handsome Giles, letting myself be seduced over a plate of spaghetti amatricia . . .

'Thanks,' I wrote back, 'I'd love to.'

*

The truth was, Giles had been kind of avoiding me since our night out and that makeout session in the taxi. He was a busy man, of course, and every time I ran into him he was in a rush, heading for a meeting or an appointment. I wondered if he was keeping aloof because I bored him. I hadn't been one of his easy conquests.

But when I met him down in the lobby, he looked genuinely pleased to see me. 'Glad to see you've got a warm coat now,' he said, opening the door and ushering me out ahead of him into the bright, cold sunshine. 'You're the only girl I know who actually looks sexy wearing down.' He whistled for a cab and we headed towards the Upper East Side.

The restaurant was Italian, very elegant, all pale pinks, golds and whites. The maitre d' and all the fawning waiters knew Giles and called him 'Mr Travaille'.

'*Aperitivo*?' the maitre d' asked, whipping the napkin from my place setting, giving it a shake, and placing it in my lap.

'Negroni?' Giles asked me.

'What's that?'

'Equal parts gin, vermouth, and Campari,' Giles said. 'You'll love it.' He ordered two of them. When the waiter had gone, Giles smiled at me and said, 'You know, all I have to do is ask you to model for us and this meal becomes a business meeting and can all go on my expense account.'

'You'd better ask me then.' I thought he was joking.

'OK. Why don't you model for us?'

I smiled, keeping my mouth closed, and shook my head.

'You're exactly what I'm looking for,' Giles said. 'Look, we have this huge audience in the Armed Services. Fighting over in Iraq and Afghanistan and wherever else they're sending the poor buggers these days. So I want to do a special issue called "The Girls Back Home". Every race, every nationality, and here's the revolutionary part – *real girls*. Not porn stars and airbrushed Barbie dolls. Real. Natural.'

'And that's revolutionary?'

'In my business it is. And look, Venus, you'd be perfect as, say, a farm girl from the Midwest.'

'But I'm not a farm girl from the Midwest.' I was kind of hurt by the suggestion. 'I don't even know what a farm girl looks like.'

'We'd have you riding a huge John Deere tractor, out in a cornfield,' Giles said. 'Or standing with a pitchfork, like that painting *American Gothic*. Only topless, of course.'

I sipped my delicious negroni, feeling pleasantly guilty to be drinking at lunchtime. Giles kept his eyes on me, studying me as if I were already nude and ready to jump into the hay. 'Giles,' I said, 'I'm flattered that you think I'm sexy enough to be in *Peeper*. But I just don't want to do it.'

'Two grand?' he said, draining his negroni and ordering another.

It was suddenly very tempting. But then I remembered those hundreds and hundreds of porn and semi-porn magazines for sale on the racks at Phantastic Phantasy. The guys furtively scanning them, looking for their perfect sex fantasy. All those winking, pouting, beckoning models, gleaming under cellophane covers like so much meat in the supermarket. After awhile, that whole business just seemed so sleazy and depressing, today's titillations and tomorrow's trash.

OK, I'd danced topless and modelled lingerie in Portland, back when I was really hard-up for cash, so it wasn't like I was a prude or anything. And a couple of years ago, I probably would have accepted Giles's offer and enjoyed the attention. But now? I just couldn't see myself naked atop a John Deere tractor in an Iowa cornfield.

Oh, he worked hard to persuade me. At one point I felt his knee against mine. He smiled and spoke low, his voice full of promise. I would be one of his famous discoveries, he said.

'Like Cupcake Cassidy?'

'I didn't discover Cupcake. She already had a big career before I met her.'

'Yeah, really big.'

'Cupcake has very talented breasts,' Giles said. 'They've earned her lots of money.'

'What happens when they start to sag?' I asked.

'Well, they already have, a bit. That's why she's moving into the next phase of her career, as a writer.'

How was it possible that a woman who had big bazooms and gave blow jobs on screen could get a book published but a really talented writer like Josh could not even find an agent? It seemed grossly unfair.

'Well,' Giles said as our antipasti arrived, 'I can tell you're going to drive a hard bargain.'

'I'm not playing hard to get,' I insisted.

'But I'm getting hard just sitting here with you,' Giles said. 'OK. I'll back off for now. But just tell me you'll consider it.'

'OK,' I said, 'I'll consider it.'

On the fourth day she was out of the office, Susanna sent me a text message asking if I'd stop by her apartment later that evening. It was bitterly cold and the subway wasn't running because of a terrorist alert, so I gamely set out on foot, swaddled in my Michelin-White Queen down coat, mittens, fur-lined boots, and Chinese aviator hat.

This walking-in-all-weathers thing was a whole new phenomenon for me, and I was really getting into it. Nobody walked in Portland. Everyone walked in New York. And though I wasn't consciously trying to lose weight, the combination of aerobic exercise and reduced rations was doing wonders for my figure. That sluggish lassitude that used to make me feel so fat and tired was gone. Now I always felt alert, alive, ready for another cup of coffee.

Susanna's doorman knew me by then and ushered me into the vast hallway of her building. 'Wouldja mind bringin' her this, since you're goin' up?' He handed me a white paper bag.

I looked at it as the elevator made its way up to the fourteenth floor. It was from a pharmacy. The bag wasn't sealed, so I peeked inside. Prescription medications. Painkillers. Percocet and Tylenol 4.

It took her for ever to answer the door, and when she finally did, the sight of her gave me such a shock that I gasped.

'Yes, I know,' she said, turning to shuffle back down the darkened hallway. Her voice was low and mumbly, not as distinct as usual. Maybe she'd been drinking. She was wearing a white terrycloth robe and slippers, and her hair looked like it hadn't been washed for days. The apartment had a stuffy, closed-in smell.

'Are you all right?' I asked, following her in.

'My tits are killing me,' she moaned.

I thought: oh my God, she's had chemo or a lumpectomy for breast cancer and didn't tell anyone. My heart flooded with tenderness. 'The doorman asked me to bring this up – from the pharmacy.'

She turned back around, giving me a better look at her face. The hallway was unusually dark, but I could see that something had happened to her face. Her upper lip was swollen, as if she'd been punched. But there was something different about her eyes, too, and her skin had a shiny, almost waxen glow.

'Oh, thank God.' She shuffled back and snatched the bag from my hand, extracting the two orange pill bottles. 'I'm going to sleep well tonight if it kills me.'

I followed her into the sitting room, where she slowly eased herself into an overstuffed chair fitted out with extra pillows and blankets. Strewn on tables and the floor around her were a laptop, a landline telephone, her BlackBerry, another cell-phone, a small printer, typewritten pages, dirty teacups and dishes. 'Get me a glass of water, will you?' she croaked. 'Evian. In the fridge.'

Whatever was physically wrong with her, Susanna was apparently not going to talk about it. So I didn't feel that I could, either. I got her water and watched as she popped the painkillers.

'Listen,' she said, 'you're not going to tell anyone about this.'

'About what?' I said. 'Susanna, are you sick?'

'I don't have time to be sick,' she snapped. 'I've got to finish this book, in addition to everything else.' She tilted her head back and placed an ice pack on her upper lip.

'A new book?'

'No, the one I've been working on. I've been paid a fortune for the damn thing and it has to be completed chop chop. But just when I'd almost finished it, I had a brainstorm. Utterly brilliant. So I've been rewriting like mad, every night, after work. Now it's more of a memoir, and I've added a real sizzler. They'll absolutely love it but it's a total rush to stay on schedule for the April pub date.'

I looked at the stuff scattered around her, saw the discomfort she was in, heard the fatigue in her voice, and could only wonder at the strength or fortitude needed to keep *Aura* running while writing a book and dealing with surgery.

'It's going to be big,' Susanna said, sounding tired but pleased, shifting her ice pack. 'Very big. *Huge*. And I'm going to need your help when it comes out.'

'My help?'

'Stuckey's doing a big promotion – sending me around on a book tour. I negotiated an assistant. You.'

This was big news and took a moment to sink in. 'But what about the office?'

'We'll find a way to deal with that. Yes or no?'

I had no reason to say no, so I said yes.

'Good. It won't be until next spring – April.' She removed the ice pack, stretched her neck, and took a deep breath, one hand fluttering protectively in front of her chest. 'Oh. That Percocet works quickly. They didn't tell me there'd be this much pain.'

I was dying to ask her just what, exactly, had been done. But before I could work up the courage, Susanna untied her robe and looked down at her breasts. I stared, horrified. They were covered with painful-looking bruises and encased in a weird-looking black latex bra that would have set a fetishist's heart ablaze.

'Oh my God!' I cried. 'Were you in a car crash?' Maybe it wasn't cancer. I envisioned her in a speeding taxi, hurled forward and smashing her chest against the acrylic divider as the driver slammed on his brakes to avoid a collision.

Susanna gave me a puzzled look. Or maybe it was a stoned look from the painkillers. 'What are you talking about?'

'Your –' I pointed at her bruised breasts.

'I had them do a lift at the same time.'

Now it was my turn to look puzzled. 'A lift?'

'A breast lift. After my augmentation mammoplasty.'

I sat down, speechless. I couldn't believe that someone as pretty as Susanna, someone with nothing wrong with her, would *choose* to put herself through this kind of ordeal.

'I had them do everything at once – tits, lips, and eyes. And microdermabrasion.'

All I could say was, 'Wow.'

'Why didn't you tell me there was so much pain?' Susanna asked.

'How would I know?'

'From having yours done!'

'I've never had mine done.' And, I thought, I never will.

'Oh, please. The bruises they told me about. But not the pain.' Again she looked down at her chest, jutting out her lower lip as she gently prodded the tender tissue. 'They do look nice, though, don't you think? Much larger. Better shaped.'

I couldn't think of anything to say.

'By the time I enter that party on the arm of Lord Stuckey, my titties will be the prettiest at the ball. And I've got the most gorgeous gown to show them off.'

She was sinking fast. 'You wanted me to stop by for something,' I prompted.

Susanna's eyelids fluttered. 'Did I? Wha— oh yes. Listen, Nick Burden's going to be your date for the Christmas party.'

'I've already got a date. My mom's coming out from Portland.'

'Your *mom*?' She made the word sound alien, ludicrous. 'Sorry, you've got to take Nick, too. It's the only way he can get in.'

'Why?'

Susanna sighed at my ignorance. 'Because he's been banned.'

'Banned?'

'Oh, you're too naïve to understand any of this.'

'If I have to sneak someone into a party because he's banned, I want to know why.'

Another sigh, this one edging off towards slumber. 'Because Lord Stuckey likes to protect his image. He doesn't allow his picture to appear in any tabloid that's not his own.'

I fought back a wave of foreboding. Was she asking me to do something I shouldn't? It sounded like espionage.

'And listen,' Susanna said, barely able to keep her eyes open, 'nobody's to know. Unnerstan? 'rase any e-mails with Nick's name in 'em. Delete 'em. You never heard his name.'

'Who am I supposed to say he is? At the party.'

Susanna slowly waved her hand. 'Say – say he's your husband.'

On the day that my mom was due to arrive in New York the temperature took a nosedive and it started to snow. I stared through the dirty window of the M60 bus at the thick slurry of flakes, hoping that her flight wouldn't be delayed.

The bus to LaGuardia took for ever but it cost two dollars instead of the thirty I'd need for a cab. As we lumbered along, I thought of Josh O'Connell and what a bore it was to be poor in New York.

I'd run into Josh in the Garden of Eden, an upscale deli-supermarket on 108th and Broadway. The store was generally out of my price range, but I'd go up there periodically for the free samples. Some nights by wandering through the different departments I could graze an entire meal – appetizer, main course, and dessert. The portions were tiny, but they took the edge off my hunger. The trick was never to look furtive and never to grab too much.

I was in the cheese department, toothpick in hand, about to spear a free cube of New York cheddar, when another hand, reaching for the same cheese, brushed mine.

We looked at each other and smiled. Well, I smiled. I hadn't seen Josh since that evening when I'd helped him celebrate the completion of his novel – the night we'd met at L'Albatross and I'd had to relay the news that Susanna was dumping him. I'd been hoping that he'd call but he hadn't, and the couple of times I tried to call him on his cellphone, I got a message that the number was no longer in service.

He looked thinner, almost gaunt, and hadn't shaved for a couple of days. I've always been a sucker for that haunted look. His long black coat, with its upturned collar, looked too thin for the current wind-chill factor.

Josh said he'd moved again, this time into a friend's apartment near Columbia. 'He's letting me crash there for awhile,' he said, 'but there's no heat. The boiler burst and the landlord won't send anyone over to fix it.'

'What's happening with your novel?' I asked.

He made a dismissive face. 'I'm working on something else.'

'Another novel?'

'A memoir. That's what's selling.' He turned away to cough that New York winter cough I heard everywhere I went.

'I thought you said your novel was sort of a memoir.'

'It was – well, it could have been. But this is a real memoir.'

'That's interesting,' I said. 'Susanna's writing a memoir, too.'

His green eyes narrowed. 'I thought she was working on another one of her sex books.'

'Well, she was, but she had a brainstorm and ended up turning it into a memoir. They gave her a huge advance and she's doing a big book tour.' I didn't tell him that I was going along as her assistant.

Josh lowered his head, a wounded expression on his gaunt, whiskery face. 'What's it about, this memoir, do you know?'

I shrugged. 'What's any memoir about? Her life, I guess. With some new sizzler she's added.'

'I wonder if it's about us.' Josh looked at me as if I might know. 'She hinted once that she was going to do that. Write about us.'

'Is there a lot to write about?' I imagined the two of them locked in a wild embrace. And then wondered what Josh would think if I told him about Susanna's bruised breasts and swollen lip and all her recent cosmetic surgery.

'Do you know the title?' he asked.

I did, because Susanna, now back at the office, had told me. But should I tell Josh? I didn't want to give away any of

Susanna's secrets . . . even if it meant that doing so might make Josh more interested in me. 'It's called *Puppy Love*,' I said.

'*Puppy Love*,' he repeated, barking out another unhappy laugh. The laugh segued into another fit of coughing. This time he couldn't stop. He spun away from me, hunkered down, and coughed as if his lungs were going to explode.

'Josh, are you all right?'

He swung back, trying to be comical about it, his hands clamped over his mouth, and nodded. 'Just a cough,' he wheezed.

I don't know why I did it. I untied my long wooly scarf and wrapped it around his neck. When he protested, I lied and said, 'I've got dozens.' I just couldn't bear the thought of him being cold and sick and poor and hungry and alone.

'Can I call you?' he asked.

'Sure. Do you have my cell number?'

He didn't, but neither one of us had anything to write on, so Josh said he'd try to remember it if I said it out loud. We repeated it back and forth several times. 'OK,' he said. 'Well, look, I'd give you mine but they stopped my account. Just because I hadn't paid it for three months.'

'I guess you'll have to call me, then.'

'OK,' he said. 'I will. But if you don't hear from me for a while, it's because I'm trying to finish this new book.'

'I hope the heat comes back on,' I said. 'If it gets too cold, you can come over to my place to warm up.'

'Thanks. I might have to take you up on that.'

We both popped a cube of cheese into our mouths and said goodbye.

I pondered and replayed our entire encounter as the stuffy, crowded M60 slowly made its way out of Manhattan into Queens. I'd felt such a deep sympathy for Josh and wondered if he had picked up on that.

He was a writer, obsessed with putting words on paper. I understood that need in a way that I never had before. I'd seen it with Whitman but it never really registered because I'd never known my faux pa as anything *but* a writer. But now I was working in a place that dealt with words, and I was writing for a woman who was a writer herself. And when you start writing, I'd discovered, it kind of takes over. One idea leads to the next and that one leads to another. I was beginning to understand how writing could become both a skill and an escape.

And I also knew how difficult and frustrating it must be when you couldn't get your work published. The competition was murderous. Everyone had something to say, a story to tell, an idea to pitch. Before I started to work in publishing I didn't have a clue how any of the books or magazines I read got to be books or magazines. When you're not a writer, you don't think about those things. But now, in my limited way, I *was* a writer, like Josh, like Susanna, like Whitman. I didn't go out on dates with people. I was dating *words*. It was a whole new adventure.

I wasn't obsessed with writing like Josh seemed to be. I was just dipping my toe in the water. But even so, I was aware of a very strong undertow, tugging at me, a current so powerful that it could suck me in and sweep me away. That's why I could empathize with the frustrations and humiliations Josh had to put up with. He was in way deeper than I was. He'd taken the plunge and was battling the current.

In his single-minded determination to succeed, he reminded me of Tremaynne. And that, of course, was part of his attraction.

As I threaded my way through the crowds at LaGuardia, fretting and anxious, waiting for my mom's delayed flight to arrive, I suddenly realized that I was doing what my dad used to do when I flew to New York, by myself, as a kid. This memory stirred up something inside and made me feel horribly emotional. It was so weird to realize that I'd grown up and was now living in New York and doing for my mom what my dad used to do for me.

Flying was different then, of course. There were no security restrictions. You could wait and fret right at the gate, which is what Daddy did. I remembered how his anxious face would bloom with relief when he finally saw me coming out of the jetway, accompanied by a guardian flight attendant.

I was anxious, in part, because Mom had hardly ever travelled outside of Portland, and then only by car. She knew nothing of big cities because she was afraid to visit them. Flying had always been out of the question. I guess you could say that she was agoraphobic. Or maybe just fearful in general. That she had actually gotten on a plane and flown for over six hours, just to see me in New York, was a feat of monumental importance.

The arrival time of her flight kept changing. I heard people from other flights talk about high winds and rough entries. There was a backup of planes waiting to land. But finally I saw on the monitor that her flight had arrived.

The airport was worse than Penn Station at rush hour, packed with holiday travellers and endless snaking lines. I'd told Mom exactly where to meet me but now I was afraid that she'd be so overwhelmed by the crowds that she'd have one of her 'attacks' and forget where I was.

Then I heard her voice – 'Venus?' – and scanned the crowds until I saw her, nervously clutching a huge shoulder bag and grasping the extended handle of her carry-on.

When we were finally hugging, Mom hoarsely whispered three words in my ear: 'I did it.'

She had conquered, or at least confronted, one of her biggest fears.

'I flew,' she said, with a kind of breathless, pre-sob wonder. '*In an aeroplane*.'

She looked a little gray, her ashen face offset by the whirly rat's nest of her freshly tinted red hair.

'I want to hear all about it,' I said, tugging her through the dense throngs of travellers. 'But first let's get out of here.'

'I have to pick up my luggage,' Mom said.

She already had the largest carry-on you can carry on, plus her capacious purse, big enough to stuff in a whole frozen salmon and an entire grocery store of non-perishable food items.

'You have more?' She was only going to be here for three days.

'Well,' Carolee said, 'I had to bring *clothes*, didn't I? You said it might be ten below or seventy above, so I figured an *assortment* was best. Plus my party dress, of course.'

Well, of course her checked luggage wasn't on the plane. Mom's anti-anxiety medication was starting to wear off and this news caused the first stirrings of panic. 'Oh my God, what am I going to do?' she wailed. 'All my clothes are in that suitcase!'

A tight-lipped and obviously unhappy airline employee told us they'd deliver the suitcase when it arrived.

'But how could it be lost?' Mom whispered as we made our way back out into the congested terminal. 'I didn't have any connecting flights. That means it never got put on in Portland!'

'Don't worry about it,' I said, leading her on, trying to take charge of her anxiety. 'There's nothing we can do about it now.'

'But—' Mom let out a sharp gasp as we stepped outside. 'It's *freezing*!' She began to shimmy with the cold. 'My coat's in the suitcase! What am I going to do?'

Pay thirty bucks for a cab, is what. There's no way I could get this woman on to a public bus that would take almost an hour to get to the Upper West Side.

'Where are your cleaning supplies?' Mom asked the next morning as I was getting ready for work. By then her suitcase had arrived and she was looking a lot better. 'Mr Clean, and a sponge, and a pail, and rubber gloves, and the vacuum cleaner.'

'Does the apartment look dirty or something?' I tucked the sheets into the Murphy bed, strapped the pillows down, and lifted it into its cabinet, a procedure Mom viewed with wonder.

'Well, no,' she said, heading for the kitchen as I headed for the bathroom, 'but I thought I could clean while you're at work.'

'You didn't come to New York to clean, Mom.' I turned on the shower and prayed for hot water.

'But I want to,' she said. 'Cleaning always helps me concentrate.' I heard her rummaging around on the shelves beneath the kitchen counter. 'Where's your toaster, sweetheart?'

'It's down there somewhere,' I called. 'I never use it.'

'Because I brought some of those English muffins you like so much. And a jar of marionberry jam.'

Now that was strange because I had no memory of ever eating English muffins with marionberry jam with my mother. 'Did you find the toaster?' I called.

'I think so. It looks awfully *old*, sweetheart. Are you sure it's safe?'

'It's fine,' I assured her.

A minute later I heard a piercing scream and rushed, dripping, from the shower. 'Mom! What happened? What's wrong?'

'Ahhh!' She pointed. I saw.

Hundreds, maybe thousands, of dark brown cockroaches were pouring out of the two slots in the toaster, fleeing a comfortable, crumb-filled haven that had suddenly turned into a sizzling inferno.

'Ahhh!' I screamed.

'Ahhh!' Mom screamed, running into my arms.

'Ahhh!' we both screamed, dancing up and down, terrified that a roach would run across our feet or up our legs.

An army of fleeing roaches raced across the counter top, streaming across kitchen utensils, darting into crevices. Mom broke loose and started wildly beating at them with her slipper. I grabbed a big wooden spoon and did the same. We were like a demented percussion act. But the roaches were faster than we were and disappeared into those dark, hidden cavities that no one likes to think about.

By the time Mom's toasted English muffin popped up, we were both slightly hysterical and I put in an emergency call to Mary-Joseph Capistrano.

Everyone at work was excited about the big party that night. I felt the buzz myself. I'd never attended an office party before, and this one promised to be full of glamour and intrigue. Through Susanna, I was privy to some of the high-level machinations that would be played out in the Twilight Ballroom at the famous Park Avenue hotel where the party for Stuckey Universal Media was to be held.

Susanna wasn't in the office that day. At Lord Stuckey's behest, or maybe through her own string-pulling, she'd become terribly involved with planning the party. This led to major clashes with Prill Rosenbaum from Human Resources and Sybilla Lansgaard in Public Relations, who thought they were in charge. And probably they were, until Susanna entered the picture and began to criticize and override their decisions. If Susanna's power hadn't come directly from Lord Stuckey himself, there's no way she could have pulled any of this off.

She was, by now, something of a new woman, at least on the outside, as I could see from the publicity photographs I went to pick up from Giles Travaille. Susanna wanted me to deliver them to various gossip columnists that afternoon.

'Wow,' was all I could say when Giles handed me the photographs.

'I know,' he said. 'It's a miracle. She almost looks sexy.'

She'd obviously been professionally made up – maybe by Giles himself. Susanna wore a low-cut dress that showed off her firm, uplifted, saline-stuffed breasts. Her lips were big and glossy, her teeth straight and gleaming, and her new larger eyes held a twinkly star of light. Botox and careful lighting had effectively erased the wrinkles on her forehead and around her eyes. In a weird way, she'd erased the very character that had made her face interesting.

'Those should be good for about a year,' Giles said, gesturing towards the photos. 'After that, she'll have to go back to Santa's workshop for reassembly.'

I slipped Susanna's photos into an envelope, aware that Giles was looking at me.

'Given any thought to my offer?' he asked.

I had – the idea of earning two grand for baring my all was financially appealing, and I'd even gone through a few issues of *Peeper*, trying to envision myself in its glossy pages. But I couldn't. Not even for two grand. 'Thanks, Giles, but the answer's no.'

'I suppose you're proud to be the first woman who's ever turned me down,' Giles said.

'I'm sure you'll discover the farm girl of your dreams, Giles.'

'I'm sure I will. But she won't be as farm fresh as you.'

'Are you going to the party?' I asked, starting for the door.

'Mm. With Cupcake. You?'

'I'm taking my mom. And I have to smuggle Nick Burden in.'

'Ah. Right. St Nick's in town.'

'Do you know him?'

'Nobody knows Nick. They only know his fees.' I was on my way out when Giles called my name. The way he said it, the sexiness of his voice, the accent, stopped me in my tracks. I turned around. 'About St Nick,' he said. 'Be careful. Once you've got him inside, let him go. Don't have anything more to do with him.'

'You make him sound like a criminal,' I said nervously.

'He's worse than that,' Giles said. 'He's a photographer.'

*

'I thought I'd *die*.' Mom was relaying the cockroach story to Mary-Joseph Capistrano as I walked in. 'I pressed down the toaster handle and suddenly – *suddenly* – millions of them just poured out. *Millions*. I mean I've never seen a cockroach in my entire *life*. We don't have cockroaches in Portland.'

'Yes we do,' I corrected her under my breath, smiling at Mary-Joseph. My super looked awfully cute in her knit cap and workclothes. She stood in the kitchen, holding a big silver canister with a spray hose, politely waiting for my mom to stop talking.

'They ran *everywhere*,' Mom went on. 'They're laying eggs this very minute, I just know it. I scrubbed everything in the kitchen – *everything*.'

'That won't do it,' Mary-Joseph pointed out. 'It ain't about just being clean, see? They can eat anything, roaches. They can eat codboard.' She turned to me. 'We gotta regulah fumigatuh comes every month but he couldn't get in here the last two years.'

Whitman had instructed me never to mention Dingding Wang, his illegal subletter, so I merely smiled and shrugged to indicate it was all a mystery to me. I was worried about time and told Mom we had to start getting ready.

'I'll just spray and get outtayuh way.' Mary-Joseph squirted some liquid under the kitchen shelves, unleashing a reassuringly nasty chemical smell.

'Would you like to have a glass of wine while you're fumigating?' Mom asked. She refilled her own glass. 'I brought it all the way from Oregon. It's Venus's favorite Chardonnay.'

I'd never tasted it.

'Nah, better not,' Mary-Joseph said. 'Gotta drive home. And the roads suck in this weathuh.'

'Does your family celebrate Christmas?' Mom asked as she began to disrobe, right there in the living room.

'Oh yeah. Big time.'

'Does your family accept you?' Mom asked. Shivering, clad only in panties and bra, she took a sip of her Oregon Chardonnay.

'Accept me?' Mary-Joseph asked.

'I know when Venus had *her* first lesbian experience—'

'Mother!'

Mom turned to me with innocent eyes. 'What? I'm talking about JD. She was a darling girl,' Mom said to Mary-Joseph. 'She sang in a rock band. What was it called? The Tough Slits, or The Mean Clits or—'

'The Black Garters,' I said.

'Oh right, The Black Garters. Well, anyway, JD was the lead singer . . .'

'Mother, please, just get ready.' I could see Mary-Joseph's eyes trying not to stare at us.

'She was about your size,' Mom said to Mary-Joseph. 'Now when I had *my* first lesbian experience, it was with an older, taller woman. An artist.'

'A potter,' I said, remembering Jerri and her ugly pots and her uglier alcoholic rages.

'Yes, she threw pots,' Mom said. 'Sometimes at *me*.'

'No kidding,' Mary-Joseph said.

'Oh yes.' Mom nodded solemnly. 'Abusive. One time she actually struck me.'

'I don't believe it,' Mary-Joseph said politely, squirting, looking at me.

'Mm-hm. Well, it was such a *shock*,' Mom said. 'You can imagine. I thought it was just men who abused women. I never knew women abused other women.'

'You nevuh lived in Brooklyn,' Mary-Joseph said.

'That's why I'm writing my memoir,' Mom babbled on. 'I think it might help other survivors.'

'Excuse me? You're writing a memoir?' It was the first I'd heard of it. What was it that made everyone think they had to write a memoir this year?

Mom nodded and stepped into her party dress, pulling it up as far as what used to be her waist. 'I'm taking a class. "Unleashing Your Inner Memoir". I just love the teacher. She used to be a crack addict who robbed houses for drug money. So inspiring.'

I couldn't get her to shut up but I managed to keep her on track with dressing. I was getting really nervous because I was supposed to meet Nick Burden in the hotel lobby in less than an hour.

When Mom was in the bathroom, Mary-Joseph asked me where we were going. I told her about the party and how I was afraid we'd be late. 'I can give you a lift,' she said. 'If you want.'

'That would be really sweet.' I slipped into the bedroom to put on my black low-cut dress, the one that looked like a satin negligée. It was the dress I'd worn to my wedding with Tremaynne. I'd lugged it out to New York with me like a teddy bear, to give my aching heart some false comfort. But now, holding it in my hands, a flood of Tremaynne memories washed over me and I let out a strange sound, half moan, half suppressed sob. And then sternly told myself to get over it.

Get over him.

Move on.

It was time.

'Jeez,' Mary-Joseph said when I stepped back into the living room.

I'd lost weight and the dress wasn't quite as tight as it was on the day I was wed. 'Do I look all right?'

'Yeah,' Mary-Joseph nodded. 'You look all right, all right.'

'It's old. I couldn't afford a new dress.'

'Old on you looks new,' Mary-Joseph said.

'Thanks.' I could see her interest and felt my cheeks get hot. But that was OK, because I *was* hot, or trying to be. You know how sometimes the way you look all comes together for one night? Everything just seems *right*? That's how it was with me that night. I was determined to be a wow.

I stepped into those fabulous black heels Daddy had bought me last summer at Bergdorf's. I artfully mussed up my hair. I used eyeliner and mascara and a kind of silky sheeny subtle eye shadow and swabbed on some lusciously red lip gloss.

'I didn't know you had tattoos.' Mary-Joseph stared at the heart above my heart. 'My ma woulda killed me.'

My cellphone rang. I was afraid it was Susanna, who'd come up with some last-minute errand or task. But it wasn't. It was Josh.

'Hey,' he said. 'I was wondering if your invitation for leftover pizza was still good.'

It's all in the timing, as they say. He *would* call tonight. 'Oh, Josh, any other time would be great but tonight's my office party.'

'Oh. *She*'ll be there, of course.'

'Everyone who works for Stuckey will be there.'

'OK. Another time.'

Just as I put the phone down, the bathroom door opened and Carolee appeared in a cloud of perfume so strong that it almost cancelled out the bug spray. Her dress was red and sparkly. Her high heels were red and sparkly. And her face was red and sparkly. Or half of it was. Don't ask me how or why, but she'd applied a swath of red glitter diagonally across one cheek and up over her eyes and forehead. Big earrings shaped like Christmas wreaths blinked on and off in her ear lobes. 'Ready to boogie!' she cried. 'New York, here I come!'

It was freezing outside and not good high-heel weather. Mom hadn't been in heels for years and I'd learned first-hand the perils of wearing them on New York's cracked and grated streets, but I had to wear them with my dress or go barefoot (as I had on my wedding day) because the dress would have looked ridiculous with low heels. Mom and I shivered and clutched one another for support as we followed Mary-Joseph down the icy sidewalk to her van. She swung open the side door and helped Mom with her blinking earrings climb in.

'There's plenny a room,' she said. 'Just shove them pipes off the seat.'

Then – so sweet! – she opened the passenger door for me. I climbed in. Mary-Joseph hopped into the driver's seat, started the ignition, and a CD of Christmas music blared to life. I looked back at Mom and we started to laugh – just at the adventure of it all, I guess. I couldn't do anything but laugh –

unless it was to cry. I was so mortified by Mom's sparkly red face and blinking earrings that I didn't know what emotion was appropriate.

Mary-Joseph was a fast, aggressive driver. 'Fuckin' asshole!' she screamed when a cab cut in front of her. I was barely able to hear her above the deafening strains of 'The Little Drummer Boy'.

'Heat'll come on in a sec!' she promised, her breath frosting the windshield. It never occurred to her to turn down the volume, and I was too polite and grateful for the ride to ask, so we were forced to shout for the entire trip.

'How you doin' back there, Mrs Gilroy?' Mary-Joseph shouted.

'I'm fine!' Mom shouted. 'Thank you for asking!'

'This yuh first time in New York?'

Mom said something incomprehensible so I nodded on her behalf.

'How you like it so far?' Mary-Joseph asked.

'I don't know,' Mom said, leaning forward to shout in Mary-Joseph's ear. 'I haven't seen anything yet. Except cockroaches.'

Nor did she see much on the ride over to Park Avenue because there were no windows in the back of Mary-Joseph's van. But at some point, Mom began to sing along with the Christmas tape. That meant she was happy. She waved her finger like a conductor, indicating that I should join in. So I did. And so did Mary-Joseph. We sang 'Deck the Halls', 'We Wish You a Merry Christmas', and 'We Three Queens of Orient Are'.

'What a darling girl!' Mom exclaimed as we scurried towards the hotel entrance on Park Avenue. 'Have you slept with her?'

'No! She's my super, for God's sake!'

'What does that have to do with anything? She's obviously totally infatuated with you.'

'I'm not sleeping with her,' I said.

'Well, who *are* you sleeping with?'

'Nobody.'

Mom let out a sound – maybe surprise – and I didn't know if it was because she didn't believe me or because we'd just entered the hotel lobby and was overwhelmed. 'Oh!' she exclaimed, stopping to stare. As she was taking it all in, she said, 'What about that person on the phone?'

'What person on the phone?'

'Someone called while I was in the bathroom. Josh, was it?'

'You sure have good ears,' I said.

'Is he someone special?' Mom asked.

'Yes. Sort of. We've gone out a couple of times.'

'And you haven't slept with him either?'

'No.'

'But he's tried to –?'

'Actually, Mom, he hasn't. He was sleeping with my boss, if you want to know the truth.'

'Susanna Hyde?' Mom turned her glittering face to me, eyes wide, eager to hear more. 'Did he drop her or did she drop him? I won't tell a soul,' she whispered.

'Mom, we've got to hurry, OK? Please. I'll tell you later.'

'Everyone's always hurrying here,' she complained. 'Who is it you're meeting?'

'Just a guy.'

'Just a guy. Someone you're dating?'

'No – I'm just bringing him up to the party. Hurry, will you?'

'Sweetheart, I can't walk any faster in these heels. What's his name?'

'Nick Burden?' I said to a short man wearing dark glasses and a stylish suit. He was waiting, as planned, near the giant Christmas tree in the lobby.

Nick Burden didn't say anything but stepped towards me and headed towards the bank of elevators.

'Wait!' Mom said. 'I have to use the little girls' room.' She darted away before I could stop her.

So we waited, silently, Nick Burden and I.

He had a manner – or a non-manner – that warded off any attempt at conversation. He was a very short man with an almost palpable air of arrogance that he used to puff up the space around him and make himself look larger, or maybe just unapproachable. His pitted face was covered with some kind of flesh-colored make-up that was probably supposed to hide the pits but only made them more noticeable. His dark wraparound sunglasses were so dark that it was impossible to tell what he was looking at. He gave me the creeps, but we were bound together because I'd let Susanna talk me into smuggling Nick Burden into a party he'd otherwise be banned from attending. It was through me that he'd be able to take those photos of Susanna arriving with Lord Farrell Stuckey.

Why on earth were those photos so important to her? Did she need them to prove to herself that she'd truly scaled the highest pinnacle of social and professional prestige?

The hotel lobby was blissfully warm so I slipped off my quilted coat. The moment I did so, I was aware that Nick Burden's head flicked in my direction and he was staring at me behind those impenetrable dark glasses.

I cleared my throat. 'So where's your camera?'

He turned away, as if I'd deeply offended him by speaking.

'If you're a photographer, you have to have a camera, don't you?' For some reason I'd pictured him with a bunch of cameras slung around his neck. But I didn't see a single one.

Nick Burden reached into his trouser pocket and pulled out what I thought was a cellphone. He flipped it open. Turned in my direction. Pressed a tiny button. 'Gotcher,' he whispered. 'Too bad you're not a celeb.'

Standing in the back of the elevator, behind a laughing, chattering, excited crowd of partygoers, we silently made our way up to the Twilight Ballroom. We were packed in as tight as the subway at rush hour, so I wasn't sure if Nick Burden's hand was pressed against my thigh on purpose or because he had no room to move it. But I had my suspicions.

'Oh my God!' Mom cried as we stepped off the elevator. 'It's gorgeous!'

And it was. For once she wasn't exaggerating.

The Twilight Ballroom had just been reopened after a two-year refurbishment to restore its original Art Deco splendor. Back in the 1920s and 1930s it had been the most glamorous nightclub in Manhattan. Then, as fashions changed, it had all been covered up. They'd rediscovered it, completely intact, hidden behind an ugly Fifties façade.

Mom took my hand and we gazed up at the enormous crystal chandeliers, the high, vaulted ceilings, the twenty-foot-high windows hung with velvet curtains. There was a dance floor and a bar where people were lined up for drinks, and a second floor reached by a long curving gold staircase cordoned off with a golden rope.

Suspended from the ceiling were enormous full-color images of the covers of all the magazines and best-selling books published by Stuckey Universal Media. The high-res images, projected on giant screens, were constantly changing and switching from one screen to another. The December cover of *Peeper* featured Cupcake Cassidy wearing a Mrs Santa Claus outfit that would have been quite chilly in the North Pole. Then I spotted a giant image of Susanna – the new Susanna, the Susanna of the publicity photos taken by Giles Travaille and distributed by me to celebrity gossip outlets earlier that afternoon. I couldn't quite figure out why Susanna's image was up there until publicity photos of other celebrity authors began to appear.

The room reverberated with the hum of voices and laughter. A band was playing a medley of holiday tunes.

Mom turned and stared at everything like a little girl. 'It's like a dream,' she whispered, squeezing my hand. 'I never in a million years thought I'd finally get on a plane and come to New York and see – this.'

I knew what she meant. For a moment I was caught up in the magic of New York and a world lived on a far grander scale than anything I'd ever known. There was a sense that powerful forces were at play, forces that were allowing us, mere mortals, to glimpse and participate in their power.

Over a thousand people were scheduled to attend and

security was tight. Lord Stuckey, because of all the media he controlled, was one of the wealthiest and most powerful men in the world. That meant he had enemies, seen and unseen.

Mom and I checked our coats and then, with Nick Burden wedged between us, made our way towards the barricade of tables where we had to register before moving past the security guards.

The puffed-up arrogance Nick Burden emitted downstairs vanished as we approached the check-in table. He donned an affable smile that I knew was fake and stayed partially hidden behind me.

'Venus!'

I turned and saw Dorcas and Sharanda standing way back in the line.

'Who?' they were asking through facial expressions and hand signals. They meant who was the short ugly man in dark glasses and who was the plus-sized woman with blinking earrings and red glitter on her face. I made a vague gesture indicating that I'd meet them inside and then turned back around.

I was both excited and apprehensive and my heart was beating fast. Four women and a man were handling the registration, working from laptops. I didn't know any of them, which was good. Our turn came. We got the man. I smiled and gave him my name.

'Venus Gilroy,' he repeated, scrolling through a list on his laptop. 'Here it is. And your guests are?'

'Her mother.' Mom stepped forward and introduced herself. 'Carolee Gilroy. From Portland, Oregon.'

The man stared at her glittery red face as if he weren't quite sure what he was seeing. 'OK. And he's –'

I leaned forward, trying to evade Mom's hearing. 'My husband.'

'Mr Gilroy?'

Nick Burden nodded and smiled.

Mom opened her mouth and said, 'Sweetheart, did I hear you say—?'

I whirled around with a high-pitched laugh, drowning her out before she could say more. 'Ready to boogie, Mom?'

She squinted at me through her supersize glasses. 'Did you say—?'

'Come on, let's go through and get a drink.' I turned back to the guy checking us in. 'I work for Susanna Hyde. She told me I could bring both of them. She said she'd arranged it.'

He looked at his screen. 'You're all set. Open bar at the end of the dance floor. Dinner upstairs but not served until nine. They'll make an announcement.'

Nick Burden scooted in front of me, smiling at the security guards eyeballing everyone who passed by. By the time Mom and I passed them, the mysterious Nick Burden had vanished into the crowd.

'Where did your *husband* go?' Mom asked as we crossed the dance floor on our way to the bar.

'I just had to say that to get him in.'

'Why?'

'As a favor to someone. Just forget it now, OK?'

'I'm glad you're not married to him,' Mom said. 'He pinched my ass in the elevator.'

'He did?'

'Well, more like fondled it. I'm glad he wasn't being unfaithful to you.'

We nabbed a couple of hors d'oeuvres – smoked lox and cream cheese on crunchy little crackers – from a passing server and then waited in line for drinks. I was hyperaware that people were staring in our direction, but I wasn't sure if it was because Mom looked ridiculous or because I looked fabulous.

'I think you're happy with your life in New York,' Mom said, picking something off the back of my dress.

'I like it here. I've learned so much.'

'It's changed you,' Mom said. 'Or maybe you've changed you.'

I wasn't going to dispute that.

'Don't worry,' Mom said reassuringly, misinterpreting my artfully mussed hair and trying to smooth it down. 'Someone new will come along.'

I pushed her hand away. 'I'm not worried about it.' And I realized, with a jolt of something that felt like pride, that I wasn't. Tremaynne was gone, out of my life, and no amount of wishing would bring him back. That left a big empty space at my side, just waiting to be filled by . . . Josh, maybe? Or Giles, possibly? Or Mary-Joseph, conceivably?

Or maybe all three. Whitman said I was a 'serial monogamist', gluing myself on to one person after another. Maybe now it was time for me to change that old pattern and adopt a multi-lover approach.

'I've learned so much from writing my memoir,' Mom said. 'You should try it.'

'Right,' I said. 'What would I call it? *My Three Husbands*?'

'You have nothing to be ashamed of,' Mom said. 'Lots of women have been married three times.'

'Before they're twenty-five?'

'Rita Hawley, my teacher, says that writing a memoir is the best way to forgive yourself.'

Finally we reached the bar. Mom ordered something called a Tequila Mockingbird. I asked for champagne. We took our drinks and headed back into the crowd milling around the dance floor.

'I can't wait to boogie,' Mom said, surveying the crowd with a hopeful smile. 'There weren't any men in my ecstatic dancing class. It was all women.'

'Maybe you should try women again,' I said. 'Get back into the swing of things. If a man's not available—'

'Well, you know me, sweetheart – open to alternatives. The goddess will provide. But none of those women appealed to me, somehow. There has to be a spark. You know, like what you have with Mary-Joseph or that Josh person you're so tight-lipped about. I'm sure there are others, too,' she hinted, 'that you haven't had time to tell me about.'

'Hey!' Giles, with glazed eyes and a drink in his hand, made his way towards us. He looked a little unsteady on his feet. 'Venus!' he said, eyeing me up and down. 'You look ravishing.'

Which prompted a loud, high-pitched titter from Mom, who stared like an infatuated schoolgirl at Giles and said, 'She does, doesn't she?'

'You look stoned,' I said to Giles.

'Do I? Well, I'm actually stoned and drunk with a coke chaser.'

Mom let loose with another round of high-pitched laughter and turned to me. 'Better be careful of this one, sweetheart. He looks dangerous.'

Giles looked at her, trying to focus his gaze. 'Who's this glittering approsition – appasition – apparition?'

'This is my mother, Carolee. Mom, this is Giles Travaille. He's an art director.'

'Ooooh!' Mom was highly impressed. 'An artist!'

'No,' Giles shook his head, 'an art director.'

'What's the difference?' Mom asked.

'A pay cheque.' Giles leaned forward and said in a low, confidential, boozy-smelling voice, 'Not that you'll be impressed, Venus, but you're looking at the man who's soon to be executriv – *executive* group design director for all of Stuckey Universal Media worldwide.'

Mom let out an appreciative gasp. 'Wow! That sounds important!'

'You're leaving *Peeper*?' I asked.

'*Peeper*?' Mom drew back and looked at me. 'Isn't that a girlie magazine?'

Giles ignored her. His eyes were busy licking me up, like I was a big piece of eye candy. If he hadn't been so high and slurry, I would have enjoyed his attention. 'I am leaving *Peeper*,' he said to me, 'but *Peeper* is not leaving me, if you get my drift.'

'I don't,' I said.

'I will determine the look and control the image content of every magazine that Stuckey publishes. *Aura*, *Peeper*, *Lifestyle Home*. The whole lot.'

'That's quite a promotion,' I said.

Giles half closed his eyes, took a deep breath, and smiled a huge, rapturous smile that illuminated his entire face. 'Only, look here, it's not public yet, so you mustn't breathe a word. Promise?'

'Promise.'

'Cross your heart if you've got one.'

I crossed my heart.

'I'll cross mine too,' Carolee said.

Giles looked from her to me and back to Mom, his head weaving a bit. 'Seeing the two of you's given me a fantastic idea. A mother-daughter spread. Whudayou think?'

'I think it's kind of disgusting,' I said.

'Have to go.' Giles gave me a smooch. 'Cupcake's waiting.' He gave Mom a kiss too, and walked away with glitter on his lips.

Mom and I turned to follow his departure. 'What a handsome man,' Mom said. 'I love that accent.' When I didn't reply, she turned and gave me a Meaningful Glance. 'He seems to like you an awful lot.'

'He likes a lot of women an awful lot.' I watched Giles weaving and glad-handing his way into the crowd and I wished he wasn't drunk and stoned and coked up, because for some weird reason that made me feel sorry for him instead of infatuated, which I might otherwise have been. He was someone who could have it all if he didn't self-destruct along the way. I recognized that self-destructive streak because I'd seen it in JD and other friends who were creative and cool until they sank into alcoholism and drug addiction. In a fairytale Giles would fall in love with me, and only me, and I'd help him to change his ways (right, said a mocking voice in my head, you're so good at moderation) and I'd walk through this sophisticated New York crowd on his arm, both of us proud and happy and flush with success. A couple. Maybe one of those power couples the gossip columns reported on.

But I had a feeling that Giles had already forgotten me. He was like a kid in an eye-candy store, and I suspected that the very last thing he wanted to do was change. Right now the world was his, or about to be.

Cupcake may have been waiting for Giles but she certainly wasn't waiting alone. She was wearing the skimpy Mrs Santa Claus outfit she wore on the December cover of *Peeper* and a crowd of men had clustered around her, smiling like lucky elves in Santa's workshop.

'What a cute outfit,' Mom said. 'I wonder if she made it herself.'

I was sitting in a stall in the busy ladies' room, taking a breather from Mom and the endless rush of the day, when I heard a loud, aggrieved voice out by the mirrors say, 'I just wanna know why *her* photo's up there and none of the other editors.'

'It's not because she's an editor,' another voice said, 'it's because she's an author.'

'It's because she's a fucking bitch,' the first voice said bitterly. It sounded like Eldora Button but I couldn't be sure.

'She's got another book coming out,' the second voice said, 'and Sybilla told me Stuckey ordered them to do a major PR campaign.'

'Well, she's fucking him, isn't she.' This was a statement, not a question. 'How the hell do you think she got to be editor? She doesn't give a shit about *Aura*. It's just a stepping stone.'

'She got the advertising revenues up,' the second voice conceded.

'She got old Stuckey up, that's what she did.'

They shared a soft, nasty titter.

'Is his wife going to be here tonight?' the second voice asked. 'Lady Stuckey? I heard she always comes to these things.'

'Yeah. They like to enter like they're royalty.'

'They are, aren't they?'

And the rest was lost as they opened the door and their voices were sucked into the general roar of the party.

*

You know how it is with big events. As drinks were drunk and the mingle factor escalated, so did the noise level. It was so crowded that I managed to avoid meeting Dorcas and Sharanda until just before nine.

'That's an interesting effect,' Sharanda said, indicating my mom's glittery face.

'Isn't it fun?' Mom said. 'It's called GlitterUp. I found it online.'

'So where's Susanna?' Dorcas asked me.

'Yes,' Mom said, 'I want to meet the famous Susanna Hyde. I just love her column,' she said in a confidential aside to Dorcas and Sharanda, clueless that they hated Susanna's guts. 'I've learned so much from it.'

'Like what?' Sharanda asked. 'How to have fun with an enema bag?'

'Apparently a lot of men like that,' Mom whispered, shaking her head. 'I never would have known. That's what I mean.'

'Who was the little guy in dark glasses?' Dorcas asked, insatiable as ever for details.

'Oh,' Mom said, 'that was Nick—'

'*Rick*,' I said quickly, giving her a shut-up look. 'Rick Frick. He's an old friend.'

'Well,' Dorcas said, 'there he is.'

I looked over and just managed to catch a glimpse of Nick Burden edging his way towards the grand staircase when the lights suddenly went down. Startled, the crowd fell silent for a fraction of a moment, just long enough for an amplified professional announcer's voice to excitedly proclaim: 'Ladies and gentlemen, your host and hostess for this evening – Lord Farrell Stuckey and Miss Susanna Hyde.'

As the band played the first few bars of 'New York, New York', a spotlight bloomed at the top of the staircase and there they were, Lord Stuckey and my boss, Susanna, standing side by side, beaming down at the crowd below.

And there they were, too, on all the giant, suspended screens, their images projected and magnified like pop stars.

Dorcas, Sharanda, and women all around me gasped in disbelief.

It was perfectly engineered. The employees had to applaud for their generous employer, Lord Stuckey, and, by extension, for Susanna. All those gasping, gawking women may have despised her, but now they'd also been officially advised that Susanna was their hostess.

Lord Stuckey was handed a microphone, but I can't remember what he said. Something about 'the pride of our Stuckey universal family' and 'raising the bar of excellence worldwide', and 'embracing the changing media landscape'. He wasn't a great or particularly inspiring speaker, but everyone acted as if he were. It was so quiet you could hear a pin drop.

My attention was focused on Susanna, standing beside him like a silent, smiling presenter at the Academy Awards. She truly was transformed, and that was partly why the women around me gasped. She'd made herself into someone who knew she would be looked at. She'd created for herself a reproducible media image. Her hair was up, her décolletage prominent, her face – at least from this distance – oddly youthful.

I wondered if Lord Stuckey would let her speak.

He did.

She did her best to defuse the jealousy, derision and incredulity she must have felt emanating from a sizeable portion of the crowd. She made a couple of self-deprecating jokes and then spoke briefly of her 'truly honest thrill' to be associated in such a 'hands-on way' (this phrase provoked some unintended laughter) with Stuckey Universal Media.

In some weird way I was proud of her. I think I was probably the only one who felt that way.

She handed the microphone back to Lord Stuckey and stepped back, out of the spotlight, as he invited his thousand guests to come up to the second floor and enjoy a good roast beef dinner.

As the crowd surged towards the staircase – Lord Stuckey

and Susanna were waiting at the top to shake everyone's hand before they were seated – I looked around and saw Nick Burden slip away, a phantom gliding through darkness before daylight arrives.

How could I have known? There's no way I could have known. About Nick Burden's photos, I mean.

Now, of course, I know. But, as the old year was fading into the new, and I was still finding bits of red glitter left behind by Mom, I didn't know. It's not that I was naïve, exactly. I simply couldn't imagine the lengths some people would go to in their quest for money, power and fame.

There was a huge hoo-ha at Stuckey Universal Media when the photos surfaced. First the newspaper images were passed surreptitiously around the office, then scanned and sent as e-mails. When I received one from Dorcas, with the terse message 'Screwing up?' in the subject line, I knew she was suggesting that Susanna had slept her way to the top. I wasn't outraged, as Dorcas apparently was. I knew Susanna was friends with Lord Stuckey, and maybe his mistress. Why the big fuss? All the images did was confirm what everyone had already seen at the party: the two of them standing together, as a couple.

I was Susanna's accomplice in all this, sworn to secrecy. And though I didn't believe I'd done anything wrong, all the fuss made me wonder if Susanna had left out some essential piece of information when she'd first enlisted my help. Because what I found out later on was that Lord Stuckey was protective of his public image to the point of paranoia. The lord of media did everything in his considerable power to prevent his image from being captured and reproduced.

Exceptions were occasionally made for his own publications, but if the occasion was a public one, he was *always* seen in the company of his wife. So a picture showing him side by side with Susanna, both of them smiling and royally waving, was a major breach of Lord Stuckey's privacy, and Susanna must have known that.

Some of Nick Burden's photographs appeared in the New York papers (with headlines like 'Stuckey Steps Out'). Others were published in various London tabloids, accompanied by brief stories suggesting that Lord Stuckey was leaving his wife of fifty years for Susanna Hyde, who was usually called a 'sexpert' or a 'sexpot' or a 'sex columnist'. Her role as editor of *Aura* was never mentioned. One article, with the headline 'Hair Apparent' and a photo of a perfectly coiffed Susanna laughing at Lord Stuckey's side, hinted that Lord Stuckey was going to make Miss Hyde editor-in-chief of his entire New York media operations.

Susanna didn't seem particularly concerned by her sudden notoriety and the innuendoes in the press. She seemed to enjoy it. 'It sells papers,' she said matter-of-factly.

That was true. It was also true that it splashed her new image and her name into the public viewfinder. And that, of course, wouldn't hurt when the time came for her to do her cross-country book tour for *Puppy Love*.

Her memoir, I soon discovered, had a subtitle: *Loving a Younger Man*. I found this out when all those New York gossip columnists I was always delivering her notes to began to mention Susanna's 'eagerly awaited memoir' in their columns. Was Josh that 'younger man' in the subtitle? He'd suspected that Susanna was writing about him, or them. I was dying to know, but Susanna was keeping mum about the book, at least to me.

One day, while all this was going on, Josh called me at the office. 'Sorry I haven't been in touch,' he said. 'Between working and writing, I just don't seem to have any time.'

'You have a job?'

He let out a scornful huff. 'Pph. Yeah. Cleaning apartments. Fifteen bucks an hour and all the dirt I can eat.'

'That's more than I make.'

'It sucks,' Josh said, 'but at least it's not a career job where they want me to work sixty hours a week and pay me for forty.'

He asked if I'd like to meet him for coffee after work. It was one of the rare nights when I was actually free to leave before seven, so I said yes. And smiled as I hung up the phone.

It was mid-January by then, and everyone was complaining about how cold, gray and miserable New York was. I suppose it was – but those New York midwinter blues just didn't get to me. Everything was still a fresh adventure, exciting, eternally new.

Except for the emotions that got stirred up when I left work and hurried down a dark midtown street to meet Josh. Those weren't new. I recognized them for what they were – a kind of romantic longing. That surprised me. And kind of irritated me, too, because I realized what I was doing: trying to ignite Josh into a flame that would warm and illuminate my heart.

I saw Josh before he saw me. He was outside the Starbucks on Fifth Avenue, across from the library, pacing back and forth like a caged animal and blowing into his gloveless hands to keep them warm. My heart gave a little stutter. Josh was wearing the wool scarf I'd given him.

I whipped off my Chinese aviator's hat and shook out my hair, which was now so long I could wear it in a thick, easy-care ponytail. But when I saw my image in a shop window, some old insecure voice in my head said, You look terrible, lose the ponytail. My hand flew up and grabbed the elastic band. And then – it was the weirdest thing – this conflicting voice or feeling or whatever it was told me not to touch or change a thing. If Josh liked me, a ponytail wasn't going to change his mind.

But old habits die hard, and I found myself fretting about my clothes – what Josh would see when I removed my Michelin-White Queen down-filled coat. I had on red woollen tights beneath a black one-piece Mod dress from the Sixties that I'd found for twenty-five dollars in Bygone Fashion, a used clothing store way downtown. The dress was wool, mid-thigh, with red leather piping down the sides and at the top. My fur-lined, rhinestone-studded cowboy boots were too clunky for the sleek style of the dress, but they kept my feet nice and toasty.

'Venus.' He didn't smile. But those green eyes looked greener than ever, inviting as a summer field where you just want to lie down and loll.

'Hi, Josh.' I gave him a quick peck on the cheek, New York-style. 'How are you?'

'Freezing,' he said. 'Let's go inside.'

Josh ordered the cheapest thing he possibly could, a small cup of filtered coffee, so I did the same, even though I was already buzzing with caffeine. 'I'll get this,' he said, pulling out a woefully thin wallet. 'I'm a rich man now that I'm cleaning apartments. I can almost afford to eat.'

'Thanks, Josh.'

'We could even split a chocolate chip cookie if you wanted to.'

'Sure.'

I was hyperaware of how thick my coat was and how loud it rustled as we made our way to a table. When I took it off, I felt like I was emerging from a thick, soft cocoon.

'So – ' Josh said when we sat down. 'How are things with Susanna?'

'Fine. Hectic.' I didn't mention the photographs or the frenzy of speculation they'd created in the office. Not everything had to revolve around Susanna.

Josh sipped his coffee, munched his half of the cookie, and silently studied me over the rim of the cup. 'Do you know who her agent is?' he finally asked.

'Her name's Grace Glickman. Why?'

'Just curious.' He threw me a curious, inquisitive glance. 'I see her name in all the rags.'

Now I was silent.

'So she's Stuckey's mistress, huh?'

I shrugged, wondering if he saw me at all. Or was I nothing more than a conduit to gain information about Susanna?

'She was fucking him when she was fucking me,' Josh said, studying me like a prosecutor.

'Josh, I don't know.'

'And why was she fucking me? So she could write about it.'

'How do you know she *did* write about it?'

'Because someone I went to college with works in the books division at Stuckey Universal Media, and he happened to get his hands on a bound galley of Susanna's memoir. Haven't *you* read it?' Josh asked, and made a face of surprise when I said no. 'Well,' he said, 'she doesn't use my name, of course. But it's me. It's us. Susanna and me.'

'And what? It's horrible? Embarrassing?'

'Yeah, and completely untrue,' Josh said.

'Then how can you say it's you?'

'Because there's enough there to figure it out. But most of it's fabricated. Whole conversations made up, situations altered, time frame compressed. She comes out the winner, of course.' He gave the scarf around his neck – my scarf – a sharp, angry tug.

I put my lips to my coffee but couldn't drink it; eyed my half of the cookie but couldn't bring myself to pick it up. I was trying to figure out a way to extricate myself before I got pulled in any deeper. Josh wasn't interested in me. He was obsessed with Susanna. I was nothing more than his sounding board. He probably didn't even remember that I'd given him that scarf.

'Jesus,' he said, shaking his head, 'was I a fool or what? I think I'm helping her out at a party, but she's just using me to serve drinks. A butler! Her lover, serving drinks to her other lover. It's like some weird French novel.'

I gathered up my hat, scarf and mittens. 'Josh, I have to go.'

His face fell with what looked like genuine disappointment. 'Hey. You just got here.'

I nodded. 'Josh, I'm sorry about what happened between you and Susanna. But I don't want to sit here and talk about it. She's still my boss. And you know' – I hesitated, then decided I had nothing to lose – 'your motives weren't exactly spotless either.'

He stiffened. 'What do you mean?'

'I mean that you went after Susanna the same way she went after you. Only she wasn't material for a memoir –'

'Not then,' Josh said under his breath.

'She was someone you thought might help you get your book published.'

'More fool I,' he said bitterly.

'So no one's motives are pure here. You were both after something.' I didn't say any of this in an angry way. I wasn't judging Josh. I was just pointing out to him something that he had conveniently overlooked.

'It's just fucked, that's all.' Josh jammed his hands in his coat pockets and sat back scowling in his chair. 'And it wasn't like she *pretends* it was, in her memoir. Because you know what? Susanna Hyde, who spends her life writing about sex, and portrays herself as this earthy, artful, experienced lover, is totally frigid.'

'Josh, I have to go –'

'Wait.' One of his hands shot out and grabbed my arm. 'I'm sorry. Stay.'

His voice was soft. He sounded like he meant it. I sat back down.

'Venus, I really like you,' he said.

That was a toughie. Four words so fraught with meaning that they could dissolve resolve and jumpstart a rusting heart.

'You're everything she's not,' he said, his eyes aglow. 'You're real. Honest.'

My heart was like a dry sponge soaking up the liquid of his words. Would he tell me I was beautiful, too?

'What you said – about our motives – was really insightful.'

I tried not to glow.

'I'm as big a shit as she is,' Josh said thoughtfully. He looked at me and smiled. 'So thanks.'

'For what?'

'Helping me see that. It's going to make it so much easier.'

'Make what easier?'

Those green eyes were staring off into space – the inner

space where writers go when they're mentally composing. 'I've already got the first line,' Josh said.

That January, Susanna's schedule went from fast to frenetic. Which meant that mine did, too.

It's what happens when a person becomes a celebrity. It was like a giant wave just took her up and shot her forward and she had to balance on its crest, like a surfer.

I don't know when she slept, or how, given all that was going on. A whole new deluge of names and telephone numbers and e-mail addresses had to be programmed into our matching BlackBerries. The phone rang constantly. She was in for Nonna, out for Caspar, on another line when Fenicia rang. These were the very same gossip columnists I'd been delivering her 'notes' to.

'I don't speak to assistants,' Susanna informed me. 'Got that? *No assistants*.'

One morning after her editorial meeting she called me back into her office and asked if I knew how to drive.

'Sure. Why?'

'If I got a town car, would you be interested in driving it?'

I looked at that strange new Susanna-but-not-quite face of hers, trying to figure this one out. 'What do you mean, driving it?'

'*Driving* it,' she said. 'Driving *me*.'

'You mean, like your chauffeur?'

'My *driver*.'

'What about the office?'

'When it's time, I'll hire someone else to take care of the basics. You'll move up a notch. We'll call you senior administrative assistant.'

I was really befuddled and didn't know what to say. Driving the boss around didn't seem like it would fit into any job description for senior administrative assistant.

Susanna must have sensed my confusion, for she said, in that impatient way of hers, 'It's just a *title*, for God's sake. With more pay. An extra hundred dollars a week. You'll still be my

PA, do all the scheduling, and continue writing "Nothing to Hyde", but you'll also drive me around when I need to go someplace.'

Four hundred extra dollars a month. It seemed like a fortune – but then it would, to me, who'd never earned more than minimum wage before moving to New York.

'You're going to be doing this sort of thing on the book tour,' she reminded me. 'It will be good practice.'

I heard Frank Sinatra singing that famous line from 'New York, New York': 'If I can make it here, I'll make it anywhere . . .' I thought of all I could do with four hundred extra dollars a month. I thought, with a ping of excitement, of driving again, this time in New York.

'I'll do it for five hundred,' I said, amazed at my audacity.

Susanna was startled, I think, but that new face of hers wasn't terribly good at registering surprise or emotions of any kind. 'Five hundred what?'

'Dollars. A month. One twenty-five a week more.'

'You drive a hard bargain,' she said.

'I'm a good driver.'

Was that a smile? The newly enlarged lips seemed to move up a notch in the corners. 'All right. But the secret to all bargaining is never to leave the table feeling bested. So I'll give you the hundred and twenty-five if you'll agree not to tell anyone in this office building about the car or your driving it. It's none of their bloody business. You work for me, not for them.'

Again I had that fleeting sense that she was withholding some essential piece of information, as she had when she first enlisted my help with Nick Burden. But it faded when she put out her hand and said, 'Deal?'

'Deal.'

Picture me then, behind the wheel of a shiny black Lincoln town car, expertly navigating the pothole-strewn streets of New York in all weathers and all traffic conditions. I, who had barely been able to make the monthly payments on my battered wreck of a used Toyota, now glided down Fifth Avenue or Park behind tinted windows, glancing at the global positioning system or programming Map Quest on the dashboard computer if I got lost.

Which I never did, so long as we stayed in Manhattan, which was almost always.

Despite my new commitment to walking and using public transportation, the West Coast girl in me was secretly thrilled to be behind the wheel again, even if it was just to pilot my cosmetically enhanced boss around a city that had become her playground.

Susanna always sat in the back, of course. She was usually on her BlackBerry, talking or texting as we went. She rarely spoke to me except to schedule appointments or issue orders. Her incoming calls still came through my BlackBerry so I was kind of a mobile receptionist, putting through the important calls and taking messages. I wore an earclip for this task so my hands would be free for driving.

Where did we go? To appointments in midtown that Susanna could have walked to in less time than it took to drive. To special stores and boutiques and salons and spas and restaurants and museums and theatres and grand apartment buildings and exclusive townhouses and famous hotels. To lots of black-tie galas and red-carpet charity events.

An air of exclusivity now permeated everything Susanna did. She'd become celebrity-mad, the way all celebrities do. I heard her excitedly dropping names and relaying pieces of gossip in what sounded like an endless game of Who's Important Today. Important was important in Susanna's life. Fame was the yardstick by which everything was measured. People would lure her to parties or charity events with the promise of meeting a celebrity. Famous Names were dangled like diamonds.

I was the conduit to Susanna, and Susanna was the conduit to Lord Farrell Stuckey, one of the richest and most powerful men in the world. It wasn't too hard to figure out that a large part of her heightened celebrity appeal was based on the assumption that she was Lord Stuckey's soon-to-be wife. Susanna herself did nothing to disavow that notion and at times even encouraged it. She was like a royal mistress impatiently waiting the death of the queen so she could ascend the throne.

To be fair to Susanna, she did have a measure of celebrity status before any of Nick Burden's Stuckey-Susanna photos appeared. But in the cruelly competitive world of Big Name Fame, she was relegated to the minor leagues. 'Mid-range on the B-list,' as Whitman later put it.

All that had now changed. Her life had changed. It was interesting and informative to watch it happen, to see how the mechanics of fame operated, to note all the planning and manipulation it took to gain celebrity and then retain it.

From what I could tell, people who played the Fame Game were obsessed with seeing their names in print and having their images recognized. They lived for photo ops and spent obscene amounts of money to make themselves presentable to any interested camera. Some of them had talent, even major talent, but many of them did not. Some of them had once done something but no longer did anything except be famous. Some had nothing to recommend them for the celebrity circuit except money or an inherited name or title. There were several ex-wives of billionaires, the ex-husband's name their only calling card. There were ex-convicts and victims of high-profile crimes, like the cheating garden-store owner who, after his wife lopped off his *penis erectus* with a hedge clipper, had it reattached and went on to star in a porn film called *Cock on the Walk*. People under criminal investigation were always welcome, provided their case was big enough to warrant the front page of the Metro section. Politicians were plentiful.

Lots of these people drank a lot or did drugs. Lots of them were really mean.

Well, fame is a cruel mistress everyone adores. If they knew what an awful person fame was, they'd still adore her.

As Susanna's driver, I was one of those invisible minions who help the famous play their game. I discovered there were hundreds of us, probably thousands, unseen behind every scene. Drivers, caterers, waitstaff, florists, electricians, lighting specialists, bartenders, coat checkers, red-carpet layers and erectors of event tents. While the famous bared their sparkling teeth and posed for photographers and waved to one another and picked at their food, the rest of us waited for their famous night to end and maybe snuck a quick smoke outside the service entrance. The dregs were ours. We spirited away the leftover chicken cutlets, the half-empty bottles of wine, the stray goody bag left behind on a chair.

The waste. Oh my God, the waste. You could get fat on it.

After dropping off Susanna at an event, I was free until she called for me to pick her up again. That meant finding a place to park and killing anywhere from fifteen minutes to four hours. Sometimes, at special events, parking places were provided, and all the drivers would hang out together. I liked most of the guys, and they seemed to like me, maybe because I was the only female. I shot the bull with them but shut my mouth when the subject turned, as it always did, to employers.

Some of the drivers were called butlers but treated like indentured servants, given room and board in exchange for being on call 24/7/365. They described, with a mixture of admiration and resentment, their employers' lavish lifestyles, one-upping one another with their descriptions of spectacular country estates, fabulous apartments, enormous yachts and celebrity-laden parties where they'd had the honor of mixing special Martinis for some drunken movie star or celebrity.

More often than not, their bosses were abusive, vindictive, miserly (except when it came to their own endless wants), selfish, and incredibly petty. The richer they were, the worse they behaved. But the guys working for them – the drivers and butlers – put up with the mean-spirited cruelties as if that behavior was all right so long as you were rich and famous.

I learned a lot from those guys. Like, I never wanted to turn into one of them.

And I got really tired of their stories and what their stories told me about them and the world of the super-rich. When you're looking in at the rich and famous from the outside, you see only their 'glamour'. But when you're watching them from the inside, like I was, you see how heartless and horrible most of them really are.

I liked the drivers, but they reminded me of hamsters on a wheel, always running but getting nowhere. So instead of hanging out with them, I found someplace else to wait for Susanna.

While I was waiting, I opened my laptop, and wrote.

Or tried to.

By then I was pretty good at ghosting Susanna's 'Nothing to Hyde' column. I'd read her books and enough of her old columns to be able to mimic her style. If there was one thing I knew about, after three marriages, it was sex. I enjoyed it so much – the writing, I mean, but also sex – that I was several months ahead of schedule with the column.

That left me time to work on something else. Because – it occurred to me one day like a flash from heaven – *I was no longer a slacker*. The sad, aimless girl I'd been in Portland, continually broke and living on the edge of crisis, hoping that some man would come along and save her from herself, that girl was gone. I missed her occasionally, but less and less. Even Mom had commented on the new me. Before she left, after our Christmas together, she looked at me and shook her head and said, 'You're a different person. You seem to have so much more *control*.'

Well, it was far more intriguing to live the life I was leading now, working for Susanna, than to spend my entire existence looking for a new mate and slogging away at some repetitious, minimum-wage job.

In my free minutes and hours, sitting in the Lincoln town car, I began to write something that was not for Susanna but for me.

I didn't try to label it and I didn't inflate it with high-minded literary hopes. I just wanted to get it down on paper, to see if I could do it. I called it *My Three Husbands*. I guess you could call it a memoir, in that everything in it had happened to me.

On paper, or rather on the computer screen, the life I'd lived looked unbelievable. It was a weird, weird, *weird* experience and it gave me a new appreciation for writers. For the first time in my life I was on the inside of a book instead of the outside. Creating it out of me. Fumbling along. Deleting sentences, paragraphs, whole pages. Daring myself to write it down as it had happened. Looking for humor that I hadn't felt at the time.

Analyzing myself in the process. Externalizing what I'd lugged around in private, locked in my heart and soul.

I told no one. Not even Whitman or Daddy. They were both in it, and so was my mom, and so were my three ex-husbands and my one lesbian lover, JD.

One cold, sleety night in early February, I was scheduled to pick up Susanna at a SoHo nightclub called Loose, where she'd been attending the launch party for a new rock CD produced and distributed by Stuckey Universal Media. I pulled up and waited with the doors locked and the heater on but Susanna didn't show.

It was late, I was tired, and the stuffy warmth of the car made me so sleepy I could barely keep my eyes open. Until someone suddenly banged on the passenger-side window and shouted, 'Hey! Open up!'

It was a wet, womanless Giles. When I unlocked the door and he stuck his head in, the smell of booze and cigarettes rushed in with him.

Once I loved that stale, bar-roomy smell. Don't ask me why, but I found it comforting. And it still held some lopsided romantic memories for me.

' 'Ey, love,' he said in a deep, hoarse voice, sliding into the front and slamming the door. 'What are you doin 'ere?'

'Waiting for Susanna.'

'Oh. Right.'

'Did you see Susanna? Is she on her way?'

Giles laughed. 'Ar' mate, Susanner's on 'er way. We bofe are. On our fuckin' way.'

The booze had really transformed him. I could barely understand a word he said. I figured he was putting on a working-class accent for fun.

'I hope she comes soon,' I said, yawning. 'I'm tired and I want to get home.'

'Oh, she's not –' He pursed his lips and blinked, trying to remember something. 'She's stuckey with Stuckey. 'E's bringing er 'ome.'

'You sure?'

'Hey, Venus, do a line with me.' He fumbled in his coat pocket and drew out a packet of white powder.

'No thanks. Look, if she's not coming, I'd like to get going.'

'Well,' he said with a wave of his hand, 'less go.'

I sat there not knowing what I should do. 'I mean, I want to get the car back to the garage, so I can go home.'

'I'm on East 81st Street, juss off Madison. Less go.'

'You mean I should drive you home?'

'You're a drivuh, ain'tcha?'

'I'm Susanna's driver.'

'Yeah, well, Susanner's stuckey with Stuckey an' said you'd tike me 'ome.'

'Giles, the garage is on 44th Street. If I take you home, that's almost forty blocks out of my way.' He sat there, tapping his packet of coke, not saying anything. 'Then I'd have to drive back to the garage and take a subway from there.' He remained silent. 'How about if I take you up to 44th Street and you get a cab from there. Then I can get home at a reasonable hour.'

'What the fuck's a reasonable hour? There's no such thing as a reasonable hour in New York.'

'There is when you have to be at work by eight.' With Susanna's coffee yogurt.

'What are you,' Giles said, 'some Christian fundamentalist?'

'Me?' I had to laugh. 'No way.'

''Cause that would be a bloody shaime,' Giles said, patting my knee. 'A beuwiful girl like you.' He slowly drew his hand up my thigh.

I took his hand – it was surprisingly warm – and placed it on his own knee.

'Find me old and disgusting, do you? Well, I could make you famous, you know.'

I laughed again. 'Jesus, Giles. Don't you ever give up?'

'Show me your breasts.'

'No!'

'I know they're beautiful. I've got a sixth sense about these things.' He put a finger to his forehead, like a mindreader. 'They're full and creamy white. With large pink nipples. Am I right?'

'Giles, please stop this.'

'You're easily aroused,' he whispered. 'I can tell that. But you're –'

'I'm what?'

'Afraid. Am I right?'

'I'm not afraid when I think it's the right person,' I finally said. 'But all the people I thought were right – weren't.'

'Yeah.' He nodded and sniffed. 'How does one find the right person?'

'I don't think you could ever be interested in just one person, Giles.'

'You don't, eh?'

'No.'

He sighed and looked down at his packet of coke. 'It's all a bloody fake, you know.'

'What is?'

'Monogamy. If men had their way, they'd be screwing night and day and it wouldn't be their wives and there wouldn't be any responsibility attached. It would be just plain sex. Nobody wants to admit it, but that's how it really is.'

'Not for everyone.'

'Ah. You're a romantic.'

'I suppose I am.'

'Well, love, romantics are like Christian fundamentalists. They put all their faith in what isn't there.'

'Maybe. But I'd rather be romantic than cynical.'

Giles nodded, once. 'Well, Venus, I'll leave you to your romance.' A flood of cold air raced in as he opened the door. 'I've got more cynical fish to fry.'

Home Sweet Home.

I never appreciated the sentiment behind those three words the way I did now, as winter grumbled towards spring and planning for Susanna's impending book tour took over most of my waking hours and some of my sleeping ones as well. I felt home-deprived.

The logistics of the *Puppy Love* tour were daunting, to say the least. Eighteen cities in two weeks (that was all the time Susanna could take off from her job as editor of *Aura*). A hair-raising itinerary was mapped out. The tour would wrap up in Chicago, where Susanna was scheduled to be the featured speaker at a big 'Women and Sex' conference at the University of Chicago.

Sybilla Lansgaard, head of PR for Stuckey Universal Media, was supposed to be in charge of 'event tours' like this one, but she and Susanna locked horns almost immediately. Office grapevine (maybe grapeshot would be a better word) had it that these two alpha-gals had been at one another's throats ever since Susanna interjected herself into the planning for the holiday party.

'Dumb move on Susanna's part,' Dorcas the observer observed. 'Susanna pissed *off* Sybilla and now Sybilla's going to piss *on* Susanna.'

Back and forth it went. Sybilla would submit an itinerary and Susanna would scotch it. Sybilla would counter by saying the itinerary was based on the schedules of the superstores where Susanna would be reading and signing. Back and forth. Susanna said she would only fly on direct flights, in first or business class, with a window seat. Sybilla said in some cases it would probably be easier to take a train than to fly. Absolutely not, said Susanna. No trains. Period.

And then the hotels. Only five-star luxury or new and hip would do. She had to have a suite, of course.

And for her personal assistant? The cheapest single room available.

What about media? Sybilla was to set up interviews with every major newspaper in every city Susanna visited. The newspapers were to be told in no uncertain terms that any story on Miss Hyde had to be a front-page feature.

It was exciting but oh, sometimes it made me so tired. It was a war of details. Susanna the multitasking micromanager thought of everything and demanded the impossible. And – again, from office grapevine – because Stuckey was behind her, she had the upper hand.

'Poor Sybilla,' Dorcas sighed. 'If she doesn't do what Susanna tells her to do, it's off with her head. After fifteen years with the company.'

That was the 'old' company she was referring to. The one that Lord Stuckey had bought and consolidated into his global media empire. I'd never worked for the old company, so I didn't have the sense of loyalty and outrage that roiled the ranks of the old guard. Things were changing, and they hated it. Editors were fired and senior staff let go or given new positions. Departments were merged. For the old guard, it was like working on quicksand. Because I worked for Susanna, I was spared a lot of that stress. But I felt sorry for the employees who had families and stiff mortgages and who had come to assume that a certain lifestyle would always be theirs.

Susanna didn't seem terribly concerned, but then she wasn't from the old guard either. She was part of the new Stuckey regime. And every spare moment she wasn't in a meeting, she was shopping on a vast new scale. She *had* to have new luggage. New travelling clothes were essential. Book signings required designer outfits. And to counteract all that dry, miserable air in aeroplanes and superstores, special hydrating exfoliating stress-reducing hypo-allergenic creams and unguents were needed.

I got dizzy just trying to imagine what her monthly credit-card bills must be. Then, one night, when I was cat-sitting Regina, I happened to see a credit-card statement lying open on a table. I had to peek.

During that statement period, Susanna had racked up over forty thousand dollars in charges. I saw the names of all the stores I'd driven her to and dozens more that I hadn't, including some luxury men's stores. And then I glanced at the billing name and address. It wasn't a name at all. It was a trading company with a post-office box in the Cayman Islands.

Home Sweet Home. Every night I looked forward to returning to my comfy little apartment, far away from the frantic battlefield of fame and fortune. Those few free hours were bliss. Hot baths with all-natural holistic bubbles, courtesy of product samples sent to *Aura*. A nice little meal, served to myself on Whitman's family china. With the extra five hundred a month I didn't have to limit myself to pizza, hot dogs, and salads. I could now afford take-out from Empire Szechuan, Mexican Rose, Falafel Frenzy, or any neighborhood restaurant I felt like.

Then, instead of turning on the television, I'd open my laptop and get back into my memoir. This was just for me. It *was* me. The world it described was totally different from the one I was living in now. At times it almost wrote itself. When that happened, I felt like I'd finally achieved some distance from the events it described.

And speaking of memoirs, I finally got a chance to read Susanna's. She hadn't offered to let me read it, so I snuck out one of the bound galleys I found in her office. I figured I'd read it and return it the next morning before she arrived.

That night I took it out of my purse and studied the blue paper cover with a curious feeling of trespass and excitement.

This was the first book I'd ever seen before it was published. 'Uncorrected Proof' was printed at the top. Then the title: *Puppy Love: Loving a Younger Man*. Below it, Susanna Hyde. Below that, all the publishing data: trim size, number of pages, ISBN bar-code number, genre (Memoir), rights, and publishing date.

I opened to the first page and read: 'I met him at a party. He was with another woman, one his own age . . .'

If the younger man she was writing about was Josh, as he claimed, then the 'other woman' was me. Because I was the woman Josh was standing with when we first met Susanna at that party the previous August.

I closed the book and thought about this for a moment. My heart was racing. This wasn't like my memoir, confined to the hard drive on my laptop. This was soon to be published, in hardcover, with a huge amount of flash and fanfare.

And I was in it. *In the first sentence*.

But that was my only appearance, as it turned out. I was never mentioned again because Josh, according to Susanna's memoir, was immediately infatuated and began trailing her around like a new puppy. Pestering her for dates. Sending her romantic e-mails (usually with quotes about love written by great writers).

Josh, if it was Josh, was called Jimmy. A young, idealistic writer from an impoverished family, he'd worked his way up through scholarships, attending Boston U and then the creative writing program at Columbia. 'Sexually, Jimmy was not inexperienced,' Susanna wrote, 'but he was certainly inept and unsophisticated.' Overeager, uninterested in foreplay, ejaculating too soon, smelling of greasy fast food, he bores Susanna sexually and she tries to break off the relationship. But Jimmy begs her not to discard him. He says he will be her slave. He agrees to let her tutor him in the bedroom arts.

On and on. Jimmy is hopeless. He sulks when she deconstructs his sexual performance. He cries when she rates him as a 4 on a scale of 1 to 10. He's incensed when she continues to insist that he wear a condom.

Susanna dwelt on Jimmy's social ineptitude, something I could really identify with but which Susanna always viewed as a humiliating embarrassment. Like the time Jimmy escorted her to a fancy publishing party, got drunk, and 'slobbered all over' her in front of her colleagues. 'Part of me was flattered', she admitted, 'that Jimmy found me so desirable that he couldn't keep his hands off me in public. His puppy-lovingness made him impulsive and unpredictable and occasionally adorable. But I also found his immaturity to be a sad commentary on the American male of today. At some level, I think most women respond more favorably to subtlety and sensitivity and sweet suggestion. But these traits are associated with maturity and thoughtfulness, and women today, no matter what their age, are forced to deal with a world of eternal Peter Pans.'

Poor Josh. Susanna hadn't robbed him of his virility, exactly, but she poked fun at his sexual ineptitude and emotional immaturity every chance she had.

And yet, for all its limitations, their brief affair was more sizzle than fizzle. At least that was how Susanna presented it in the later sex scenes, when she was tutoring Jimmy in the bedroom arts. (Some of those scenes were amazingly steamy.) Altering her book to include her fling with a much younger man was a smart marketing move on Susanna's part and added to the hype and anticipation that already surrounded it. In the end, though, when I finally finished it, I had the feeling that Susanna had never taken Josh, or Jimmy, very seriously. There was a curious lack of feeling and a condescension towards him that I found off-putting. He wasn't a man, he was an overeager puppy.

Around the same time, in my own life, Mary-Joseph Capistrano was becoming a bit overeager, too. She called to ask if I wanted a new terlet installed (yes), then called to ask if the roaches had returned (no), then called to say she'd noticed a leak in a corner of the bathroom ceiling and thought she'd better take care of it before it got any worse. She had a key to the apartment and could have done any of these jobs during the day, while I was gone, but she always scheduled herself to come over on a Saturday, when I'd be there.

'Don't lemme get in yuh way,' she'd say, setting down her tool box and pulling off her flannel jacket and tiny canvas gloves. She'd taken to wearing a dark, musky perfume and sometimes a dab of lipstick. But she was so petite and naturally pretty, with dark, dark hair and big, big eyes, that she really didn't need any make-up at all. She just didn't know how pretty she was, that's all, and she'd obviously never taken *Vogue* seriously.

Saturday was my morning to sleep in, so Mary-Joseph *was* in my way, but I didn't mind and even welcomed her visits. I didn't really have any close friends, and Mary-Joseph's working-class reality was refreshing after all the pretension and power plays I lived with at Stuckey Universal Media.

I was comfortable with her because I didn't have to pretend. I could just be myself. I could pad around in my comfy old robe and slippers, or sit on the sofa and read, or wash my hair, or sit and stare out the window.

One Saturday she arrived with a bag of pastries from a famous Italian bakery in Brooklyn. 'Thought you might be hungry.'

I gained weight just peeking in the bag. A buttery, sugary smell rose from its depths. 'I'll make some coffee.'

It was so sweet, sitting there with her at the little walnut dining table, sipping coffee and sharing Italian pastries. Outside it was foggy and wet. The trees in the garden glistened and dripped. Inside it was cozy and warm.

'Your ma's a trip,' Mary-Joseph remarked, taking a big slurp of her white, sugary coffee. 'You real close with huh?'

'Sometimes.'

'I liked huh. She's not uptight about nothin'.'

I was trying not to be too critical of Carolee at that point, so I nodded and smiled like a proud daughter. My attitude towards my mom had changed a lot since I began writing about her in my secret memoir. 'She's always full of surprises,' I said.

'She's got a wild side,' Mary-Joseph laughed. 'Like huh tattooed daughtuh.'

I lowered my eyes and smiled, feeling oddly shy. 'What's *your* mom like?' I asked.

'She's OK,' Mary-Joseph said without much conviction. 'Religious though. Nutty like.'

'Are you close?'

'Nah. Not really. My dad, I was closer to him. My grandpa, Carmine? I'm real close to him.'

'My dads always liked Carmine. They said he really knew what he was doing.'

'Yeah.' Mary-Joseph was obviously pleased and proud to hear this. 'He always let me hang around with him and taught me how to do stuff. I was nevuh innerested in *dawls* and stuff like that. Nevuh. I liked fixin' stuff. *Hated* school. Maybe it was the nuns I hated. They were so mean. Half of 'em were dykes, you could just tell, but they couldn't admit it. That makes people fucked up, you know, when they can't admit who they ah.'

'Mary-Joseph, you're gay, right?'

She nodded. 'For as long as I can remembuh.' She took a tiny bite from a pastry. 'How 'bout you? That rocker chick your mom talked about.'

'JD? She was beautiful, but she was so fucked up.'

Mary-Joseph's voice was very quiet. 'Were you in love with huh?'

'Yeah, I was. Or thought I was. Same thing, I guess.'

Mary-Joseph nodded. 'Hard to tell sometimes.' She smiled and glanced shyly into my eyes. 'Love's weird, huh?'

'Weird and wonderful.'

'Yeah. It can make you so happy and so sad.'

'You know one thing I've learned though?'

'What?'

'Not to rush into it. I always rushed into it. I always made the other person into my fantasy of who I wanted them to be, and didn't see who they really were.'

'Yeah,' Mary-Joseph said. 'Shits.'

'No, not shits. Just people like me who didn't want to be alone.'

'Nobody wants to be alone,' Mary-Joseph remarked with another tentative glance.

Kenny, the snake charmer up in 2B, met someone, and the floor above my bedroom would sometimes shake and I'd hear the squeaking thump of bedsprings and howling moans of pleasure. Little Andy and fat Candy in 1A never seemed to tire of screaming, hurling and copulating in rapid succession or at the same time. Sheba Fleischbaum up in 3A was dating someone she'd met online – 'an honest-to-Gawd gentleman who is *not* afraid of a plus-sized tuches and a laugh-line or two'. Sharanda at work had met a new guy and wouldn't stop rhapsodizing about his sexual prowess.

I guess it's almost inevitable after a dark, cold winter. People start mating. And in Manhattan, as the air turned soft and balmy and heavy winter coats were shed, the sense of longing was almost palpable.

I felt it myself. A kind of surge in the blood. A desire to hold hands and smooch and tease and tickle and laugh and make love. Or just to sit on a bench in the warm sun and talk quietly with someone special.

So I had mixed feelings when Mary-Joseph Capistrano called one evening and shyly asked if I'd be interested in going out for some pizza. I knew she was interested in me, and was flattered. With JD I had been infatuated, hypnotized by her local punk-rock fame and reputation as Portland's hottest lesbo. JD was a challenge. I had to work to get her attention and then worried constantly that she'd dump me. Lovers were essential but expendable to JD. A lot of her girlfriends ended up in her harem, unable to see how she manipulated them to her own ends.

It was completely different with Mary-Joseph. She was tough on the outside but sweet, maybe gooey, on the inside. The way I used to be.

'I'd love to have some pizza,' I said to Mary-Joseph. 'But I won't have a lot of time to hang out.'

'Oh, shu-uh,' she said excitedly. 'That's fine. I just thought – you know – it would be fun.'

'I don't know if I'll recognize you without your tool kit,' I teased.

'Those are just my work clothes,' she said. 'You think I dress like that all the time?'

I said I'd take the subway out to Brooklyn and meet her, but she insisted on driving in to pick me up. 'Mary-Joseph,' I said, 'that's nuts.'

'Why? I gotta cah. Might as well use it.'

Then I had a brilliant idea. 'I've got a car, too,' I said. 'How about I drive out there and pick *you* up.'

She was silent. 'You'd do that?'

I would, and did. Susanna was away that weekend. OK, I did feel a bit guilty. But it wasn't like I was stealing the car or anything. I was just borrowing it for a couple of hours. Even so, I felt a little weak in the knees when I got to the garage.

'Hey, Venus.' Frankie Silvestra, the guy in charge, waved and smiled. 'Where's her highness headed tonight?'

'Brooklyn.'

'Give my regahds to Borough Hall.'

Stupid to be trembling like a thief. I punched Mary-Joseph's address into Map Quest, buckled up, and slid the Lincoln out of the garage into Manhattan's Saturday-night traffic. It was always a thrill to nose out into the stream of cars and become part of the parade.

My heart was pleasantly fluttering as I headed up the ramp and began crossing the Brooklyn Bridge. Sometimes New York is so impossibly beautiful that it makes you excited just to be there. It was a clear, breezy night, not exactly warm, but you could sense that spring was on its way. The East River was vast and black and carried a salty fragrance from the harbor and the ocean beyond. Stretched and twinkling along the opposite shore were the lights of Brooklyn Heights, where Mary-Joseph lived. A few minutes later I was parked and walking towards her building.

I'd gone through a ridiculous 'what should I wear' thing, the kind of crazy insecurity that generally takes hold about an hour before you're going out on a date. I pulled on a pair of jeans and my old rhinestone-studded cowboy boots and one of Daddy's old Brooks Brothers shirts, which I'd found in the closet, and a rather cool wool blazer that would keep me warm. I put on some new organic make-up that had come to the *Aura* offices as free samples and bunched my hair back into a ponytail.

Mary-Joseph lived in an old brownstone on a pretty cobblestone street lined with nineteenth-century brick townhouses and lit by old-fashioned street lamps. I rang the buzzer for her apartment on the top floor and got buzzed in.

'Just a sec!' she called from behind the door. I heard her rushing to complete a last-minute task. Then she opened the door.

I stared, dumbfounded.

Mary-Joseph Capistrano, whom I'd never seen in anything but denim and flannel work clothes, was wearing a short leather skirt with a white silk blouse and a red-velvet bolero jacket. She had on black fishnet hose and the tiniest high heels I'd ever seen. Her hair was swept up in a kind of gelled punky style, and her beautiful dark eyes were shadowed with peacock blue. She looked adorable and pathetic, like a little girl playing dress-up.

'Wow,' I said.

She held up one of her small, strong hands. 'OK. This ain't how I usually dress, right? I just figured I'd try, you know? Just try, and see if I liked it.'

'OK. Cool.'

'Do I look . . .' She didn't finish the question, so I didn't know what adjective she had in mind. Beautiful? Ridiculous?

'You look great,' I said.

'Do I really?'

'What do you think? That's what matters.'

She looked down at herself as if she weren't quite sure what she was seeing. 'I dunno. I guess I think –' She bit her lip, inadvertently scraping off some of her lipstick. 'I guess I think I look kinda – hot?'

'Like you eat chillies for breakfast,' I said.

'Didja find a good place to pahk?' she asked as we headed down the stairs. Mary-Joseph was wobbling severely on her stilettos but acting brave about it. On the old sidewalks it was even worse. I was a lot more surefooted in my old cowboy boots, so I offered her my arm.

'Hang on, girl, or you'll be sprawled on the ground flashing your thong.'

Mary-Joseph giggled. Well, she didn't exactly know how to giggle, so it came out as a kind of low, muffled snorting. 'I can't believe women walk in these things every day,' she said, firmly latching hold of my arm. 'It's like balancing on twenny-penny nails.' She gasped when we reached the Lincoln. 'Oh my Gawd! That's yours?'

'For tonight.'

'Jeez,' she whispered, settling in, gazing at all the gadgets, stroking the finishes.

We had a ball, and she gave me a fabulous tour of Brooklyn. She'd grown up in Carroll Gardens, and most of her family still lived there. Mary-Joseph was the first Capistrano to 'move away'.

'I just wanted something bettuh,' she told me over a luscious pepperoni pizza. 'Something prettiuh. And I guess I wanted to get away from my muthuh. But I didn't wanna leave Brooklyn. I like workin' in Manhattan but I can't see myself livin' there.'

After dinner we drove around her old neighborhood and she pointed out the local landmarks. 'That's where Mrs Signorelli hung huhself. Her husband come home and found huh in the laundry room, just hangin' there from a piece of clothes line, and St Joseph's wouldn't even say a Mass for huh, even though she went to that church her whole life.'

'Why wouldn't they say Mass?'

''Cause she killed huhself,' Mary-Joseph said. 'Catholics can't do that.'

'Oh. I thought everyone could kill themselves if they wanted.'

'Well shu-uh, they *can*, but if they do, the Church says it's a mortal sin. That means you don't get into heaven.'

'Oh.' I nodded as if it all made sense.

'Now, see that house there?' Mary-Joseph pointed. 'That's where Mr Locatello lived with his othuh wife.'

'He had two?'

'Mm. Maybe more. And ovuh there was the witch's house. That's what we called it. An old lady with a hunchback lived there. She'd come out and yell at us kids all the time. And there's St Joseph,' she said, pointing to a derelict-looking church.

'It looks all boarded up.'

'Yeah, they had to close it. They had to pay out like three hundred million bucks to settle all the sex-abuse charges against the priests. Now they're broke. So ha ha, and who's goin' to hell this time?'

She showed me the Catholic elementary and high schools she'd attended, and pointed out the parks and street corners where she'd hang out after school to smoke and get into trouble. 'I mostly hung out with the guys,' she told me. 'I thought the girls were stupid. All they wanted was to get married. That was it. Get married. Have kids. Take a vacation in the summuh.'

After the home tour, we went to a bar and talked some more. Mary-Joseph was a little giddy. She'd had a glass of wine with the pizza and another glass at the bar. I was stone sober, afraid to drink because I was responsible for Susanna's car. When a slow song came on and Mary-Joseph asked me to dance, I hesitated.

'It don't have to *mean* anything,' she said, looking up at me with hopeful eyes.

'OK,' I said, 'but then I've got to get going.'

Mary-Joseph was tiny, even in her heels, and only came up to my chest. She was pretty stiff, the way a guy who doesn't know how to dance is stiff. But she was so cute and sweet, with her short leather skirt and red velvet jacket and her gallant attempt to feminize herself. When she laid her head against my shoulder, I could smell her fruit-scented hair gel and musky perfume. And I wanted to be tender with her.

'I like being your friend,' I said.

She raised her head. 'Do yuh?' she whispered. ''Cause I think you're wonduhful. And I'm gonna get you a new stove and fridge.'

When we got back to the car, one of the tires was flat.

'Oh, those fuckin' shits!' Mary-Joseph cursed. 'They still do this?'

'Who?'

'Kids. Homophobic fag bashers. They pound nails into the tires.' She looked up, furious, as two dark shapes darted out from behind a dumpster and ran laughing down the street. 'You fucking ass-wipes!' Mary-Joseph screamed, taking off after them. 'I'm gonna kick yuh asses so hahd yuh balls're gonna fly out yuh nose!'

I didn't know what to do so I took off after Mary-Joseph. She couldn't run very far in her stilettos, and when I caught up with her she was holding on to a street lamp for support as she sprayed the now-vanished homophobes with her juiciest Brooklyn vitriol. When I put my hand on her shoulder, she turned and looked at me, her dark eyes blazing. 'I coulda caught 'em if I wasn't wearin' these damn stupid shoes.'

We walked back to the car, Mary-Joseph bristling beside me.

I looked at the flat tire and felt the first stirrings of panic. I'm not totally inept with cars, but I knew nada about this one. In New York, nobody changed their own flat tires. A garage did it for you. The fact that the car wasn't mine, that I'd snitched it for the night, made me really nervous. How was I going to explain this to Susanna if she found out? What if the police somehow became involved?

I could lose my job.

'I don't know what to do,' I said.

Mary-Joseph, bless her soul, immediately took charge. 'Open the trunk,' she said.

I'll never forget the sight of her, in her short skirt and heels, jacking up the car, unbolting the flat tire, and replacing it with the new tire in the trunk. She was focused and methodical, the way she was when she tackled any maintenance problem. She wouldn't allow me to lift or carry anything, even though I was more comfortably dressed than she was.

'This is my penance for dressin' up like this,' she joked.

Sweet, good-natured Mary-Joseph Capistrano. As I stood there by the side of the car, watching her, my thoughts drifted back to selfish, self-centred JD and the excitement I used to feel riding around on her big black Harley. Vehicles, I realized, had figured prominently in all of my romances. Sean Kowalski with his souped-up Grand Prix. Peter Pringle and his Pet Away van for hauling dead animals. Tremaynne didn't have a car, but we rode off to our fateful encounter at Pine Mountain Lodge in the dads' SUV, and then were almost killed when those rednecks locked us in cages and threw us in the back of their stinking pick-up.

So much moving around and going nowhere.

And what had I learned from all of it?

That once I figured out where I wanted to go, a car wouldn't be the vehicle that would take me there.

March came in like the proverbial lion, with Susanna astride and flying high. She was riding high, too. Every time I picked her up from an 'event', she was half-soused, with a thick tongue and a belligerent or arrogant manner that wasn't very pretty.

Giles accompanied her to some of these to-dos and came out looking and sounding worse than she did. Sitting in the back of the town car, laughing, arguing, picking to shreds everyone they'd just met, rhapsodizing over the celebrities, Susanna and Giles reminded me of two drunken, spoiled teenagers. Sometimes they seemed completely oblivious to the fact that I was sitting in front, driving them, and would talk about things as if I weren't even there.

That's how I learned that Susanna was finally going to fire Evan Bevins, *Aura*'s veteran art director. She pleaded with Giles to leave *Peeper* and work for her. 'Haven't you had enough tits and slits to last you a lifetime? How many ways can you make a pussy look in'neresting, for God's sake?'

'You want *me* to work for that New Age shit?' Giles laughed. 'I'm not into spirit photography, darling. And Stuckey likes *Peeper*. He tol' me it's his favorite magazine.'

'Can't you do both? *Peeper* and *Aura*? Just until our new appointments?'

'Right, and when's that going to be?'

'No later than June. Start of the new fiscal year. That's when he'd logically do it.'

'But he still hasn't made any promises, right? It's just talk.'

'Giles, you have to trust me. I know what I'm doing.'

'Do you?' Giles said. 'That's good. But do you know what *he*'s doing?'

'Of course. We talk every day.'

Giles said, 'You know what I heard tonight?'

'What did you hear tonight?'

'I heard he's going back to his wife.'

The silence that followed this remark was so intense that I glanced into the rearview mirror to see what was going on. Susanna was sitting there with a weird expression on her face. Stunned, maybe.

'And if he goes back,' Giles continued, his voice turning belligerent, 'then what? Eh? Then what?'

'Giles—'

'He won't bloody name you editor-in-chief, I can tell you that!'

'Don't say that. Don't put it into words. Don't even think it.' She sounded frightened.

'You promised me,' Giles said. 'Executive group design director for Stuckey Universal Media.'

'You'll get it, Giles, you'll get it.'

'A position that comes with a salary of half a million before perks.'

'Giles, for God's sake, I'm doing everything I can.'

'And so is she, love.'

'Who?'

'Lady Stuckey. She won't give him up without a fight, you know.'

'She's too old to fight,' Susanna said. 'And she's never once stood up to him, not once in her entire life.'

'Well, darling, you'd be amazed at the inner strength people find when billions are at stake.'

Finally, in the third week of March, the huge, glittery launch party for *Puppy Love* drew near. Sybilla, who should have been in charge, was basically cut out of the loop when Susanna hired a flashy freelance PR firm to plan the event.

Hardly anyone from Stuckey Universal was invited, but the list of celebrities who were asked to come was prodigious. All of Susanna's bold-face compatriots were sent special invitations that featured the titillating new book jacket photograph Giles had devised: Susanna, wearing tight jeans and a fancy bra, leading a naked young guy on a leash.

At the last minute, I was invited too. Or, rather, asked to work. 'Just stay close by,' Susanna told me. 'I'll signal if I want you.'

Oh my. I'd be *signalled*.

'I'll be sticking pretty close to Lord Stuckey,' Susanna said, 'and I'll be leaving the party with him.'

But on the day of the big bash, Lord Stuckey wasn't answering his phone. Susanna kept getting his new personal valet, and the valet refused to tell her where his master was or let her speak to him. All he'd say was, 'Lord Stuckey is unavailable at this time.'

'Fucking asshole!' Susanna screamed after her fifth attempt. But an hour later she was on her cellphone again, again talking to the valet. 'Listen, would you please give him a message?' she said, her voice tense but cordial. 'It's quite important, so can you *please* give me your word that you'll pass this on to Lord Stuckey? Thank you. Tell him, please, that the launch party begins at seven o'clock. I would like for him to pick me up no later than half past six, so we can arrive together. We've discussed all this, so it's just a reminder. And tell him that I've arranged a small dinner party afterwards. We'll go there about nine. In *his* car. Tell him – well, just tell him I *know* he understands how important this is to me.'

After the call, she was ominously silent. We were driving up Central Park West towards 'Dr Gail's' office, which meant Susanna was getting a Botox cocktail in order to be wrinkle-free for her big party. I glanced in the rearview mirror and saw her staring out of the window and idly stroking her temple. She looked pensive, vulnerable, and determined, all at once.

*

The Germans have a word for it: *schadenfreude*. It means taking pleasure in other people's misery. It's scary to see it in action, even scarier to realize how prevalent it is in the celebrity world Susanna was courting.

I don't know German, but Whitman does. He's the one who told me about *schadenfreude*, many a long year ago.

I mention it here because there was a shitload of *schadenfreude* at Susanna's launch party. It was supposed to be a fun, upbeat, gala celebration of her new book – and of her, now raised to celebrity status. She'd micromanaged every last detail, as exacting as a film director. That night she was to be the star. And with Lord Farrell Stuckey at her side, she would be invincible as well.

But oh-oh. Lord Stuckey was a no-show.

I'd stayed close by all afternoon, ferrying her from 'Dr Gail's' to her apartment on Riverside Drive, and then hanging out there while she got ready. There were endless calls but Susanna didn't take any of them. She said she was waiting for Lord Stuckey to ring. He was the only one she'd talk to.

But she couldn't talk to him because he never called.

Even I, who was totally on the outside of this private drama, knew what a terrible dilemma she was facing. She was like an actress who has to go on stage and perform despite some horrible personal calamity.

At six-thirty, when Lord Stuckey still hadn't called, Susanna came out of her bedroom and said quietly, 'Venus, you'll have to drive me.'

She looked great in her tight, sexy dress. She'd been working with a personal trainer to tone up her body and hired Marc André, an obscenely expensive celebrity stylist, to give her a youthful new coif (short, blonde, carefree) and advise on make-up schematics.

But I realized something really simple and really important the moment she appeared. Beauty – real *glowing* beauty – comes from within. You can't fake it, no matter how perfect the externals.

'Wait,' Susanna said before we left. She went to the kitchen and returned with a champagne flute and an open bottle of Veuve Cliquot. She poured a glass and lifted it – toasting herself, I guess. 'To whatever it takes.'

She continued to drink and made a couple of phone calls as I drove her to the hip new club in Tribeca where the launch was to be held. She cranked up her voice to make it sound like nothing was wrong. 'Giles? Where are you? Listen, it looks like Farrell's stuck in a meeting and may not be able to make it to the launch for an hour or so. Would you be a darling and meet me there? Thanks, love.'

The second call was to Eileen, head of the flashy PR firm that had helped her to plan the event. 'Farrell's going to be late,' she reported with a disappointed sigh. 'Tell the photographers to wait until nine.'

'Darling! You look fabulous! Where's Lord Stuckey?'

'Susanna, darling, congratulations! Where's Lord Stuckey?'

'What a marvellous party, my dear! I thought Lord Stuckey was going to be here.'

On and on, over and over. Susanna smiling and prevaricating and enduring the humiliation.

'Sweetheart, I can't *wait* to read your naughty new book. What does Lord Stuckey think of it? And where is he, by the way?'

'Susanna, so *daring* of you to write about teaching a younger man to fuck you. I can't wait to ask Lord Stuckey if he's jealous. Is he here?'

'Sweetie, you're an absolute *inspiration* to old hags everywhere. But why didn't you write about your romance with Lord Stuckey? That would have been far more interesting.'

From my post near the table stacked with free copies of *Puppy Love* I could keep my eye on Susanna and wait for her *signal*. I hate to disillusion anyone who thinks the rich and famous aren't cheap – this crowd was like vultures. Bony old hands with long red talons and giant diamond rings grabbed copies, *everyone* grabbed copies, sometimes two or three. Canapés and glasses of champagne were snatched from trays.

There was the usual posing and acres of smiles and lots of flash and sizzle because celebs were in attendance and Susanna was a celeb herself . . . or was she? Everyone there was expecting to see her with Lord Stuckey, whose presence would have given Susanna's book launch a triumphant boost.

Giles, acting as Susanna's escort, kept the two of them well supplied with champagne, and as the evening wore on, Susanna began to weave and slur a bit.

I was gnawing on a short rib nabbed from a passing tray when a voice said, 'Hello, Venus.'

I whirled around and saw . . . oh my God . . . Josh O'Connell. He picked up a copy of *Puppy Love*, flipped through the pages, and tucked it under his arm.

'Josh! What are you doing here?'

He flashed a smile. 'Well, it's my party, too, isn't it?'

'How did you get in?' Because it was invitation-only, and everyone had to show their invites at the door. Security was discreet but tight because Lord Stuckey was supposed to be there.

'I'm good at crashing parties,' Josh said. 'Especially my own.'

He looked incredibly handsome and – what was it? Charismatic. Still gaunt, but now using it to his advantage. Wearing a gorgeous suit that fit him perfectly, a soft gray shirt, and a dark, rich-looking tie. With a smile and a wink, he could probably get past any security guard in the world.

Before I could say anything, or stop him, Josh walked over and planted himself in front of Susanna. Her eyes widened in surprise, maybe fear, and she took a faltering step backwards. 'Josh,' she said.

'You fucking skank.'

Susanna kept her smile but her eyes turned hard and flashed left and right to ascertain if anyone had heard him. 'Let's have lunch,' she said placatingly.

'No more puppy chow,' Josh said.

'Give me a call and we'll set it up,' Susanna said.

'Hey!' Josh suddenly yelled, so loud that the room fell

silent. He waved a copy of Susanna's book over his head. 'Do any of you dogs know who I am?'

'Yeah, mate, you're an asshole terrier,' Giles said, taking an unsteady step forward. 'Come on, give it up. Get out of here.'

'What are you, her new stud service? Filling in for the old billionaire?' Josh smiled and did a slow turn, obviously not worried about Giles. 'Listen!' he yelled to the now riveted crowd. 'I'm the puppy in *Puppy Love*. Me! I'm her puppy fucker!'

Susanna signalled to someone, but it wasn't me. I followed her line of vision and saw Eileen, the PR woman, standing with a frightened look on her lifted face. She squinted and nodded and turned to signal a security guard.

Everyone just stood there, not knowing if Josh was a madman or on the level. 'My name isn't Jimmy! It's Josh. Josh O'Connell,' Josh shouted. 'And I'd be happy to sign copies of this book for you, even though it's full of lies. Because you know what? This isn't a memoir, it's not even a *roman-à-clef*. It's complete fiction!'

I heard Susanna say in an undertone to Giles, 'Get him out of here.'

By this time the security guard was slowly walking across the room. He wasn't a policeman, and he was so overweight that you just knew he'd be useless in a real emergency. The only weapon he wore was a really stern expression.

I was aware, suddenly, that people were taking photographs. Some with their cellphones, professional photographers with their big cameras.

'Stay away from me,' Josh warned the approaching security guard. 'I bite!' He turned his attention back to the crowd. 'Just so you all know, I'll be coming out with my *own* memoir about what it's like to sleep with an old, wrinkled, lying bitch like Susanna Hyde.'

Giles lunged.

They fought.

Susanna screamed.

It was the most exciting book launch I would ever attend.

*

Then it was time for damage control, and lots of it, but Susanna didn't get any help from her publishers. When contacted by reporters, spokespeople for Stuckey Universal Media (such as Sybilla Lansgaard) 'refused to comment' or 'did not return calls'.

The photos were embarrassing but the publicity turned out to be useful for sales. The incident did raise awkward questions, however, that Susanna wanted to avoid – like how much of what she was calling a *memoir* was actually *fiction*. The whole thing might have blown over except that Josh, highly photogenic, had become something of a media magnet, always ready with a comment and a smile for the camera. He was now attached to Susanna and her book like a dog to a juicy bone.

And still no word from Lord Stuckey.

It turned out, though, that Lord Stuckey wasn't even *in* New York on the night of Susanna's book launch. He was at his estate in Gloucestershire.

The London tabloids reported that when Lady Stuckey got wind of her husband's straying behavior she acted 'swiftly and decisively' to rein him in. Sources close to the Stuckey family, who chose to remain anonymous, reported that Lady Stuckey was 'absolutely furious' to discover that after fifty years of marriage, her husband had been 'lured' from the nest by 'an unprincipled harlot'. If Lord Stuckey ever saw this 'publicity-seeking tart' again, sources close to the Stuckey family said, Lady Stuckey was prepared to sue for divorce and claim half of her husband's estate . . . currently estimated at 1.3 *billion* pounds.

All this was happening as Susanna worked her usual sixty-hour weeks as editor of *Aura* and fought with Sybilla over the final details of the *Puppy Love* tour. I had to admire her. She just kept going. But there was a tinge of fanaticism about her now, like a general fighting without any troops.

It's enough to make you believe in astrology. I mean, those times when absolutely *nothing* goes according to plan. Some planet, usually Mercury, is going backwards or aligning with some other pissed-off troublemaker, usually Saturn or Mars. During these periods of Saturn Return or Mercury Retrograde or whatever they are, you should expect the worst, be prepared for *anything*, and wear full-body armor instead of underwear.

The warning was right there, in Petra Darkke's 'Celestial Navigations' astrology column. During April, it said, all those born under Susanna's sign were in for a great big celestial pie-in-the-face.

But Susanna didn't believe in astrology.

Not even when she woke up on the morning we were scheduled to fly to Boston on the first leg of the *Puppy Love* tour and found a huge honkin' cold sore on her lower lip.

'I look like a freak!' she cried, obsessively touching the swollen mound of herpes simplex. 'I can't do a book tour with this monstrosity on my face!'

But of course she had to, and she knew it. Too much was at stake. Cold sore or no cold sore, the show had to go on.

I was in charge so I took charge. I calmed Susanna, who was obviously hung over, tricked Regina into her kitty-carrier, and got all of us and all our luggage downstairs and out to the waiting taxi. I told the driver what our two stops would be and that we were in a hurry.

I was really excited. This was a big deal. Eighteen cities in fourteen days. I had a lot to keep track of, but I'd had two triple-shot lattes and was wired for efficiency.

'Want to say goodbye to Regina?' I asked Susanna when the driver pulled up in front of Hôtel Chat, the exclusive cat hotel where Regina would be boarded while we were away.

'Who?'

'Regina. Your cat.'

'Oh.' Susanna tapped distractedly on the door of the kitty-carrier. 'Bye-bye, darling. Be good.'

Regina hissed and lunged for her finger.

'Ow! Stupid fucking – oh *no*!'

I left Susanna swearing and examining her broken nail and ran into Hôtel Chat. The check-in clerk couldn't find Regina's reservation and had no sense that life, for some, could be urgent. I glanced at my watch. We had to be at LaGuardia in less than an hour.

'Hello, Regina,' cooed the reception clerk, peeking through the door of the carrier. 'My, aren't you pretty.'

'Fffff,' came from a back corner of the kitty-carrier.

'Let's just take you out and see . . .'

I was distracted by a text message from Susanna, out in the taxi. When I looked up, Regina was flying out of the carrier and the startled receptionist was turning away to avoid those sharp little claws.

'Regina! Goddamn you!' I bolted after her and the receptionist bolted after me. We raced around the lobby, scrabbled under a table, and I even caught hold, briefly, of Regina's tail, but she was fast and determined to elude capture. Finally, panting, we cornered her and I managed to pick her up under her front legs and stuff her twisting, squirming, hissing body back into the kitty-carrier.

'She's just a little upset,' the receptionist said nervously. 'She probably thinks you're abandoning her.'

I smiled noncommittally, signed the papers, and ran back outside.

'It's getting bigger!' Susanna cried as I jumped into the cab.

She'd pulled out her mirror and was staring in horror at her fat lip. 'Call Dr Gail! Tell her I have to see her. Chop chop. Tell her it's an emergency.'

'If we stop at Dr Gail's we'll miss the flight.'

'Call her!'

So I did. And we ended up detouring to Dr Gail's. Susanna darted in and dashed out five minutes later, her eyes swimming with tears from a painful shot directly into the cold sore. Dr Gail had given her a salve to rub on the infected area. 'If I keep applying this, Dr Gail said, it should be gone by tonight,' Susanna said, touching the hot fat lump as she studied herself in her mirror.

But at the airport, as part of the new security precautions, they confiscated the salve. A luggage scan detected the four-ounce metal tube in Susanna's purse and a security screener told her she couldn't bring it into the cabin with her.

'But that's ridiculous!' she cried.

'I'm sorry, it has to be three ounces or less.'

'You can't take that!' she insisted. 'I need it for my lip! It's medicine!'

'Then you'll have to check it, ma'am.'

Of course there was no time to check it. We'd arrived late and had already checked our luggage at the curb.

'Please,' Susanna pleaded. 'I'm very ill. I must have this medicine. I'm on a book tour and I—'

'You're holding up the other passengers, ma'am,' said the security screener. 'If you want to talk to a supervisor . . .'

'Oh for God's sake!' Susanna snatched the tube of ointment. 'All right, then! I'll just have to rub it all on now, won't I?' Which is what she did, squirting the entire tube on her lip. She slammed the empty tube back down on the table and said, 'There! Now are you satisfied?'

I prayed she wouldn't be led off in handcuffs. Nowadays they arrest passengers who exhibit erratic behaviour.

'Call Dr Gail,' Susanna told me as she angrily grabbed her heels from the big plastic bin and slipped them on. 'Tell her to FedEx more salve to our hotel in Boston.'

*

Luckily, some of the 'big' reviews had come in before the book launch, which meant that the reviewers had not questioned *Puppy Love*'s pedigree as a memoir. Women tended to review the book more sympathetically, picking up on its tone of 'caustic humor' and praising Susanna's candor and understanding of male/female relationships. Plus, they loved the sex scenes, those private tutorials Susanna gave to her ardent but inept lover. Male reviewers were more guarded and grouchy, as if Susanna's characteristic frankness in matters of sex was somehow insulting to their manhood.

Most of the advance press was pretty good, though, and full-page ads featuring Giles's photo of Susanna leading the naked young man by a leash had appeared in the *New York Times* Sunday Book Review and other prominent papers and magazines. The superstores were behind the book. The store in Boston had ordered an unprecedented two hundred copies.

But tell that to Mercury and Saturn and their heavenly cohorts. They didn't care if the advance press was good or that the bookstore had ordered two hundred copies or that Susanna Hyde was scheduled to make her first author appearance at Copley Square that evening at eight o'clock.

First, the flight – for mysterious reasons no one could ascertain but which seemed to be related to a terrorist alert – was delayed four hours. Forget about finding another flight: they were all full and all grounded, just as we were.

Then: 'Uh. Ladies and gentlemen, this is your captain speaking. We've encountered some unexpected difficulties as we approach Boston's Logan Airport . . .'

A sudden and very nasty snow squall had whipped up off the Atlantic and the air traffic controllers weren't letting any flights land.

'Uh, folks, this is your captain again. Just to give you an update. We've been circling for, oh, about fifty minutes now. And we still haven't been cleared for landing. Uh, folks, we don't know at this time if *any* flights will be allowed to land . . .'

Susanna was up in first class and I was back in economy, so

I didn't know how she was taking this news. Since we were airborne, there was no way I could call the bookstore to tell them we might be late or not arrive at all.

But finally, after some horrible turbulence, the plane landed. I got our luggage and managed to finagle an illicit cab (an hour's wait otherwise) to take us to Copley Square. The cab moved at a snail's pace through the clogged, snow-packed streets. We dashed into the bookstore at two minutes to eight, breathless, having no time to change, Susanna's lip risen to soufflé proportions.

Only to find the store practically deserted.

'It's this weird storm,' the events manager apologized, unable to keep her eyes off Susanna's lip. 'People just stayed home.'

I looked at Susanna, wondering if she was going to blow. Her face was red and her expression difficult to read, though her dilated nostrils offered a clue. The swollen lip made her look like she'd just been socked in the mouth. 'All right,' she finally said, 'I'll sign every book you have and we'll call it a day.'

'Well, since so few people showed,' countered the events manager, 'I think if you signed fifty that would be sufficient.'

'After what I have been through, trying to get here,' Susanna said slowly, enunciating every word, 'I intend to sign every copy.' She was insisting on this because she knew that bookstores can't return books that have been signed.

'You'll have to read first, for the people who did show up,' the events manager said.

We all looked over to the forlorn sea of empty chairs. I counted five people, one of them probably homeless.

In Philadelphia there was a gratifyingly large audience – but no books.

The frantic bookstore manager said she'd been on the phone all afternoon trying to figure out what the problem was. Apparently there had been some breakdown in communication between Stuckey Universal Media and the warehouse. The books should have been shipped two days earlier and arrived the day before, but the order had never been received.

All that arrived was the 'stand alone', a life-size cardboard replica of Susanna in her jeans and sexy bra leading the naked young man on a leash.

At five o'clock, when we discovered this, Susanna got Sybilla Lansgaard on the phone and started screaming. I mean *screaming*. I've never heard anything like it.

'I want *you*, Sybilla,' Susanna concluded, 'to get your fucking ass down to that fucking warehouse and pick up two hundred copies and drive them to fucking Philadelphia *yourself* by seven fucking forty-five p.m.!'

But the gods – and probably Sybilla – just laughed at her request. The books didn't arrive until the day *after* the book signing, by which time we were already on our way to Washington, D.C.

Every day presented a new crisis. Like the day Susanna was scheduled to give telephone interviews to newspapers in cities where she would not be appearing. Interviews were scheduled for every half-hour, right up to the time when we had to leave for our next flight. The interviewers were to call Susanna's private BlackBerry number.

After an hour had passed and no one had called, Susanna said, with ominous calm, 'Ring Sybilla.' It took an hour, but I finally tracked down the problem: Sybilla's assistant, who had arranged all the interviews, had given the journalists the wrong phone number.

Hmm.

'From now on,' Susanna said, when the screaming (hers) had died down, 'we don't trust *anyone*. Got it? We're on our own. So from here on in I want you to double-check every detail. Call every warehouse to find out when the books are scheduled to be shipped. Call every bookstore to find out if the books have been received. Call every reporter on our media list to find out if they've got the right time and place for the interview.'

I nodded briskly and jotted down her instructions. I would do what I could to grease the complicated machinery of the *Puppy Love* book tour.

But maybe this was just a glaring example of really bad karma. Or dirty chakras.

And that horrible blog that suddenly appeared, who was behind that? We wouldn't have known about it except that a virus insinuated into Susanna's personal website flipped everyone visiting www.Susannahyde.com over to www.hideSusannahyde.com.

Susanna was a staunch supporter of new media technology. She checked her website every day, monitoring the number of hits as if they were gains in her personal stock portfolio. The number of hits had increased significantly since the release of *Puppy Love*, and there was a bookstore link that allowed visitors to order the book instantly and online, so she could check sales figures, too.

My job, when we arrived at the hotel, was to remove her incredibly expensive and super-sophisticated laptop from its padded leather case and set it up on the desk. It was up to me to fiddle with telephone plug-ins or wi-fi cards because the laptop had to be turned on and ready for her to access cyberspace anytime, day or night.

I'll never forget the sight of her face the first time she typed in www.susannahyde.com and got flipped over to www.hidesusannahyde.com.

'What is going on here?' she said.

I went over to take a look.

The graphics were awful. A low-budget amateur, obviously.

> Welcome to www.hidesusannahyde.com, where Freud meets fraud and we sleuth out the facts behind the *fiction* that Susanna Hyde is pawning off as *Truth* . . .
>
> Join us as we travel with Susanna on her book tour (click here for a list of cities and stores) to promote what she calls 'a memoir' . . . Visitors to this site are invited to submit *un-retouched* photos of Susanna and to share their own Susanna stories . . .

'Call my webmaster,' Susanna said in a breathless whisper, staring with horror as an old photograph of herself morphed into a glamorous image that drew attention to her reconstructive surgery. 'Dr Jekyll and Susanna Hyde' appeared in red horror-movie lettering below the two images.

Susanna began to drink way more than she should.

In Cleveland she had one too many glasses of wine (on an empty stomach), got flustered during her reading, and lost her place. My stomach clenched as I watched her fumbling. 'Uhh,' she said, flipping pages, 'umm.' A woman seated in front of me leaned towards to her friend and whispered, 'She's drunk', in a voice loud enough to be heard by everyone in the audience.

The next morning, when I checked www.hidesusanna hyde.com, there was a blurry photograph of Susanna standing at the podium, her eyes half closed, looking half crocked, with the caption: 'Drunk on success in Cleveland!'

In Minneapolis she stumbled on her way up to the stage and fell flat on her face. Soooo embarrassing. Luckily, the bruise on her nose was barely visible on the ghastly photo that appeared on www.hidesusannahyde.com with the caption 'What a trip!'

The fact-or-fiction controversy caught up with her in Atlanta. Up until then, it hadn't really registered on the national radar, probably because *Puppy Love* hadn't yet become a bestseller. The fracas at her book launch, and Josh's claim that *Puppy Love* was fiction, not fact, had been confined to the New York tabloids and to the scurrilous blog.

But now, somehow or other, the fact-or-fiction story got picked up by a wire service and a wily reporter in Atlanta just happened to see it. This reporter, and not the one on our media list, showed up at the hotel to interview Susanna. He was a balding, middle-aged dude with wire-rimmed glasses, big yellow teeth, and a major attitude.

When confronted by a hard-hitting veteran reporter, Susanna's media-focus training didn't do her a bit of good. She hemmed and hawed but the reporter would not drop the essential question: had she made up portions of *Puppy Love*? Susanna grew flustered, then belligerent.

'I don't see why I should even answer that question,' she snapped, 'when obviously all you want to do is twist it around to your own meaning.'

We saw the story – oh, what a horrible story – before we left the next morning. Sybilla herself called to alert us. Yes, there it was, right on the front page, a feature story with the headline: 'If Her Lover's a Puppy, She Must Be A Bitch'.

And of course the reporter was nice enough to mention the blog, alerting readers everywhere to its existence.

After a week of non-stop travel and non-stop catastrophes, I was in a state of permanent high alert. But oh, I still felt so damned competent. There was nothing I couldn't deal with. I was super-nanny and Susanna was my charge.

Of course I noticed things. Like how Susanna would get on the plane long before me, because she had a seat in first or business class, and then completely ignore me when I entered with my fellow inmates in economy. There'd she be, all settled into her wide, comfy seat, sipping something, making calls or texting or working on her laptop as I filed past with the other prisoners.

I forgave her a lot because she was under incredible strain. I wasn't there to insinuate my personality but to soothe and validate hers. And despite all the problems, despite the back-breaking schedule and the petty humiliations and the fact that I was so inundated with details that I could barely sleep at night . . . I had a ball. It was a *private* ball, the pleasures of which I kept to myself because I sensed that Susanna wouldn't like it if she discovered I was enjoying myself when she so obviously was not.

I'd never travelled so far and wide or so fast. Every day we were in a new city, sometimes two. Charlotte, North Carolina; St Louis, Missouri; Atlanta, Georgia; Houston, Dallas, and Austin, Texas.

Susanna, I discovered, hadn't travelled much in the United States. 'And now I know why,' she grumbled. 'Everything looks exactly the same wherever you go.'

She meant the airports, and the freeways into the cities, always lined with the same fast-food restaurants and motel chains, and the sprawling suburbs with the giant malls and humongous parking lots and even the superstores where she gave her readings.

'Where are we?' she'd ask. 'It looks just like the last place.'

She didn't notice how the sky was different in every city. She didn't smell the different airs. If there were mountains or rivers or lakes, she didn't see them. She was an urban creature, like me, suspicious of nature, nervous when she wasn't within shouting distance of a Starbucks.

But I was a girl of the golden West, too, and was always looking for the mountain peak beyond the mall. That just seeps into your consciousness when you grow up in a place like Oregon. Tremaynne had been the one who really opened my eyes to what was still to be found 'out there', beyond the commercial strips. When he disappeared on our honeymoon, I'd been forced to go out into the wilderness, on my own, to find him. That experience, which I was trying to describe in my ongoing memoir, *My Three Husbands*, had given me a new respect for nature's power and a new responsiveness to its beauty.

But Susanna? Nah. For all her complaints about the sameness of everything, it was the sameness that made her feel safe. She was not interested in hacking new trails to reach her destination. She wanted a smooth, paved road.

Fat chance, with Mercury at the steering wheel, driving backwards and laughing hysterically.

'Who are all those unattractive people?' Susanna asked as we turned a corner in the mall and approached the bookstore. She was limping a little because she'd twisted her ankle the night before. She'd had a glass of wine in her hotel room 'to ease the pain'.

I squinted to read the signs. 'Do Not Suport Moral Coruption', 'God Hates Harlots', and 'If Not Married, Abstain'.

'They look like fundamentalists,' I reported.

'What the hell are they upset about?'

'You, I think.'

'Me? Why? I'm not gay.' She stopped and looked more closely. Five women and one man were standing in front of the bookstore's air door, waving signs and talking eagerly and angrily to a young woman holding a microphone, a news-cam behind her.

'Oh my God,' Susanna said. 'Are we in one of those horrible red states? Where they don't believe in evolution?'

'Or sex outside marriage, from the looks of it.'

'That,' Susanna said with a note of disgust, 'is ridiculous. Pre-marital sex is the only way a woman can tell if she's chosen the right partner.'

'It didn't work for me, but I'm with you in principle.'

'Well, they look like bullies and I'm not afraid of bullies,' she said staunchly. 'But do you think there's another entrance?'

'Look! There she is!' cried one of the women, pointing in our direction. 'Harlot!' she called. 'Child molester!'

'You bloody fat stupid cow!' Susanna hobbled angrily towards her. 'How dare you—'

'She promotes promiscuity!' shouted a woman who looked about my age but weighed about a hundred pounds more.

'I promote sexual equality for women,' Susanna said. 'I always have and I always will.'

'Do you approve of pre-marital sex?' The reporter shoved her microphone in Susanna's face.

'Of course I do!' Susanna said.

Oh, she shouldn't have had that glass of wine. She got angry and lost the hocus-pocus of her media-focusing skills. She should have known that that exchange ('Do you approve of pre-marital sex?' 'Of course I do!') was what they would pick up and air.

*

I always thought that somehow, somewhere, sometime I'd get to know Susanna better. You know, that she'd open up as a person, and tell me stuff that would make her more human.

I wanted that, I really did. Because the truth is, I knew next to nothing about her. She avoided talking about anything personal with me. Was that an English thing? A class thing? An employer/employee thing? Or was she simply incapable of any kind of intimacy – she who had made her name writing about sex?

I'd begun by thinking of her as my mentor, but now she wasn't pointing me in any direction I wanted to go.

The only time that came close to happening was one night, after a reading, when she coaxed me into the quiet, low-lit bar of our hotel by offering to buy me a drink. Susanna *never* offered to buy me a drink, so of course I said yes.

We slid into a booth. Susanna ordered a vodka stinger and I ordered a cosmopolitan.

She looked pleased and a little pensive. 'The reading went really well.'

I nodded. 'Not a single screw-up.' I didn't mean her, I meant the event itself. Maybe the planets were finally taking a rest from their retrogrades and returns.

'I signed a hundred and four copies.'

'Out of a hundred and twenty-five ordered. That's great.'

'I just wish I didn't have to do those awful question and answer things. I'm sick of answering their stupid questions.'

'The audience always likes that part.'

She was quiet for a moment, then said, with a note of wonder in her voice, 'You actually like people, don't you?'

'Well, not everyone – but overall – yeah, I do. Don't you?'

She shrugged. 'Not really. I do like *some*. People who make something of their lives. But in general? No.'

The waiter brought our drinks. Susanna said 'Cheers' and drained half her glass in one go.

'What about your audience,' I said, sipping my totally delicious cosmo. 'The people who come to your readings and buy your books?'

She sighed and settled back, relaxing for the first time that day. 'Oh, they're all right, I suppose.'

'You look like you enjoy being up there.'

'Actually, I loathe it. Horribly shy, if you can believe it. But I knew if I was ever going to get anywhere in life, I'd have to learn how to do things like that. Stand in front of people and exude confidence.' She finished off her stinger and signalled the waiter for another.

'So you overcame your shyness –'

'Shyness is visible insecurity. Have you ever known a shy person to get anywhere in life? It's a kind of pathology. It's disgusting.'

'Were you always shy?'

'Yes.' She sipped her fresh drink. 'Except when I was drunk, of course. You don't drink much, do you?'

'No.'

'Drugs?'

I shook my head. 'Not since I was a teenager.'

'I used to drink a lot,' Susanna said. 'Giles and I. My God we put it away.'

'I suppose Giles was shy, too,' I said teasingly.

Susanna let out a big hearty laugh. 'Giles? That's very funny.'

'You two've known one another for a long time,' I said.

Susanna smiled, secretive as a cat. 'Don't you think Giles Travaille is the most attractive man you've ever met in your entire life?' she asked.

'He's pretty cute,' I said.

'Cute is not an adjective that applies to Giles.'

'OK. Handsome.'

'Sexy, wouldn't you say?'

I shrugged. I no longer found Giles that sexy. He was looking more and more like a faded, jaded party boy to me. One of those coked-up guys desperate to believe that forty-something was the new twenty-something. But I didn't want to say any of this to Susanna because I detected a softening in her armor and I suspected it had to do with Giles.

'I think he's just the most incredibly sexy and charismatic

man I've ever known,' she said, with the dreamy relish of a schoolgirl. 'I've thought so since the first moment I laid eyes on him.'

'You went to the same college or something,' I hinted.

'Has that ever happened to you?' she asked. 'You look at someone and it's almost like you're hypnotized. You'd do anything they asked.'

I nodded. 'Tremaynne. My last husband.'

'That sensation', Susanna said, 'is the most primal sexual attraction in the world. And woe to the woman who gives in to it. Because once she does, she's lost.'

I nodded. 'I know.'

'She evaporates. Her life becomes his. But his life never becomes hers. So she's doomed.' She finished her second stinger and signalled for a third. 'That's why it's dangerous to be a shy girl. Shy girls are always looking for the man who'll release them from the spell. And of course he never does, because it's in his best interest not to.'

I just had to ask. 'So are you in love with Giles?'

Susanna narrowed her frosty blue eyes and looked down at the table. 'It's rather more complicated than that.'

I sipped my cosmo and waited for her to say more, then wondered if that was it, if she'd spilled all the beans she was going to. But then she said, quietly, 'Giles and I are soul-mates. We understand each other. We're partners, but not in any . . . conventional sense.'

And maybe she would have said more, or maybe I would have gotten up the nerve to probe further, but just then two guys approached our table. Twins. I mean, identical. They looked younger than me, college age, very cute but with a smart-ass preppy look about them. They were dressed in blue jeans and blazers and wore loafers with brightly colored socks. They looked weirdly glossy, with their buzz-cut blond hair and chiselled Nordic faces, like iconic American male dolls you might see staring out of boxes in a toy store.

'Hey,' first one, then the other, said shyly, looking from Susanna to me.

I smiled, Susanna didn't. Neither of us said anything.

'Um, we were at your reading,' said one of the twins.

After a long pause, Susanna said politely, 'I hope you enjoyed it.'

'Oh, man, it was awesome,' said the other. 'Really sexy.'

'We loved hearing you read about fucking that guy.'

'Young enough to be your son.'

Susanna said, 'Did that turn you on?'

'Sure did,' said Twin A.

'Then I suggest you go home and rape your mum.'

At this their mouths flew open and they laughed, showing their big milk-white perfectly formed teeth. 'Wow,' said Twin B, looking at his brother. 'Is she hot or what?'

'Actually,' said Twin A, 'we were wondering if we could be your new puppies.'

Susanna said, 'Not my breed, I'm afraid.'

'Actually,' said Twin B, 'what we were wondering is, would you like to be a guest on our reality show? *Doubletake*. It's really cool. See, it's all about twins. We share this small house and . . .'

'I don't think we inhabit the same reality,' Susanna said.

'Because you're so old, you mean?' Twin A looked at me. 'Maybe you'd like to be in our show.'

'No thanks.'

'Why not? We've got the camera equipment. We've just gotta shoot some footage before we pitch it to the networks.'

'I think I know what kind of footage you have in mind,' Susanna said. 'And I know exactly where you can pitch it.'

'I simply *adore* Los Angeles,' Susanna gushed to the young reporter from the *LA Times*.

Susanna was star-struck, like everyone else in LA. She looked great, like everyone else in LA. Nothing on her body was swollen, sprained, or sprouting. The moment we arrived she'd gone to our hotel's high-end salon for a facial, manicure, pedicure, massage and body wrap in heated grape skins. 'I'm utterly *exhausted*,' she complained. 'If I don't take care of myself, I'll simply collapse.'

I didn't say anything. Relaxing for a couple of hours and getting a full-spa treatment would have been a deeply religious experience for me just then.

My boss exhibited more excitement in LA than she had in any of the other cities we'd been to. This was due, in part, to a phone call from Grace Glickman, her agent, telling her that a production company had 'expressed interest' in her book. That meant a possible movie version of *Puppy Love*. That meant that Susanna might be played by a famous actress.

'Who would you like to play you?' the reporter asked, after Susanna told her she was 'in discussions' for an adaptation of her book to the screen. 'Helen Mirren?'

Susanna's smile looked a little strained. 'Helen's a great actress. But she's in her sixties now, isn't she?'

'And how old are you?' asked the young reporter, flipping her straight blonde hair out of her face. That face – it spooked me. Like so many faces in LA, it looked too perfect for its own good. I suddenly had the weird thought that maybe the reporter was an actress playing a reporter.

'I'm forty-three,' Susanna said, shaving off a couple years.

'Oh, then you won't have any trouble finding an older actress to play you,' the reporter said. 'You can have your pick. In Hollywood, every actress who hits forty is a has-been.'

'Yes,' Susanna said, rather sharply, 'but that's the whole point of my book. That women are just reaching their sexual prime at forty, and—'

'I thought the whole point of your book was that you, as an older woman, want desperately to stay sexually active, and you couldn't find anyone your own age, so you—'

'Did you actually *read* my book?' Susanna asked.

'Skimmed it. Got the gist. So let's talk about Jimmy, your puppy love. Who do you think should play him?'

'I hadn't really thought about it,' Susanna said.

'What about this guy – this' – the young reporter skimmed her notes and innocently blinked her big eyes in Susanna's direction – 'Josh O'Connell.'

'Who?' Susanna feigned ignorance.

'Is he the real Jimmy, as he claims?'

'Of course not.'

'Then why is he making these claims?'

'I have no idea. To get attention, I suppose.'

'Who *is* the real Jimmy?' the reporter asked.

Susanna gave her a guarded smile. 'Jimmy is – well, he's the young man I describe in *Puppy Love*. That's all I can say.'

'But he does exist?' the reporter asked.

Susanna shifted in her chair. 'Of course he exists. *Puppy Love* is a memoir about our time together.'

'If a reader asked you for some kind of proof that this *is* a memoir, that these events, this May-December love affair between an old woman and a young boy, actually happened, that it's not a complete fabrication, as some have claimed, what would you tell them?'

'Good question,' Susanna said, deflecting the reporter's hostility. She reflected for a moment before giving her answer. 'I'd tell them that *Puppy Love* came from my heart. I'd tell them the book is about my experience as an older woman with a younger man. It's bittersweet, and not without humor.'

Her 'sincerity' was as sincere as anything I heard in Los Angeles. It answered the question by not answering the question at all.

San Francisco was the only place where Susanna did something 'touristy'.

'I've always wanted to ride that bloody cable car,' she said. 'I don't know why. It's totally irrational. But I want to do it.'

So there we were on California Street, on a bright windy afternoon, jammed in a cable car with all the other tourists, thrilling to the sight of the Golden Gate Bridge and San Francisco Bay in the distance.

Well, I was thrilled. I don't know what Susanna felt. She'd been relatively quiet and unusually task-free all morning. A little pensive, maybe, now that we were nearing the end of this calamitous book tour. She'd walked the gauntlet, I have to say. My job, I realized, was easy in comparison, because I was not on display, as she was. She looked a little tired, as if some of her usually abundant energy had been sucked out or used up.

Being or becoming famous is a battle. I saw that now. There was nothing glamorous about being glamorous. It was hard work carried out against impossible odds in a world full of monsters.

I felt the wind tearing through my hair and smelled the bright, salty air and thought how lucky I was to be alive and doing something interesting with my life. That was one thing I would always be grateful to Susanna for: that she took me on and gave me an opportunity to learn what I could do.

When we returned to the hotel, she said she was feeling tired and wanted to rest. The wind had given her a slight earache.

That evening she gave a good reading to an appreciative audience. I could tell that her energy level was still low, but everything had gone well that day and I was lulled into thinking that maybe the worst was behind us. There were only two cities left: Portland and Chicago, where she was scheduled to be the star speaker at the University of Chicago's 'Women and Sex' conference.

After the signing, we headed back to the hotel a couple of blocks away. In the hotel lobby Susanna was stopped by a woman, probably in her mid- to late-sixties, wearing big dark glasses, a belted raincoat, and carrying an umbrella.

'Susanna?' the woman said in a deep voice.

We stopped. Susanna cocked her head, as if she wasn't quite sure if she knew this person or not.

'Don't you recognize me?' the woman said, removing her dark glasses.

'No – I –' But she kept staring, unable to draw her eyes away.

'I'm your husband,' the woman said.

'Keep it zipped,' Susanna said the next morning when I came in to pack her things for the trip to Portland. She didn't mean her suitcase, she meant my mouth. I knew without asking that she wanted me to keep quiet about the encounter she'd had the night before in the hotel lobby. 'I can trust you to keep your mouth shut, can't I?'

'You should know that by now.' I watched her out of the corner of my eye. She looked both dazed and agitated, like a boxer who'd taken one too many hits in the ring.

The flight was uneventful. It was a brilliantly clear day and from my window seat back in economy I gazed out at vast stretches of forest and the giant, snow-covered peaks of the Oregon Cascades. My heart gave a tug. Was Tremaynne down there, hiding somewhere in that wilderness?

At the Portland airport, Susanna flung herself on Whitman, who'd come to meet us, like a long-lost lover. 'Darling! Oh, I can't begin to tell you how *horrible* everything's been!'

She didn't look too pleased when Whitman disengaged himself to embrace me. 'Hello, sweetheart.'

'Hello, faux pa.' Whitman, just back from a press trip to another 'sacred beach' somewhere in the South Pacific, looked fit and fabulous, with a bronzy tan and golden streaks glinting in his blond hair. His casual dress was impeccable, as usual, and his overall elegance made him stand out from the crowds in the airport. Suddenly I could see why Daddy had fallen in love with him.

'Your real pa's hog-tied in a meeting for that new resort he's designing,' Whitman said, gathering up our carry-ons.

'No!' Susanna stopped him before he could take our laptops and hung her own on my shoulder. '*She*'s the laptop girl.'

'Oh.' Whitman turned to me with a look of amusement. 'I guess I didn't read the job description.'

'My entire *life* is on that bloody computer,' Susanna said. 'If it's ever lost or stolen –'

'I'm to blame,' I said. But no one laughed, maybe because we all knew it was true.

As he ushered us down to the luggage carousels, Whitman turned his attention back to me. 'Your mother sends her love and says she knows you probably don't have an extra minute for her.'

My mom, I knew, was beside herself with excitement that I was coming back under what she called 'such glamorous circumstances'.

'My my,' Susanna said sourly, keeping an eye on us as she scouted the carousel for her Louis Vuitton suitcase, 'I had no idea you were such a close-knit family.'

Whitman kept his arm around me, squeezing me close, something he usually didn't do. 'Looks like you've held up well, sweetheart.'

'Just barely!' Susanna cried before I had time to answer. 'My God, Whitman, if you're ever a successful book author I hope you *never* have to go through what *I've* been through.' She pointed to her precious suitcase. 'That one, darling. Snag it before someone steals it, will you?' Whitman, my fellow porter, hauled her heavy suitcase off the rack, flipped up the pull-handle, and started to arrange Susanna's heavy carry-on on top of it.

'No, darling,' Susanna said, 'the carry-on has to be carried.'

Whitman looked at her, then at me. I nodded.

'I don't want it to scratch my poor Louis Vuitton.'

Without saying a word, Whitman hoisted her carry-on up on his shoulder. Susanna clutched his free arm and cast her frosty, disapproving eyes around the terminal as we headed up to the parking garage. 'I've never seen so many obese people in my life,' she said. 'How can you stand it, darling, not living in New York? You must feel like Oscar Wilde visiting the miners out here.'

'The West has its charms,' Whitman said as we made our way through the parking garage.

'Like what?' Susanna wanted to know.

'A partner who loves me.'

That shut her up – for a second.

'But you'd have more of a career if you lived in New York,' she said.

'Maybe.' Whitman smiled at her. 'But would I have a life?' He led us to his sleek new silver Acura, opened the passenger door, and helped Susanna in. I squeezed in back, behind Whitman, because Susanna immediately extended and reclined her seat, leaving no room to sit behind it.

'Frankly, darling, you look knackered,' Whitman said to Susanna as we sped towards town.

'Do I?' Susanna whipped down the sun visor and slid open the mirror, examining herself with a look of alarm. 'Well, I'm exhausted. *Totally exhausted*. And I think I may be coming down with something.'

'I'll take you to your hotel so you can lie down.'

Susanna stroked his arm. 'Will you lie down with me, darling? I need a friend. Someone to talk to. An *adult*.' She cast a sidelong glance at me, sitting all hunched up in the back seat.

'I'll come back to the hotel this afternoon,' Whitman said. 'I thought I'd surprise Carolee and bring Venus over to—'

'No,' Susanna snapped. 'She can't go. I need her.'

Whitman caught my eye in the rearview mirror. 'Would you like to stay with us tonight, sweetheart? Or with your mother? So we'll have a little more time together?'

'She *can't*,' Susanna insisted. 'I *need* her.'

'Sounds like you've become invaluable,' Whitman said to me.

'No one's *invaluable*,' Susanna said with a dismissive huff.

I was so accustomed to her snide, cynical remarks that I

hardly thought anything of it. But Whitman gave her a sharp, rebuking glance, as if she'd offended him instead of me. But Susanna didn't see it. She yawned, let out a vague groan, and closed her eyes.

'I guess you'll have to wait until the reading to see your mother,' Whitman said quietly to me. 'And she'll be at the party afterwards, of course.'

Susanna's eyes snapped open. 'What party?'

'Susanna, I told you. John and I are hosting a reception for you. After the reading.'

'Oh *God* – how many people?'

'Fifty,' Whitman said. 'The caterers are at the house right now.'

'Who are these fifty people?' Susanna asked suspiciously.

'Friends. People who want to meet you and see Venus again.'

'Are they buying my book?' Susanna asked.

'Yes,' Whitman said, 'they're all buying your book. And you're going to do a private signing. And we're providing hors d'oeuvres and champagne and music.'

'They have a beautiful house,' I chipped in from the back seat. The dads' parties were always special, and I was excited to go.

'Well,' Susanna said frowningly, ignoring me, looking at Whitman, 'I suppose I could do that. Just for you, darling. If they'll all buy the book.'

As soon as we'd checked in at the hotel, Susanna handed Whitman her room key and, taking his arm and pressing close as a newlywed, let him escort her up to her suite. 'We don't want to be disturbed,' she informed me at her door.

'Can't Venus join us?' Whitman asked.

'No. I desperately need to talk to *you*.' She gave him a Meaningful Look and turned back to me. 'Call room service and order a bottle of Chardonnay and two glasses to be brought up.' Before she closed her door I caught a glimpse of Whitman, standing behind her. He shot me a perplexed glance and shrugged his shoulders, as if to say he had no idea what was going on with Susanna.

Was Susanna trying to make me jealous by usurping Whitman's attention? Was she attempting to seduce Whitman, my faux pa, right under my nose? Was it business? She was his boss, after all. Or did she just need to unload on her old friend in a way she never could with me?

We'd been booked into adjoining rooms but the walls were too thick to hear clearly what was being said. I got a glass from the minibar, held it up to the wall, and heard the sound of Susanna's voice, sometimes rising to a fevered pitch, once breaking into heaving sobs (was that possible?), and Whitman's low, measured tones as he responded.

Hmm. I called room service and ordered Susanna's bottle of wine and a glass of red wine for myself. I was standing there, holding the water glass up to the wall with one hand and sipping my wine with the other, when my cellphone rang. I didn't need the caller ID to tell me who it was.

'You're here!' Mom cried. 'Oh, sweetheart, I can't wait to see you. How's Susanna?'

Mom had met Susanna once, for all of five seconds, shaking her hand at the holiday office party, but she made it sound like the two of them were best buddies. 'She's OK,' I said. 'She's holed up with Whitman.'

'I told all the women in my ecstatic dancing class about her reading tonight,' Mom said. 'They're all coming.'

'I thought you quit that.'

'I did,' Mom said, 'but I missed the twirling. So I thought it would be cute if we all came to the reading wearing our dancing veils.'

I took a big sip, almost a gulp, of my wine. 'Mom, please don't do that.'

'Why not? Susanna boogies with the goddess every day of her life! That's what *Aura*'s all about.'

For the next half-hour I pleaded with her not to wear her dancing veils to Susanna's reading. The last time Susanna had met her, Mom had red glitter all over her face and blinking earrings. Susanna had kept her professional poise but her glance – sliding from Mom's smiling face to my own – spoke volumes.

An hour later, as I was unpacking and freaking out because I had absolutely *nothing* to wear to the dads' big party, there was a knock on my door. When I opened it, Whitman slipped in. He stood there, saying nothing but breathing deeply, as if trying to regain his composure.

'Whitman, what's wrong?' I asked.

He shook his head. 'My God,' he whispered. 'This is the stuff of memoirs.'

'What happened?'

'I've been sworn to secrecy.' He strode excitedly into my room, stopped at the window, and turned to look at me. 'But I feel I should tell you. Actually, I feel like I should write it down, right now, before I forget.'

'*Whitman* –'

His face turned serious. 'Look, sweetheart, things might be getting a little ugly for Susanna, and you might be right in the thick of it.'

I sat down on the bed and looked at him. 'Is it about that woman who came to the hotel last night?'

Whitman nodded.

'She said – this woman said – she was Susanna's *husband*.'

Whitman nodded again. 'She is.' And then he told me the story of what happened to the man Susanna had married years earlier and whose apartment on Riverside Drive Susanna now called her own.

He'd run off to San Francisco to become a woman. But the situation was complicated by the fact that halfway through the gender realignment process he discovered that the hormones that gave him breasts were also poisoning his liver, so he'd stopped before the critical cut. He lived as a woman, but still had what Whitman called 'his male equipment'.

'Does that make him Susanna's husband or wife?' I asked.

'I think it makes him a little of each,' Whitman said.

Until their encounter in the hotel lobby, he went on,

Susanna hadn't seen her husband since 1995. Back then, when her husband told her he was leaving New York, Susanna didn't try to stop him. In fact, she encouraged him to go. Because by that time she was a US citizen and the apartment, now a co-op, was registered in both their names. Since theirs was purely a marriage of convenience, she didn't much care where he went or what he did.

It was only when things heated up with Lord Stuckey that her marriage of convenience became an inconvenience. If she married Lord Stuckey without first divorcing her husband or having him declared dead, she'd be guilty of bigamy. But how could she divorce a missing person? Where was he? She didn't have a clue.

Meanwhile, her long-lost husband had seen all the media hoo-ha about Susanna's memoir and the book tour and her relationship with Lord Stuckey, and decided he wanted to move back to New York. Back to the co-op apartment on Riverside Drive, which was still half his.

'But that wasn't what he really wanted,' Whitman said.

'What did he really want?' I asked breathlessly.

What he really wanted was money. Now, at the height of New York's overheated housing market, when the value of their New York co-op on Riverside Drive was three million dollars, he wanted Susanna to buy out his share. If Susanna did that, he'd be able to buy a nice little place in Hawaii and live out her/his twilight bi-gender years in comfort. And he'd let her divorce him without any further settlement.

And if Susanna didn't fork over the million and a half dollars?

Why, she/he would blab to the blog and to every tabloid in the US and UK. Imagine the headlines Lord Stuckey would see in the papers . . .

Susanna was desperate. Oh my God, she wailed to Whitman, why was nothing going right? Why was everyone out to get her? Why was the past coming back to haunt her? *Now*, of all times, when she was so close to reaching her goal?

'What did you say?' I asked. 'What did you tell her?'

Whitman shook his head. 'Nothing. She'll have to find her own answer, just like the rest of us poor mortals.' He looked at me. 'These are dangerous days for her, sweetheart. She's right on the edge, as I'm sure you know.'

The tone of his voice made me a little nervous. 'What should I do?'

'Just watch your back, sweetheart, and be prepared for anything.'

The 'events' room at the bookstore was packed for Susanna's reading. She did a pretty good job, considering all she was going through, but I detected a kind of feverish glitter in her eyes. She was pushing too hard, hamming it up in a way she never had before and losing her place a couple of times.

Afterwards, while she was signing books, I dashed back to change for the party. 'I'll meet you in front of the hotel,' I told Daddy. He was going to drive Mom and me, and Whitman would bring Susanna after she'd finished her store signing.

Any party at the dads was a special event and the big question, as always, had been what to wear. I was *totally* sick of all the sensible ensembles I'd mixed 'n' matched while on the road with Susanna. And for once – just once – I wanted to out-glam her. 'Susanna thinks the party's all for her,' Whitman had told me before he left that afternoon, 'but it's for you, too.' And it was *my* hometown, after all, and *my* family.

So when Whitman left and while my employer napped, I'd snuck out and made my way over to Rethreads, a funky used-clothing boutique just a couple of blocks from the hotel. There, amidst the sweet, familiar smells of mothballs, vanished perfumes, and old clothes, my eye immediately fastened on a silk hostess gown with a black strapless top and long slits up the sides of a billowing, wine-colored skirt. 'They used to wear Capri pants underneath,' the clerk told me, picking at her pierced eyebrow, 'but a pair of fishnets would be cute, if you ask me.'

With the fishnets and open-toed high-heeled sandals, the whole get-up set me back almost a hundred dollars. But I didn't care. When I slipped on my new ensemble I felt like a gorgeous, glamorous movie star from the Fifties. The bodice of the dress was a little too tight, forcing my boobs up, and I noticed a stain on the skirt which the sales clerk hadn't pointed out, but it was definitely me. I knew that the moment I made my entrance in the hotel lobby, holding up my skirt so I wouldn't trip, and the doorman said, 'Just say the word and I'm yours for life.'

It was weird driving up to the dads' house with both my biological parents in the same vehicle. They'd been divorced for over twenty years, since I was five years old. That was when Daddy finally realized he was gay – by falling in love with Whitman. Mom, who found it difficult to hate anyone, had always tried to be supportive, even when she felt abandoned and betrayed. 'I knew your father was gay when I married him,' she once confided to me. 'I think that was partly why I fell in love with him. But like a fool I thought I could change him.' Over the years, the two of them – three, I should say, since Whitman was involved – developed an amicable relationship. But my linear, left-brained Dad simply could not 'understand' his free-flowing, right-brained ex-wife. 'Your mother doesn't seem to have any – *filters*,' he once told me.

What a mystery love is, I thought, squeezed into the back of Daddy's BMW and studying my parents. At one time they must have been happy, however briefly, and seen themselves as a workable couple. It was almost impossible to imagine now.

Daddy was wearing a dark suit. Mom had heeded my pleas to leave her dancing veils at home and instead worn a violent yellow tent dress covered with what she claimed were ancient fertility symbols.

'Well, Gilroy,' Mom said, turning to Daddy, 'our little girl's done pretty well for herself, wouldn't you say?'

Daddy glanced at her and smiled. 'Yes, I would say.' He seemed a bit preoccupied, as if he were still coming down from a tense meeting.

With difficulty, Mom shifted around to look at me.

'Susanna's lucky to have you. Has she ever been married, by the way?'

'Um – I really don't know,' I lied. 'Why?'

'She seems awfully close to Whitman,' Mom said, looking at Daddy.

'Old friends,' he said.

'Yes, I know. And of course she's going to marry Lord Stuckey and everything, but she just seems so – I don't know – *clingy* with Whitman.' She paused. 'Were they ever lovers?' she asked Daddy.

'Whitman and Susanna?' Daddy laughed. 'Not that I know of.' He cast his ex-wife a sidelong glance. 'Why?'

'A woman just *notices* certain things, that's all,' Mom said mysteriously.

'Like what?' Now Daddy sounded concerned.

'Oh, just little things. The way she acts around him. It's always "*darling*".'

'That's just New York,' Daddy said.

'And this party Whitman's throwing,' Mom went on. 'It must be costing you a fortune. He told me champagne. And a jazz combo.'

'Whitman likes to do things right,' Daddy said. 'Anyway, the party's as much for Venus as for what's-her-name.'

'Susanna,' Mom said. 'Her name's Susanna.'

Her name was Susanna, but my name was Venus, and that's what I heard ten minutes later when I entered the dads' fabulous glass-walled house high in the hills overlooking Portland.

'Venus!' they cried. 'There's Venus!'

You know how maybe once or twice in your life you get to make a perfect entrance? Everyone stopped talking and looked over at me as I took Daddy's arm, sort of carelessly bunching up my long, wine-colored silk skirt with my other hand, and swept down the three long stone steps into the giant wood-panelled room with the lights of the city sparkling beyond it.

For once it wasn't Susanna hogging all the limelight. And a rush of emotion, or exhilaration, came over me as everyone gathered round to greet and welcome me back to Portland.

Marielle and Fokke, the dads' super-rich and highly cultured Dutch friends, beckoned me over to them. Or maybe I was just pulled by the sight of Marielle's famous yellow diamonds, sparkling on her neck, ear and hand. Beneath her diamonds, she wore tight black leather pants, a scoop-necked leather tunic with a wide, soft, yellow-leather belt, and spike heels that added several inches to her already-Amazonian height. Fokke, about a foot shorter than his auburn-haired wife, had on a soft gray suit. They vigorously kissed me the Dutch way: first on one cheek, then the other, then on the first again.

'You need some jewelry with that dress,' Marielle said, appraising me. And before I could say anything, she slipped off her yellow diamond earrings and clipped them on to my ear lobes. 'Just for the party, eh? Don't shake your head too much.'

'Oh my God, Marielle.' I tightened my neck, terrified that one of the long, dangling earrings would fall off, and stiffly turned to look at myself in a mirror.

'Marielle, you're being too generous again,' Fokke said, giving his thinning hair an anxious swipe.

'Oh shut up. That's my nature.' Marielle peeked over my shoulder into the mirror. 'That's Venus's nature too, eh? To be generous. Sometimes a little too generous.' She leaned close, fiddling with my hair, and whispered in my ear, 'I'm sorry the last husband didn't work out. But you were too good for him, eh?'

'Dat last husband of yours turned out to be a *loser*,' Fokke said.

'Oh shut *up*,' Marielle scolded.

'Now dat you're single again,' Fokke said, eyeing the heart tattooed above my heart, 'I suppose you play night and day. Out dere in dat Big Apple dat never sleeps.'

'Actually, I work a lot.'

Fokke laughed. 'Ven you're not playing, you mean. Going out to clubs and dose wild parties.'

'Right,' I said. And for a moment, the glamorous creature I saw in the mirror, the one wearing a strapless silk gown and yellow diamond earrings, became the carefree playgirl Fokke was imagining.

'Veeeee-nus.' Lordy Mallory, the cadaverous old society columnist who showed up at every Portland event whether she was invited or not, fastened a skeletal claw on my arm and led me away. 'Always such a striking girl. Who designed your gown, my dear?'

'Oh, it's—'

'Some famous New York couturier, no doubt. You know, my dear, I used to wear gowns like that. But *always* with Capri pants.'

'Oh look, it's Venus looking Venusy.' Snobby Rory Schnab, heir to a tire fortune, stroked my arm with his pudgy hand. 'I'm going to New York next week, honey. What are the hot restaurants I absolutely have to try?'

'Well, I like Gray's Papaya at 72nd and Broadway,' I said. 'Two hot dogs and a medium-sized papaya drink for under three dollars.'

Rory tittered, thinking it was a joke.

'Or L'Albatross,' I said knowingly. 'That's on everyone's BlackBerry.'

'I want your life!' Thisbe Nesbitt with her short brown bob and pixie face sidled up and clutched my hand, as if we were two contestants in a beauty pageant. 'I'm sick of boring old Portland. I want to live in New York and have fun like you.'

'Doesn't she took fabulous?' Rory said.

'Fabulous,' Thisbe agreed. She looked pretty great herself, in a black leotard top and a skirt that flared out like stiff layers of crinoline, 'Of course Venus can get away with anything.' She heaved a sigh. 'I'm just a boring old Boomer, but Venus is a gorgeous Va-Va-Voomer.'

'Is your husband here, my dear?' Lordy asked. 'I seem to recall one of your fathers telling me that you'd married again.'

'No,' I said, hating her for asking, 'he's not here.'

'He was a tree-sitter or something,' Rory remembered.

'An environmentalist,' I said.

Thisbe stroked my arm and gave me a sympathetic glance. 'God knows we need 'em with this administration.'

Lordy prided herself on remembering every name that had ever been dropped in her direction, but she seemed to be having a memory lapse. She frowned as much as her severely lifted face would allow. 'I can't quite recall his *name*, my dear.'

'Tremaynne,' I said, and added bravely, 'we're divorced.'

'Divorced?' Lordy looked confused. 'But I thought your fathers said you just got married.'

Thisbe quickly and tactfully changed the subject, lowering her voice to a confidential undertone. 'Everyone's dying to know what she's really like, Venus. Is she a horrible bitch?'

'Is who a horrible bitch?' Mom asked, handing me a flute of champagne.

There was a moment of silence as the others took in her dress and her question.

'Susanna Hyde,' Thisbe said.

'Oh, no, Susanna's a *lovely* person,' Mom said, sipping her champagne.

'Have you met her?' Rory asked.

'Oh yes,' Mom said grandly. 'In New York. At the Twilight Room. Susanna was there with Lord Stuckey. You know, the media baron she's going to marry.'

'I thought I read somewhere that he dumped her,' Rory said.

'Oh no,' Mom said. 'I don't think so. I'm sure I would have heard.'

'What about her puppy love?' Rory asked.

'Her puppy love was my son's age,' Thisbe said, looking up as her tall, silver-haired husband Ed slid in beside her. 'Not that I hold it against her or anything.'

'Hold what against whom?' Ed asked in his deep, slow, lawyer's voice. His eyes wandered over to eye-lick my uplifted breasts.

'Nothing,' Thisbe said forlornly. 'If she's over forty and can still get boys to play with her, more power to her.'

Lordy Mallory's eyes, old but lifted and pulled tight in a look of perennial surprise, had been fastened on Mom's searingly yellow tent dress for some time. 'My dear,' she said, squinting, 'what *are* those figures on your gown? You appear to be covered with—'

'Fertility symbols.' Mom lifted her arms and turned in a circle, showing off her dress. 'Isn't it cute? They handprint them over at Gaia Gals. These are the male organs and these are the vulvas.' She pointed out what looked like unfolding flowers.

'The what symbols?' Lordy was a little hard of hearing.

'Vulvas!' Thisbe shouted.

'Volvos?' Lordy frowned. 'Why they don't look like cars at all. They look like—'

But everyone's attention was distracted just then by the appearance of Whitman and Susanna. 'Here we are!' Whitman announced as they swept through the front door.

Guests applauded, the jazz combo started playing, and the party instantly moved into higher gear. Susanna, accustomed to making an entrance, stood at the top of the three stone stairs and positioned herself under a light that illuminated her as if she were on stage. She allowed Whitman to remove her coat, then smiled up at him, just as she had with Lord Stuckey at the office party. Taking Whitman's arm, she regally descended into our midst.

When she saw me, standing in a knot of friends, in my silk gown, with Marielle's yellow diamonds sparkling in my ears and a flute of champagne in my hand – *at home in my dads' home* – a look passed over her face that almost scared me.

'Let's get you set up at the escritoire,' Whitman said.

For about an hour Susanna sat at Whitman's small, portable, seventeenth-century French writing table – the only old piece of furniture allowed in the dads' severely modernist house – and signed books while Whitman brought her champagne and delicious little delicacies from the buffet table. She completely ignored me until Whitman left her side to take care of some party details. Then she motioned me over.

'That's the first time I've seen that dress,' she said.

'It's the first time I've worn it.'

'Where did those earrings come from?'

'Do you like them?' I asked.

Susanna didn't respond. 'Get me some aspirin,' she said. 'I feel awful.'

And up close she looked pretty bad, too. Her face was pinched, her skin had lost its glow, and her eyes had a feverish sheen, as if she was fighting off a major virus. I lifted my skirt and rustled off to find some aspirin. Upstairs, in the dads' huge, open, impossibly neat bedroom with its low Italian bed and minimalist furniture, I ran into Daddy. He was just ending a call.

'Damn clients.' He pocketed his cellphone and held out his arms. 'Hello, my sweet. Did I tell you how beautiful you look tonight?'

I snuggled in his strong, safe arms. 'Thank you, Daddy.'

'Well, she's certainly a piece of work, isn't she?'

'Mm-hm.'

'The way she acts towards Whitman,' Daddy said. 'I find it kind of irritating. It's like she's just taken him over.'

'That's how she is with men,' I said.

'The sooner she leaves the better, as far as I'm concerned.'

I looked at him and smiled. 'You're jealous, Daddy.'

'Is that what it is?' He released me from his embrace. 'Well, don't tell Whitman.'

When I returned with two aspirin in my hand, Susanna's temper flared. 'In your sweaty palm? Why didn't you bring the bottle, for God's sake?'

My eyes caught Thisbe's, who was standing there waiting for her book to be signed. 'Remember that question I asked you earlier?' she said. 'I think I know the answer now.'

After her grouchy hour signing books, Susanna put her hand up and hailed Whitman as if he were a taxi. I watched as she pulled him close and whispered in his ear, shaking her head and touching her forehead.

Whitman didn't look too happy but, always the gentleman,

he steered Susanna through the room one last time, explaining to his guests that she had to leave. Watching their progress through the crowd, I remembered Susanna once telling me she did not like people 'in general'. I could see now how hard it was for her to connect with strangers. She held herself aloof and acted like a queen among rather distasteful commoners.

Finally Whitman led her over to the group I was standing with and reintroduced Carolee and some other friends.

'Oh, right, you're the mother,' Susanna said, glancing not at Carolee but at her dress. 'Why are you covered with all those flying cocks?'

'Fertility symbols,' Mom said. 'I wore this in your honour.'

'Excuse me?' Susanna said.

'Because you write so openly about sex,' Mom explained. She turned to Marielle and the others in our group. 'Have you read Susanna's "Nothing to Hyde" column in *Aura*?'

No one had. They all politely shook their heads.

'I think it's got *so* much better,' Mom said. 'It's so much – I don't know – *fresher* now.'

Susanna looked at me with daggers in her eyes. She was the only one who knew, of course, that I now wrote her column.

'Maybe we could get together some time and exchange notes,' Mom blithely suggested. 'I'm going to be writing my own memoir, you know.'

'Really,' Susanna said, folding her arms and audibly sighing.

'I thought I'd call it *Giddyup, Goddess*.' Mom snagged another glass of champagne from a passing tray. 'For the spiritual awakening part. What do you think?' she asked Susanna.

Susanna shrugged.

'Of course, writing a memoir is really a *healing* process,' Mom said, 'isn't it?'

'I suppose so,' Susanna said. 'If you're sick.' She turned to me. 'I really need to go. Fetch my coat. Chop chop.'

I was having a great time and I wanted to stay. But Susanna suddenly looked as if she might collapse, so I hurried off to get her coat.

'You can stay, can't you?' Mom said, following me around as I collected Susanna's things. 'Whitman can take care of her.'

I shook my head. Duty called. It had been wonderfully fun, but my short time at the ball was over. At the dads, I'd been treated like returning royalty. I, as much as Susanna, had been the center of attention. But now, from across the room, Marielle tapped her ear lobes to signal that it was time for Cinderella to return her borrowed jewels.

Susanna stood to one side, watching impatiently as I hugged Carolee and Daddy goodbye. 'I hardly got a chance to see you!' Mom cried, folding me in her arms.

'Can we please *go*,' Susanna said crossly from the doorway.

Susanna barely said a word as Whitman drove us back down through the hills of Portland. Finally Whitman said, 'Susanna, are you all right?'

'No,' she said in a tired, cranky voice. 'I told you, I feel absolutely wretched. Feverish, spacey, and the whole right side of my face is all sort of tingly.'

'You need to get some rest,' Whitman said. 'You may have picked up something on one of your flights.'

He escorted us into the hotel lobby. 'Stay longer next time,' he said, hugging me. When he turned to Susanna, she reached up and pulled his face to hers, kissing him on the lips. She didn't say a word but there was a pleading look in her eyes, as if she was afraid to let him go.

'Take care of yourself,' Whitman said to her. He turned to me. 'You too.' He gave me another quick hug and a smooch before hurrying back to his car.

'Does my face look *odd*?' Susanna asked in a raspy voice when we were back in her room.

'No, but you look tired.'

'Oh,' she sighed, kicking off her heels and collapsing into a chair, 'I am mortally knackered. All those awful people, clamoring for my attention.'

'They're not awful,' I said, 'they're really nice.'

'And I have to be up for Chicago tomorrow. And then back

at *Aura* the day after that – because this has been my bloody *holiday*.'

I knew Chicago was important to her. They were paying her a fortune to be the keynote speaker at a big 'Women and Sex' conference at the University of Chicago. 'You'd better go right to bed,' I said. 'It's a big day tomorrow.'

'I need to go over my speech first.'

'The speech is fine,' I said. She'd been working on it obsessively, having me retype it day after day until I practically knew the whole thing by heart. 'Just go to bed.'

She sighed and looked at me in an oddly childlike way. 'Yes, Nanny.'

When she was safely tucked in, I went to my room, changed clothes, and headed back down to the lobby. I stepped outside and took a long deep breath.

The April air smelled soft and delicious.

Oregon.

I was back in Portland, city of my birth, the place I'd mostly called home for all of my life. I felt weirdly sentimental about it, reconnected to . . . what? My old life?

I thought of Mary-Joseph, and the tour she'd given me of her old neighborhood in Brooklyn. If she'd been here, I would have returned the favor and shown her a bit of my home turf.

I started walking. When I lived here, I drove everywhere. But now I took pleasure in being on foot, moving at my own pace.

What struck me first was the richness of the air. It smelled real, smelled of rain and blossoming trees and grass, a fragrant green smell that I don't think I'd ever appreciated as much as I did now, after two weeks of breathing the stale, recycled air of aeroplanes and shopping malls and superstores and hotels with windows that couldn't be opened. The air was like champagne. So unlike New York, where I always felt like every breath I took, even in Central Park, had already seen the insides of seven million other lungs.

I walked down streets I'd never bothered to look at, passing quiet downtown parks without a soul in them. Here, as in the downtowns of all the cities I'd just seen, there was little sign of street life after 6 p.m. It wasn't like non-stop New York. It felt kind of deserted, and there was a loneliness to it. It wasn't a city for singles, like New York. It was a city geared for couples, for families, for people who went home to big houses instead of tiny apartments, and stayed home because no one thought of the street as a place to hang out. Except, maybe, those forlorn-looking Goths I saw creeping around in their long black coats and big heavy boots, and the homeless, pushing their shopping carts. In New York, the streets were the living breathing theatre of life. Everyone shared them.

My heart gave a sudden lurch when I turned a corner and saw the county courthouse. I stopped and stared, lost in a welter of emotions. Because it was there, on the second floor, that I'd first met Tremaynne. I was coming out of bankruptcy court and he was going in.

Tremaynne. The man I'd loved more than any other. Suddenly my heart was struggling with the pain of losing him.

He couldn't afford to buy me a wedding ring, and wasn't interested in buying one, either, so I'd had one tattooed on my finger. It was still there, only now there was no person attached to the symbol. Without Tremaynne it was just a line of ink. It looked like my ring finger had been severed and stuck back on.

I'd wanted nothing more than him. And if I'd gotten my wish, if he'd loved me the way I'd loved him, if we'd stayed together . . .

If, if, if. The middle letters of life.

Let him go, something in me urged. *Let him out. Free him from the cage of your heart. That would be real love.*

But I didn't want to say goodbye to that dream. I didn't know if I could let him go, finally, once and for all, for ever.

But I had to, if I was ever going to move on. I knew that. So, standing there in front of the courthouse where we'd first met, I said goodbye.

And not just to Tremaynne, but also to my two earlier marital mishaps, Sean Kowalski and Pete Pringle, and to JD. I'd loved all of them, in a blind, grasping-at-straws kind of way. With each of them I thought that I'd found happiness.

But I hadn't. And I couldn't. Because I didn't love myself. I'd had no idea who I was. I'd had no idea what I was capable of. All I'd wanted was someone to take care of me – but instead, every time, I ended up taking care of them.

All those flaring passions, all the crazy drama and impossible nuttiness of love, I'd been trying to describe in the memoir I was calling *My Three Husbands*. But how much of the slippery truth of life could I or anyone really capture in a memoir? Once the love or horror or comedy is over, all you've got is the memory. And memory is always trying to reinterpret, to make you believe that you're in the driver's seat of your fate.

Is it fate that we meet the people we meet? Or is it simply an accident?

Something else occurred to me as I stood there in front of the courthouse. It was one of those 'moments' when an inner eye opens and you quietly realize something about yourself.

I was a different person. The Venus who'd left Portland was not the Venus standing there now. There was no way to reconnect to a life I no longer lived or a person I no longer was. There was no need to. In fact, it would be wrong to even try. It would be like trying to stuff myself back into a dress I'd worn as a child.

No, the only way to reconnect with the past, and make sense of it, and make sense of me, was to write about it. And that was just what I was going to do.

That night I made a vow and baptized myself . . . as a writer. It seemed crazy, illicit, to think that I had a 'voice' or that anyone would ever pay attention to me because of it. Maybe they wouldn't. But I was going to do it anyway. For myself. To prove that I could.

When I got back to the hotel and fell asleep, Tremaynne appeared in my dreams. We made love just as we used to, so intense and attuned that I had an orgasm. Make that two. I wanted to hold on to the physical sensation, keep him inside me, but he said, 'It's time for you to go.' And I said, 'Yes, it's time for me to go.' And I went.

It was the last day of the tour. That evening, Susanna would be delivering her speech in Chicago in front of a thousand people. After that she'd sign copies of *Puppy Love*, and then it would all be over.

I tried to imagine what she must be feeling as she approached the grand finale. It was a big deal for a shy girl who had taught herself confidence.

The flight was three hours long. I bought my snack box and enjoyed my plastic cup of cranberry juice while up in First Class Susanna was served a glass of champagne and lunch on a linen-covered tray. In Chicago she disembarked before me, as usual. When I saw her again, out in the arrivals area, she looked different. Deflated. Exhausted. Something. Her eyes looked like dry, old, hard-boiled eggs.

'Susanna, you don't look so hot.'

'That's funny,' she said, 'because I'm burning up.'

I touched her feverish forehead. 'Do you want me to find a doctor?'

'No.' She wearily shook her head. 'I just need to sleep.'

When we got to the hotel and up to her room, she headed straight for the bed, not even bothering to take off her clothes, and was out like a light.

Dilemma. Should I call the people in charge of the conference and tell them their keynote speaker was ill? Or would the keynote speaker rebound after a couple of hours' rest and go on as planned? She *was* indomitable, after all.

During the past two weeks she'd plowed on despite all manner of calamities and catastrophes.

I wanted to have everything ready to go when she woke up. There would be no fuck-ups. While she was conked out, I went down to the hotel's business centre and printed out the final copy of her speech. Then I got directions and walked over to the building where she'd be speaking, just so I'd know exactly where to go.

The 'Women and Sex' conference was officially underway and the place was jammed. Everyone seemed to be talking at once. I guess most of them were academics, but how can you tell an academic from a normal person? The conference was 'cross-disciplinary', which sounded kind of kinky.

I decided I'd better call Dr Ellerby Schrick, our liaison, to let her know we were here. Dr Schrick wasn't picking up, so I left a message and tried Gaylen Stroudel, our back-up liaison. Dr Stroudel was in, but frantic. Dr Schrick's six-year-old daughter had just come down with chicken pox, and Dr Schrick couldn't find a sitter, so Dr Stroudel was handling everything herself. She reeled off a breathtaking list of everything that had gone wrong so far – from the confusion over panel discussions and seminars listed as taking place in one room but held in another to problems with backed-up and overflowing toilets.

Not a good idea to add to her palette of woes. She sounded guilty that she couldn't meet me and relieved when I told her she didn't have to. 'I'll be there tonight to introduce her,' she promised.

All I had to do was get Susanna from the hotel to the auditorium.

I didn't hear from Susanna all afternoon and started phoning about two hours before we had to leave for the conference. She didn't pick up, so finally I headed up to her suite. There was no answer when I knocked on the door. 'Susanna?' I knocked again.

Maybe she'd gone out. Unlikely, but possible.

I dug out the electronic key and slid it into the lock. We always got two keys to her suites because I was forever running in and out and Susanna didn't want to have to get up from whatever she was doing to open the door.

The lights were out. The room was dark. Maybe she was still sleeping. She'd looked utterly exhausted.

'Susanna?' I said quietly, entering the bedroom. 'It's almost seven.'

She was still in bed. I saw her shape under the covers. She was turned away from me.

'Susanna?'

She didn't move. And for one horrible moment I was gripped by a sudden fear, no, terror.

I slowly moved closer to the bed. 'Susanna? Are you all right?'

I thought I heard something like 'Nnn.'

'Should I turn on the lights?'

Again, that pathetic sound, like someone who doesn't want to get up or a child who's sulking.

Instead of switching on the lights, I went over to open the curtains. It was a softer way to wake her up. 'I don't want to rush you, but if we're going to –' I turned around. I was going to say 'be on time', but the words got sucked away by my gasp.

She was sitting up on the bed, facing me, her clothes wrinkled and her hair dishevelled. There was a kind of hopeless, helpless, pleading look in her eyes. And I immediately saw why. Half of her face was normal but the other half was drooping, almost comically. She reminded me of one of those Roman theatre masks with half its mouth smiling for comedy and the other half turned down for tragedy.

'Oh my God! Susanna! What happened to your face?'

All she said was, 'Nnn.'

Under the circumstances, it sounded almost eloquent.

Well, neither Susanna nor I knew what the hell had happened. Half of her face was paralyzed, like a Botox treatment that had gone really bad. She couldn't lift the drooping right side of her mouth. When she spoke, she sounded like a stroke victim. She drooled when she tried to drink. She had trouble closing her right eye.

Her brain was still functioning, so she ruled out a cerebral haemorrhage. She was tired, yes, but she didn't feel physically ill. Emotionally, however, she was a total wreck. She'd awakened knowing that something was wrong but it wasn't until she looked in a mirror that she saw what it was.

I could almost smell her panic so I tried to remain very calm. 'What do you want me to do?' I asked.

She sat on the bed and threw up her arms in a gesture of hopeless despair and began to cry. She looked like a sad, weeping monster.

'Do you want me to call an ambulance?'

She shook her head.

'Do you – I don't know, do you feel up to –' I glanced at my watch. She was due on stage in forty-five minutes. 'Should I call and cancel?'

Susanna let out a horrible wail and began to pummel the bed with her fists.

I punched in Dr Gaylen Stroudel's number. No answer. 'Listen,' I said, 'if you're not desperately ill, if you don't need a doctor this second, I think I'd better run over to the hall and tell someone you won't be—'

'No!' Susanna suddenly jumped out of bed and ran for the bathroom.

I paced. Every couple of minutes I stood by the bathroom door and asked if there was anything I could do. She didn't answer, but inside I could hear the tap running and a toilet flushing. I looked at myself in the full-length mirror next to the door. Looked closely at my face. Opened and closed my mouth and moved my facial muscles. Then drew half of my mouth down and tried to simulate what had happened to Susanna.

Horrible! Something like that would change your life for ever.

She emerged at a gallop, moving so fast I hardly had time to take in what she'd done to herself. She was wearing her black Chanel dress and had wound several scarves around her neck. 'Let's go.' At least I think that's what she said. I grabbed her speech and we headed out the door.

Susanna let out a weird noise when I told her we couldn't get to the place by cab and would have to walk. She was in heels but I – the new Miss Sensible – had on low-heeled leather boots.

It was almost dark as we raced across campus, through blooming pools of street light where I'd look over and try to catch a glimpse of Susanna's disfigured face. She pulled the scarves up as high as she could, to obscure her grotesque mouth, but there was no way to disguise that drooping eye.

By the time we arrived, all the ticket holders had been seated and the auditorium doors were closed. I grabbed Susanna's hand for the final sprint through the lobby, past the table stacked high with her books, past the life-size cardboard 'stand alone' of her in jeans and sexy bra leading the naked young guy on a leash. We burst through a door at the far end of the lobby and started down the aisle towards the stage.

The moment we entered the auditorium Susanna disengaged her hand from mine. I thought she was following me as I raced towards the stage, but when I turned back to make sure, she wasn't there.

I stopped, bewildered, then spotted her hanging back in the shadows by the door. I started back but she frantically shook her head and made a motion that I took to mean, 'Go ahead. You. Do something.'

So I did.

In front of a thousand puzzled people I made my way up to the stage and over to a very confused Dr Gaylen Stroudel. We conferred, in full view of the audience, for approximately one minute. Then Dr Stroudel made the announcement and nodded at me.

I stepped up to the podium. Felt the warmth of the lights. Cleared my throat. Smiled as I looked out into the sea of faces. My heart was racing, my hands were trembling, my palms were wet.

'Um. I guess I'm here as Susanna's voice tonight,' I said. My amplified voice sounded high and wobbly because I was breathing shallowly.

A disappointed rustling and whispering filled the hall.

'She's very ill, but she's worked really hard on this speech, and I'd like to read it to you in her place. If that's OK with everyone.'

A few audience members got up and left. Where was Susanna? Now I couldn't see her at all. Maybe she was pissed. Or shocked. Maybe this isn't what she had in mind when she had gestured for me to go up to the stage instead of her. Maybe she was saying, 'Get away from me.'

But now I was up there. I placed her speech on the lectern. I'd read it through dozens of times. The trick was to remain calm and remember that I wasn't the Venus Gilroy I used to be. I was a Venus Gilroy who could cope with emergencies great and small and talk to anyone.

That's what working for Susanna had taught me.

So I took a couple of deep breaths and dived in. I'd watched Susanna closely during her readings and noted all the little tricks she used to make a connection with the audience. She gave herself authority. She didn't drone on in a monosyllabic tone but *acted* with her voice, giving it nuance, subtlety, and sharpness, periodically glancing up from the page and out into the sea of faces. The tricks a shy girl had learned to give herself confidence.

Her speech was actually quite funny and drew a lot of laughs, and at the end of it I accepted the applause that was for Susanna, not for me.

I felt flushed and triumphant, like I'd crossed some kind of magic line. I, Venus Gilroy, had stood on a stage and given a speech without fainting or losing my voice. I'd never thought of myself as Susanna's 'understudy', but in a way, I was. I'd gone on in her place.

Dr Stroudel stepped up to the mike and said that a question and answer period had been scheduled, but under the circumstances . . .

'Oh, I can do that,' I said brazenly. I knew as much about women and sex as the next person. Maybe more than Susanna did. I'd been writing Susanna's column for months now, listening to the questions posed after her readings. 'I can try anyway.'

'Well . . .' Dr Stroudel hesitated.

'I don't have a *degree* in sex,' I said, 'but I do have a lot of *life experience*.'

With a nervous smile, Dr Stroudel stepped away from the mike and a hand shot up in the audience.

And that was when I really connected with the audience. It was the most wonderful feeling. I just tried to be myself and give answers based on what I knew. I didn't try to be intellectual. I spoke from my heart, not my head. At the end of it I reminded people that Susanna's new book was for sale right outside.

During the final round of applause I looked out and saw Susanna standing in the shadows beneath the balcony overhang. I thought, foolishly, that she might be relieved, or even proud. But, in fact, she was staring at me with what looked like utter hatred.

It's called Bell's palsy, after the nineteenth-century Scottish doctor who first described it, but in San Francisco, I later found out, it was known as 'cable-car disease' – apparently because so many people riding the cable cars along windy San Francisco streets came down with it.

Poor Susanna. While riding the cable car, her one and only tourist activity during the entire *Puppy Love* tour, a virus had blown into her ear, crept down her Fallopian canal (not tube), and attacked her seventh cranial nerve, the one that controls facial expression.

Some doctors believed that herpes simplex caused Bell's palsy, so that nasty cold sore on her lip might have been an early warning sign. And stress probably weakened her immune system and made her more susceptible.

But nobody could say for sure. Even though forty thousand Americans came down with Bell's palsy every year, doctors knew next to nothing about it. There was no 'cure', no standard course of drug treatment.

All Susanna could do, the doctors said, was rest. Facial massage and electrical stimulation *might* help prevent loss of muscle tone, and there were other unproven therapies that *might* prove beneficial: relaxation techniques, acupuncture, electrical stimulation, biofeedback training, and vitamins (B12, B6, zinc). But basically, all she could do was wait it out. She *might* regain use of her face in two weeks or it *might* take six months and – best to be prepared – there *might* be permanent disfigurement, such as a drooping eyelid or contorted mouth.

Naturally she didn't come into the office. Who could blame her? If I turned into a monster, I wouldn't want anyone to see me, either. If she showed herself, there was always the possibility that someone would surreptitiously take her photo and post it to the blog. I was under strict orders not to tell anyone what had happened.

Rumors – insidious as airborne viruses – began to fly.

Susanna could do some of her work at home, but not all of it. If she took an extended leave of absence, Larry Weiner, the editor-in-chief of all Stuckey Universal Media magazines, would have no choice but to appoint an interim editor for *Aura*. Eldora Button and Petra Darkke were already being mentioned as candidates.

Susanna could have weathered this storm if Lord Stuckey had been behind her. But the lord had definitely returned to his lady, whisking his magic cloak of power and protection from Susanna's shoulders.

Bad-news pies kept splatting her in the face. *Puppy Love* had *not* become the bestseller she desperately hoped it would, but it did become kind of notorious after it was mentioned in a prominent *Arts & Culture* story called 'The Miming of Memoir'. Web versions of this story raced through the network of office computers like digital wildfire. Josh's name was mentioned, but 'Ms Hyde did not return calls or e-mails regarding this story.'

I checked the blog. Sure enough, under the headline 'Ripping Off Reality', the baleful blogger was cackling over Susanna's latest humiliation.

Then an e-mail from Closeup Cinema, the Hollywood production company that had expressed an interest in the book, curtly informed Grace Glickman, Susanna's agent, who forwarded it to Susanna, that Closeup would 'not be pursuing this project'.

Oh, it was all such a big fat mess, and Susanna was, as they say back in Oregon, 'up shit creek'.

*

One night about three weeks after our return, Susanna sent an e-mail asking me to stop by her building and drop off some layouts. She called and e-mailed me constantly, but she hadn't set foot in the office since her return, or did so only late at night when everyone else was gone. I hadn't actually seen her since we'd got back, so naturally I was curious, though I felt some trepidation, as I headed up to her apartment in the elevator.

I rang the bell, expecting Susanna to answer, but a woman with thin, dyed-blonde hair opened the door. She looked oddly familiar. Dressed in slacks, slippers, and a twin-set, she eyed me through large square glasses that magnified her suspicious gray eyes.

And then I remembered where I'd seen her. In the hotel lobby in San Francisco. Wearing a raincoat and dark glasses. Susanna's gender-bent husband.

I went to Susanna's bedroom door and knocked, got no response, knocked again. 'Susanna?'

A peeved voice within said what sounded like, 'All right!', so I opened the door.

Her room was a mess. I mean a *disaster*. Susanna was lying in the midst of it, on her bed, wearing a black eyepatch and pressing something that looked like a wand or a very skinny vibrator to her drooping cheek.

'Clothe the door,' she said through the good side of her mouth.

I did as she asked but wished I could leave the door open because the room smelled unpleasantly stale. 'What are you doing?' I asked.

'Thtimulating my faythal muthels.' She sat up and held out her free hand for the envelope I'd brought.

'Is your eye all right?'

She didn't answer, and wouldn't look at me. She pulled out the layouts and studied them.

'Where's Regina?' I asked.

'Put down.'

'What? Why?'

The side of Susanna's face that could still register emotion stiffened into what appeared to be loathing. 'Becauth *he'th* alleryick!'

I looked towards the door. 'What's he doing here anyway?'

Her uncovered eye glared at me. 'Living!'

'Oh.' I didn't say more. I wasn't even supposed to know about Susanna's husband or his/her claim on the apartment. 'Well, I'll let you rest.'

Susanna spat out a bitter laugh.

'Be prepared for the end,' Whitman calmly warned me. It was around midnight in Manhattan, six hours earlier in Maui, where he was researching a Hawaiian beach once used to heal royalty. I thought I heard steel guitars in the background.

I'd finally called and told him everything that was going on at *Aura*. 'You think they'll fire her?'

'Now that Lord Stuckey's gone, she's a sitting duck,' Whitman said. 'She won't be replacing Larry Weiner as editor-in-chief, but she *has* turned *Aura* around, and made it a lot better, so they may keep her on as editor.'

'But she's alienated so many people –'

'Poor thing,' Whitman said. 'She let power go to her head before it was even in place.'

'Her head?'

'Her *power*. She used it – misused it – before she earned it.'

'If they fire her, I'll have to find another job.'

'You're not the only one,' Whitman said. 'You realize if she goes, I go, too.'

I'd worried about losing my job, but it had never occurred to me that Whitman might lose his. Heads rolled, he said, every time there was a regime change at a magazine. If they fired Susanna, a new editor would probably jettison everything and everyone associated with her tenure. First to go would be the freelance writers she'd hired for the magazine's monthly columns.

Suddenly I realized how fragile, complicated and interconnected it all was. I'd never sympathized with Whitman's life because it was so unlike mine. If anything, I'd regarded it as glamorous because he didn't have to sit in an office and he got to travel. But now I had an inkling of how tough it actually was to live the life of a freelance writer. This was the first time in Whitman's career that he'd had the financial security and professional cachet of a monthly column.

'Well,' he said gamely, 'it's been a great gig and it's not over yet. But listen to me, Venus. Be prepared. OK? This is how publishing is. It's changing and shifting all the time.'

'Like life,' I said.

'Like life,' he agreed. 'A hard shake that love makes a little easier.'

'Or shakier.'

He laughed. 'Anyway, you know my philosophy: if one door closes, another will open. Being fired might finally give me the opportunity I've been waiting for.'

'To do what?'

'Finish my memoir, of course.'

That thing called love. Was I ready for it?

That thing called sex. Was I ready for that?

I wanted both, the way a kid wants chocolate, but was I ready?

There were signs that I was. Reciprocal flirting, for instance. I've always liked men, but in New York I'd soon picked up the really bad habit of avoiding their eyes. I'm talking about that awful nose-straight-ahead, horse-blinkered gaze New York women adopt the minute they step outside and hit the lewd reality of the streets. It comes from a fear that we'll accidentally make eye contact with *the wrong man* – a murderer, a psycho, a nerd – who'll misinterpret the merest flick of an eye as an open invitation to proceed with harassment or abduction.

To break myself of this habit, I developed a flirt plan. I rated guys from 1 to 10, and every time a flirt-worthy fellow (8 and above) gave me a full-frontal once-over, I gave him one in return. There was no reason why I shouldn't appreciate a guy's well-shaped ass, crotch bulge, and overall physique – even hidden beneath a suit – the same way he might appreciate my legs, chest or bottom.

Sometimes it was just eye meeting eye, a passing glance of appreciation, nothing more. They made me smile, those ardent, fleeting glances. And smiling, I discovered, was one of the most potent aphrodisiacs in New York. Why? Because so many people looked miserable. Men, accustomed to being ignored or shot down by every woman they looked at or propositioned, are suckers for a smile.

And once I started smiling, my sense of fun kicked in. That was a good sign. It meant that something was loosening up inside me. I was ready to laugh. So if a flirt-worthy guy made a comment like, 'Mmm, I'd love to see the inside of your laptop,' I'd shoot back with, 'It's for registered users only.'

New York has this incredible verbal energy because everyone's talking all the time, and talking is a kind of flirting. Guys in New York can come up with some really funny pick-up lines. If you're a politically correct sourpuss, like Dorcas, you'll tsk your tongue and call them childish and demeaning. Which they often are. But a girl should never take a pick-up line *personally*. If a comment is tossed in her direction, she should have the brains and skill to scoop it up and toss it back.

So that was my flirt plan: to look, smile, and practise repartee. And as the weather turned warmer, I felt more and more alive to . . . what? The possibilities of love, sex and romance, though not necessarily in that order.

'It's impossible to meet a straight man in this city,' Dorcas complained on one of our lunch breaks. It was warm and muggy, and we were strolling down Fifth Avenue without coats. 'I've been trying for years. *Everything*. Yoga classes. Bars. Mix and match singles events. Dating services. Online chat rooms. Nothing works – except maybe flashing your thong at a homeless bum in Times Square.'

Sharanda was equally pessimistic. Her red-hot affair had turned cold when her boyfriend demanded that she let him rear-end her. When she refused, he grew bored and drifted to other back doors.

'I am just so not into that,' she said with an indignant huff. 'What is this thing about men and assholes anyway?'

'Men *are* assholes,' Dorcas said.

Girl, I thought, with that attitude you are doomed to spinsterhood. A passing flirt-worthy in a pinstriped suit winked at me and lifted his eyebrows in a classic 'Are you available?' gesture. I smiled and shook my head without missing a step. My office mates were totally oblivious to this non-verbal exchange.

'They watch porno flicks,' Sharanda complained, 'and think all women are like those whores.'

'Right,' Dorcas chimed in. 'Intellectual achievement means *nothing* compared to a pair of big – oh my God.' She stopped and pointed in the window of a bookstore.

There was Cupcake Cassidy's memoir, *The Naked Truth*. Cupcake's signature cupcakes, pumped up to impossible proportions, dominated the glossy cover.

'They should have put smiley faces on them,' Dorcas said.

She stared in frozen apprehension as a delivery man, dark-eyed and dishy, clicked his tongue in passing and said in a low voice, 'Whoa, baby, you've got what I call a ten-digit figure.'

'That's right,' I said, 'it takes two hands to hold me.'

'Oooo!' he laughed, hurrying on with his deliveries.

'Venus,' Dorcas hissed disapprovingly.

'What?'

'He was a delivery man!'

At that minute I felt really sorry for her.

The offices of Stuckey Universal Media were undergoing a radical downsizing. People were being fired left and right. I kept anxiety at bay by working on *My Three Husbands*, trying to capture the facts of my life as I'd lived it before moving to New York. But late at night, staring at the words on my laptop screen, I'd wonder how on earth any writer conveyed 'truth'? Parts of my story seemed unbelievable, even to me . . . and I had lived them.

'This really happened to you?' Mary-Joseph asked in wonder. I'd given her a section of the manuscript to read. 'A *moose* chased yuh on yuh honeymoon?'

'I think it was a moose. But it might have been an elk.' These were the sorts of details that drove me crazy. If I was going to write about an animal or a bird or a tree, I had to know what it was, and before that fateful third honeymoon I'd never paid much attention to nature. Now I had to know the exact names of things. I made a note to ask Daddy if the animal that had charged me was a moose or an elk. 'It wasn't a deer, anyway,' I told her.

'And the second guy yuh married –'

'Pete.'

'Yeah. He worked for a pet-disposal company? And you'd go out with him on his rounds, pickin' up *dead pets*?'

'I didn't say it was fun, I just said I did it.'

Mary-Joseph cocked an eyebrow. 'OK, so whennayuh gonna write about the one person yuh *didn't* marry?'

'Who? JD?'

'Yeah. That punk rocker chick. Yuh gonna write some hot sex scenes with huh?'

'Well, it's a memoir,' I said. 'I can't just make it up. It has to be true.'

'So it's not true that yuh had hot sex with huh?'

The truth was, JD was hot on stage but cold as a popsicle in bed. But I didn't want to get into any of that with Mary-Joseph, who, as usual, was angling for something more than friendship. 'I haven't gotten to that part yet.'

'I wanna be the first to read it,' Mary-Joseph said eagerly. 'Try'n make it as hot as the scenes with yuh last husband, will yuh?'

Needless to say, the sex scenes with Tremaynne had been the easiest to write.

On a fearsomely hot afternoon in mid-May I got into the subway at Times Square and headed downtown to meet Josh at L'Albatross.

For lunch.

He'd invited me.

'I always keep my word,' he said. 'I told you I'd take you there one day. I promised. Remember?'

Of course I did. But I hadn't been expecting it so soon.

The air-conditioning in the crowded subway car was on but not doing much. After days of monsoon-like rainstorms, the temperature had shot up to almost a hundred and Manhattan was steaming. I thought cool thoughts and tried not to sweat.

'If this ain't global warming,' the perspiring man next to me said, 'I'd like to know what is.'

I smiled sympathetically, not sure whether or not it was a pick-up line.

I'd dressed up, of course. L'Albatross was an epicenter of chic. It required a certain *je ne sais quoi*. And I hereby admit that I wanted to impress Josh, too.

I was all in white. Immaculate, impeccable white. The kind of white that you never see anyone wearing in grimy, black-clad New York. The kind of white that makes you stand out in a crowd. I'd had my hair cut, too, into a kind of vampy, old-fashioned bob. Short for what promised to be a long hot summer.

At L'Albatross, I lowered my fake Gucci sunglasses and said to the maitre d', as if I were just as important as everyone else, 'I'm meeting Josh O'Connell.'

'Of course. Miss Gilroy, yes? Follow me, please.'

I won't pretend I didn't notice the stares. Maybe it was my white dress with its form-fitting bodice and wide, pleated skirt. Maybe it was my broad-brimmed white straw hat or my white, open-toed platform heels. Maybe it was my white-gloved hands clutching my white bag. I wondered what the starers would think if they knew I'd found the entire ensemble at a second-hand shop on Flatbush Avenue in Brooklyn for under seventy-five bucks. Mary-Joseph had taken me there because she knew I liked vintage clothes. 'You're a woman creates huh own style,' she said.

'Venus!' Josh stood, a big smile on his face, and kissed me on the cheek. Very grown-up. A sophisticated Manhattan greeting. 'Wow, you look – fantastic.'

'Thank you.' I'm extremely susceptible to compliments, but tried to sound as if Josh's comment was no big deal. I took off my sunglasses and smiled at him. 'You look great, too.'

And he did. Gone was that gaunt, haunted, half-starved look of the winter before. He was wearing a linen jacket and a green tie that drew attention to those eyes of his, shining green as clover under thick black lashes. His curly black hair gleamed with some kind of gel.

'Well,' he said, beaming. 'Wow. How about a drink?'

I pulled off my gloves, one finger at a time. 'Just water.'

Josh lowered his voice. 'Hey, we don't have to do that this time. I'm treating.'

'Sparkling water, then.' More than anything, I wanted a lovely glass of chilled white wine, but in this heat it would put me under, and I had to go back to work after lunch. Plus, it would make me horny.

Josh kept smiling at me, which was confusing and a bit disconcerting. He spread his arm out along the back of the banquette, not quite touching me but so close I could feel his body heat through the linen.

'So,' he said.

'So.'

'I'm glad to see you.'

'Really?'

'Really.' He gently clinked my tumbler of Pellegrino with his wineglass. 'I was thinking about it yesterday. About you. How you'd been there, each step of the way.'

'Each step of what way?'

'Everything that's happened. I mean, in a way, it's all because of you. You precipitated the whole thing.'

I just wasn't following. 'What whole thing?'

'Oh – you know. The Susanna thing.'

I sipped my fizzy water and shrugged. 'The Susanna thing?'

'I was with you when I met her,' Josh said, 'and I was with you when she dumped me. You're the one, in fact, who delivered the news.'

Apparently my fate with Josh was not to have a fate, or only a peripheral one, through Susanna. I thought: give it another ten minutes. If he was still talking about Susanna then, I'd leave.

'So, you see,' Josh said amiably, 'none of this would have happened without you.'

'It still would have happened,' I said, 'just differently.'

'You think?' The question seemed to bemuse him. 'It's an interesting theory. That the major events in a person's life have to happen no matter what.'

I was starting to feel grouchy. 'I take it you're saying that Susanna was a major event in your life.'

'Of course she was. In yours, too.'

'I'm still working for her,' I said.

'Not for much longer.'

My stomach did a flip. I looked at him.

'Maybe I shouldn't tell you,' he said. 'But if it was me, I'd want to know.'

I waited, my eyes glued to his.

'My friend at Stuckey Universal? He's pretty tight with – what's her name – Sybil?'

'Sybilla Lansgaard? Head of the PR department?'

'Right. So this Sybilla told my friend that Susanna's not long for this world.'

I could almost feel the blood draining from my face. A cold shudder ran down my spine. 'Josh – oh my God – you mean –'

'I mean, start assembling your resumé. She's on her way out.'

I couldn't help it. I started to cry. The shock of it was too much.

'Hey, Venus. It's just a job,' Josh said.

'It's not that. It's S-s-susanna.'

'What about her? That bitch deserves every evil that comes her way.'

'Josh, for God's sake. How can you say that about someone who's dying?'

'Dying?' He drew back in surprise. 'Is she dying?'

'Isn't she? You said she wasn't long for this world.'

'I was speaking metaphorically. I meant they're going to fire her foam-filled ass.'

'Oh.' I let out a big sigh of relief. 'I didn't think you could die from Bell's palsy. Although you might want to.'

'Bell's palsy?'

'That's what she has.'

'What is it?'

So, hesitantly, trying to infuse some sympathy in his outlook, I told him about Bell's palsy aka cable-car disease. 'It paralyzes half your face. Half your tongue. Makes your eye droop and your mouth.' I tried to show him but, horribly, he started laughing. Then, horribly, I did, too.

'I wish I could get a picture of that for the blog,' Josh said.

I stopped laughing. 'Oh no, Josh. Are you Hide Susanna Hyde dot com?'

'Part of it,' Josh said. 'My friend at Stuckey Universal—'

'Josh, that blog is so damn cruel.'

'And she's not?' Josh picked up his menu and began to scan the lunch offerings. 'I don't think you'll ever understand, Venus, what that bitch did to me. How she used me. I mean, *used* me. And then lied when the truth didn't suit her.'

We had to stop talking because the waiter came to tell us what the daily specials were. When he'd left, I said, 'You're like a dog who can't stop licking a sore spot.'

'Not even a dog,' he said, 'a puppy.'

'Why can't you just give her up and move on?'

'Oh, I *am* moving on,' he said. 'I'm moving on big time. With her help, actually. Actually, *because* of her.'

I stared at him, trying to decipher his meaning and get a handle on my feelings. I was trying to digest a lot and I hadn't even ordered yet. First there was the news that they were trying to fire Susanna. With that came the daunting realization that I'd have to find another job. Then came the shock of learning that Josh was behind the blog. And now Josh was telling me that he was 'moving on' with Susanna's help. What did that mean?

'You are looking at a published author,' Josh said, trying to keep his smile within manageable proportions.

'What?'

'Well, a soon-to-be-published author.' His face was glowing so brightly it made his eyes sparkle.

'Josh, that's wonderful. Someone's publishing your novel?'

'They're publishing what *was* my novel until I rewrote it. And it didn't take a lot of rewriting because it was basically a memoir all along, only disguised as fiction. So I took out the fiction and put in the facts.'

'What's it called?'

'*Sleeping With Older Women.*'

He didn't need to tell me who the older woman was. And I didn't need to ask.

'That's all you're having?' Josh said when the waiter came and I ordered the seasonal leaf and flower organic salad, the cheapest thing on the menu. He leaned close and whispered, 'Order anything you want, Venus. I've got it covered this time. Really.' He told the waiter he'd start with the medley of ancient grains followed by the veal filet with pomegranate reduction. Oh, and another glass of pinot grigio.

'OK,' I said, 'I'll have the same, only salad instead of the ancient grains.'

'I was so naïve,' Josh said, sipping his wine and shaking his head. 'I thought talent was what mattered. But it's not. It's publicity.'

'The publicity doesn't mean anything if you don't have talent to back it up.'

'No. Sorry. You're wrong. I just had a long talk with Grace about this.'

'Grace?'

'Grace Glickman. My agent. She said the publicity I received – you know, after I crashed Susanna's book launch – added at least a hundred grand to the advance. Because publishers knew my name.'

'Oh.'

'I didn't know any of that at the time,' Josh said. 'I was just pissed off, that's all. I wanted to embarrass her the way she'd embarrassed me.'

'Get even,' I said.

'Yeah. But I had no idea that it would turn into what it did.'

'So *your* memoir tells the truth about—'

Josh smiled and raised a finger in recognition of someone

across the room. 'My memoir corrects the distortions of hers. I mean, it's my story, of course.'

'Your version.'

'It's pretty graphic. You'll probably be shocked.'

'Why?'

'Well, you'll see her in a new light.'

'What about you?'

'What do you mean?'

'How do you portray yourself? That's the hardest part of writing a memoir.' As I now knew first-hand, from trying to write about myself in *My Three Husbands*.

'I just tell the truth,' Josh said.

'Whatever that is.'

Josh leaned back so the waiter could put down his medley of ancient grains. I leaned back and received my organic salad. And as the waiter ground fresh pepper on my seasonal greens and flowers, I looked over and saw Susanna pull open the restaurant door.

I was so shocked I couldn't speak. My first thought was, she's gone mad. Because she looked mad. Crazy mad and angry mad. She was dressed all in black and wore running shoes that made her feet look larger than they were. Her punky haircut, created to foster a more youthful and rebellious image for the book tour, had gone haywire. It stuck up and stuck out all over the place. The black eyepatch gave her the cruel, dangerous look of a one-eyed pirate queen. There was no way to disguise the drooping mouth or the sagging cheek.

She got into some kind of altercation with the maitre d', who was attempting to keep her from entering the restaurant. I could hear the angry tone of her voice and his firm, placating response. Susanna was peering around him, hot and determined, and finally she caught sight of me and her face blazed with fury.

I wanted to crawl under the table.

Susanna pointed at our table, dodged around the maitre d', and headed straight for us. By that time Josh had seen her, too. 'Jesus,' he whispered. Was it because of the way she looked or because of the obvious fact that she was on the warpath?

Knocking into waiters and patrons, seemingly oblivious to the stares and whispered remarks, Susanna barged over and stood in front of us. 'You fuck!' she hissed at Josh. Her good eye darted over to me. 'What the hell are you doing here?'

'She's having lunch,' Josh said. 'With me.'

'I won't let thith happen!' Susanna vowed.

'What? You won't let Venus have lunch with me?'

'Your *book*, you louthy fuck!'

'Oh.' Josh nodded. 'You just heard.'

'From Grayth! That fucking bitth!'

'I wish you wouldn't talk that way about my agent,' Josh said.

At this Susanna let out a disgusted grunt and stamped her foot in frustration. She rounded on me again. 'You knew about thith!'

'Susanna,' I said nervously, 'I didn't know a thing. I just found out.'

'You're fired!'

It was a shock to hear the words. There's no way you can ever really prepare yourself in advance. I drew back and for some reason my hands flew to my hair, smoothing it back, holding on to it as if I was afraid my head was about to fly off. I wanted to say something but I didn't know what to say. I looked at Josh.

But he only laughed.

'You're firing her?' he taunted. 'Because she's having lunch with me?'

'Sheeth been helping you. Feeding you information.' Susanna pointed a chipped fingernail at me. 'I'll thue your ath.'

And then I thought: After all I've done for her, after all my hard work to make her life easier, why am I just sitting here and taking this? 'You'd better watch your mouth,' I said – yes, an unfortunate choice of words, given Susanna's disfigurement, but I was worked up, and I wasn't speaking literally.

Susanna let out a funny-sounding squawk, as if she couldn't believe that I was talking back to her. 'You thtupid cunt!'

That did it. She'd pushed me over the edge. 'I guess I'll have to put this scene in *my* new memoir,' I said.

'You're *not*—'

'There seems to be a big market for them.' Oh, I loved seeing her squirm. I was way beyond shame or *schadenfreude*. All the humiliations I'd endured and overlooked came rushing back to me, a big dark dangerous storm cloud that opened up and drenched me with resentment. I was furious with myself, with my simpleminded acceptance of her 'superiority'. I thought of all those drivers, butlers and valets who put up with their employer's abuse because they thought, for some reason, that they deserved it. 'I'll have to put in the part about Nick Burden, too,' I said. 'And all the other stuff. It'll be kind of sticky, all the stuff about Stuckey.'

Susanna just stood there, frozen. 'Thith ith how you repay me?'

'Speaking of repayment,' I said, 'you owe me about a thousand dollars for all the tips and cab fares and teas and bottles of wine and all those things I had to pay for because you just never seemed to have any cash. I'll make up a list.'

While all this was going on, Josh had put up a finger, smiled, and signed to the maitre d'. Susanna flinched when the man appeared behind her.

'This woman is threatening us,' Josh said amiably. 'Would you kindly remove her from the premises?'

'Chop chop,' I added.

The maitre d' leaned down and said, 'Madam? Will you come with me, please?'

Susanna twisted her head around to look up at him, then turned back to us. Quick as a striking snake, she grabbed my tumbler of Pellegrino and dashed the contents in my face. 'You'll be thorry,' she said. Then whirled around and stormed out of the restaurant.

I was too surprised to do anything. I sat there with the water dripping from my face, aware that the entire restaurant was staring. How did a girl extricate herself from a situation like this?

'I think that was meant for me,' Josh said. He poured another glass of Pellegrino and flung it in his own face. Then we had lunch.

How do you end a memoir?

I thought about this as I walked the dogs.

How do things end in real life?

Do they ever?

Isn't the end always a beginning?

In a way, being fired by Susanna Hyde was the best thing that ever happened to me. True, I panicked about money. New York is one of the most expensive cities in the world, after all, and I hadn't been able to save much.

But I was lucky. The rent on Whitman and Daddy's apartment was ridiculously low. And if you're ingenious and determined, weird, well-paying jobs in New York are relatively easy to find. I wasn't into cleaning apartments, though, the way Josh had when he was so broke. I wanted something a little more interesting.

Daddy and Whitman told me not to worry. If I wanted to stay in New York and live in the apartment, they said they'd help out if I became strapped for money. It was wonderful to feel this nudge of encouragement because I wanted to stay. I couldn't imagine moving back to Oregon.

'Enjoy New York while you're young,' Daddy said. 'It's a city to be young in.'

Susanna was not about to give me a good recommendation, so that narrowed my job search. And did I really want to be in an office?

What I really wanted was time to write. I wanted to finish *My Three Husbands* and develop this idea I had for a book. I was going to call it *The Happy Camper Guide to Sex*.

Not that I was getting any.

Anyway, cash flow was imperative. What was I going to do?

I'd made lots of friends working for Susanna. They weren't people in publishing, they were people in the 'service industry' (doormen) and 'retail' (store managers). I started with them.

The doormen were the most helpful. I printed up sheets describing my services and they distributed them to select tenants in their buildings (what Susanna would have called 'targetted marketing'). That's how I got the dog-walking jobs.

My rates were high but I was trustworthy and reliable and I didn't just walk, I *played* – those boring games that New York dogs never tire of but their cerebral owners do. I was Dog Nanny. I took my charges to the fenced-in runs in Central Park and Riverside Park and threw sticks and wrestled and ran with them. They loved me, waiting eagerly by the door in their little hats and rain capes or holding their leashes in their mouths, wriggling and groaning with excitement when I came to liberate them from their stuffy apartments for ninety minutes of down and dirty fun.

Caring for two sets of five dogs, Dog Nanny raked in two hundred bucks a day. Cash. More, if Dog Nanny was required to take Max or Fifi to a salon or veterinarian.

So I got lots of exercise and got to be outside instead of sitting under fluorescent lights in an office module, and had time to finish *My Three Husbands* and begin *The Happy Camper Guide to Sex*.

If you want to meet guys, get a dog and 'walk it reguluh' as Mary-Joseph would say. This was one trick that Dorcas hadn't tried. There were tons of dog owners out there, most of them single, many of them male.

There was Noah Ahrens, owner of Mickey, a snorting English bulldog.

There was Marcel Lamartine, owner of Colette, a wired wire-haired terrier.

There was Owen Williams, owner of Boone, a giant, drooling Lab-Weimaraner mix.

There was Ernesto Principe, owner of Lorca, a shivering, anorexic-looking greyhound.

But it wasn't just guys I met.

There was Vicki Gollasky (dachshund), Germaine Prongler (English setter), Bobbi Lewis (chihauhau), Charlene Montefiore (bichon frise), Sarah Cohn (shi-tzu) and Willamine Stoll-Friedrich (golden retriever).

OK, I won't say they were close friends, but they were 'reguluhs' in my daily life as Dog Nanny. And eventually I knew them well enough to begin asking the questions that served as background for *The Happy Camper Guide to Sex*.

'A vooman is happy during sexual intercourse only vhen she trusts *completely* the man she is vith,' declared 75-year-old Willamine Stoll-Friedrich. 'She must know he loves *all* of her, not only her flesh.'

Bobbi Lewis wasn't quite so romantic. 'He's gotta be a man about it, ya know? Take charge. If he knows what he's doing, I come real quick.'

'My happiest sexual experiences', confided Owen Williams, 'are pre-penetration. The lead-up for me is sexier than the let-down.'

'E-mails to my e-zones,' was Charlene Montefiore's cryptic comment about what constituted good sex.

And so on.

That summer I got to know Whitman and Daddy's garden in a way I never had before. As a girl, visiting, I'd always thought of it as pretty, and unique, and also a little scary. Now I saw that it was enchanted.

The dads had drawn me a detailed map so I'd know what plants were where and when they bloomed. Whitman claimed there were over a hundred different varieties and he'd always ask about them.

'Are the snowdrops out yet?' he'd want to know.

'I don't know. What are they?'

'*Galanthus nivalis*. There's a patch of them over in the north-east corner. Little white flowers that look like three drops of milk. They're usually out by now.'

I'd go look. There they'd be.

Or Daddy might say, 'Be on the lookout for that Red Crown Imperial.'

'What's that?' It sounded like beer.

'A fritillaria. It comes back year after year. Whitman and I planted it the first year we were together. Big red bells under a green crown. You can't miss it – it's about three feet high and comes up just to the right of the birdbath, in front of the forsythia.'

Et cetera.

I'd never realized how much love, care and artistry they'd put into that 450 square feet of earth. In one corner of the garden wall, scratched into the stucco, I found their initials – WW & JG.

Yes, that little walled garden in the middle of Manhattan truly was enchanted. It seemed to breathe with the serenity of shared love. It seemed to have its own secret existence and a special pact with nature, drawing to it things that you just never saw on the loud, crowded streets of New York. Butterflies flittered in and fanned their wings on purple flowers. Birds (not pigeons and not sparrows) sang in the trees and hopped down to forage for insects, berries, and worms. Squirrels scampered along the top of the walls. In the middle of a hot afternoon, cicadas let loose a dry, rattling shiver of sound. At night, fireflies blinked and floated like tiny green dirigibles.

It was my own little garden of Eden.

Josh, when he saw it, was almost speechless. 'This is all yours?'

'My dads made it.'

'You don't have to share it with anyone? Any other apartments?'

'No.'

'It's like being in the country,' Josh marvelled. He sat down at the old round garden table under the bittersweet vine. It was a blaringly hot afternoon and he was dressed in loose shorts, a sleeveless T-shirt, and flip-flops. I couldn't help but notice his strong-looking legs and nicely developed biceps and the tendrils of curly black chest hair against his pale skin. But it was always Josh's green eyes that fascinated me. I was drawn to them like a cow to clover.

During that lunch at L'Albatross, before Susanna barged in and fired me, I'd decided that smart, cute and sexy as Josh was, he wasn't boyfriend material. At least for me. I saw his ambition and what he was prepared to do with it and I couldn't imagine him fitting me into any of his calculated career moves. I wasn't important enough, rich enough, smart enough.

But when he poured that glass of Pellegrino and dashed it in his own face, something in my heart made room again for the possibility of Josh O'Connell. I read his willingness to make a fool of himself in Manhattan's snootiest restaurant as a gesture of solidarity. And he did pay for lunch.

The encounter with Susanna had made me upset and jittery, but Josh was there for me, sympathetic to my predicament as a suddenly unemployed New Yorker. He laughed and joked to get me over the hump of my initial shock, then calmed the adrenalated anger that came after.

In the days that followed, those first strange days of unemployment, Josh called to check up on me. Gave me pep talks. Assured me that I'd done nothing wrong. 'You didn't deserve to be treated that way,' he said.

'Not after I worked so damned hard for her!' That's what I couldn't get over and obsessed on and occasionally cried about – that there was absolutely no recognition for all that I'd done to make Susanna's life easier. I was completely expendable, as invisible as a servant, useful only while I was useful.

'That's how Susanna treats everyone,' Josh said. 'I should know.' He reminded me of the cocktail party when Susanna tricked him into serving drinks. 'Look,' he said, 'the world isn't about rewarding you for what you've done or giving you a medal for being a nice person. The ones who should give you your due, don't. So you have to give it to yourself.'

'Believe in yourself, you mean.'

'Yeah, totally. Then, if you're ambitious, you have to figure out ways to get what you want. And just go for it. Not be afraid and not be held back by all the crap you've been taught about being nice and polite and humble.'

'But then you just turn into another Susanna,' I said. 'Don't you?'

'Maybe,' Josh said. 'Sometimes.'

It was too early to tell if he would turn into one of those awful people himself. It was a distinct possibility.

I felt the stirrings of old-fashioned lust every time I was with him. After a year of drought, my juices were starting to flow again. But I was being cautious. And because I'm not cautious by nature, it was difficult to keep myself from signalling my desire: brushing a finger along his bare neck as I passed by, say, or giving his ear lobe with its silver stud a playful little tug. And Josh, though I'd catch him following me with his eyes, or resting his glance on my breasts or legs, wasn't the aggressive lover of my fantasies or the clumsy, clueless stud in *Puppy Love*. I wondered if his sexual self-esteem had been so scorched by Susanna's book that he was now hesitant to expose himself to any situation where his performance in bed might be judged and found wanting.

Which, frankly, made him even more attractive. If we ever made love, it would be an opportunity to give him back his manhood. And for that he would be eternally grateful.

Wouldn't he?

'This heat,' Josh said, sitting at the round table under the bittersweet vine. 'If you were writing about it, how would you describe it?'

I thought for a moment. I was, in fact, writing about it, but I'd never mentioned *My Three Husbands* or *The Happy Camper Guide to Sex* to Josh. He had no idea that I was a wannabe writer. 'Something like "tropical swelter",' I said, 'or how about "a relentless French-press of humidity"?'

Josh laughed and looked at me as he swirled his iced coffee. 'How about "a lubricious inflammation of the earth"?'

'Lubricious?' I racked my brains trying to remember what it meant.

'Great heats do awaken great fires in the loins of men.'

'Is that Shakespeare?'

'No, me.' He smiled and laid his hand lightly on my thigh.

My temperature suddenly shot up a few more degrees.

His voice was low. His hand began stroking. 'If you knew how much I love saying your name. *Venus* –'

I was going to say something like, 'Josh, I'm not sure about this,' but I couldn't bring myself to speak. The air was like molten glass – or was that my body? Not a leaf stirred, yet everything in the garden seemed to shimmer.

Josh's hand slowly slid up my thigh, across my stomach, over my right breast, down my arm. He lifted it to his lips and licked the drops of moisture that had collected like rainwater in the bend of my elbow. I closed my eyes and shivered. 'Josh –'

'Venus –'

I couldn't move. I hadn't been touched like this in a year.

'Venus,' he whispered, leaning over and kissing my neck. The soft, grazing heat of his lips made me catch my breath. 'I have to leave tomorrow.'

'Where are you going?'

'Meat Loaf.' Last year he couldn't attend this famous writer's workshop because he couldn't afford it. This year, on the basis on his forthcoming book, he'd been asked to lead a seminar called 'Memoir Noir'. 'I won't see you again for over a month,' he murmured, his lips nibbling, his tongue licking.

It would be autumn then. A whole new season. A different city. A different me.

'I hate to say goodbye,' he said.

My heart gave a lurch. I hated to say goodbye, too.

'So soft, so sweet.' Josh's breath was hot against my neck. And then finally, at last, he was kissing me.

I was in one metal chair, he in another. It couldn't have been more awkward, but we just sort of overcame the obstacles. His tongue tasted like coffee. I opened my eyes just enough to be able to see those long black eyelashes. I felt his fingers move up into my hair. I felt his fingers gliding along my breasts.

'Venus,' he whispered again. 'So beautiful.'

'You're beautiful too.'

'I've dreamed about this,' he murmured. 'Touching you. Kissing you. Making love to you.'

'Keep talking,' I sighed. 'I love the way you talk.' No man had ever talked to me like that, oiling me up with words, and I'd never realized until that moment how erotic words could be, how effective they were in foreplay. I made a note to myself to remember that. It was something I could use in *The Happy Camper Guide to Sex*.

So Josh talked. Whispered. Coaxed. Cajoled. Teased. Flattered. He was playful, he was ardent, he was serious, he was lubricious – I finally remembered what the word meant.

Above us, in the bittersweet vine, I heard a faint crackling, as if something were slowly moving through the dark tangle of leaves and berries. Maybe a squirrel or a little bird. The vine, planted many years ago by the dads, was enormous, its grasping tendrils so thick that they shaded one whole section of the back garden.

A leaf fluttered down.

'Tell me you want me,' Josh whispered in my ear. 'Tell me you want me inside of you.'

The old Venus? She would have moaned yes, yes, yes, a thousand times yes, I want you, take me, take me, oh yes, yes, make my life exciting, add some drama and sensation to what is otherwise so friggin' boring.

The new Venus? She held back, without knowing why. She breathed heavily but didn't say a word. The urge was there, the desire for abandon.

'I want to lie down beside you,' Josh whispered. 'I want to take off your clothes, one piece at a time, and –' His hand slid into my halter top and teased my nipples. He sucked my tongue into his mouth.

I was so hot, so sticky, so aroused. I tried to talk sense to myself. He doesn't want *you*, I insisted to the dull, ugly girl who always made her appearance at times like this. Another awful voice, maybe unconsciously picked up from Susanna, said: You're free to play the same game, you know. Why not? Your clitoris has needs, too, doesn't it?

I laid my hand on his thigh, felt the hot bare flesh, the soft hair, the play of the muscles. I did a little exploring of my own.

I was slowly inching my fingers up towards Josh's crotch when I heard more rustling in the bittersweet vine, just behind us, then faint music coming from Kenny's apartment directly above. He must have opened his balcony door. What if he walked outside and saw us?

'I'm going to miss you,' Josh murmured. 'I'm not going to think of anyone but you.'

Right, I thought, as his tongue slid along the erogenous rim of my ear. While you're hobnobbing in Vermont with all those literary luminaries, you're going to be thinking of *me*. Why? Because I was great in bed?

My head wouldn't shut up. I couldn't turn off the doubts and leap into pure carnality. In the 'old days', I would have blindly obeyed the desires of my body and wilfully ignored any interfering internal voices. Now, it was completely turned around.

'Let's go inside,' Josh said. 'Let's go inside and fuck.'

'Josh, I—'

'Come on. I can't wait any longer.' He was bearing down on my mouth again, getting more excited, breathing in short, excited gasps.

'No, listen—'

'Come *on*.' He pulled the straps of my halter top down and began feasting on my oh-so-sensitive shoulders.

It was the coup de grace that broke the camel's back. Or something. With a gasping moan I threw my head back. All systems were go. Every light turned green. But just as I made up my mind to give in and join in the fun my body was longing for, I made the mistake of opening my eyes.

And saw, dangling above me, not a foot away, a giant snake.

A huge snake.

A boa constrictor.

Esmerelda.

My scream, Josh later e-mailed me, was heard by a friend of his in Hoboken.

Esmerelda seemed to be extruding herself from the bittersweet vine. She dropped another foot, lifted her head, wove back and forth, and then landed gracefully in the garden, almost at our feet.

Well, you can put the blame on Mame, as Rita Hayworth sings in that old movie, but in this case it was Esmerelda who put the kibosh on Josh. Her appearance was like having a pail of cold water suddenly splashed on us.

After Kenny heard my scream and rushed down in his nun's habit to fetch his lost darling (she'd slithered out his open balcony door while he was getting dressed for an afternoon of roller skating), Josh and I just looked at one another with disbelief – another impossible New York story! An urban legend in the making – and began to laugh. We hung out together for another couple of shell-shocked hours and when he left, I kissed him goodbye.

The next day he was gone.

One October afternoon I was walking my charges in Central Park, around the pond where rich kids and fanatic men race their electronically controlled toy boats. Autumn in New York. We were back to that again. Shimmering clouds, glittering crowds, falling leaves of sycamore. The whole enchilada.

My dogs had all attended the very best schools and held their heads high as they pranced along beside me. I was thinking about my new book, *The Happy Camper Guide to Sex*, and not paying a lot of attention, when Charlotte, the ten-year-old standard French poodle, suddenly stopped to give one of the benches ringing the boat pond a delicate sniff. Her tug tugged me out of my reverie and I looked up.

Sitting on the next bench, not ten feet away, was Giles Travaille.

He was bent forward, hands dangling between his knees, watching as a toddler excitedly threw a leaf into the boat pond.

I resisted the urge to turn away before he saw me. 'Giles?'

You know how sometimes you meet a person you haven't seen for awhile and their face has changed? That's how it was with Giles. His hair had receded. There were deep wrinkles around his eyes and dark bags beneath them. His face was paunchy. He looked up and smiled. 'Venus!'

'I saw you sitting there and –' And what?

'Are those your dogs?' he asked.

'No, I just walk them.'

He nodded and looked back towards the boat pond, where the little boy with the bored Hispanic nanny was pointing to his leaf in the water and laughing excitedly. Giles appeared to be totally caught up with the scene. He began to laugh. 'Look at that,' he said.

'What?'

'That kid. He's so bloody happy.'

I nodded and smiled dumbly, wondering why something like that would be of interest to him.

'Sit down,' he said, patting the bench. 'Can you? For a moment?'

I sat and told my charges to sit, too. There was an awkward moment of silence. I didn't know what to say.

'So you're walking dogs now, eh?' Giles scratched Charlotte behind her ears.

'Yeah.' I hesitated. 'And – um – writing.' There, I'd actually said it.

'Writing? That's a dangerous occupation.'

I didn't say anything. I wasn't sure I knew what he meant.

'Poor Susanna,' Giles said. He looked at me as if he expected me to agree with him. 'You heard she was let go, yes?'

'No.'

'Yes. It was nasty. Very nasty indeed.'

Stupid old resentments suddenly rose up and almost choked me. Was Giles aware that 'poor Susanna' had treated *me* like dirt and then fired *me*? But I didn't want to rag on about Susanna – that chapter of my life was over. 'How's her face?' I asked.

'Oh, the –' Giles distorted half his face, trying to simulate the downward droop of Bell's palsy. 'That's better. At least she's not suicidal about it any more.'

'How are things at *Peeper*?' I asked, just to move the subject away from Susanna.

Giles tightened his lips into a nervous smile and looked back at the boy beside the boat pond. 'I left,' he said.

'What?'

'Well – to be honest – I was asked to leave.'

'Why?'

'Silly little thing, really. Caught me using coke.'

'Oh.'

'Stupid, really. Miss Peeper for November. How was I supposed to know she was a Jehovah's Witness? She alerted someone. Claimed I was sexually harassing her.'

'Oh.'

'Which I most definitely was not. I've never sexually harassed anyone in my life. I've never had to.'

'So what are you doing now?' I asked.

'Sitting in Central Park watching a little boy being happy.' He sighed and squinted as the sun came out from behind a fat white cloud. 'All he's got is a leaf and a pond. A leaf floating in the water. That's all it takes to make him happy. Can you imagine?'

Well, what does it take to make any of us happy?

I asked myself that question the following spring, as I lugged another carton of *The Happy Camper Guide to Sex* out to my rental car.

How can we be happy if we don't know what happiness is? Or if we've forgotten what it is?

And how terrible that we do forget. Because without happiness, life is dark, cold, and uncomfortable. Something to be endured rather than adored.

'Last box,' Mary-Joseph called from the stoop. She hoisted it to her shoulder and carried it down to the car, neatly stacking it in the trunk with the others.

I wasn't taking any chances. I'd learned a lot on Susanna's book tour, and even more by talking to Josh about his. The biggest problem was having the books arrive on time.

'How fah yuh hopin' to make it today?' Mary-Joseph asked.

'Just to Boston.'

'Wish I was goin' with yuh.'

'Maybe next time.'

'Yeah. When I can take some time off.' She crossed her arms and leaned back against the car. 'Jeez, Veen, I really envy you. Just takin' off. Free as a bird. Seein' America.'

'I'm not *that* free.' But, actually, I was – or felt I was. The small publisher who'd taken *The Happy Camper Guide to Sex* didn't have any money for advertising, so I'd planned out the book tour myself. It was not what you'd call grand. It was probably stretching things to even *call* it a 'book tour'. I was the one who contacted the bookstores and arranged the times. I was driving around the country with several cartons of my new memoir in the trunk. I had to feed myself, house myself, pay for my own gas. When I arrived, I'd bring the books with me.

I had no help of any kind, but I didn't care. Because I had actually done it. I had written a memoir and found (with Josh's help) a publisher to publish it.

The dads, Carolee, everyone I knew was absolutely dumbfounded. Because I hadn't told anyone along the way what I was doing. Once I finished *My Three Husbands*, which I didn't show to anyone, I began *Happy Camper*.

It started out as a guide to what does and what doesn't make sex satisfying. It was something Susanna Hyde might have written. But during the course of writing it, it changed into something else. My voice just took over. It became a memoir of my new life in New York. The irony, of course, was that there was no sex in *The Happy Camper Guide to Sex*.

'I already ordered my copy,' Mary-Joseph said. 'They said it won't be available for a couple a weeks. Some problems with the distributuh.'

I popped the trunk and pulled a book from one of the boxes. 'Here. Advance copy.'

Mary-Joseph's eyes opened wide. 'Really?' She took the shiny paperback and stared at it with an almost religious reverence. 'Oh my Gawd. *Veen*.'

'You're in it, OK?'

'OK,' she whispered. 'Oh my Gawd. I'm in a book. Did you write any sex scenes?'

'No sex scenes. Just heavy petting.'

'Will yuh sign it?'

'Sure.'

Mary-Joseph yanked a pen from her shirt pocket, clicked it, handed it to me. 'Say somethin' nice.'

I wrote: To Mary-Joseph Capistrano, good friend and super duper super.

She read what I'd written, then said in a choked voice,

'Jeez, I'm gonna start bawlin'.'

'Why?'

'*This*,' she said, holding up the book. 'And you. Goin' away so long.'

'I'll be back.'

She looked at me with hopeful eyes. 'Will yuh?'

'This is my home now. I've got a garden to take care of. And a cat.'

Well, a part-time cat. Maybe. For guess who'd appeared at the top of the garden wall just a week before? Yes, the very same tom who'd been squatting in the apartment when Whitman, Daddy and I first arrived. He looked fairly clean and was no longer limping. Someone had obviously been feeding and taking care of him. He sauntered along the top of the wall with a wary stare, sizing me up, trying to decide whether or not to jump into the garden – and my life. He hadn't, yet, but he was out there every day, and if he was still out there when I got back, I'd know he'd been waiting for me and I'd invite him to stay for good.

'I'll keep an eye on things till yuh dads get here,' Mary-Joseph said.

'I warned them about Esmerelda.'

'Oh my Gawd. I woulda hadda heart attack!'

We went on making the kind of small talk you make to postpone saying goodbye. But I had to get going. It was time.

I put my hand on Mary-Joseph's shoulder. 'Well –'

'Yeah. So call me – will yuh call me?'

I nodded. Mary-Joseph sucked in a deep ragged breath and lurched into my arms. 'Drive safe.' She threw her arms around me and squeezed, then abruptly turned away and headed down the street to her van.

So how do you end a memoir?

And where does the last one end and the new one begin?

I nosed my rental car out into the traffic on Broadway and headed north.

I thought: My old memoir has just ended.

I thought: My new memoir is about to begin.